P

"Hoffmann's d
It's
— on *The Charmer*

"Fully developed characters and perfect pacing make
this story feel completely right."
— on *Your Bed or Mine?*

"Sexy and wildly romantic"
— on *Doing Ireland!*

"A very hot story mixes with great characters to
make every page a delight."
— on *The Mighty Quinns: Ian*

"Romantic, sexy and heartwarming"
— on *Who Needs Mistletoe?*

"Sexy, heartwarming and romantic…a story to settle
down with and enjoy—and then re-read"
— on *The Mighty Quinns: Teague*

Dear Reader,

Welcome to the second book in my MIGHTY QUINNS trilogy, featuring youngest brother Danny.

About ten years ago, I happened across a small blacksmith shop near my hometown and decided to stop in and see what was going on. I'd nearly forgotten that place until I was looking for a profession for Danny Quinn and it just popped into my head.

I was so impressed by an artist using fire and tools to coax beautiful shapes from reluctant iron. It took strength and patience and creativity—exactly the qualities I wanted for Danny.

I hope you enjoy *The Mighty Quinns: Danny*. And don't miss the final book in the trilogy next month, when eldest brother Kellan meets his match.

Happy reading,

Kate Hoffmann

THE MIGHTY QUINNS: DANNY

BY
KATE HOFFMANN

First published in Great Britain 2012
by Mills & Boon, an imprint of Harlequin (UK) Limited,
Eton House, 18-24 Paradise Road, Richmond, Surrey TW9 1SR

© Peggy A. Hoffmann 2011

ISBN: 978 0 263 89392 2
ebook ISBN: 978 1 408 96944 1

14-1112

Harlequin (UK) policy is to use papers that are natural, renewable and recyclable products and made from wood grown in sustainable forests. The logging and manufacturing processes conform to the legal environmental regulations of the country of origin.

Printed and bound in Spain
by Blackprint CPI, Barcelona

Kate Hoffmann began writing for Mills & Boon in 1993. Since then she's published sixty-five books, primarily in the Mills & Boon® Temptation and Mills & Boon® Blaze® lines. When she isn't writing, she enjoys music, theater and musical theater. She is active working with high school students in the performing arts. She lives in southeastern Wisconsin with her cat, Chloe.

Prologue

DANNY QUINN PULLED the pocketknife from his jacket
and opened the blade. He carefully cut into the piece of
soap he'd stolen from beneath the kitchen sink, hoping
his mother wouldn't notice it was missing before he had
a chance to finish his carving.

A brisk breeze blew off the sea, scattering the flakes
of soap in the sand. He'd come down to his favorite spot,
a spot he'd named Smuggler's Cove, to get away from
his brothers. There weren't many places the youngest
Quinn had all to his own, but this was one of them.

He'd spent a lot of solitary time in the area. Beyond
the cliffs was the old haunted castle, a place his older
brothers always talked about. He hadn't quite gathered
the courage to venture inside; but he had found this spot,
far enough from the ghosts and goblins that guarded the
old tower. Though it was a five-kilometer walk cross-
country, it was worth it to put distance between him
and his tormentors.

Today, just after breakfast, he had sneaked away
from home, his rucksack packed with a lunch, scraps
of driftwood and soap and his pocketknife—ready to

enjoy a day alone. Who needed older brothers anyhow? He was just grand on his own.

"I saw him go down here!"

Danny looked up to see his eldest brother, Kellan, standing thirty feet above him. He scrambled back to hide himself against the rocks, but he wasn't fast enough. "He's down at the bottom," Kellan shouted.

"Go away," Danny yelled. "This is my place and you can't come down."

"How did you get down there?" Kellan called.

"I jumped," Danny shot back.

Riley appeared beside Kellan. It was now two against one, the typical breakdown between the three brothers. "Bollocks!" Riley said. "Tell us how you got down or we'll tell Ma you were climbing on the cliffs."

They wouldn't go away. His older brothers were merciless. "Find the rock that looks like a duck," Danny finally said. "The path is on the other side of that." He watched as Riley and Kellan searched for the right spot and then slowly descended through the rocks. As they both leapt down onto the sand, Danny watched them warily.

"How did you find this place?" Kellan asked, looking around in wonder.

"I was searching for driftwood in the rocks. I just found it." He cursed. "How did you find me?"

"We followed you," Kellan said, a wide grin on his face. "We were curious where you were off to in such a rush."

"What are you doin' down here?" Riley asked. He pointed to the bar of soap that Danny held to his chest. "What's that? Are you plannin' on a bath, then? Tryin' to smell grand for your girlfriend, Evelyn?" Riley laughed, jabbing Kellan in the side with his elbow. "That's why he's hidin' out here. Danny has a sweetheart. Maybe she's meetin' him here for a bit of snogging."

"You in love with Evelyn, Danno?" Kellan asked, circling around him.

"No," Danny muttered. "I don't have a girl."

"Then why are you holdin' so tight to that soap?" Riley asked.

Danny tried to shove it in his jacket pocket, but Kellan was waiting to snatch it from his grip. Danny cursed as his brother retreated a safe distance.

"What are you doing with this?" Kellan said with a laugh, looking down at the dragon's head that Danny had begun to carve. He immediately went silent. Riley frowned, then walked over to Kellan's side. "What is it?"

"Where did you get this?" Kellan asked.

"It's mine," Danny murmured. "Now give it over."

"Who did you steal this from?" Kellan demanded.

"No one. I told you, it's mine."

Riley held up the soap, pointing to the dragon's head. "You carved this?"

"I did," Danny said, grabbing the soap back from his brother.

"Shut yer gob," Riley said. "You can't carve like that. You're just a baby."

Danny's eyes narrowed. "I'm eight years old."

"Prove it," Riley challenged. "Prove you carved that."

"I don't have to do anything you tell me," Danny said. "You're not my da, so feck off, the both of you."

"Maybe he did," Kellan said. "He's a clever little shite. After all, he found this place, didn't he?"

"I did," Danny insisted. "And I'll show you." Plopping down on the sand, he opened his rucksack and began to pull out all the carvings he'd done in the past few months. His collection was always changing—some he kept, some he gave to school chums and some he threw into the sea when they looked too crude against the others.

Riley and Kellan watched him, silently, suspiciously. But as his menagerie of animals and insects and mythic creatures grew, they leaned in more closely. "Will you look at that," Kellan murmured. He reached out and picked up a beetle that Danny was particularly proud of, carved out of a palm-sized piece of driftwood. "How do you do this?"

"I have to find a good piece of wood first," Danny explained. "Then I stare at it for a while, and pretty soon I see what I want to carve. Then, I just take away everything that isn't the beetle. My teacher says that's how the great sculptors do it."

"Look at this," Riley said, grabbing a dinosaur. "He's even got the spikes on the tail."

They sat down on either side of him and examined all of Danny's carvings, their comments filled with awe and respect for his talents. This was the first time in his whole life that his brothers had taken him seriously. Usually, they just ignored him and left him behind. But now, he could do something they couldn't. And that was like gold.

"Would you like one, then?" Danny asked.

His brothers looked at each other. "We can have one?"

"Sure," he said. "Any one you like."

"Can ya make me something?" Kellan asked.

Danny nodded. "I can. If you find a picture, I can carve it." He rummaged in his rucksack until he found the photo he'd torn out of a magazine. "I'm going to make this troll for Ma's garden, for her birthday, but I have to find a big piece of wood."

"We'll help you find one," Riley said. "There's got to be a good piece around here somewhere."

He and his brothers searched the beach for a long time, climbing over the rocks and talking about Danny's carvings. It was the best day of Danny's whole life, better than any day he could remember. Somehow, he knew things had changed, that he was someone important to Riley and Kellan now. The duo was now a trio.

"I can show you something else," Danny offered. "It's a secret and you can't tell Da or Ma or they'll take the strap to us all. And you can't tell anyone else. None of your friends. It has to be for Quinn brothers only."

"We swear," Kellan said.

"You have to make a blood oath," Danny said. He opened his pocketknife and held out his hand. Without flinching, he cut the tip of his index finger, then handed the knife to Riley. "Do it," he said. "Or I won't tell you."

Reluctantly, both Kellan and Riley cut their fingers, then let the blood drip onto their palms. Then the three brothers grasped hands, mingling their blood. Riley grinned at Kellan. "He's a brave little bugger, isn't he?"

"Let's see it," Kellan said, drawing his hand away.

"It's a cave," Danny said. "In the cliff. It's deep and

I didn't go all the way in because the tide comes up into the opening. But I think that smugglers might have used it." He pulled a tiny flashlight out of his jacket pocket and turned it on. "We've only got an hour before the tide starts coming in. We'll have to hurry."

"Are you sure we should do this?" Riley said. "What if it's dangerous?"

Danny gave him a look. "If you're afraid, you can stay on the beach."

As he walked across the sand to the rocky outcropping, Danny smiled to himself. Though he was only eight, he felt like a full-grown man. Maybe now, he'd have enough courage to talk to Evelyn Maltby.

1

"So this is Ballykirk," Jordan Kennally murmured to herself, peering through the windshield of her car at the picturesque village below.

She'd been in Ireland for nearly sixteen months now, working as the project manager on the Castle Cnoc renovation. And though she'd seen a lot of the countryside, she was still amazed at how every sight managed to look exactly like some picture-postcard. Ireland was nothing if not quaint.

She glanced at the clock on the dash, then calculated the time it would take her to find Danny Quinn, discuss their business and get back to the castle. She wasn't used to chasing around the countryside looking for workers, but she'd been told that Danny Quinn was the best. And Jordan needed the best.

She steered her car down the winding road that led into Ballykirk, following the carefully drawn map that Kellan Quinn had provided. The town was like so many others along the coast of County Cork—a pretty collection of colorful buildings set against a stunning landscape, this time the blue waters of Bantry Bay.

When her father had assigned her the project at Castle Cnoc, she'd looked at it as both punishment and reward. It was her first project as manager, solely in charge of a five-million-dollar budget and pleasing one of her father's wealthy clients. It was also a way of putting her firmly into her place at Kencor.

She'd been doggedly scratching her way up the corporate ladder of her family's multimillion dollar real estate development firm, working hard to carve out a place for herself. But with four equally driven and talented older brothers above her on the ladder, just the process of getting noticed was impossible.

She'd begged for good projects to manage, but had always been given a secondary role, usually as the interior designer, for projects that her brothers headed. She'd been sent to Ireland to oversee the restoration of a once grand manor house and castle keep, because no one else could be bothered to come. They were all too busy with hotels and shopping malls and office towers.

"Whistler Cottage." No street, no number, just a name. Jordan studied the map. "Behind the bakery and up the hill to the blue cottage," she read. The bakery was easy enough to find and when she did, Jordan parked her car, grabbed her bag and jumped out of the vehicle.

There were blacksmiths scattered all over Ireland, their skills ranging from amateur to competent artisan. But Danny Quinn was known as one of the best ornamental blacksmiths in the country, a true artist, and she intended to hire him for her project.

His brother, Kellan, had served as the architect on the Castle Cnoc restoration and Jordan had assumed that Danny would jump at a big-budget job so close to home. But he hadn't returned any of her calls. So Jordan had decided to force the issue. She needed an answer, one way or another, or she'd be put off schedule.

The pressure to bring the job in on time and under budget was immense. If she did, her father wouldn't be able to ignore her anymore. The next logical step would be the boutique hotel they were developing in SoHo and after that, progressively larger projects. They wouldn't think of her as the company "decorator" anymore.

Jordan cursed softly. They all looked at her like some swatch-wielding cream puff, unable to exert any power with the mostly male contractors on the job sites. Maybe she didn't curse and throw tantrums and berate the workers, but that didn't mean she didn't get the job done. Jordan had always preferred a quiet confidence to a raging temper. You get more flies with honey. That's what her grandmother had always said.

But she'd been pleasant to Danny Quinn, polite on all the messages she'd left. Maybe it was time to get tough. If he didn't want the job, he needed to tell her outright so she could find someone else. Trouble was, she didn't want anyone else. Kellan had shown her a portfolio of his brother's work and Danny was exactly who she needed to provide some of the authentic details she sought for the project.

As the map indicated, a cobblestone path led between the bakery and the adjacent building. After walking through a narrow alleyway, she saw the sign for the smithy—a decorative iron anvil and tongs attached to the side of an azure cottage set on the low hillside.

The front door to the cottage was wide open and she walked inside. Two black-and-white dogs lying near the fireplace immediately leapt up and began barking at her. They scampered across the room, driving her against a battered breakfront.

"Shh," she urged, working her way back to the front door. "Settle down. I'm not going to hurt you." Jordan held out her hand as she made her retreat. But just as she turned to step outside, she ran face-first into a wide, muscular and naked chest.

A tiny cry slipped from her lips as she stumbled back. The dogs got behind her legs and she felt herself losing her balance. And then she was on the floor with the dogs climbing all over her, licking at her face and nuzzling her hands.

"Finny. Mogue. Away now."

The dogs retreated a safe distance, then sat down and peered at her with curious blue eyes, their tongues hanging out, their heads cocked. They looked so pleased with themselves. "Thank you so much for the lovely welcome," she muttered to the dogs as she struggled to her feet. A moment later, the man grabbed her hand and helped her up. It was only then that Jordan got a good look at the elusive Danny Quinn.

The family resemblance was keen. At first glance, he looked like his older brother, Kellan. But upon more careful study, she saw that where Kellan was handsome in a cool, sophisticated way, his brother oozed raw sex appeal.

He wore torn blue jeans that rode low on his narrow hips, and an old work shirt, open at the front and missing its sleeves. A sheen of perspiration covered his sinewy arms and chest. His hair, nearly black, stood up in unruly spikes. But it was his eyes, pale blue in color, that caught her complete attention. She forced herself to look away and her gaze drifted to a narrow strip of hair that traced a line from his navel to beneath his—

"Sorry about the dogs," he said with a boyish smile. "They'll herd anything that moves." He paused. "How they could mistake you for a sheep, I'll never know."

Jordan looked up, her face warming with embarrassment. Sheep? What was she doing? Quinn was a business associate. "You—you must be Daniel Quinn."

"I must be," he said. "And who must you be?"

"Oh." She held out her hand. "Jordan. Jordan Kennally."

He seemed taken aback by her introduction, but then wiped his hand on his jeans and took her fingers in his. "You're Joe Kennally?"

"Jordan," she said. "Your brother calls me Joe. He thinks it's funny." She cleared her throat, determined to stay on the subject at hand. "I've been trying to contact you for the past two weeks now and haven't gotten a call back. So I decided a visit was in order." He stared at her silently. "What?" she asked, an impatient edge to her voice.

"I'm just surprised you're a girl. Kell neglected to mention that."

Jordan felt her temper rise. That comment had been thrown at her regularly since she'd begun working for her father's development company. Why couldn't she be a girl? Women had every right to work in the construction industry these days. And Jordan wasn't a name reserved exclusively for boys.

"Is that a problem?" she asked, snatching her hand

back and fixing him with a cool look. Obviously, the only way to keep this conversation on track was to present a tough facade.

Danny shrugged. "I can assure you, that's never been a problem with me. And had I known you were a woman, I might not have dodged your calls for two weeks." He chuckled. "And had I known that you were so beautiful, I'd have turned up on your doorstep in less than a day."

"You could tell I was a woman from the messages," she said.

Danny frowned. "I really wasn't paying attention. I usually just ignore my phone messages."

"That's always a good business practice," she murmured.

He stepped out of the door and motioned for her to follow him. "Come on then, I'll show you around."

To her consternation, he didn't bother to button up his shirt and she found herself fixated on that thin line of hair, this time following it up from his belly to his collarbone. Maybe she should offer him a chance to put on something more appropriate for a business meeting. When her attention shifted to the sculpted muscles of his upper arms, Jordan stifled a groan.

She stepped past him, her shoulder brushing against his body as she walked outside. The contact sent another current racing through her. Jordan wanted to scream. What was happening to her? After just a few minutes, this man had her completely off balance. There was no way she'd be able to negotiate a contract with him in this state. He could ask for a million Euros and her naked body in his bed and she'd sign on the dotted line.

"Just follow the path to the back," he said, pointing.

Since she'd been in Ireland, Jordan had lived the life of a nun. The first year, she'd made a point to return to New York at least once a month, in an attempt to maintain a romantic relationship with her last boyfriend. But after their breakup, it had seemed like a waste of time and money.

Though she'd made a few acquaintances in the area, she'd kept to herself. In truth, she wasn't very good with friends. Work always took precedence and she often turned down invitations to socialize because of that. She put all her energy into her job.

"Did your brother tell you about the project?" she asked as they walked to a small stone barn set behind the cottage.

"I know the place," Danny replied. "Castle Cnoc. We used to go out there when we were teenagers. It was a grand spot for a party if you could avoid getting caught by the peelers."

"Peelers?"

"The gardai. The…cops. People around here think it's haunted, you know."

"Yes, well, a lot has changed," she said, risking a sideways glance. "We've finished with most of the renovations. But we still have a lot of the details to get right. Your brother showed me your portfolio. I like your work. A lot of the original ironwork was stripped out of the place after it was abandoned, but we do have photos from early in the twentieth century and some samples we managed to find. So you'd do some new fabrication and some restoration of existing work. We want to put everything back the way it was."

"It's a big job of work," he said. "That place is huge."

"We haven't done anything to the castle itself. That will be done later. It's the attached manor house that we're working on."

"That's still a big house," he said. "And the last time I saw it, it was a ruin."

"Nine bedrooms. Nearly ten thousand square feet. Built in 1860 with a major addition in 1910. I know we haven't talked money, but I figured you'd want to see what's required before you give me a quote. And I wanted to meet you, to see if we…well, if we could work together."

They reached the door to the old stone barn and he stopped and stood in front of her, staring at her in a brazen way. She pressed her hand to her chest, wondering why her heart was suddenly beating so fast. Was it the smile that made his mouth seem more kissable? Or was it the sheen of perspiration that made her long to touch his bare skin? Or was it—

"So, this is kind of like a first date for us," he commented. "We're just feeling each other out, trying to decide whether we want to get involved, is that it?"

Jordan felt her cheeks blaze again. This was crazy! She'd dealt with handsome men like Danny Quinn all her adult life. What was it about him that had turned her into a silly teenager? "It's purely a business transaction, Mr. Quinn. It has nothing to do with my feelings for you. Not that I have any feelings at all for you. We just met."

"Oh." He nodded. "Then it would be more like I'm a brasser and you're my customer?"

"A brasser?"

"A prostitute? A hooker, I think you Americans call it."

"I'm not making you do anything illegal, unless making hinges and gates will get you arrested in Ireland."

"You haven't seen my hinges," he said with a grin. "They're obscenely sexy. Erotic, some would say."

She had to put a stop to this—this playful, but highly suggestive banter. "Mr. Quinn, I—"

"Oh, Jaysus, can we stop with the Mr. Quinn? No one ever calls me mister. And it makes you sound like a snootypants."

"Do you want this job?" she asked, her eyes narrowing in frustration. "Because I get the feeling you're doing everything in your power to get me to turn around and walk back to my car."

He raked his hand through his tousled hair. "Now don't be doing that. I'm just having a bit of fun," he cajoled. "And you're right, I'm not really sure I want to take on a job like this. Copying someone else's work doesn't appeal to my creative sensibilities at all."

"But you'd be a part of a really wonderful project. The castle is going to be restored to its former grandeur."

"Why? So some rich American can live there and pretend he's a nineteenth-century lord, looking down on all the locals? Oh, count me in on that. And while you're at it, do you have a few red-hot pokers you'd like to stick in my eye?"

Jordan stared at him, baffled by his response. She'd gotten the impression from Kellan that his brother really needed the work. But it was clear that Danny Quinn required more than just a decent paycheck before he took a job. He needed inspiration.

"So who is it that bought the old castle?" he asked. "Everyone in the county has been speculating. Whoever it is must have money to burn."

"I'm really not at liberty to—"

"If you expect me to take the job, I'm going to want to know who I'm working for."

"You'd be working for me," Jordan said.

"And who would you be working for?" He pointed inside the barn. "After you."

She opened her mouth to counter his sarcastic query, but as soon as her eyes adjusted to the dark interior of the barn, Jordan was silenced. From every rafter, in every nook and cranny, there were beautiful objects made of iron, twisted into shapes she'd never thought possible. She saw gates and railings and balustrades and a beautiful sundial that she immediately wanted for the garden at Castle Cnoc.

But it wasn't just architectural items that she found. Along one wall were a series of small animals, hedgehogs and rabbits and squirrels, clever little creatures made of cast iron. She wandered over to a crooked shelf tacked to a crossbeam and examined a collection of small carved objects.

"You did these?" she asked, glancing over her shoulder.

"When I was a kid. The cast-iron animals are for the tourists. They're small enough to fit in a suitcase and make a nice remembrance. You wouldn't believe how many good jobs I get because of those bloody hedgehogs."

Jordan smiled. "They are cute."

He reached down and grabbed one and handed it to her. "Then take one with you. They make a proper doorstop or a decent paperweight. But they're pure hell if your toe runs across one in the dark."

"Thank you," Jordan said.

He stared at her for a long moment. "You have a lovely smile," Danny said.

Jordan quickly turned away, crossing the dirt floor to the forge. The massive stone fireplace, set at waist level, was located against the far wall, banked with coal, red embers glowing inside. Soot stained the stone above the hearth. Tools lined the walls surrounding the forge and a battered anvil sat in the center of it all.

"This is amazing," she murmured. She walked to a spot where an iron gate was propped against a post. The decorative ironwork was so intricate, so artistic that Jordan immediately knew she wasn't in the presence of a craftsman but an artist. She pointed to a huge rosette sitting beside it. "What is this for?"

"That's just a try," he said. "The two I finished were set into the stone wall of a formal garden, kind of like a window."

"I want you," she blurted out, spinning around to face him. "I don't care what it takes, but I want you."

A slow smile curved his lips. "That's always nice to hear."

Jordan groaned inwardly. Never in her life had she been so befuddled by a man. Yes, she found him wildly attractive. What woman wouldn't, him standing there with his shirt unbuttoned to the waist and his gorgeous body tempting her?

But there was something else at work here. He was incredibly talented and impossibly charming and nothing like the men she was usually attracted to. Yet the attraction was undeniable. If he agreed to work for her, she'd have to keep that attraction in check.

Maybe she ought to just walk away. Having him in close proximity was a disaster waiting to happen. What she really needed was a blacksmith who was old and wrinkled and didn't have all his teeth. That kind of man would be so much easier to resist. Danny Quinn was the human equivalent of catnip.

"How much do you want me?" Danny asked.

"What I meant was that I want you to do this job. I can see your talent and I think we can work out a way that your needs—" She cleared her throat. "Your *artistic* needs can be met." Jordan drew a deep breath. "As far as compensation, I'm willing to be generous if you're willing to put all your time and effort into the project until it's finished. Ten-hour days, six days a week if necessary."

"And what kind of compensation are we talking about?"

"Well, it depends on how long you take to finish the job. But I can promise you that it will be very generous. Well worth your while."

"You'll have to include living expenses. I can't work from here."

"Why not?"

"Because I don't want to spend my time making the drive back and forth every time I need to fit something, dragging iron from here to there. We can set up a forge on-site. It will be more efficient. I'll need a place to sleep."

"You don't want to sleep at home?"

"I have to tend the fire and I sometimes work late into the night. I don't need anything posh, just a bed and a shower."

"All right. There's a cottage that you can use."

"And I'm bringing my dogs, too. And I eat three meals a day."

"You expect me to cook for you?" Jordan asked.

"I expect you to feed me," he replied.

The thought of having a man as sexy as Danny around 24/7 was a bit disconcerting. But she was a very capable woman with finely honed self-control. And this was business. Nothing would happen if she didn't want it to happen. "That can all be arranged," she said. "We don't have a cook at the house, but I'll open up an account for you at the market in the village."

"I can live with that." He smiled and a shiver skittered down her spine. "Well, I suppose I ought to see the place, make a few notes and figure out if this is really a job I want to do."

"The sooner the better. I'd like you to start as soon as possible." She paused. "And I should warn you, I'm a very hands-on—" Jordan swallowed hard. In such a highly charged atmosphere, her admission could probably be misconstrued—again. "I meant to say, I'm very concerned with details, so I will be involved in all important decisions."

He cocked his eyebrow, then shrugged. "I have some things to finish up here. Why don't I drive over this evening and you can show me around?"

"That would be fine."

They stood facing each other, an uneasy silence growing between them. Now that their business was completed, Jordan realized she should leave, or risk looking as though she was interested in something more than his blacksmith skills. She held out her hand again. "Well, it was a pleasure meeting you, Mr.—Danny."

He took her fingers in his, his touch so gentle that it was more a caress than a polite gesture. "You have no idea what a pleasure it was for me, Jordan," he murmured.

For a long moment, she wasn't sure what to do. His touch felt so good she didn't want to pull away. Neither one of them took a breath or even blinked, and when he took a step closer, Jordan was certain he was about to kiss her. She yanked her hand back and clutched at the purse slung over her shoulder.

"Later," he said with a crooked smile.

She wasn't sure whether he was referring to their meeting at the castle or his intention to kiss her. "I look forward to it," she stated curtly. "And please don't blow me off this time."

"I wouldn't think of it," he said in a low voice.

Jordan gave him a nod, then strode out of the barn. As soon as she had put a reasonable distance between them, she cursed softly. Had it really been necessary to add that last part? It made her sound like a complete bitch. But from the moment she'd set eyes on Danny Quinn she'd found it impossible to separate pleasure from the business she meant to do with him. She'd have to toughen up if she was going to deal with him—and with the unbidden attraction she felt.

"He's not *that* cute," she said to herself in a feeble attempt to mitigate her feelings. "All right, maybe he *is* really cute. But he's probably just like all gorgeous men—full of himself. And I've always hated men with big egos."

Hopefully, by the time she got back to Castle Cnoc, she'd have convinced herself that Danny was just like all the other workmen wandering about the place—ordinary guys, there to do a job and nothing more.

But as she pulled away from the bakery, she realized it would take a whole lot more than the drive to make that happen.

Maybe a ride to Dublin and back would do it.

DANNY TWISTED THE rearview mirror around to check his appearance. After he'd finished work for the day, he'd grabbed a quick shower and a shave and put on a decent shirt, then set off for Castle Cnoc. He'd thought about walking. Along the coast the castle was not more than an hour's hike. But he didn't want to arrive all sweaty and knackered. For any other girl in County Cork, he wouldn't have bothered to worry. But Jordan Kennally was not just any girl.

She was—well, what the hell was she? he wondered. Sophisticated…and ambitious…and American, three qualities he hadn't really dealt with in his love life to date. No wonder he'd acted like such a fool. Even the best of his pathetic charm had had no effect on her. He'd tried to be cool and he'd sounded like a bleedin' culchie instead. And she'd left acting as though she'd stepped in something with a big stink on it.

"So just keep your gob shut," he muttered. "Smile and nod and let her do all the talking."

He jumped out of the battered Land Rover and slammed the door behind him. He probably should have borrowed Riley's car, just to create a better impression. Hell, he probably should have gone out and bought some new clothes and maybe even stopped for a haircut. And while he was out, he could have bought himself a clue as to how to act around a woman like Jordan.

He stared up at the facade of the old manor. The castle was attached to the huge Georgian house on its north side—the tall stone tower constructed to look out over the surrounding countryside and the sea to the west. Smuggler's Cove was right below the castle, at the bottom of the rocky cliff.

With all the construction around, it was difficult to tell where the front door of the manor house was anymore. Danny wandered over to a scaffold covered in plastic and found the door behind it. He pushed it open and stepped inside the spacious entry hall.

He felt as if he were stepping back in time. His last visit had been during a drunken birthday celebration for one of his schoolmates. At the time, he'd been just shy of eighteen and the manor had been rundown and open to the elements. But now the windowpanes had been replaced with sparkling glass and the crumbling plaster restored to its former beauty. Wainscotting had been polished and floors waxed.

As Jordan had promised, Castle Cnoc's manor house had nearly been restored to its former grandeur.

"Hello?" Danny called.

A soft melody drifted from the rear of the house and he followed the sound, the Irish tune luring him closer.

The imposing dining room at the rear of the ground floor had also been restored, the floor-to-ceiling paneling refinished and shining softly in the late-afternoon sun. A new chandelier hung from the ceiling in the center of the room, crystals twinkling.

The music grew louder as he traced it to the small breakfast room that adjoined the dining room. Danny felt a tiny thrill race through him when he saw her. She was standing on a ladder, her back to him, polishing a stained-glass medallion in one of the leaded windows. A Cara Dillon song played from a small radio.

Jaysus, she was beautiful, tall and slender, but with curves in all the right places. Her dark hair and pale skin made her appear delicate, but Danny already knew better. He suspected that Jordan was the kind of woman who liked to get her own way, and pity any man who wasn't willing to comply. He smiled to himself. Hell, he could stand to be bossed around a bit—especially in the bedroom.

She'd changed out of the turtleneck jumper and jeans that she'd had on earlier and now wore a pretty flowered dress with a green cardie over it. His gaze fixed on her backside and he found himself speculating on the color and style of her knickers.

"White," he murmured to himself. "With lace."

Danny leaned against the doorjamb and continued to watch her, listening to her hum along with the tune. She seemed so relaxed, completely different from the businesslike woman he'd met earlier that morning.

Danny knew it was crazy to want her the way he did.

She was about to become his boss, never mind the fact she'd be leaving Ireland as soon as her work was done at Castle Cnoc. Yet, he couldn't seem to help himself. From the moment he'd set eyes on her, he'd felt a wickedly powerful fascination.

He'd always done his best to avoid lengthy romantic entanglements with women. An occasional one-night stand with an attractive girl was plenty for him. He'd just never been any good at commitment.

His mother had always said it was because he was constantly searching for his muse, the perfect woman who could push his art to greater heights. "Hard work," she'd say, shaking her finger at him. That was the only thing that would bring him true success. But that hadn't stopped him from looking. Still, as he observed Jordan, Danny suspected she was more like one of the enchantresses from the old fairy tales, the *leanan sidhe.* Everything about her was meant to make him ignore reason and surrender to her magic. But the *leanan sidhe* were dangerous. If a man tried to leave such a powerful being he was doomed to death.

Danny slowly walked into the room, taking in the tiny details: the stained glass, the carved rosettes in the dark wood paneling, the decorative plaster medallion on the ceiling. "This is brilliant," he said.

Startled, she clutched at the ladder then glanced over her shoulder. "You scared me! How long have you been standing there?"

"Two verses and a rather lovely chorus." She wobbled on the ladder and he rushed to offer his hand. When he'd captured her fingers in his, Danny grinned. "Look at what you've done to this place. It's a deadly miracle."

"It is?" she said, excitement suffusing her tone. "It's…deadly. Yes. I've been so wrapped up in all the details that sometimes I forget to look at the big picture. It's going to be beautiful when it's all done."

"And you're in charge of all this?"

"Yes. I'm the project manager. The boss." She paused, sending him a suspicious look, then slowly climbed down the ladder. "Is that going to be a problem?"

He held on to her hand, smoothing his fingers over the back of her wrist. "You being in charge? Why would that be a problem?"

"Some men don't like working for women. I've had to fire a handful of them on this project because they wouldn't listen to me. They were…insubordinate. And dismissive. And rude."

"This isn't the type of job that women usually do," Danny said. "But in all honesty, I usually work for the woman of the house so there's no problem that I can see."

She slowly withdrew her hand from his. "Come on, let's go to my office. I've got a lot of the old hardware there and a list of what we need done."

Danny followed her through the dining room and down a narrow hall behind the stairs. She stopped to open a door, but it appeared to be stuck. As Jordan struggled with it, Danny reached around her to help. "Here, let me give it a try."

"No," she insisted. "I can get it." She shoved her shoulder against the door, but it wouldn't budge. "It's as if someone locked it from the inside."

Jordan turned to face him and they found themselves

in an odd embrace, his hands flat against the door on either side of her, trapped in the small alcove of the doorway. He drew a deep breath, the scent of her perfume touching his nose, and leaned closer. A woman didn't wear perfume like that unless she wanted to attract a man.

There was no helping it. Nothing to be done. Without even a second thought, Danny brushed a kiss across her lips. It was a tentative contact and he waited for her response, bracing himself for a slap across the face or a verbal dressing-down.

But to his surprise, Jordan threw her arms around his neck and kissed him back, desperately, hungrily, as if she'd gone without for far too long. At first it was a clumsy kiss, but then Danny took her face between his hands and softly tempered her frenzy with a carefully measured assault.

Almost immediately, she melted against him, her body going limp. A tiny groan slipped from her throat and he drew back and looked down into her flushed face. Her eyes were still closed and he couldn't tell from her expression what she was thinking. Was she embarrassed by her actions? Or well-pleased?

"Jordan?"

She opened her eyes and stared up at him. "Oh, God." The word slipped out of her on a gasp. She twisted out of his embrace and nervously smoothed her hands over her clothes. "That was...unexpected."

He reached out and ran a finger along her flushed cheek. "Now don't get yourself all mortified over it. It was a kiss and nothing more. A very lovely kiss at that," he said.

"Yes." She nodded nervously. "Well, maybe we should just focus on the business at hand."

As far as Danny was concerned, the only business at hand was the business of kissing her again. In truth, he had an entire business plan unfolding in his head. First another kiss, then a caress, and then, maybe full-on seduction. He didn't care a whit about the job, he wanted this woman.

He slipped his hands around her waist and moved her out of the way, then firmly grasped the doorknob. When he turned it and pushed, the door easily swung open. He chuckled softly. "Clever," he said. "If you wanted me to kiss you, you should have just asked."

"It was locked!" Jordan cried.

"And now, it's unlocked."

Jordan gave him an odd look. "I wasn't trying to get you to kiss me," she said, walking past him into the library. "These things happen around here all the time. Doors are locked, then they aren't. Windows are closed, then they aren't. Things go missing and then they turn up a day later."

"Sounds like brownies," Danny said. "Or leprechauns."

"Don't be ridiculous."

"Or ghosts. Or fairies. We have all manner of fantastical creatures here in Ireland. And none of them up to any good at all."

"I don't believe in any of those things," Jordan said.

Danny followed her into the library, making a careful study of the backside of her beautiful body. He fought the urge to slip his arms around her again and pull her into another kiss. Instead, he distracted himself with exploring the interior of the old library.

A memory flashed in his mind and he chuckled softly. "I do remember this room," he murmured. "I lost something here."

"Well, I don't think you'll find it after all these years," Jordan said. "But you're welcome to look."

"I don't think I'd want to find it," he said. "She was seventeen and I was fifteen. And I thought I knew everything about girls. After that night, I realized I knew nothing."

"You mean you—"

Danny nodded. "I lost my virginity right about—" he stepped to a spot in front of the fireplace "—here, I believe. I was drunk on whiskey and she was looking for a bit of fun. The minute she put her hands on me, I knew the world would never be the same."

"Right here?"

Danny nodded. "God, that seems like just yesterday."

"How old are you?" she asked.

"Twenty-six. How old are you?"

She tipped her chin up and, for a moment, he thought he'd insulted her. "Twenty-seven."

He grinned. "I've always gone for older girls." Danny continued his stroll around the room. Instead of books, the shelves were filled with pieces of decorative plaster and wood carvings, doorknobs and ceramic tile, and an entire wall of iron hardware.

"We've collected samples of all the hardware that needs to be replicated," she said. "It's on these two bottom shelves." Jordan turned and searched the cluttered surface of the desk, then glanced nervously over her shoulder.

"What's wrong?" Danny asked.

"Nothing," she murmured with a frown. "I just misplaced something."

"I can help you look," he said. "What is it?"

"No," she said. "It's probably gone."

Danny walked over to the desk. "What was it?"

"An old door knocker, made of cast iron. It was really beautiful. I found it half-buried in the garden. I was hoping that we could make them for all the exterior doors." She sighed, shaking her head as she braced her hands on her hips. "I don't know who's been in here, but I'm about to put in a surveillance system to find out."

"Leprechauns steal things from houses. Brownies like to live with humans and torment them for amusement."

"I told you, I don't believe in leprechauns or brownies."

"You should. You're in Ireland," he teased. "You've got to let the country into your bones. After all, with a name like Kennally, I'd wager you have a drop or two of Irish blood in you."

Jordan laughed softly. "I'm a quarter Irish. My father's father." She shook her head. "I probably just misplaced it. It'll turn up later." She picked up a paper from her desk and held it out to him. "Here's the inventory of what we need. They're numbered to correspond with the samples on the shelf." She opened her mouth, then snapped it shut again.

Danny gave her a curious look. "Was there something else?"

"About what just happened outside in the hallway. I want you to know that that kind of behavior is absolutely inappropriate and I'm sorry that I let my—my—Whatever. I'm just sorry. And it will never, ever happen again."

"Jaysus, don't say that. It's really the only thing that makes me want to take this job," Danny admitted. "Replicating hinges isn't nearly as exciting as kissing you."

"But we can't," she insisted.

"Why not?" He backed her up against the edge of the desk and braced his hands beside her hips. Once again, he met no resistance when he kissed her. If anything, she seemed to enjoy it even more this time. He took care to make the kiss deliciously tantalizing, invading her mouth with his tongue.

"See," he whispered against her lips. "It's very simple. I lean forward and you lean forward and it happens."

"We can't," she said again.

"Yes, we can," he said. "Forget the job. I don't need the job if that's what's standing in the way."

"But I need you to do the job," she insisted. "Much more than I need you to do…this. We need to keep it strictly business."

"I don't do business," he said. "It's art. There are no rules. And I refuse to consider you my boss. You can, however, be my muse."

A smile quirked at the corners of her mouth. "I'll be a muse for hinges and gates?"

Danny nodded. "I'll need one. The job itself promises to be a bit of a snore."

"Mr. Quinn, you are completely full of shite."

He stepped back as she fixed him with an irritated glare. "I see you've picked up the language, if not the mythology," he said. Sure, he'd pulled the last straight out of his arse, but right now, he'd say just about anything to get her to kiss him again.

"Will you do the job?"

"Are you going to let me kiss you again?"

She shook her head. "This project is very important to me, Mr. Quinn."

"If you call me Mr. Quinn again, I'll walk out of here and you can get Neddy O'Doul to do your work. He usually shoes horses and he makes a hames of that."

"Danny," she said. "My future depends upon this project. It has to come in on time and under budget. You have no idea how much is riding on this. We can't have any distractions."

He wasn't going to get any closer to Jordan sitting at home. He'd have to take the bad with the good. "I'll do the job," he said. "You won't have to worry." He pushed away from the desk and saw relief flood her features. All the tension in her body eased. "Tell me why this is so important."

"I have a lot to prove to my boss, who just happens to be my father. If I do a good job here, then maybe he'll finally recognize that I'm competent and trustworthy. And as good as any son he has."

"You work for your father?"

"Yes. I've worked for his real estate development and construction firm since I was in high school. Some day, I plan to run it." Jordan paused, then smiled weakly. "I'll just have to find a way to get rid of my four older brothers first, but I'm working on that."

"Well, I'll have to make sure that you get what you want while you're here," Danny said.

She nodded. "Yes. Fine. I suppose we should talk about compensation."

"I don't like to talk about money," he said. "That's business. And it will be difficult to know how much this will cost until I buy materials and get started."

"But I have to have some idea," she said, concern furrowing her brow.

"What's your budget?"

"Thirty thousand plus materials," she stated.

"Materials. There's where the budget could go to hell. You'll have to decide if you want iron or steel."

"What's the difference?"

"Iron is authentic to the time period but very expensive. Steel is cheaper, but it doesn't have the same look."

"Iron," she said. "When aesthetics make a difference. Steel, when practicality is important. This has to be an authentic restoration."

"The labor budget sounds more than reasonable," he said. In truth, it was enough to live on for a good year. Once he completed this job, he could spend the next twelve months working on his art instead of working in the smithy. "You've got your man."

She relaxed and smiled. "Good."

"Now, why don't you show me where I'm going to live and where I'll set up the forge."

They made a quick tour of the house, upstairs and down, then walked outside to tour the collection of stone buildings that surrounded the manor. There was a stable, a barn and a huge garden with a newly restored drystone wall. "You'll need a gate for this?" he asked, peering over.

An elderly man and woman were inside, wearing wide-brimmed hats and wellies, standing among huge piles of earth. They stared down into a hole in the ground, not noticing Danny and Jordan. "What are they doing?" he asked.

"That's Bartie and his friend, Daisy. They run the garden club in Glencairn. They showed up one morning and volunteered to do the work for free if I paid for the plantings. Bartie claims that he played in the garden as a child."

"Folks around the county weren't very happy to hear that an American bought this place," he said. "They're kind of suspicious of outsiders."

"I know. But I'm employing a lot of local craftsmen and once they find out who bought the place, they'll be fine. The person is of Irish descent. In fact, she can trace her family back to the original builders of the castle."

"Are you going to tell me who it is, then?"

"You have to promise not to say anything. Until she moves in, she'd like to avoid publicity."

Jordan leaned forward and whispered a familiar name into his ear. There weren't many actors living in County Cork, and now they were about to gain a certified American movie star. "Holy Mary, now there's some news."

She pressed her finger to her lips and shook her head. "Don't tell."

He pressed his own finger to his lips. "Silent as the grave, I'll be." Danny glanced back inside the garden. "So, what are they doing in there?"

"Some Irish thing. Purifying the soil, I believe he calls it. Something about the peat and the sea air and leachings from limestone. I don't really understand it. But he promises I'll have a beautiful rose garden in the end."

"Where do I stay?" Danny asked. "And where do I set up the forge?"

Jordan pointed down the path as they continued on. "There's an old laundry cottage back there with an existing hearth. I think that will do for the forge. And there's the cottage you can use for your living quarters. It was the first place we renovated," Jordan explained. "I used it as my home and office until the manor house had a decent roof and plumbing. It's very comfortable."

She unlocked the door and walked inside. Danny followed her to find a cozy place not much different from his cottage in Ballykirk, a bedroom on one end and a kitchen and bath on the other, with a large living area in between.

"I hope it's all right." Jordan motioned to the bedroom. "The bed is brand-new. There's electric heat and a shower in the bathroom. And a functioning kitchen."

"This will be fine," he said. "I can start moving in tomorrow."

"Good," she murmured.

He reached out and took her hand in his, weaving their fingers together. "So, I guess that would be it, Miss Kennally. Everything is settled between us?"

"Yes," she said, watching him play with her hand. "I—I look forward to working with you, Mr.—I mean, Daniel. Danny. Dan?"

"Danny," he said. He took her hand and turned it

over, then placed her palm on his chest, covering her hand with his. He wanted to do so much more. "I would kiss you, but now that we've come to an agreement, we'll have plenty of time for that later."

"Well, you got what you wanted," she said. "And I got exactly what I wanted. That's what makes a good business deal, don't you think?"

"I got the first thing I wanted. But there's always room for renegotiation." With that, he let her hand drop and turned to the door of the cottage. It took all his will-power to walk away. "I'll see you tomorrow, Jordan."

He left her standing in the center of the room, her green eyes wide, her lips parted. As Danny strode back to his car, he couldn't help but wonder if all that had happened between them had simply been a way to secure his services. When she'd come to the smithy that morning, she'd been determined to convince him to work for her and here he was, ready to drop every-thing and move into her caretaker's cottage.

No, Danny thought to himself. He knew how to read women and she was just as attracted to him as he was to her. There was a lot about this job he was going to like, Danny mused. And spending more time with Jordan Kennally was top on the list.

2

Jordan rolled over in bed and stared at the alarm clock
on the bedside table. It was almost 8:00 a.m. and she'd
only managed a few hours of sleep. She was always up
early, supervising the workmen, putting together the
daily schedule, checking on supplies and invoices. This
morning, she'd risen at sunrise, unlocked the doors, then
crawled back into bed.

After what had happened yesterday with Danny
Quinn, her whole routine had been thrown into a tail-
spin. Now, all she could think about was the way he'd
kissed her and touched her, the feel of his chest beneath
her palms, the way he seemed to ignite her desire with
just one look.

Jordan groaned and pulled the pillow over her head.
"I've been in Ireland too long," she murmured. "I need
to get back to my real life in New York."

But she knew she was only kidding herself. The
longer she'd stayed in Ireland, the more she'd grown to
enjoy the feelings of freedom. Here she didn't have to
worry about pleasing her father or competing with her

brothers or avoiding her mother's endless attempts at matchmaking. Here, she did her job and she enjoyed it.

That had been easy until now. She hadn't had any trouble keeping her mind on business. But after her encounter with Danny, maybe the effort had finally become too much to handle. The stress of devoting her every waking moment to this project had finally made her crack.

Never, ever, in her life had she thrown herself at a guy the way she had with him. He was, admittedly, the most handsome man she'd ever met. That dark hair and those incredible blue eyes. And that smile that sent shivers racing through her body. Undeniable lust was only a natural reaction.

But it was more than that. It felt good to be wanted. She'd spent so much time trying to make her way in the men's club that was Kencor that she'd almost forgotten she was a woman. Danny had reminded her that she was pretty and interesting and maybe even a little sexy.

He was a charming bloke, as the Irish would say. Talented, too. She'd always admired artistic people. Though she'd possessed a knack for design, she'd majored in business in college. And her eye for choosing fabrics and furniture wasn't nearly as interesting as that of a painter or sculptor.

But this project would be done in less than three months and she'd be ready to move on to something bigger and better at Kencor. Her father was in negotiation to buy an old Manhattan hotel and she wanted that project more than anything. She wasn't about to allow herself to be distracted by a man—even one as sexy as Danny.

Jordan had sought her father's approval from the time she knew what it was. But he'd never really noticed her, devoting his attention to his four sons. In truth, Jordan had always felt that she'd been born to satisfy her mother's need for a daughter.

She'd spent her entire life trying to hide the fact that she was a girl. As a child, she'd dressed just like her brothers, in jeans and T-shirts, trying desperately to keep up with them in every activity from football to fishing. As a teen, she'd turned her competitiveness toward her education, refusing to take anything but the honors courses that her brothers had completed before her. And though she'd longed to major in interior design in college, she'd chosen business instead, like her brothers.

This was the project that would finally prove she was just as competent as any son Andrew Kennally had. He'd tossed this project to her, deeming it a good job for a girl. The fact that it was in Ireland made it even better. It would get Jordan out of the way for a year or two. But she'd determined that Castle Cnoc would prove her worthy of so much more.

Jordan snuggled back beneath the covers. If she could just catch a few more hours, she'd be ready to deal with the arrival of her new blacksmith. "Danny," she murmured. "Danny Quinn." She closed her eyes and an image of the handsome Irishman swirled around in her head.

It wasn't wrong to indulge her attraction in private. Though sleeping with an employee was against every code she followed, sleeping with the fantasy of him was perfectly acceptable—as long as she didn't tell anyone.

The sound of barking dogs invaded her waking dream and she brushed it aside. But then she heard a car door slam and that brought Jordan upright in bed. Tossing the covers aside, she raced over to the window that overlooked the front drive.

Two very familiar dogs ran around Danny's battered Land Rover. "Oh, shit!" she muttered, running her hands through her tangled hair. How was it possible that he was here already? Had he stayed up all night packing? Somehow, she couldn't imagine a man like Danny being so excited about moving in that he couldn't sleep through the night. No, only silly, infatuated, desperate women did that.

Jordan scrambled to get dressed, pulling on a pair of jeans and a T-shirt, with no time for underwear. As she slipped on a pair of loafers, she ran her hands through her tangled hair. Today she'd regain her footing with this man. She'd act professionally and she wouldn't let anything he said or did tempt her. Time to get back to business. "Stay strong, be firm," she murmured to herself.

Jordan grabbed her sweater, then raced down the stairs and ran though the entrance hall. Opening the plywood front door, she expected to find Danny waiting on the other side, but he wasn't. She walked beneath the scaffolding and pushed the plastic aside to find him sitting on the tailgate of his Land Rover, staring up at the facade of the manor house as he chatted with Bartie the gardener.

The dogs saw her first and they came trotting up.

"Hi, puppies," she mumbled. What were their names? Mogue was one. "Finny," she said. "Finny and Mogue."

"They seem excited to move in," Danny commented.

She glanced up at him, blinking against the morning light. "I'd prefer that they didn't come in the main house," she said.

"No problems," he said. "They sleep with me."

Another image of him flashed in her head, naked, lying in her bed, the covers tossed aside. What did he mean by that? Had he decided he wasn't interested in sharing her bed? Jordan closed her eyes and banished the erotic fantasy from her head. "Morning, Bartie. You're here early." She glanced down to find the old man holding what looked like a metal detector. "What's that?"

"Special thing it is. Got it from a gardener friend of mine. Supposed to measure the ferrous metals in the soil. Ferrous metals. Very bad for roses, I'm afraid."

"Yes, well. Good luck with that. You're not paying rental for it, are you?"

"No, no. 'Tis a loan." Bartie nodded at them both, then strode off around the side of the manor house, his pace sprightly for a man of his years.

"Ferrous metals?" Danny asked. "What are those?"

Jordan shrugged. "I have no idea. Something Irish I suspect. According to Bartie, it's a wonder anything grows in Ireland."

"My mother has a beautiful rose garden at our family cottage," Danny said. "I never heard her complain about…"

"Ferrous metals," Jordan said. She held her hand up

to the sun, squinting at him. "I was just going to make a pot of coffee. Would you like some?"

He pushed up from his seat on the tailgate. "Actually, I'm going to start unpacking my things. My brother Riley is going to bring my anvil and tools. And I've set up a coal delivery for today. Steel is coming in tomorrow. Can I drive around to the back?"

"Of course," she said. "Well, it seems as if you have things under control."

He chuckled softly, shoving his hands in the back pockets of his jeans. "Appearances can be deceiving. Right now, all I can think about is kissing you again. I'd say control is the last thing on my mind."

"The hours from eight until five are considered work hours," she said. "With an hour for lunch." But though her warning effectively shut him up, Jordan was secretly pleased he was still thinking of her as a woman rather than a boss. Maybe they could stretch the rules a bit. A kiss here and there couldn't hurt, could it?

"After I get some coffee, I'll come and help you unload." She groaned inwardly at her choice of words. Everything she said to him sounded sexual now.

"Bring me a cup and I'll meet you there," he said.

She nodded. "Fine. I'll come in just a—" This was ridiculous! "I'll be just a moment." Jordan turned on her heel and walked back inside the manor. When she reached the safety of the kitchen, she clapped her hands to her warm cheeks. "Get a grip," she muttered to herself. At this rate, they'd be in bed by lunchtime and exploring their deepest sexual fantasies by dinner.

If this was the way it was going to be every day that he was here, she wondered how she'd survive. Her heart was beating double-time and her nerves were so jangled she wanted to scream at the top of her lungs.

The coffeemaker had been set up the night before and Jordan simply pushed a button and waited as the glass pot began to fill. Sitting at the huge worktable in the center of the kitchen, she cupped her chin in her palm and considered the men she'd allowed into her life—and into her bed.

Though she'd had a number of lovers in the past, none of them had really moved her. The relationships had always been enjoyable, the sex interesting, but she'd always held something back. And Jordan was self-aware enough to put the blame for this on her relationship with her father.

Though she'd struggled to win his approval, she sometimes resented the control he held over her life. Andrew Kennally could snap his fingers any time of the day or night and she'd come running, ready to do his bidding. But she had refused to do the same for any man in her life. And in the end, they'd never wanted to compete with a man as powerful as Andrew Kennally.

Jordan wondered what it would be like to let go of all the baggage she carried around. Just to set it down and feel completely at ease for once. What harm could a little romantic fling do? There were few people around to witness any dalliance, just a workman here and there. Bartie and Daisy were too preoccupied with the garden to pay any notice. And everyone left at five, giving her all evening alone with Danny on this remote seaside estate.

The coffeemaker clicked off, startling her back to reality. It was a risk, pure and simple. If her father found out, he'd be furious. Sex with an employee was forbidden by company policy. She could be sued for sexual harassment, putting her entire professional future at Kencor in jeopardy.

Jordan grabbed a pair of mugs from a nearby cupboard and filled them, then put sugar and creamer in one and left the other black. After this morning, she'd know exactly how he liked his coffee. And by the end of the day, Jordan was certain she'd know a lot of other things about Danny.

Anticipation mixed with fear as she walked out the kitchen door and toward the caretaker's cottage. The dogs were romping along the garden path and joined her, trotting along behind. "I don't want the two of you digging up any of the new plantings in the garden," she ordered. "And if you have to poop, run out along the cliff to do it."

Finny and Mogue looked up at her as if they understood everything she was saying. But she made a mental note to repeat the rules to their owner as well.

When she reached the cottage, she found Danny inside, his belongings tossed in the middle of the living area. He emerged a few moments later from the kitchen, his canvas jacket gone. He wore a faded T-shirt that hugged the muscles of his chest and dangled loosely around his waist.

"There's beer in the fridge," he said.

"I stocked the refrigerator last night." She frowned. "Do you drink your beer warm?"

He crossed the room to stand in front of her. "No. Cold is fine. And I drink my coffee hot and black." She handed him the proper mug. "That was nice of you. Very thoughtful…for a boss."

She knew immediately that he was teasing. There was a definitely a twinkle in his eye and a devilish smile playing across his lips. "I just wanted to make sure you were comfortable," Jordan said.

"I have drink. What about food?"

"You're on your own there," she said. "I set up the account for you at the market. They'll have everything you need to make meals."

"You're not going to cook for me?" He put on a pout. "I thought that was part of the deal."

"No, I think I made it quite clear yesterday that I don't cook."

"Ah, but I do," he said. "Good thing."

Jordan had been surviving on sandwiches and cereal for most of her stay. A few nights a week, she went into town and had a decent dinner at one of the pubs there. But she'd longed to explore a bit further. She just needed a dinner partner. "I'll pay for dinners out whenever you care to go," she said.

"If you come along, it's a deal."

Danny rested his hand on her hip. Jordan's breath caught in her throat. Were they at that point already, that he could touch her without even having a good reason?

"It's a deal," she repeated.

"I'm gummin' for a decent breakfast. Why don't I finish unpacking and we'll go out and get something. My treat."

Jordan was tempted by his offer. She usually didn't leave the worksite during the day. But the men who were scheduled knew their jobs and would keep an eye on the house. "All right," she said. "Let me just make a few phone calls."

"Fifteen minutes?" he asked.

"Yes. I'll be back."

The minute Jordan got out of the cottage, she ran. Back to the manor house, up the stairs and into her room. Fifteen minutes was just enough time for a shower. She hadn't shaved her legs in a week, but that would have to wait. Though it was just a simple breakfast, Jordan couldn't help but be excited. Any excuse to spend time with Danny was worth celebrating.

"TELL ME ALL ABOUT YOURSELF," Danny asked, staring at Jordan over the rim of his coffee cup. "And spare no details."

There was no doubt about it. He found her endlessly fascinating and they didn't even know each other yet. He watched as she spread jam on her toast in a precise manner, then took a tiny bite out of it. It wasn't just her body, he mused, although that was just grand. He found himself caught up in the chase, the desire to possess a woman who was equally determined to avoid him.

Sure, they'd shared a few kisses, but according to Jordan, it would have to end there. But that wouldn't stop him from trying. He wanted to know what she looked like naked, how her body felt beneath his hands, what she talked about in her sleep. But even that wasn't enough. He wanted to know about her life, the people she loved, her dreams, her fears.

Danny had usually satisfied himself with the superficial and left it at that. But there was something about

Jordan that made him want to know more. Was it just curiosity or was there some deeper connection?

"Are you going to eat that toast or paint a portrait of the Mona Lisa with raspberry jam?" He grabbed her hand and took a bite, then grinned.

"Hey! Eat your own toast."

"I like yours better," he said. Though she did everything to perfection, from buttering toast to renovating the manor house, there was one thing that seemed to escape her—flirting.

"What do you want to know?" she asked.

"Tell me about your family," he ordered.

"Only if you tell me about yours," she countered.

"Agreed. You first."

"All right. There's not much to tell. I have four older brothers who work for the family business. My father thinks I should decorate houses but I think I should get the same chance to run Kencor as my brothers have. So I work as hard as I can."

"You and your father don't get on?" Danny asked.

Jordan shook her head. "I'm sure he loves me just as any father would. But he doesn't really trust me. I think I remind him of my mother. She drives him crazy." She took a bite of her eggs. "I suppose you have a normal family life?"

"As normal as it gets," Danny replied. "Two sisters, two brothers, all older. I know what it's like to be on the trailing end. I was always following my brothers around. My folks own a pub in Ballykirk. The Speckled Hound. My sisters are both married, both teachers. You know Kell. He's the oldest boy and then there's Riley. He's a musician and he helps my folks with the pub."

"And how did you become a blacksmith?" she asked.

"I went to art school and studied sculpting and along the way I started working in metal. It was the next logical step. I saw a demonstration at one of the heritage festivals and went to a few workshops. Then I spent my summer holiday working for a smith up in Galway."

"It seems like such hard work to make that iron do what you want it to."

"It is. It's a slow process. It gives you time to think and plan and visualize what you want it to be. All the architectural stuff is just to pay the bills. Someday, I'd like to focus entirely on sculpture."

"I saw the work in your portfolio. The willow tree that you did, the one that was blowing in the wind, that was one of the most beautiful things I've ever seen. I want it for the garden here."

"You'll have to steal it from the lady I sold it to in Dublin," he said. "It's sitting in the lobby of her posh hotel."

"You should show in a gallery," she said.

"I have a few things in a show opening next month. And I've had my own show a few times at a gallery one of my friends runs." He paused, observing her from across the table. "What about a boyfriend?"

His question took her by surprise and Danny cursed inwardly, knowing he should have waited. But there was no reason not to be honest about his interest in her.

"Sorry," he said. "Just curious."

"You first," Jordan countered. "Do you have a girlfriend? Or do you have five or six?"

"I have no girlfriend," he said. "There was someone about a year ago, for about a month, but that ended. No hard feelings. Most women are looking for a little bit better than I'm able to provide. Now you."

"There is a guy I used to see in New York. But we were never in a committed relationship. We were just…" She cleared her throat. "Friends."

"You're just dating then?"

"Well, no." She frowned. "Yes. At least I was. I'm sure we'll see each other again when I get back to New York."

"Naked?" he asked.

She gasped. "What?"

"Will you see each other naked? It's a simple question."

"That's none of your business," she replied.

"Well, it is. I don't want to cause any problems between you and your man."

"He's not my man. I don't have a man," Jordan said. "I'm single and that's all I have to say about it."

"You sound a wee bit prickly there," he said. "Did I touch on a sore subject?"

"You're awfully nosy for someone I've just met."

"Curious," he said. "That's a better word for it. So, now it's your turn. Ask me anything you like. Anything at all."

He picked up a slice of bacon and bit off the end, then waited for her to come up with an appropriate question. But she seemed to struggle. "You want to know whether I can be discreet," he finally said. "You want to know that, if we indulge, it won't blow up in your face. And you really want to know what I look like naked."

A nervous laugh burst from her lips. "No," she said, shaking her head.

"Yes," Danny countered, reaching across the table to capture her hand. "You do." He opened her fingers and placed a kiss on her palm. "I look feckin' fabulous, just to let you know."

Jordan gasped, pulling her hand away. "Are you always so bold?"

"Absolutely."

A pretty blush stained her cheeks. "I'll take your word for it."

"And I can be discreet, too," he said.

"I don't need complications," Jordan murmured.

"It's very simple, then. Whenever we're alone, I have permission to kiss you. And we'll see where it leads? Sound good?"

"It sounds very good. I'm just not—"

He reached out and pressed his finger to her lips. "Leave it at that," he said. "Talking about it isn't nearly as much fun as doing it." He picked up a piece of toast from his plate and held it out to her. "Can you put some jam on this?"

Jordan stared at the toast. "What?"

"I like the way you do it. You spread it out right to the edge. Perfectly perfect without any drips."

"Are you making fun of me?" she asked.

"A little bit. But I fancy what I see."

"And in between all this kissing, you're going to get your work done?"

"That's what I'm here for," he said. "I thought I'd start with the big projects first and cross them off the list and—"

"No," Jordan interrupted. "No, we have to have the

hinges first. The doors will be back next week and they all have to be hung. The hardware comes first."

"All right," he said, nodding. "Hardware first."

"I have it all laid out on a spreadsheet," she explained. "And a flowchart. I can show them to you if you'd like. I'll make you a copy."

"No need," Danny said. "I'm sure I can get along without." He smiled at her. "I like a woman who takes charge."

"All right. I'm a little obsessive-compulsive. But that's not a bad thing. I wouldn't have gotten where I am if I didn't care about details."

"You've been in Ireland for how long?"

"Sixteen months," she said. "But for the first year I went back and forth to New York once a month."

"You've spent too much time shut up in that house. We're going to have to loosen you up, woman. Show you what Ireland is really like. I'll wager you'll become so fond of the place, you'll never want to leave."

"And how do you propose to do that?"

"I have my ways," he said.

The rest of the breakfast passed in lighthearted conversation. He learned more about the project and about Jordan. Though she spent most of her free time working, it wasn't for lack of interest in the surrounding countryside. She'd visited many of the estates open to the public and spent time at museums and shops in Dublin, Galway and Cork. But she'd never been out to a pub on a Saturday night.

They'd have two, maybe three months together. If he couldn't provide her with a bit of fun and excitement in that time, then he didn't deserve to be called an Irishman. "So what do you do for fun if you're not out at the pubs?" he asked. "When you need a break or you want to relax, what do you do?

She gave him an odd look. "I have fun."

"How?" he said.

Jordan seemed reluctant to tell him. "I read, I listen to music."

"That sounds like fun," he said, grinning.

"And now I'm looking for the brownies that keep stealing things from the house," she said.

"You believe in brownies now?"

"I don't know what to believe. But things disappear in the middle of night. I found an old ring in one of the bathrooms. I set it on the sink and a day later, it was gone. Then it turned up in the bottom of a cabinet."

"Hmm. I suppose I could spend the night with you and we'd search out those brownies soon enough," Danny suggested.

Jordan met his gaze. "You're a nice guy, Daniel Quinn. But we won't be sleeping together."

"You don't even know me yet," Danny teased. "If you did, you'd realize that I'm far from nice. In fact, I'm very, very naughty. As for sleeping together, it's a little soon to be makin' a statement like that, don't you think?"

BY THE END OF THE DAY, Danny had managed to get the old laundry set up as a temporary forge. It had been impossible for Jordan to get any work done and she found herself standing at the second-story windows and staring out over the garden, hoping to catch a glimpse of him in the yard beyond.

By the third visit, when she'd brought him a glass of lemonade and a ham sandwich, he'd finished hanging all his tools from a chain stretched across the old laundry.

The coal was delivered by truck after lunch, and she stood and chatted with him as he filled a wheelbarrow full and dumped it beside the hearth. It was almost too much to bear, watching the play of muscle beneath his smooth skin as he worked. She wanted to reach out and run her hands over his shoulders and down his back; but she was left to pretend that his shirtless state had no effect on her at all.

She was thankful that the two dogs were a constant presence; when she ran out of things to say, she'd toss them a stick or rub their bellies.

The sun was beginning to descend in the west when Jordan decided to ask about Danny's plans for dinner. She'd promised to provide him with a decent meal and she couldn't think of anything else that might provide them with more time together.

She grabbed the bag of dog treats she'd purchased in the village that afternoon and headed out to the temporary smithy. Finny and Mogue were asleep in the doorway and she called to them, then tossed a treat up in the air. To her surprise, Finny leapt and caught it in midflight. When she tossed one Mogue's way, Finny cut the smaller dog off and grabbed a second bite. "Don't be so greedy," she cried. "You've already had one."

"You're spoiling them," Danny called from the doorway.

Jordan glanced up, then straightened. Every time she saw him, a tiny thrill raced through her. She wondered when they'd kiss again. "I like them," she said. "We always had dogs when I was young. Golden retrievers, mostly."

"Why not get one now?"

"With my schedule? I wouldn't have time to spend with a pet. It wouldn't be fair."

"Well, you can have these two for as long as I stay. If you keep feeding them treats, they won't listen to me anyway."

She closed the bag. "So, how are things going?"

"I'm ready to start. Iron and steel stock is coming tomorrow. I've finished patterns for the hinges and I should be able to start work on those as soon as I get materials. Here, let me show you."

She followed him inside to a scarred wooden table he'd found in the stable. "I've looked at the doors and they weigh a ton. I'd recommend that you use modern-day hinges for strength. They'll last longer, they'll operate more smoothly and I can make dummy straps, so they'll look like the originals."

"If you think that's best," she said. "I'll trust your judgment."

"I think that's best," he said. "And it will save you some money."

"Good. I like that." Her gaze scanned his naked torso. "Are you finished for the day?"

He nodded. "I was just going to take a quick shower."

"Come with me. I want to show you something."

"It's past five," he said. "I'm knackered."

She reached out and grabbed his hand. "This isn't work. You'll like it. I promise."

She pulled him outside, reveling in the feel of his

fingers laced through hers. Just the simple act of touching him was enough to send a surge of need through her. She wondered what it might be like to be able to touch him at will, to have the complete freedom to explore his body.

They walked through the house and then down a narrow hallway behind the butler's pantry. Jordan opened a door and flipped on a light switch before leading him down a short flight of stairs. The air was moist and a familiar scent teased at her nose.

She flipped another switch and the lights illuminated a huge room with an arched ceiling. Set below them was a swimming pool, the underwater lights creating strange shadows on the walls.

Danny gasped. "Jaysus, has this been here all along?"

Jordan nodded. "The water was drained, of course, and it was full of musty old wicker furniture when I got here. And all the plumbing was rusted, but it's all functioning now." She stared up at the ceiling. "The tiles were hand-painted by an artist in Belfast. And they were installed by workmen who worked on the *Titanic*. Luckily, they were in perfect condition. Replacing them would have been ridiculously expensive."

Danny stared up at the ceiling. "Half-naked fairies must have been pretty racy for the turn of the century."

"I'm sure they were," Jordan said. "There are mermaids beneath the water."

"You shouldn't have brought me here," Danny said, shifting his gaze to the water. "It's like holding out a bottle of water to a man dying of thirst."

"You want to swim? Go ahead. It took forever to fill.

Nearly a week, but the new heater is working and it's warm enough to use now."

"Really?" Danny didn't wait for her answer. He tugged off his T-shirt as he kicked off his shoes and socks. But when he reached for the button on his jeans, Jordan sucked in a sharp breath. Danny glanced up and she quickly tried to compose herself. "Sorry. I figured boxers were just as good as a bathing suit."

"Oh, no," she said, "that's fine. Go right ahead."

"Turn around," he said, twirling his finger in the air. "I wouldn't want to make you blush. Unless, that was your plan all along in bringing me here. Getting me starkers."

"That's exactly what I was thinking of," Jordan said. "Go ahead, what are you waiting for? I'm looking forward to the superhero underwear."

He glanced down then winced. "To tell the truth, I seem to have forgotten my underwear this morning," he replied.

She quickly covered her eyes and a moment later, she heard him jump into the shallow end of the pool. When she looked again he was submerged and swimming to the deep end, his naked form visible beneath the wavering water. As he came closer to the surface, she turned back around.

"All right," he called. "You can look now."

She peered through her fingers. Danny bobbed at the far end of the pool, his arms stretched out along the tile deck. "Are you going to come in? The water's beautiful. Warm enough to be comfortable, cool enough to be refreshing."

"You're naked," she said.

"I promise, I'll stay on this end. And if you're shy, just leave your clothes on."

"I'm not going to jump in with my clothes on."

"Then take your clothes off. I won't look." Danny watched her face as she considered her options. "Oh, I can see those wheels turning. Should I cast aside my inhibitions and give it a go? Or should I pretend like I'm a good girl? I know you're not a good girl, Jordan. There's a wild woman under that proper dress and cardie."

"Don't presume to know what I'm thinking," she warned.

"We're both adults," he said.

"I'm your boss, you're my employee."

"I'm your artist, you're my muse," he countered.

"More like I'm a canary and you're a hungry cat," she said.

"All right, don't come in." He pushed off the side and submerged, kicking and stroking beneath the water before he came up in the middle of the pool. "This is incredible. The perfect way to relax after a long day at work. A bloke could get used to living like this. In the lap of luxury."

"Money doesn't always buy happiness," Jordan said.

"Who says that? And who even believes that's true?"

"I do," she said. Jordan kicked off her shoes and pulled up her skirt, then sat down on the edge of the pool, dangling her feet in the water. "My father has all the money in the world and he's never really been happy. He always seems to need more. When is it finally enough? When can you sit back and enjoy what you have?"

"I don't know," Danny said. "I never really thought about it."

"I do," she said. "All the time."

"Are you happy?" he asked. "I mean, right now, at this moment." She thought about her answer for a long moment, a frown wrinkling her brow. "It's not a trick question."

"It's not the money. That's not why I want a place at Kencor. I'd work for free if it were challenging work. I love my job."

He swam across the pool and stood in front of her, the water lapping at his waist. Droplets streamed over his skin and clung to his lashes. "You don't convince me," he said softly. "I want to know what makes you smile."

"Watching silly animal videos on YouTube," she said. "Eating a whole pint of chocolate ice cream at three in the morning. Getting the hiccups from drinking too much champagne."

"Do I make you smile?" he asked. Danny wrapped his arms around her legs and gently pulled her closer to the edge. "When I touch you?" He smoothed his hand along her thigh, beneath her skirt. "Would you smile if I dragged you in?"

"No," she warned. "I'd be mad. My phone is in my pocket and I don't think my watch is waterproof."

Danny stepped between her knees and reached up to slip his hand around her nape. He gently pulled her toward him until their lips were just a few inches apart.

A tiny sigh slipped from her throat when he removed her watch from her wrist and set it on the pool deck. Then, Danny smoothed his hands over the skirt of her dress until he found her cell phone. He slipped it out of her pocket and set it beside her watch, then gently pulled her into the water. Jordan didn't even bother to protest. What was the point? Trying to deny her impulses would only frustrate them both.

When her feet touched bottom, she reached for the hem of her dress and pulled it over her head, then tossed it to the pool deck. She'd chosen her underwear very carefully that morning and was satisfied that the scraps of lace and satin were enough for now.

Though it was difficult to ignore the fact that Danny was naked, Jordan decided to keep her gaze fixed firmly on his face to avoid any embarrassing moments. "It *is* nice," she said.

He slipped his hands around her waist, his attention moving to her lips. "I'm going to kiss you again," he murmured. "It's past five, so I think it's legal."

He leaned forward and brushed his damp lips against hers. A flood of need raced through her and suddenly, she felt as if her heart might beat right out of her chest.

Maybe it was the warm water or their lack of clothing, but any attempt at self-control by either one of them had gone missing. Her fingers furrowed through his hair as the kiss deepened. She couldn't breathe, couldn't think. Every ounce of her being was focusing on the wild sensations racing through her body.

She wanted to stop, or at least slow down, but she seemed unable to put together the will. When his lips trailed along her shoulder, Jordan gasped. And when he cupped her breast with his hand, a little moan sneaked out. All she could do was react.

Maybe she'd known all along that this was coming.

From the moment she'd met Danny, there'd been a powerful attraction. She ruffled his damp hair as his lips trailed from her neck to her collarbone. He drifted lower still, until he could tease at her nipple through the wet fabric of her bra.

Pleasure washed over her, so intense that she felt as if she were drowning in sensation. Jordan closed her eyes and threw out her arms, floating on the surface as he gently explored her body with his hands and his mouth. It felt like total surrender, as if the real world no longer existed. She had no worries, no doubts and nothing holding her back. She was a woman, from the tips of her toes to the top of her head, and for the first time in her life, she was truly comfortable with it.

And then a familiar sound echoed through the cavernous room. Jordan opened her eyes and groaned softly.

"Ignore it," he said, pulling her up into his embrace.

"I can't."

"What could be so imp—"

"It's probably my father. He calls every Friday about this time for a progress report. If I don't answer he gets—well, he doesn't like it." She carefully untangled herself from Danny's embrace and walked over to the edge of the pool. Bracing her hands on the edge, she boosted herself onto the deck, then retrieved her phone.

"Hello, Daddy," she said, hurrying to the stairs and away from the echo of the pool. In truth, she was almost happy for the interruption. Things were moving far too fast with Danny and she needed a chance to take a breath.

From now on, she was going to think before she ripped off her clothes and gave in to the charms of a naked Irishman.

3

Danny woke up with a start, yanked out of a deep and dreamless sleep. The dogs were at the front door of the caretaker's cottage, barking frantically. He swung his legs over the edge of the bed and stood, wondering what had set them off. Dragging the sheet along with him, he wrapped it around his naked body.

"Shush," he said, walking out of the bedroom and flipping on the lights. "What are you two about?"

A frantic rap sounded on the door and he opened it to find Jordan standing on the other side. She was dressed in just a T-shirt and her panties, her feet bare.

Pushing past him, she stalked inside, then spun around to face him. "Were you just in the house?" she asked.

He looked at her and shook his head, trying to reconcile her strange appearance at his door. "What time is it?"

"I—I don't know. Late. Maybe two?" Her expression was etched with fear. "Were you just in the house?"

Danny raked his hand through his hair. "No. I was asleep."

"Don't lie to me," she snapped.

"What the hell are you talking about, Jordan? After you left, I came right back here. I've been here ever since. Though not by choice."

"Someone was in my bedroom," she said. "I was having trouble sleeping and I turned over and opened my eyes and he was standing in the doorway. I could see him."

Danny reached out and drew her into his arms. "It was probably just a nightmare."

"No!" she cried, shoving away from him. "I reached out to turn on the light and then he was gone. But I heard his footsteps in the hall. I ran out to follow him, but there was no one there."

"Sometimes your mind can play tricks on you."

"I know what I saw."

"The doors were locked. How could anyone have gotten in the house?"

She drew a ragged breath, then sighed softly, sinking against his body. "I—I don't know. I was just so—I was sure I—"

Danny smoothed his hand over her hair and drew her closer. "Do you want me to go back and search the house for you? I'll take the dogs. If there's anyone in the house, Finny and Mogue will find them."

"No. I'm fine."

"You can stay here with me, if you like. We'll look into this tomorrow."

She glanced up at him, eyes wide. "I can't stay here."

"Why not? Nothing is going to happen." He took her hand, lacing his fingers through hers, then drew her along toward the bedroom. "I'll stay on my side of the bed and you have to promise to stay on your side."

"I don't know," she murmured. "Maybe I should take my chances in the house."

"Your choice," Danny said with a shrug. "I can send the dogs back with you. They'll protect you."

"Maybe that would be best," she replied.

Danny couldn't think of anything he wanted more than to have Jordan in his bed. From the moment they'd first kissed it had been all he could think about. But it had to be on her terms. Since her father's call, she'd been a bit more aloof and he knew exactly what she was thinking. Having an affair with him would probably break all kinds of rules that she couldn't afford to break.

"I'll walk you back and make sure everything is all right." He strode into the bedroom, grabbed his jeans and tugged them on. Then he pulled his jacket from the bedpost and when he returned to her, draped it over her shoulders. "Come on, let's go."

As they walked outside into the chilly night, he whistled softly to the dogs and they fell into step behind them.

"You probably think I'm crazy," she said.

"No. Does anyone else have a key to the house? Did you ever give one to any of the workmen?"

"No. I've always been very careful. And I lock the temporary doors from the inside with a padlock. There's no way to get in once I've locked everything."

They walked through the dark house. He could feel her tense beside him and he slipped his arm around her shoulders and pulled her close. When they reached her bedroom, he walked inside first. "I thought you said you turned on the light."

"I did," she said. "At least, I think I did. Maybe this was just all a dream."

Danny turned on the bedside lamp, then carefully surveyed the room. There didn't seem to be anything amiss. "Come on, hop in."

The dogs explored the room as Jordan crawled back into bed and pulled the covers up to her chin. Danny sat down on the edge of the bed. "The dogs will bark if anyone comes into the house."

"Stay here a little longer," Jordan said.

"Sure. Do you have any whiskey? Maybe a drink would calm your nerves."

"There is a bottle downstairs."

"I'll go get it and check all the doors and windows. You stay here with the dogs."

Jordan turned onto her side and clutched his hand. "I feel so stupid. It was probably just a bad dream. I had that curry for dinner and I always have weird dreams after spicy food." She looked up at him. "I'm sorry I bothered you."

"It's not a problem," he said. He dropped a kiss on her lips, not really thinking before he did. She was so close, it just seemed like the most natural thing to kiss her. But as soon as he drew back, Danny realized that one kiss would not be enough. "I'll be back in a few minutes."

The house was silent as Danny walked through the lower floor, checking the windows and the doors. He had to believe that Jordan had seen *something* to send her running to him in the middle of the night. When he checked the library, he noticed one of the windows was open a crack and shut it. But before he turned out the light, he spotted a muddy footprint on the floor near one of the bookshelves.

It was the print of a man's shoe or boot, a bit larger than his own, with a different pattern on the sole. Bending down, Danny ran his finger over the footprint and found the mud still damp. "What the hell," he muttered. Someone *had* been in the house, and not very long ago.

He grabbed the bottle of whiskey from the table in the library, along with two glasses and headed upstairs. For now, he'd keep his discovery a secret. It wouldn't do to scare Jordan. But he had no intention of leaving her alone in the house now—with or without his dogs.

When he returned to the bedroom, Danny found her sitting up in bed, Finny and Mogue curled up beside her. He chuckled softly as he handed her a glass and poured whiskey into it. "I usually don't let them sleep on the bed." He snapped his fingers and the dogs jumped down to the floor. Danny sat down beside her and poured himself a glass.

"Did you find anything?" she asked.

Danny shook his head. "No. Everything was locked up tight. But I'm going to stay here tonight with you anyway. Just to be certain." He wrapped his arm around her shoulders and pulled her up against his body.

She relaxed, resting her whiskey on his stomach as she nestled into the curve of his body. Danny sipped at his drink as he rubbed her shoulder, his palm smoothing over her silken skin. His thoughts focused on that part of her body then drifted back to their swim in the pool.

How much would it take to get them back to that

moment, to that instant when their eyes met and the world seemed to stand still? He nuzzled his face in her hair then pressed a kiss to her forehead. He wasn't going to go there. Not until she was ready.

"Feel better?" he asked.

"Yes," she said.

The whiskey warmed his belly and relaxed his body. But it only made the thoughts of her more intense. He ran his hand over her arm and she turned in to him, her warmth seeping through the jeans he'd pulled on. It wasn't enough just to touch her.

Danny leaned over and pressed his mouth to hers, his tongue slowly tracing the crease between her lips. When he drew back, she was watching him. They stared at each other for a long time, neither one of them moving or speaking. Then Jordan pushed up on her elbow, her hand slipping around his neck to draw him near.

A long, soft kiss was his reward for his patience. And when she finally drew back, he knew that they'd started where they'd left off earlier. In fact, to his surprise, she'd decided to jump ahead a few steps.

She worked the buttons open on his jeans, then ran her hand from his belly to his chest and back again. Her touch sent his senses reeling and he wasn't sure if he could maintain his control at this kind of pace.

When her hand dipped lower, Danny groaned. It had been a while since the last time he'd had a woman. And he'd never had any trouble taking care of a woman's needs before his own. But this woman could do things to him that had never been done before.

He waited, holding his breath, as her hand slipped beneath the waistband of his jeans. Danny was almost afraid to touch her, afraid that just the simple feel of her flesh beneath his fingers would send him over the edge. She still wore the T-shirt and panties and he was almost grateful that she was covered.

But that gratitude didn't last long. Suddenly, she got to her knees and pulled the T-shirt over her head, tossing it aside. Danny's breath caught in his throat. She was, by all standards, the most beautiful creature he'd ever seen.

He quickly stripped off his jeans and she rid herself of her panties. When they were both naked, she sat next to him, as if she wasn't sure how to proceed. "I've never been much good at this," she whispered.

"I find that very hard to believe."

"If I'm doing something wrong, I want you to tell me. Promise?"

He shook his head. "We'll show each other," he said. "Take my hand." She did as she was told. "Show me where you like to be touched." Slowly, she placed his hand on her breast.

That was all it took to start them down a path of undeniable pleasure. That simple contact, the soft weight of her flesh in his hand, the stiff peak of her nipple, sent waves of desire racing through his body.

A sigh slipped from her throat and Danny pulled her down next to him and captured her mouth in a kiss filled with overwhelming need.

He pulled her beneath him, drawing her legs up alongside his hips. She was soft and warm, every inch of her naked body like a revelation. Had he ever felt this kind of need before? Had he ever been so determined to possess a woman?

Though he wanted to lose himself inside her, Danny realized that he'd left the condoms back at the caretaker's cottage. He weighed the risks of leaving her, knowing how easily the connection between them could snap. There were other ways to satisfy them both.

He moved against her, his shaft sliding along the moist slit between her legs. Jordan gasped, arching against him in response, her breath quickening. Danny closed his eyes, enjoying the sensations racing through his body. It was as close to sex as they could get without actually having sex and he thought it would be enough.

But for Jordan, it wasn't. She shifted beneath him and his next thrust was met with a different kind of resistance. He slipped inside her once, then quickly withdrew.

"I have condoms," he murmured. "But they're back in the cottage. I can go get them."

"I have condoms. And they're in the bedside table. I bought them after we met," she admitted.

Danny stretched out on top of her and opened the drawer, then grabbed the box. He quickly sheathed himself and a few seconds later, slipped back between her legs. He kissed her softly, his hands braced on either side of her shoulders, his shaft gently probing at her damp entrance.

It took every ounce of his willpower to wait, to move against her without plunging deep. But with every stroke, she seemed to grow more impatient, her moans tinged with frustration. And when he finally gave in, the sensation of entering her warmth nearly sent him over the edge.

Danny sensed she was close and every now and

then, he pulled out and rubbed up against her for a time, before slipping back inside.

Jordan's breath quickened and he continued to tease her until she was clutching at his shoulders and delirious with need. When the first shudder wracked her body, he knew that he could finally relinquish control.

Jordan arched against him, crying out as her body convulsed in a deep and powerful orgasm. He felt her tighten around him and drove into her one last time, then let himself go, his orgasm exploding deep inside her.

They continued to rock together, slowing the pace as the intensity of their pleasure subsided. It had been so quick, yet so powerful, nothing at all like he'd planned. He'd imagined a long, slow seduction, a gentle teasing before complete surrender.

This had been nothing more than a headlong rush toward mutual orgasms.

Danny pulled her down on top of him then rolled to his side until they faced each other. "Whoever told you that you weren't good at that ought to have the shite beat out of him on a daily basis."

"I think he might have been compensating for his own shortcomings," Jordan said.

"Shortcomings? Really?"

"Yeah," she said. "Really short shortcomings."

As he wrapped her in his arms and tucked her body into the curve of his, Danny found a certain satisfaction in the notion that he'd been the best. It was a good place to begin.

THE END OF DANNY'S FIRST WEEK of work was cause for celebration, at least according to him. In Jordan's mind, they'd been celebrating every night in her bedroom. There hadn't been any question where he'd sleep at night and each evening, after a late dinner and a sunset hike along the cliffs, they'd climb the stairs and begin a lazy night of lovemaking.

Jordan glanced over at him as he steered the car through the narrow streets of Ballykirk. Though she would have been happy to find their fun between the sheets, Danny had insisted that they go out. His brother Riley was singing at the family pub and everyone would be there.

He pulled the Land Rover into the narrow lane behind the blacksmith shop and stopped it. "Now, don't worry about meeting the family. You already know Kell, though I think he's back in Dublin this week. Oh, and Ma and Da are still in Scotland. But you'll like Riley. And his fiancée, Nan, is American, so you'll have that in common."

"I'm not nervous," she said. "Why would I be nervous?"

He shrugged. "You shouldn't be. It's just that the pub can be a wee bit...well, everyone will be happy to meet you, I can promise that." He jumped out of the car and jogged around to her side, then opened her door. "You look beautiful, by the way."

She took his hand and got out of the car. "Thank you."

He let the dogs out of the back, then slipped his arm around her waist. "I know this won't be anything like the clubs you go to in New York but you'll have fun, I promise. We're going to dance and sing and have a few pints. And at the end of the night, I'm going to take you home and make love to you."

"Can't we just skip to the last part? I'm really not much of a party girl."

"If you don't like it, we'll leave. But I promise, I'm going to show you a good time."

"Then let's go," Jordan said. "I'm ready...I think."

The pub was noisy and crowded when they walked inside. Danny wrapped his arm around her shoulders and guided her through the crowd, calling out greetings to friends as he passed. Jordan pasted a smile on her face and tried to appear friendly.

Suddenly, a beautiful dark-haired girl appeared out of the crowd. "You're here!" she cried. "And you've brought a friend."

"Nan Galvin, this is Jordan Kennally. My boss and my—"

"His friend," Jordan interrupted, holding out her hand.

Nan took Jordan's hand and gave it a firm shake. "Hello. I'm Nan. Tiernan, actually, but everyone calls me Nan. I'm the soon-to-be sister-in-law. Not *so* soon. New Year's Eve. You're American. Kellan didn't mention that. He also didn't mention how pretty you are."

"Yes, I'm from New York. And—and thank you."

"Madison, Wisconsin," Nan said. "Come on, I'll get you a drink. Do you like margaritas? No one knew how to make them here. Can you imagine that? I guess they're not very Irish. Now, everyone is drinking them. I'm not a fan of Guinness. It makes me burp."

Nan took Jordan's hand and led her to the bar. She

glanced back and waved at Danny and he grinned. "How long have you been in Ireland?" Jordan asked.

"Since July." She paused and smiled. "I rented the Quinn family cottage for my vacation and decided to stay for the rest of my life. What about you?"

"I've been here for sixteen months."

"Really? That's a long time. Then I'm sure you've been to plenty of pubs."

"Just for the occasional meal," Jordan said. "I didn't really get out much…until Danny."

"Well, then, we'll have to make sure you have a grand time, won't we?" When they reached the bar, Nan shooed a man off his bar stool and offered it to Jordan. When their drinks arrived, she handed the margarita to Jordan and gave a toast.

"To the mighty Quinn brothers. The sexiest men in all of Ireland."

Jordan clinked her glass against Nan's then took a sip. The other woman wasn't at all what she had expected. Her dark hair was cropped short and curled around her face, and though she wore barely any makeup, she was strikingly beautiful in a pure and natural way. "Danny said you're engaged to his brother Riley. I haven't met him. I know Kellan, but not him."

"He's over there, on stage singing." She took a sip of her drink, then set it down. "I would warn you off about the Quinn brothers, but I think it would be wonderful for Danny to find someone."

"Oh!" Jordan was startled. "No, it's not like that. I can't fall in love with him. I'm leaving in a month."

Nan smiled. "Of course you can't. That's what I said, too."

"I'm sure that I won't—"

"Enough of this!" Danny appeared out of the crowd and took Jordan's hand. "I want to dance, woman. And there's no one in this place that I want in my arms but you. Will ya dance with me, Jordan?"

Jordan looked back and forth between Danny and Nan. Though she'd prefer to sit quietly at the bar sipping a drink, this talk of love was too much. She'd known Danny less than a week. "I'm not sure I know how," Jordan said, turning back to Danny.

"It's simple," he said. "I'll teach you."

Nan gave Jordan a wave before she disappeared into the crush of people on the dance floor. They walked past the stage and Jordan stopped to watch the singer. Riley Quinn looked like his two brothers, with the same dark hair and pale-blue eyes, the same devilish smile and to-die-for body.

Danny pulled her into his arms. "Just follow me," he said. And off they went, spinning and stepping around the floor to the crazy rhythm of the music. They bumped into a lot of people, but that seemed to be part of the fun. Gradually, Jordan picked up the steps and before long, she didn't have to think about her feet at all.

They danced three songs before the tempo slowed to a quiet ballad. Danny drew her close and wrapped his arms around her waist. "Are you having a good time?" he murmured, his breath warm against her ear.

Jordan nodded. "I am. I've never really danced like that."

"And now that you have, what would you like to do next?"

"I'd like to kiss you," she said. "But I don't think that would be a good idea."

He brushed his lips against hers. "I think it's a grand idea. What next?"

"I'd like you to do that again, with just a little more... tongue."

He did as she asked, capturing her lips with his and slowly tracing them with his tongue. He lingered for a bit, then kissed her deeply and Jordan sank against him, her knees going weak.

The sound of the music and the crowd faded around them and Jordan lost herself in the rush of desire that overwhelmed her body. It had become so easy to need him, and yet it frightened her at the same time.

She hadn't been prepared to feel this way, to completely surrender to emotion and physical need. But she couldn't help herself. His touch, his taste, it had become an addiction too overwhelming to resist. When he touched her she felt beautiful and powerful, as if everything in the world were hers to enjoy.

"What else?" he murmured, his lips damp on her cheek.

"I want you to run your hands over my body like you did this morning before we got out of bed. I want to feel your lips on my skin. And I want you to take all my clothes off and I want to take all of your clothes off and—"

"Stop," he growled.

"Why?"

"Because if you keep talking like that, I'm going to have to leave the pub with a bar tray over my lap."

Jordan arched against him, her hips meeting his and he groaned again. "Just from talking?"

"You have that effect on me," Danny said.

"Maybe we should take a walk and get some air," Jordan said. "We'll cool off a little bit."

"And that's a fine idea. Lead the way."

He grabbed her waist and gently pushed her along through the crowd, walking behind her. When they reached the front door, Danny held it open and they both stepped outside onto the street. "Come with me," he murmured.

"Where are we going now?"

"Some place where we can be alone." He pulled her into the doorway of a shop and kissed her again, his body blocking her view of the street. His fingers skimmed along her waist, then worked at the buttons of her dress. When he finally cupped her breast in his palm, he moaned softly. "Jaysus, I need you. I've never needed a woman like I need you right now." He grabbed her hand and pulled her out of the doorway. "We can't stay here."

When they passed an alleyway, he pulled her into the shadows and pressed her back against a brick wall, parting the front of her dress until he found her nipple with his mouth. He teased at the peak through the lacy fabric of her bra. Jordan's breath caught in her throat and she sighed, waves of delicious sensation coursing through her body.

His hand slid beneath her skirt and before she could catch her breath, he touched the damp spot between her legs. Jordan arched against him and he gently stroked her through her panties. She was already on the edge and it didn't take much more to make her shudder with pleasure.

Jordan tried to occupy her mind with something else, work, plans, schedules. But it was no use. He was determined to prove his power over her. She tipped her head back, her fingers clutching at his shoulders. And then, her body throbbed and wave after wave of sensation coursed through her. A moan slipped from her lips and though she knew they might be discovered at any moment, Jordan didn't care.

When the last spasm died in her body, Jordan looked up at Danny and found him smiling. He touched his lips to hers in a gentle kiss. "Sorry about that," he murmured. "I didn't realize you were so close."

"Neither did I," Jordan whispered.

"Can you walk?"

She nodded. He took her hand again and led her out of the shadows. Her legs felt boneless and it was all she could do to put one foot in front of the other. They walked past the bakery and then found the path that led to the smithy.

Finny and Mogue were sleeping on the stoop and they raised their heads as Danny opened the front door. The moment the door latched shut behind them, Jordan knew what she wanted. With frantic fingers, she stripped off her clothes and then started on Danny's.

They stumbled to the bedroom and by the time they reached the bed, they were both naked. Jordan pulled him down on top of her. How had she gone her whole adult life and never felt this desperation, this overpowering need?

He moved to find a condom in the bedside table,

but Jordan stopped him. It was her turn this time. She wanted to watch him, to bring him to his climax, to memorize his every reaction without losing herself in her own pleasure.

"Don't," she whispered. "We won't need them. Not yet." Jordan trailed a line of kisses down his chest, stopping at his belly.

Danny's fingers tangled in her hair. "What are you about?"

"You'll see," she murmured, wrapping her fingers around his stiff shaft. "Just relax. I'll take care of everything…"

"DANNY BOY!"

The shouts echoed through the empty interior of the Speckled Hound as Danny stepped inside the pub. His father was serving breakfast to the Unholy Trinity—Markus Finn, Dealy Carmichael and Johnnie O'Malley—three pensioners who were regular customers at the Hound. Kellan and Riley were sitting on the opposite end of the bar, reading the newspaper.

"There's our boy," Riley shouted. "What's brought you back here so soon?"

"Never left," Danny said. "We spent the night at my place rather than drive back."

"Too much of the black stuff?" Kellan asked.

"Something like that," Danny said. He sat down at the bar. "Can I get a couple of cups of coffee to take away and some soda bread? Warmed up. And toss some butter in the bag."

"Where's the girl?"

"Still asleep," he said.

Kellan looked up from the paper. "You've got yourself a girl?"

"Sure and he has," Riley said. "Brought her to the pub last night, though they only stayed for three dances. Then they started snogging on the dance floor and a few minutes later they were gone."

Nan came out of the kitchen, a coffee mug in her hand. Her expression brightened when she saw Danny. "Good morning, you! Is Jordan with you? I forgot to tell her last night that she should come to our engagement party. You'll tell her, won't you?"

"Wait a bloody minute," Kellan said, glancing between Nan and Riley and Danny. "This girl, the one you were snogging. It's Jordan?"

Danny winced. "Well, yes. That would be correct. Jordan and I are…involved."

"You've been working for her for five feckin' days," Kellan shouted. "How the hell is that possible?"

"Don't ask me," Danny said. "I'm as surprised as you. But there's no problem."

"You're sleeping with your boss," Kellan said.

"Not actually. She's not my boss. She's my muse." Eamon Quinn walked out of the kitchen, a coffeepot in his hand. Danny turned to him, anxious for a change of subject. "Hello, Da. How was your holiday?"

"Oh, it was grand. Got back late last night. You know how your ma loves Scotland. We expected to be back a few days ago, but there was another festival that Maggie just had to see. Bought a kilt, she did. What does a good Irish girl need with a bleedin' kilt? It's sacrilege, it is."

"I like the girl," Nan said, sitting down next to Riley.

"What girl?" Eamon asked.

"Danny's new girlfriend," Nan replied. "Or his boss. Or his muse." She giggled. "Take your pick. She's very pretty. But then, all American girls are pretty, don't you think?"

Danny grinned. "Yes, they are. You should visit Castle Cnoc and see the work she's done on the manor house. I'm sure she'd give you a tour."

"That would be lovely," Nan said. "It will give me another chance to convince her of your fine qualities and noble ambitions."

"I do believe our brother is in love," Riley teased. "Look at him. He looks besotted. He's got that well satisfied look. And he can't keep himself from smiling."

Danny shook his head. It *was* hard to keep from grinning when the only thing going through his head was thoughts of Jordan…naked…asleep in his bed. "I'm not in love," Danny assured them all. "I've only known her less than a week. And you're the besotted one in this family, Riley."

"Well, I'm happy he's found a nice girl," Eamon declared. "It's about bloody time. I was starting to wonder if any of you lot would ever settle down." He walked over to the Unholy Trinity and leaned against the bar. "We made the bet on Riley and Nan. What say we put some money on Danny and this new girl?"

"You're gambling on my love life?" Danny asked.

"We've grown bored with wagering on Dealy's ability to catch fish," Markus said. "And it's not nearly as interesting as your ability to catch women."

"Can I get in on this?" Riley asked. "What's the wager? How much are we tossing in?"

Kellan shook his head. "For a total wanker, Riley,

you managed to get yourself a great woman. Don't feck it up or you'll go back to being a total wanker." Kellan turned to Danny. "As for you, watch yourself. I happen to be fond of Jordan and I don't want you hurting her."

"Is that jealousy I hear?" Riley asked.

"No, I just know my little brother. And he doesn't have the best reputation. Jordan is a nice person. She doesn't deserve a git like you." He stood and grabbed his newspaper, then took it and his cup of coffee to a table in the corner.

"You know what your problem is, Danny boy?" Dealy asked. "You're too damn good-looking. Riley and Kellan too. Look at Markus here. Look at that face. When he was a lad, the girls didn't have such high expectations when it came to him. They knew he'd have to work harder because he was so close to ugly."

"Who are you to talk?" Markus said. "You're ugly as a bucket of toads."

"It's true," Johnnie said. "When a lad is too *flash,* he thinks he can get any girl. He's never satisfied with the one he has."

"I'm perfectly satisfied," Riley said.

"So am I," Danny added.

"Don't you get too comfortable," Kellan shouted from across the room. "It won't take her long to see her mistake. You just can't go draggin' anyone off to bed and expect them to fall in love with you."

"I didn't drag her into bed," Danny said. "In fact, she came to me. How could I refuse?" That wasn't exactly the full story. But what had he been supposed to do? She'd been frightened and uneasy and he'd just calmed her nerves in the best way that he could.

Kellan set his paper down and crossed the bar, leaning close to Danny, his voice low. "She looks like she's tough and like she's got herself together," he said, "but she's a lot more fragile than that."

"I know," Danny said. "And I'm not going to hurt her. That's the last thing in the world I'd ever want to do."

"You don't understand. She doesn't work like other people. She has this way of pulling you in, until all you want to do is make her happy. I've seen her do it. And if you fail, she doesn't yell or curse. She just acts all disappointed and then you feel lower than an earthworm's arse."

Danny nodded. "I know, I know." In truth, he didn't know. He hadn't experienced that moment with Jordan. And he didn't mean to anytime soon.

Eamon Quinn walked through the doors from the kitchen with a paper bag. "Here's your breakfast. Two black coffees and soda bread. I threw some fruit salad in there. And before you leave town, you may want to stop by and wish your mother a happy birthday. Tell her she doesn't look a day over thirty-five," he said.

Danny winced. "I'm sorry. I forgot all about her birthday today. I'll ring her later. I've been so—"

"Don't worry. Kellan told her all about your new job. You know, she's been dying to get a look inside that castle, too. You might invite her for a tour to make up for the missed birthday."

"I will," Danny said. "Once it's all finished, I'm sure Jordan wouldn't mind."

"Remember what I said," Kellan muttered.

Danny nodded. "I have to go." He grabbed the bag

and headed out the front door of the pub. As he strode back to his cottage, he drew a deep breath of the sea air and smiled to himself. Funny how his life had changed so much in just five days.

It didn't matter to him how long it lasted. He was going to enjoy himself while he could. And when it was time for Jordan to leave, he'd kiss her goodbye and regret that it couldn't go on for just a little longer.

But even as he told himself it was just a passing thing, Danny could imagine them together for more than just a few weeks or months. He found her endlessly fascinating. And she seemed to find him interesting as well. There was a lot to be said for that, wasn't there?

Danny hurried back to his cottage. The dogs were waiting and he shooed them out, then closed the door. A moment later, Jordan rushed out of the bedroom, half-dressed, her hair tumbling around her face.

"Where have you been?"

"I just went to get us breakfast," he said.

"We're late. I have to get back to the house. The workmen will be there and I have calls to make and—"

"It's Saturday," Danny said.

"I know it is. I work on Saturday. So do you. Just because we're sleeping together doesn't mean we can ignore our responsibilities."

She'd gone from lover back to boss—and she was disappointed in him. "I wasn't gone that long. I was talking to my brothers. Kellan was at the pub and my da was back from his holiday."

"You should have told me you were leaving," she said. "I woke up and you weren't there. I looked all over for you and—"

"You knew I wasn't far," Danny said, frowning. "Jordan, I wouldn't have left you here. I knew we had to get back. So come on, then. Get dressed. Let's go. You're the boss."

Jordan blinked, her expression suddenly shifting. "Don't say that."

"What? That you're the boss?"

She cursed softly. "I'm sorry. I'm really tired and I'm a little hungover and I just want a shower and a really big cup of coffee."

He took one of the paper cups out of the bag. "I brought you coffee," he said. Stepping closer, Danny dropped a kiss on her lips. "And something to eat."

Jordan groaned. "See. I'm really awful. You're right. I need to learn to relax. Why can't I do that? It's Saturday. We should just go right back to bed."

"I shouldn't have left you alone in a strange house."

"Well, don't do it again. Or I'll have to make a note in your personnel file."

Reaching out, he ran a finger along her arm, tracing a lazy path from her wrist to her elbow and back again. "You have a file on me? What does it say?"

She took a sip of her coffee and then sighed. "It says that you have trouble separating work from—from everything else, and I think that might become a problem."

He stared at her for a long moment, fighting back a surge of frustration. Would it always come back to this? Did they always have to be boss and employee? Why couldn't she see them as just a man and a woman? "Am I supposed to pretend that I don't want you? Because I do. All the time. And if that's a problem, then write it up in my personnel file. In big red letters." He walked to the door and pulled it open. "I'll be in the car with Finny and Mogue. As soon as you're ready, we'll go."

Danny snapped his fingers as he walked out the front door, and the dogs came running. He opened the rear door of the Land Rover and they hopped inside. Then, he slid in behind the wheel and waited, his anger growing with every moment that passed.

When she finally came out of the cottage, Jordan walked slowly toward the vehicle. She got into the passenger seat and looked over at him. "I'm sorry," she said. "This is all kind of new to me and I haven't figured out how to handle it yet. You might be able to separate work and pleasure, but I'm going to have to work on it a little longer."

"Then forget about the job. Don't worry. I will get it done and it will be perfect. You have to trust me. We *can* just be lovers."

She nodded, then reached out and grabbed his shirt, pulling him closer. Jordan pressed her face into his chest. "I really hope so."

4

DANNY STARED AT THE ornate medallion he'd begun for
the garden gate. He'd been working on it for three days,
fitting it in between the hinges and hardware on Jordan's list. He'd carefully copied the design from an old
black-and-white photo that Jordan had given him.

The work was beautiful, but it wasn't Irish. He suspected the original artisan was John Wellston, a British blacksmith from Galway who had done a lot of the
work in the area at the turn of the century. Wellston's
work was quite prized nowadays, found on many his-
torical homes.

At the time Wellston worked, Ireland was in the
midst of a rebellion, an attempt to break away from
British rule. Wellston worked for many of the wealthy
British families and Irish loyalists. But now that Ireland was free, it didn't seem right to put his work back
up on the gate. It should be Irish work on an Irish gate.

Danny glanced at his watch, then dropped the tongs
on the floor and shrugged his stiff shoulders. Jordan
was out for the morning, running errands to Cork and
Bantry. She'd been buying furniture for the house—

keeping a careful inventory of it in a huge book in the library.

She'd been trying to track down some of the original furnishings so she might buy them back. But she hadn't had much luck in that area. Everything she bought was carefully restored and reupholstered, then shipped to a storage facility in Cork, awaiting the moment when it would be moved to Castle Cnoc.

Danny grabbed a towel from the worktable and rubbed the sweat off his grimy face, then grabbed the medallion and hauled it outside, propping it up against an old wooden crate. Drawing a deep breath, he stretched his arms over his head, working the kinks out of his back as he stared at his work.

No, it didn't look better in the light of day. He sat down on a wooden stool set against the wall of the laundry. There wasn't much good about it, he mused. Copying Wellston's work just didn't seem right. He ought to just start over, with a design of his own. At least he'd take some pride in the making of it.

Sighing softly, Danny raked his hands through his hair, then leaned back against the wall, drawing a deep breath of the late-morning breeze.

This had become a sticky point between him and Jordan and it was about to come to a head. They'd disagreed on a few other small projects and he'd given in, agreeing to make exact copies rather than put his own mark on the work.

But the medallion would be the focal point of the walled garden. It needed to match the beauty of the house and the surrounding landscape—and it should be Irish. Maybe he could use that point to convince Jordan.

But first, he'd have to come up with a better design, one with some of the elements of the first, only in a more Gaelic manner.

A wave of exhaustion came over him and Danny fought back a yawn. It didn't help his creativity when he could barely put a thought together. Late nights with Jordan followed by early mornings at the forge were wearing on him. And though he kept assuring Jordan he was right on schedule, that wasn't the truth. He'd fallen at least a week behind and was falling further with every day that passed.

He closed his eyes and let his mind drift, searching for inspiration. But instead, his mind filled with thoughts of Jordan, her naked body, her lush mouth, her warm hands—disconnected images of pleasure that plagued him night and day.

Danny cursed beneath his breath. She had become his *leanan sidhe,* so alluring and yet so dangerous, tempting him and tormenting him at the very same time. He was a happier man when she was close, but was it worth the price he paid? He felt as if she'd already stolen a part of his soul, and the thought of taking it back brought out only a desperate ache deep inside of him.

Wanting her had become second nature, like drawing breath. He couldn't look at her without his hands aching to touch her, or his lips craving her taste. Was this simple lust or obsession? He was so wrapped up in it, Danny couldn't tell the difference, not that he'd even know in the first place. If he could just get a decent night's sleep, then maybe he could sort it all out.

But the nights were what he was living for. With

every one spent with Jordan, he learned more and more about passion and need, grew more aware of the pleasure they could give each other. Her bed had become a place to explore and experiment, a place to push the boundaries of what was possible between a man and a woman.

Danny drew a deep breath and let his body relax. Just a few minutes, a short kip, and he'd find his energy. He couldn't be bothered to walk back to his cottage or even stretch out on the grass at his feet. Just a few...

"Are you asleep?"

Startled by her voice, Danny sat up straight and opened his eyes. "No," he said, wiping his eyes. "No, I was just thinking."

"You were asleep," Jordan said, her brow furrowed deeply.

"Yes," he admitted. "Maybe I was. I'm knackered, Jordan. Give me a break. I just needed a quick kip and then back to work."

"How are you supposed to stay on schedule if you're napping on the job?" There was an edge to her voice and he could see she was upset.

He grinned and held out his hand to her. "How am I supposed to stay on schedule if I'm spending my nights pleasing you? That would be the more appropriate question."

"Are you saying I don't work?" Jordan asked.

He shook his head. How did she get that out of his comment? "Of course not. I'm saying that what we do in our spare time makes it hard to get anything done during the day. You can sleep in but I have to get up and go to work."

"You *are* saying I don't work!" Jordan began to pace back and forth in front of him. With every step she took, she was getting more and more upset and Danny stood silently, searching for a way to defuse the looming argument.

"Would you like to tell me what you're really upset about?"

She stopped and opened her mouth, then snapped it shut. "No," she said.

He reached out and grabbed her hand. "Come on, sit down and tell me about your day."

She plopped down on the stool and cupped her chin in her hand. "I bought a crystal vase a few months ago. It's an exact match for one that was pictured in the foyer. I put it in the butler's pantry and now it's gone. It just disappeared. I have no idea how long it's been gone, but I didn't imagine that I bought it or put it there. I have a receipt." She rubbed her forehead. "Sometimes I think I'm going crazy."

"You're not going crazy," he said.

She shrugged. "I know. One of the workmen must have come into the house and taken it. I need to be more careful with the locks."

"What else?" he asked.

"It's nothing. I'm just tired. Stressed. Confused." She pointed to the medallion. "It looks nice."

"No, it doesn't," Danny said. "I don't like it. The smith who designed it was a Brit. And I refuse to copy his work. There should be Irish work on the gate."

"We had an agreement," Jordan said.

"And I'm going back on it. You want a medallion for the garden gate, I'll make you one. It's going to be beautiful and it will be Irish and it will be my design. I want to leave something of my work in this place."

"I could fire you for this," she said, a defiant tilt to her chin.

He chuckled. "You could. But you won't. You wanted the best and I'm the best."

She shook her head. "Do what you want," she murmured, her voice wavering. "I'm tired, too. And everything is all screwed up. And it's all because of you."

"Me? How am I to blame?"

She looked at him, her eyes filling with tears. She'd gone from contrary to crying in the course of a few seconds. What the hell was he supposed to do now? Danny tried to grab her hand, but she turned and started back to the house.

"Oh, bollocks," he muttered. He ran after her, catching up on the stone terrace. "Jordan, wait." He caught her waist and spun her around to face him. "What's wrong?"

"Nothing," she said, shaking her head. "Just go back to work."

"No. You're in tears."

"I am not!" she cried, denying the wet streaks on her face. "I'm not crying. I don't cry."

"Then why is your face wet?"

"I don't cry!"

"You're tired. We barely got any sleep last night. I was acting like an arse. If you *are* crying, which I'm not saying you are, it wouldn't be a surprise."

"I'm not crying," she insisted.

He pulled her along to a bench and sat down next to her, wrapping his arm around her shoulders and smoothing the hair from her eyes. "Tell me what's going on."

She drew a ragged breath and brushed the tears from her cheeks. "I—I need to be done with this job. I need to go home. I have better things waiting for me and the longer I stay here, the less chance I have of getting them."

Just the mention of her leaving caused a pain, like a dagger to his heart. "So you'll finish the job and go home," he murmured, pulling her close and kissing her temple.

"But the longer I stay here with you, the more I don't want to leave. Everything is so simple here. I don't have to fight to be happy." She sniffled. "Do you know what I was just doing?"

"Threatening to fire me?" Danny teased.

"Talking to my father. He has a project that I really want to manage, a boutique hotel in SoHo. I thought, maybe, when he gave me this job, he was preparing me for that one. It's the perfect project for me and he knows it—small, unique. And I was right on track to get it. Until you."

"You're going to blame this on me?"

"Yes. Because I really don't care that he's probably going to give it to my brother. My brother who wouldn't know a sconce from a scone. I'm just so tired of this constant battle. Here, I'm happy. I don't feel any pressure and I actually like this job. And I like you."

"I like you, too," Danny said. "And I can tell how much this hotel project means to you."

"It doesn't mean anything," Jordan said with a shaky laugh.

"Of course it does. You're just angry." He cupped her face in his hands and touched his lips to hers. "We'll figure this out. You'll find a way to change your father's mind."

"What about the gate?" she asked.

"You have to trust me. You have to let me do this my way. I promise, I'll make it good."

She closed her eyes and sighed, her shoulders sagging. "Just get it done. I don't care how you do it. It doesn't make a difference anymore." Jordan pulled out of his grasp. "I really don't think it's a good idea for us to spend so much time together. Both of us know there isn't a future here. And we should both focus more on work."

"Sure," Danny said.

"Maybe you should stay at the cottage tonight."

"No problem." Danny wanted to grab her and pull her into his arms, to kiss away all her worries. He much preferred complete infatuation to utter confusion. But right now, Jordan needed a bit of space, a chance to figure out what she really wanted. She thought her problem was him; but Danny suspected there was something else at work here, something much deeper.

If she needed time, he'd give her that. She could have all the time she wanted. "Come on," he said. "Let's go make you a cup of tea. That always makes things better."

"I don't like tea," she said.

"What about ice cream?" he asked.

"I love ice cream."

"There's a place in town that has the best strawberry ice cream," he said.

She smiled. "I love chocolate."

"They have that, too," Danny said. "We'll go have ourselves a scoop."

"We should really get back to work."

"Well, if we're going to be spending our nights alone, then we'll have plenty of time for work."

She drew in a ragged breath and forced a smile. "I may have been a bit rash about that. Maybe if we just tried to get to sleep earlier, things would improve."

Danny drew her into his arms and gave her a fierce hug. "We'll give that a try," he said. "Now stop crying and we'll go get ice cream."

"I'm not crying," she insisted, her face pressed into his chest.

"Sure you're not," Danny whispered.

JORDAN STRODE DOWN the garden path, her scheduling flowchart clutched in her hands. It was about time to get this project back on track. No more distractions, no more Ms. Nice Girl.

Maybe she did need to be tougher. Obviously, whoever was stealing from the house thought she was an easy mark. And if that's what it took to get what she wanted, then she'd just have to change her ways. Bartie was a perfect example. He'd been working on the garden for months and nothing was done. Danny was doing his own thing with the gate medallions. And the filter for the pool had been nothing but trouble since it was installed.

"It's time to kick ass and take names," she muttered to herself. "Get tough. Be mean."

Cursing softly, she brushed aside the memory of her

attempt with Danny. The humiliation of breaking down in front of him yesterday still brought a flush of warmth to her cheeks. She'd never let her emotions get the better of her in her business life before. Why now?

She'd just been so overwhelmed with everything that had happened between them that she'd cracked. Too many late nights, too much time spent feeling like a wanton woman rather than a detached professional.

But this wasn't just about the job. Though she'd tried to blame everything on Danny, Jordan knew it was nearly all her fault. Ireland was changing her. She'd lived here for months, feeling like a fish out of water. But now, with Danny's arrival, this place was beginning to feel like home.

If she hadn't been so weak, so anxious to jump into an affair with him, then everything would be fine. He'd be finishing his work and she'd be getting ready to leave Ireland for a better project in Manhattan. And she'd have no regrets for anything that had happened between them.

But Danny had seduced her and at the same time, awakened a part of her that she hadn't known existed. For the first time in her life, she felt needed…wanted… desired. And that made her feel wonderful.

How many times had she heard professional women discussing the problem with trying to have it all? Was this what they meant? Did romance exist in direct competition with professional success? Could she be a woman in love and a woman in business at the same time? Or would one side always suffer?

Of course she could, Jordan mused. Women did it every day. But they didn't have four brothers to compete with, or a father who never seemed to be satisfied. Or a man who could inflame her body with just a simple touch of his hand.

Her job would have been so much easier if Danny Quinn had turned out to be fifty years old, balding and toothless. Instead, he had to be handsome and charming and sexy as sin. She'd never stood a chance. Her feeble attempt to put an end to their late nights had lasted all of about two minutes. Last night had been just as long and adventurous as the previous nights had been.

Jordan turned in to the entrance of the garden and observed the landscape in front of her. More holes. More piles of dirt. It looked as if Bartie and Daisy had turned over every single inch of soil in the garden.

Gathering her resolve, Jordan strode inside the walls and approached the elderly couple. They were bent low, peering into a deep hole. "What are you two looking for?"

They jumped at the sound of her voice and then quickly straightened, fumbling with the tools they held. "Nothing."

"Nothing?" She stepped over and looked into the hole. "If there's nothing, then why are you digging holes?"

"The soil," Bartie said. "Ferrous—"

"Yes, I know. Ferrous metals. I searched *ferrous metals in Irish gardens* on the internet last night. I didn't find anything. Not one thing about iron in the soil. And as far as roses, they can grow in almost any kind of soil with the proper feeding and fertilization."

"Yes," Bartie said, still nodding his head.

"Yes? Is that all you have to say?" Jordan paused

and schooled her temper. "I don't understand what the holdup is. It doesn't look any closer to being done than it did when I arrived here sixteen months ago. Except instead of weeds, I now have piles and piles of dirt."

"Oh, but it is," Bartie said. "I can see how you think that, Miss Kennally. But rose gardens in Ireland can be a tricky thing. The soil has to be prepared in just the right way or you'll have a catastrophe on your hands. We've had to go down a bit deeper than we planned, but it's important. To avoid catastrophe."

"I don't want a catastrophe. I just want flowers. Roses. Get it done. If—if I don't see flowers in this garden by next week, I'll need to hire a professional."

"Yes, miss."

She stalked back to the entrance of the garden, then turned back to Bartie and Daisy. "Have you been inside the house lately, Bartie?"

The old man shifted nervously. "No, miss. I spend all my time in the garden. Why would I have cause to come in the house?"

"What about you, Daisy?"

"No, ma'am."

Jordan shook her head. "Danny says we might have brownies or fairies in the house. Things keep disappearing and then reappearing somewhere else. Do you know anything about that?"

Bartie nodded. "Oh, yes, miss. Sounds like brownies to me," he said. "I'll keep a watch out for them. In the meantime, you might want to leave a little something out for them, miss. A biscuit or two, maybe a slice of tea cake."

"Or you can build a new house for them," Daisy said.

"Build a new house? For an imaginary creature?" Jordan shook her head. "I have to see some positive changes out here soon. It needs to start looking like a garden, not a construction site."

Bartie tipped his hat, then returned to the hole he was digging. Daisy gave him a worried look and Bartie forced a smile. "Flowers," he said.

As Jordan walked through the opening in the wall, she noticed new hinges hanging from the stone columns. Danny was working on the gate but she'd been reluctant to check up on his progress.

She'd accepted his refusal to copy the original gate, but she was afraid she might not like what he'd come up with to replace it. And if she didn't like it, she'd be forced to make him begin again. She started toward the forge, then decided to wait. Trust. She had to trust that he knew what he was doing.

When she got back inside the house, she headed to the library, ready to get to work on her scheduling. There was still the roof on the laundry cottage and the new gravel paving on the drive. She had to check her inventory of furniture and make a final list of the pieces she needed, and she'd have to make some changes due to Danny's slower pace. But there was still a chance to make her final deadline if she could just control her desires.

Jordan sat down at her desk, feeling much better about her options. Grabbing her calendar, she flipped through the next few weeks, searching for a few open days. A trip back to New York would be an excellent way to lobby for the hotel job. She could fly in one day

and out the next. Danny could watch over the workmen
for her while she was gone.

"Yes," she murmured. There was still time to get
everything she wanted. She'd bring her father a full
report on the Castle Cnoc renovation, filled with photos
and graphs and flowcharts. Her father loved graphs.
He would have to see she was the right one. And if he
didn't—if he didn't, she'd—

"I'll quit!" she cried, slamming her pen down on the
desk.

"Don't say that."

Jordan glanced up to see Kellan Quinn standing in
the doorway of the library. "Hello." For a moment, she'd
thought it was Danny, all cleaned up and looking like
a proper businessman. The brothers looked so much
alike. But in reality, Kellan wasn't anything like Danny.
He was cool and aloof and completely in control of his
emotions. She could depend on Kellan. Danny? Well,
she still hadn't figured that out yet.

He stepped through the door. "Hi. How is it going?"

From the moment she'd met Kellan sixteen months
ago, she'd liked him. He was talented and thoughtful
and possessed as much enthusiasm for the castle as she
did. As the project architect, he'd prepared all the plans
and drawings for the renovation, making sure everything they kept was sound and anything new was an
accurate restoration. Now that it was almost finished,
she realized how much she'd miss working with him.

"Things are going really well," she said. "I didn't
know you were coming. Are you looking for Danny?"

"No," Kellan said. "I'm looking for you." He handed
her an envelope. "My final bill. I know I could have

mailed it, but I come with a personal request. Actually, several. Nan wanted me to remind you of the engagement party. She'd like you to come. It's next Friday night at the pub. And she and my mother would like to come and tour Castle Cnoc once it's all finished, if that's all right with you?"

"I'd love to give them a tour." Jordan stood and took the envelope from him. "Sit," she said, pointing to a nearby chair. "Have you had a chance to walk through the house?"

"No, but I want to. It's been a while. When are you bringing in the furniture?"

"Soon," Jordan said. "I've got a few more things that I need to buy. Library books are next on the list." She glanced around. "I have to fill all these shelves. But I want real books, leather-bound with gold leaf."

"Where are you going to go for those?"

"I don't know. London would probably be best. It would be nice if I could put together a real Irish library, though."

"Really? I thought you were going for more of an English manor house."

"I've been convinced that I should approach this from the Irish side. After all, the owner is half-Irish, so there is good reason to go that way. And Danny—"

"Oh, so that's it," Kellan said with a grin. "Danny is pushing the whole Gaelic-pride thing?"

"No. But he's right. This is an Irish house and the decor should reflect that."

"There's a great rare books dealer in Galway," Kellan said. "I'll email you his name. He'll help you find what you need."

"Thanks," she said.

"So, Joe, tell me that Danny has been treating you well. Is it all fair play, then, or has he been a dosser?"

"Fair play," Jordan said, "I think. He's very good at what he does."

Kellan nodded slyly. "I'm sure he is. That's why women love him."

Jordan felt her cheeks warm. "Professionally. He's an excellent blacksmith. We've had a few creative disagreements, but other than that, it's been going quite well."

"I would warn you off," Kellan said, "but I suspect you know what you're doing."

This caused Jordan to laugh out loud. "I have no idea what I'm doing. I'm figuring it out as I go along."

"I will say this—if he hurts you, I'll reef the shite out of him."

"That won't be necessary. If he hurts me, I'll reef the shite out of him myself."

"And if things go well for you both and you'd consider staying in Ireland, then I have a proposal for you."

"A proposal?" Jordan asked.

"I'd like you to consider working with me. I do a lot of houses like this, here and in Europe, and I like your work. And your style. No drama. I don't know the technicalities of getting a work visa, but I'm sure that could be sorted out."

"You're offering me a job?"

"More like a partnership. If you decide to stay."

Jordan leaned back in her chair. She hadn't even considered staying. Her life was back in Manhattan. She had just always assumed she'd return. But it was nice to know that she had options. It would serve her father right if she decided to leave the company. At least *some-one* admired her talent and work ethic. "Thanks," she said. "I'll keep that in mind."

"Everything else is going well?" Kellan asked.

"If you're asking about the house, yes. Oh, except for the brownies or the fairies. We're not sure which we have. And then there's the problems in the garden with Bartie. He's been digging holes for weeks now. Big, deep holes. I don't know what that's all about."

"You have brownies?" Kellan asked.

"Yes," she said. "Someone or something has been sneaking around the house, stealing things and locking doors and windows behind them."

"You do know that brownies aren't real, don't you?"

"Of course she does." Danny appeared at the door, dressed in his leather apron and a backward baseball cap.

"Someone *was* in the house that night," Jordan said. "I know I wasn't dreaming."

Danny drew a deep breath. "Yes, someone was in the house. Maybe not that night, but sometime that day. I found a footprint."

"You did? You didn't tell me that," Jordan said.

"I didn't want to scare you. And you haven't had any more problems since I've been sleeping in the manor house."

"Except for the vase," she said.

"Right, the vase." He smiled. "Well, I think we can rule out the place being haunted. Ghosts don't carry off crystal vases."

Kellan nodded. "Yeah, it was easier to believe in

ghosts when the place looked like a wreck. Some of these old houses have secret entrances. And this house was used during the rebellion to smuggle guns. Maybe that's how your brownies are getting in and out."

Danny grinned. "Really? Where would this secret passage be?"

"I don't know. I have the original blueprints, but there wasn't anything on those. But then, there wouldn't be if it was a secret. I just never thought to look." He stood. "You need to find an undefined space. You could figure it out if you measured the rooms. Somewhere there's a missing meter or so, a space wide enough for a hall or a stairway."

"Now you have me curious," Jordan said, smiling. "Wouldn't that be a tale to tell the owner when she arrives? I think we should start looking. I want to find it."

"I'd love to help," Kellan said, standing, "but I'm off to Dublin. I need to scare up some more work." He crossed the room and held out his hand to Jordan. "It was a pure pleasure working with you, Joe."

Jordan smiled. "And thank you for the offer, Kellan," she said. "I'll think about it."

"Good." Kellan gave Danny a slap on the shoulder as he walked out the door. "You, watch yourself. Don't be an arse. Be nice to your boss."

When they were alone, Danny sat down in the chair Kellan had vacated. "What was that all about?" he asked.

"He brought me his bill," Jordan said.

"That's not what I'm talking about," Danny said. "What kind of offer did Kellan make you?"

"It's nothing," Jordan said. "Just business." She didn't

want Danny to know that she would even consider staying in Ireland. If he hadn't thought about it, then knowing that she had would likely send him running in the opposite direction. And though Kellan's offer was generous, it would take a lot to get her to give up her life in America.

Jordan jumped out of her chair. "I think we should look for that secret passage. Then we can figure out if anyone has been sneaking into the house." She walked over to the wall of shelves. "How are we going to find it?"

"Tap on the walls," Danny suggested. "Look for hidden latches or hinges." He stood and walked to the door. "I have to get back to work. I'll see you later."

Jordan watched him retreat, then frowned. He seemed a bit upset. Maybe she should have told him about Kellan's offer. But there was another reason she'd held back. What if he wanted her to stay?

Jordan drew a deep breath and closed her eyes. She could deny it all she wanted, but she felt something deep and strong for Danny Quinn. It might not be love, but it was something that wouldn't go away just because she wanted it to. Leaving him was going to be much more difficult that she'd ever anticipated.

JORDAN DREW A DEEP BREATH and smiled, a look of pure pleasure coming over her face. "I love the smell of books," she said.

Danny wrinkled his nose and looked around the used bookshop. To him, the store smelled a bit musty. "You and Nan should have come on this trip and left me home."

"Nan?"

Danny nodded. "She was a librarian back in the States. Something to do with old books and maps. She'd have loved this place."

"I thought you wanted to come," Jordan said.

Danny slipped his arms around her waist. "I did. But you were the attraction, not some old moldy books."

"What about when I get old and moldy?" Jordan asked. "Does that mean you're going to stop liking me then?"

Danny nodded. "I'm afraid so. Once you turn thirty, I'm hitting the road."

Jordan gasped, then slapped him playfully. "You're awful. I think I might hate you."

He bent to kiss her neck. "No, you don't. You're mad for me. Admit it. You can't get enough."

She sighed, tipping her head to allow his kisses to continue across her shoulder. "Well, that's true enough. Although, I'm not sure it's a good thing." She gently pushed at his chest. "We're here to look for books," she reminded him. "Not to snog in the stacks."

Reluctantly, Danny let her go. Hand in hand, they strolled down the narrow aisles between the stacks. "What exactly are you looking for?" He reached out and plucked a book from one of the shelves. "Here we go. *An Illustrated History of Faeries and Sprites.* Maybe we can find some of your wee friends in here."

"Why do you think I'm a fairy?" she asked. "I don't have wings. Or a wand."

"Not all fairies look like Tinkerbell. And you wouldn't. You're the kind of fairy that uses all her trickery to lure me in." He pointed to an illustration. "There you are. *Leanan sidhe.* See? That looks just like you."

She examined the illustration carefully. "She has wavy dark hair. That's about it."

"There's more," he said.

"She's naked and I'm fully clothed. And she has wings. And really big boobs."

Danny playfully tugged at the back of her shirt. "You have lovely breasts. And I think I've seen wings in here somewhere. Why don't we just take a closer look?"

"You need to keep your mind on business," she warned, wagging her finger at him.

"And you need to stop distracting me. Fairy magic is a powerful thing and you don't know how powerful you are."

"If I'm so powerful," Jordan said, "why can't I get rid of the brownies in the house?"

"It doesn't work that way. Fairies and brownies exist in separate worlds." He handed her the book. "Here. You can read all about it. I'll buy it for you, *sidhe.*"

"We're here to look for big sets of books with nice leather bindings. And, of course, they should be interesting. I have a lot of shelves to fill."

"So aesthetics are more important than content?"

Jordan shrugged. "I don't know. It all depends. We should get a full set of Shakespeare. Why don't we look for that first?"

"Buying books for their looks is like buying art because it matches the paint on the wall." Danny reached out and plucked a book off the shelf and held it up to her. "You should start with an Irish poet."

"Who is that?"

"W. B. Yeats." Danny leaned back against the bookshelf and closed his eyes. "'When you are old and gray and full of sleep, and nodding by the fire, take down this book, and slowly read, and dream of the soft look your eyes had once, and of their shadows deep.'" He opened his eyes to find her staring at him.

"That's beautiful," she murmured.

"I would still love you when you were old and gray," he murmured. It was an impulsive statement that startled him, as it was based on the assumption that he loved her now—or would in the future. Was that even a possibility in his subconscious? And if it was, what would that mean to her?

Her gaze softened, as if she were searching for the truth in his words. Danny held his breath, hoping that she might return the favor and provide a clue to the depth of her own feelings. Was she falling in love with him? Did she think about a future together?

"You have to have Yeats," Danny finally said, handing her the book.

She drew in a sharp breath and nodded. "Yes. Good."

Danny forced a smile. He'd given her an opening and she hadn't stepped through it. "And you'll need collections of Swift and Goldsmith. And Wilde and Joyce."

"How do you know so much about this?" Jordan asked.

"I'm Irish. We take great pride in our literary heroes. Bram Stoker and Samuel Beckett were Irish, too. And C. S. Lewis. Sister Mary Frances, my high-school English teacher, was a tyrant when it came to homegrown talent. I can still recite 'The Lake Isle of Innisfree.' It was my favorite poem."

"Say it for me," Jordan said.

Danny cleared his throat and stood up straight.

I will arise and go now, and go to Innisfree,
And a small cabin build there, of clay and wat-
tles made;
Nine bean rows will I have there, a hive for the
honey-bee,
And live alone in the bee-loud glade.

"That's beautiful," she murmured.

Chuckling, Danny dropped a kiss on her lips. "That's not the end of it. Maybe I'll finish it tonight, when we're in bed."

"Thank you, Sister Mary Frances."

"I used to think that's what I wanted. To escape my family, my brothers mostly, and find a place to be alone, in a bee-loud glade. But I'm starting to realize that life alone wouldn't be much fun."

"Not even in a cabin of clay and waddle? What is waddle?"

"Wattle," Danny said, emphasizing the *t*s. "Wattle is strips of wood held together with clay or mud. Although sometimes, in olden days, they used animal dung and straw."

"You know a lot of trivial things," she said. "I'm impressed."

"What do you know?" Danny asked. "Recite a poem for me."

"No." Jordan laughed. "Outside of nursery rhymes, I'm not sure I know a single poem by memory. Not that

I didn't at one time. Things just seem to come and go from my mind if I don't really think about them."

He leaned into her. "So you'll forget all about me soon enough?"

She slowly shook her head. "No, I don't think I'll ever forget you."

Danny cupped her face in his hands and captured her mouth with his. He loved to kiss Jordan. She was always so sweet and willing, her fingers clutching at his shirt. When he lingered over her lips, she moaned softly and Danny slipped his hand beneath her shirt to caress her breast.

His thoughts returned to the lines of Yeats he'd recited, the words drifting through his head. For the first time in his life, he could imagine spending the rest of his days with one woman. Jordan fascinated him with all her foibles and quirks. At once she was steely, yet vulnerable, serious, yet silly. With every contrast he discovered, he became more and more intrigued. Was this really the woman who could keep him interested for a lifetime?

And then there was their physical compatibility. He'd always enjoyed sex, but sex with Jordan was so much more than the simple satisfying of a need. It was how they communicated, how they conveyed the feelings that they hadn't yet put into words. Did he love her? He wasn't sure. But was he falling in love with her? There was a very good possibility he was.

"Books," she murmured when he finally drew away. "You have to stop distracting me."

"All right," he whispered. "Let's get your books. We'll continue this later."

As Danny followed her around the bookstore, pointing out volumes that belonged in her library, he thought about the time they had left together. He had at least another two weeks of work to do and he could maybe stretch it into three. But her work in Ireland would eventually end.

He tried to imagine how that would look, how it would feel. Would they just kiss each other goodbye and end it? Or would they make plans to see each other again? Though he'd always been one to make a break up clean and simple, somehow he knew it wouldn't be simple with Jordan. He was already thinking of ways they could be together, of trips to New York.

He needed time. Or he'd have to make better use of the time he had. Riley had only been given a couple of weeks with Nan. How had he managed it? Maybe it was time to find out.

5

THEY'D PACKED THE CAR with boxes of books, the scent of old leather filling Jordan's station wagon. More books would be delivered to the house tomorrow and the shopkeeper had found additional sets in Dublin and Galway that he'd ordered for Jordan and send on through a delivery service.

As they drove along the coast, the sun disappeared, replaced by steely-gray clouds and a soft drizzle. Jordan stared out the window as she listened to the gentle rhythm of the wipers.

Even on such a dreary afternoon, the countryside still looked so green and magical. Until Danny had come into her life, she'd been immune to its charms. But now, caught in an affair with a sexy Irishman, she could appreciate the place that had made him.

There was something about the light, how it shimmered over the landscape, intensifying the colors and the contrasts: soft green moss growing on weathered gray rock, white clouds blowing above the deep blue of the Atlantic. Ireland was alive.

Was it the land or was it the man she was with? Had

Danny made her more aware of her surroundings? Her senses were so much more heightened now. Smells and tastes could elicit an overwhelming pleasure for her. Back home, there was a quiet sameness to all her days and nights, as if she were just wandering from one day to the next, waiting for something important to happen.

Now it had. She glanced over at him, then reached out and ran her hand through his hair, brushing a stubborn curl away from his face.

"What?" he said, looking over at her.

"Nothing," Jordan replied. "I just felt like touching you."

Danny smiled. "I know how you feel. I pretty much think about touching you all the time."

"I know," Jordan said.

"You do? How do you know?"

"I just do." She looked out the window at the landscape passing by. "I love Ireland. I didn't think I would, but I do. Even in the rain, it's beautiful." She paused. "Have you ever thought of leaving?"

Danny shook his head. "No. Maybe for a holiday. I could imagine living in another country for a year or two. But I'd have to come back. Some of my cousins live in America," he said. "In Boston. And I have cousins in New York and California, too. But I've never met them."

"I feel like I haven't really seen a lot of the country. I've been to almost every antique store, but I haven't been to Blarney Castle."

"Blarney Castle is for the tourists. We'll go to the Burren and the Cliffs of Moher. We'll see the natural sites, not the ones with lines of tourists."

"What else will you show me?" Jordan asked.

"There is a place I could show you right now," Danny said. "I think you'll like it. And it's on the way to Ballykirk."

"It's raining," she said.

"Even better," he replied. "We may see something interesting in the rain."

"Is it a stone circle? I went to visit a stone circle here. I thought it would be like Stonehenge, but it was really small."

"Our stone circles aren't nearly as grand. But they're populated by much more interesting spirits."

"So, where are we going? Is it on my map?"

"I'm not going to tell you," he said.

"Will it have a gift shop?"

Danny chuckled. "No. No gift shop."

Jordan continued to question him, making a game of it, trying to tease the answer out of him. Danny grabbed her hand and laced his fingers through hers. "Look how happy you are when we're out of that house," he said. "We need to make a point of getting away more often. You never look like this when you're sitting in your office, worrying over your reports."

"How do I look when I'm in my office?"

He pulled a silly face and Jordan couldn't help but laugh. "I look constipated?"

"That was cheesed off," Danny said. "You look annoyed. As if you'd rather be doing anything else."

"And how do I look when I'm in bed with you?"

He made another face, his eyes fluttering and his lips parted.

"Drunk," she said. "You're not very good at faces."

Danny navigated the station wagon through brilliant green hillsides along the coast. At a rocky pass, they waited for a herd of sheep to cross the road and when they wouldn't move, Danny jumped out of the car and helped the farmer hurry them along.

No matter where she looked, there was something beautiful to see—a thatch-roofed cottage, an old cemetery filled with ornate Celtic crosses, the ruin of an ancient church.

They passed a number of signs for tourist attractions, but Danny continued on. Then he turned off the main road onto a narrow lane. Drystone walls lined either side of the road and bushes arched above them until they were driving through a tunnel of thick greenery. They came out on the other side and he pulled the car into a small parking spot, cut into the stone fence.

"This is it," he said, hopping out of the driver's side. He reached in the backseat and grabbed his jacket, then hurried around to help her out. They found a muddy footpath leading through a grove of trees.

The drizzle had turned to a light mist and Jordan pulled her jacket more tightly around her. Danny held the umbrella over her head, helping her over rocky spots along the path. And then he stopped. "This is it," he murmured.

Jordan glanced around. There wasn't much to see. They stood in the middle of some sort of circle, the earth mounded up with trees planted on either side of the small ridge. The entire circle was no more than forty or fifty feet in diameter. "What is this place?"

"This is a fairy circle," Danny said.

"It looks like a little shallow in the woods. Maybe there was a pond here at one time."

"No, it's a fairy circle. They're all over Ireland. Sometimes you find them in the middle of a meadow, just a ring of mushrooms. Or they can be made of stones. The farmers won't touch them for fear of grievous bad luck."

"Where are the fairies?"

"They're watching us. You should be able to see them, *sidhe.*"

"I'm not a fairy."

"That's what a fairy would say."

Jordan slowly walked along the elevated ridge, careful not to trip on the exposed roots from the trees. "How did this happen?"

"They say the fairies dance round and round in a circle and the earth rises up beneath them. If you walk around the circle and make a wish, it will come true."

"I don't believe that," Jordan said. "Someone piled up the dirt in a circle."

"They also say, if a man finds himself alone in a fairy ring with a fairy, then he belongs to her forever." Danny took her into the center of the ring, then stood behind her, lifting her arms up to the sky. "Close your eyes," he whispered.

Jordan did as she was told. Without sight, her hearing became more acute. At first, she thought it was merely the wind whistling through the trees, but then she began to hear singing. Soft, sweet voices on the breeze. "I hear them," she said, opening her eyes and searching the landscape.

The magic was all around them, like electricity in the

air. "I feel their presence," she said. Slowly she turned, searching the trees for a sight of them.

"I told you. You have fairy blood coursing in your veins. *Leanan sidhe.* She chooses a human to love and if the human doesn't love her, she becomes his slave. But if he does love her, then he is hers, forever. But forever isn't very long, because the lovers of the *leanan sidhe* always die young. They say that's why so many Irish writers and poets and artists die young, because they are captivated by the *leanan sidhe.*"

"I'm not going to kill you," Jordan said.

Danny reached out and smoothed his hand over her cheek, tucking a windswept strand behind her ear. "I know. But sometimes it feels that way."

Jordan closed her eyes and turned into his touch, waiting for him to kiss her. When he finally did, his mouth was warm and demanding.

"Like now," he whispered. "I feel like I'm going to die if I can't have you."

Jordan parted her lips as the kiss deepened and she felt her mind spinning with desire and her body pulsing with wild sensations. The kiss ended slowly, Danny nuzzling his face into the curve of her neck.

"You have bewitched me," he said.

"And can you escape from the *leanan sidhe?*"

"Only if I find someone to take my place," he said. "Another man to capture your fancy."

"I don't want anyone but you," Jordan whispered back.

The wind freshened and her hair whipped around her face. Danny glanced up at the sky. "It looks like it's going to rain again."

Jordan laughed as a big droplet hit her face. "You do weave a good tale, Danny Quinn. You almost had me convinced."

"How do you explain it then?" He took her hand and pressed it to his chest. "I can't resist you. All I think about, day and night, is touching you, kissing you." He wrapped his arms around her waist.

"If you really think I'm going to lead you to an early death then you'd better run away right now. Get out of this fairy ring."

"I'm not going anywhere," he said.

She chuckled. "I wonder why we don't have any mythological creatures in the States? We have ghosts. But you have fairies and leprechauns and trolls and dragons."

Danny grabbed her by the waist and drew her over to one of the trees, trapping her against it with his arms. He pressed his hips against hers and stared down into her eyes. "Can you feel it?" he murmured, his hands skimming over her damp clothes.

"What?" Jordan teased.

His lips were warm against her throat. "Your magic. I can't stop myself. You're too powerful."

Jordan laughed. "I've come to realize that you will use any excuse to get lucky. Are you saying you're under a spell now?"

"I am. And it's your fault. You and your fairy ways."

Jordan shook her head. "You don't seem particularly intent on resisting me." She took his hand and placed it on his chest. "See. It's not as though you can't control yourself."

He moved his hand back to her breast. "It does that

all on its own. I can't control it." He reached down and slipped his hand beneath her shirt, finding the warm skin beneath.

Jordan shivered at his touch, then mimicked his caress, slipping her hand under his jacket and sliding her palm up his chest. "Oh, no. I think it's contagious. Maybe we should get out of here before something else starts acting up on its own." She glanced down at the front of his jeans. "Oh dear, I think it might be too late."

He cupped her breast in his palm and ran his thumb over her nipple, drawing it to a peak. Jordan sighed softly and closed her eyes and a moment later, his lips met hers in a deep, demanding kiss.

Suddenly, the skies opened above them and the rain came down in sheets. Jordan yelped and Danny grabbed her hand and they ran back to the car. By the time they jumped inside they were both soaked to the skin.

He pulled her across the console to continue what they'd begun outside. Jordan couldn't stop touching him. Her hands shoved his T-shirt up, revealing the hard flesh of his belly. Impatient, Danny twisted out of his jacket, then yanked the T-shirt over his head.

The heat from their bodies fogged the windows and the sound of the rain on the roof was a counterpoint to their soft moans and sighs. Jordan pressed her lips to his chest. She was still fully clothed and he'd made no move to undress her, his hand still hidden beneath her shirt.

Slowly, she drew her tongue along his chest to his nipple, then circled it several times. It grew to a hard peak in the chill and Jordan continued to tease at it. He groaned softly, and ran his fingers through her hair, tangling in the rain-soaked strands.

Her hands drifted down to his belt and then lower, smoothing over the fabric of his jeans until she felt his erection beneath. Normally, she might have hesitated outside the privacy of the manor house. But they were all alone in the woods and the fairy circle had worked its magic.

Danny watched as she fumbled with the button of his jeans, holding his breath as if her touch were enough to send him over the edge. She glanced up to see him smiling, droplets still clinging to his thick dark lashes.

"I guess the fairies have spoken," he said.

Jordan slipped her hand inside his boxers, wrapping her fingers around his hard shaft. "I suppose we ought to listen to them."

"I've always wanted to make love in the rain. And we have this place all to ourselves. We could take our clothes off and lie down in the grass."

"What if someone comes along?" Jordan asked.

"They'll think we're fairies," he whispered, touching his lips to hers.

Jordan had never done anything so sexually spontaneous…except for almost everything she'd done with Danny. And what harm could it do? No one could see the spot from the road and there'd be no visitors in the pouring rain.

She wanted to try everything and anything with Danny. "All right," she murmured. Jordan began to shed her clothes and Danny watched, a look of astonishment on his face. When she was completely naked, she turned and looked at him. "Well? What about you?"

"You really want to do this?"

Jordan nodded. "When in Ireland do as the fairies do."

Jordan jumped out of the car, into the downpour. Though the air was cold, the rain felt warm on her skin. She ran, her bare feet slipping on the wet grass, until she stood in the middle of the fairy circle. Then she turned her face up to the sky, reveling in the utter and complete freedom she felt.

Danny joined her a moment later, completely naked and fully aroused. They met in the center of the circle with another kiss, this one deep and stirring, a prelude to the passion they were about to share.

They tumbled down into the soft grass, their limbs tangled together. Jordan had never felt anything like it. It was so completely natural to touch him like this. He rolled her over beneath him, his hips resting between her thighs. "We don't have a condom," he said, cursing softly.

"We don't need one," Jordan replied, pulling him into another kiss.

"Are you sure?"

She nodded. She'd always been careful about birth control, never leaving it to the moment when it was needed. And she was glad that there would be no barriers between them this time. He pulled her thighs against his hips and entered her in one smooth motion, taking her breath away.

He buried himself so completely that Jordan wasn't sure she could take anymore. Danny gazed down into her eyes, smoothing the rain from her face with his hands and kissing her softly. The air around them was alive with electricity, the leaves of the trees rustling overhead.

Slowly, he began to move above her, his gaze still fixed on hers. Jordan could see every moment of pleasure etched across his handsome face, every surge of desire and every determined denial. He drove himself close, then retreated and waited for her, moving against her until he felt her release coming.

Here, in this spot, there was nothing but her desire. The outside world didn't exist, the problems of the day had disappeared, everything in her life had been reduced to this perfect joining. He withdrew and slid against her, teasing at the damp folds until Jordan cried out beneath him.

And then he was inside her again, taking her over the edge, the spasms enveloping her body until she couldn't think any longer. Everything had become sensation: pure, powerful pleasure that raced through her body like a current.

A moment later, he dissolved into his own orgasm, his body driving into hers one last time before he lost control. She whispered his name, urging him on until he was completely sated.

With a sigh, Danny pulled her on top of him, their bodies still joined. He stared up into the sky, the rain splattering in his face. "We have to be gone in the head to be out here in this rain."

"I love it," Jordan said. "I'm not even cold."

"I'm freezing," he said. "And I have grass in places I won't even mention."

A low rumble sounded in the distance. At first,

Jordan thought it was thunder, then realized it sounded more like a car. "Someone's coming."

Danny shook his head. "It's just a car passing by on the road. They won't come out in the rain."

Jordan got to her feet and raked her hands through her hair, letting the deluge wash all the dirt from her naked body. Danny watched her, an appreciative smile on her face. "You are a mysterious creature," he said.

She began to dance, swaying slowly from side to side and—

"Don't worry, Mildred, it's supposed to be here somewhere. A little rain won't hurt ya. Come along now. Step lively."

Jordan spun around to see an elderly couple, decked out in rain gear, stepping into the grove. A tiny scream slipped from her lips and she looked down at Danny. He was already leaping to his feet.

He grabbed her hand and they ran for the car, but not before the couple caught sight of them. Jordan slipped once and Danny steadied her before racing on.

"Look, Mildred, I told you we'd see fairies. Didn't I tell you?"

"Freddie, those are no more fairies than you and I are. Fairies don't drive around the countryside in a Volvo."

Laughing, Jordan and Danny jumped in the car and quickly made their escape. As they swerved down the narrow lane, the car spitting up mud as it gained speed, Jordan pressed her hand to her heart, the laughter making her breathless and dizzy.

They'd made love in a warm, soft bed, on the sofa in the library, on the worktable in the kitchen. But it all seemed so ordinary, so controlled, compared to what they'd just done. Never in her life had she completely surrendered to her desires—until now.

"Are we going to drive all the way home stark naked?" Danny asked. "Or would you like to stop and get dressed?"

She glanced over at him. "Oh, let's have some fun. Forget the clothes."

"You're a woman after my own heart, Jordan Kennally. You know that, don't you?"

I hope so, Jordan said to herself. Because she wouldn't be satisfied with anything less.

"I'M LOSING MY MIND!"

Danny heard Jordan's shout from the breakfast nook, where he was replacing the hinges on the old wooden door. He frowned, then decided to see what had set her off. No doubt she'd just finished her daily report to her father.

There were times when Danny was ready to hop on a plane, fly across the ocean and beat the shite out of the man who made Jordan's life so miserable. How hard would it be to convince him to let Jordan go? Right now, it seemed as if her father kept her employed simply to torture her.

Parents were supposed to support their children, not torment them. He'd always taken his parents for granted, but after hearing about Jordan's dysfunctional family, it was clear that he needed to be much more appreciative of what he had.

Danny found her standing in front of the bookshelves, staring at the neatly arranged shelves of books. She'd spent most of the previous day unpacking the crates and arranging the volumes in the library. But now, she stood in front of her work, shaking her head.

"What is it?" he asked.

"It's gone," she said. "It was here yesterday and it's gone today. I counted out each of these books, matched them up with the packing lists. The Shakespeare plays have thirty-seven volumes. And now there are thirty-six. There's a spot empty right here, where *A Midsummer Night's Dream* belongs."

"Are you sure?"

"Of course I'm sure. I'm not imagining this. It was here yesterday and now it's gone. The set isn't worth anything if it's incomplete." She turned away from the bookcase and began to pace the room. "We have to get rid of these brownies," she said. "We—we need an exterminator." She reached for the phone book on her desk. "Like those ghostbuster guys in the movie. You have to have someone in Ireland who takes care of these things."

"Of course we do," Danny said. "And they're all scoundrels and cheats. They'll take your money, sprinkle a few herbs around the room and laugh all the way to the bank."

"What am I supposed to do? I didn't mind it at first, but this set cost five hundred pounds. I'm going to have to replace it."

"Unless we found the person who stole it."

"I thought you said brownies stole it."

He closed the phone book and grabbed her hand, leading her along to the leather sofa. "I don't believe in brownies any more than you do. We need to figure out how this person—and I do believe it's a person—is getting into the house. Remember Kellan told us about the secret passage? We need to find it before anything else goes missing." Danny sat down, then pulled her into his lap, wrapping his arms around her.

"Okay. So how do we do this?"

"We start by checking out the exterior and the cellars. See if we can find any entrances there. They have to come in from the outside in some way. And it can only happen from the exterior walls or the cellar."

"Contractors have been over every inch of this place," she said. "The cellars are solid stone so that can't be it."

"The pool," Danny said. "What better place to hide an entrance?"

"No. You'd be able to see an entrance down there. The walls are tiled."

"Maybe Kellan is wrong," he murmured.

"No, he has to be right. My question is, who is coming in and why? They really haven't stolen anything of value. They're just causing mischief."

"Maybe it's a kid," Danny said, smoothing a strand of hair from her temple. "Before you started working on this house, it was open for years. Maybe one of the kids who hung out here found the secret entrance and is just coming in out of curiosity."

"That makes sense," Jordan said.

"We need to let the dogs sleep in the house," Danny said. "If someone comes in, they'll bark."

Jordan thought about his suggestion for a moment. She hadn't allowed Finny and Mogue into the house since that very first night, when she'd thought someone was in her room. Danny understood her reluctance, considering all the work that had been done on the wooden floors. But the best defense against a troublemaker was a four-legged offense.

"All right. But I'm going to make them wear those little booties that I make the contractors wear."

"They're not going to like that," Danny said. "Besides, they won't stay on. I'll trim their nails. They'll be fine."

Jordan drew a deep breath. "All right. I feel better. Now that we have a plan, we're going to figure this out."

Danny forced a smile. If only the rest of their troubles were so easy to solve.

He wanted to talk about what was going to happen between them when the job was over. He needed to know where he stood. All the guessing was wearing on him and he'd grown sick of trying to interpret every little thing she said to him.

When they were together, intimately entangled, Danny knew there was something there, something much deeper than just lust. When he moved inside her, it wasn't about his pleasure, it had become all about her, as if the beauty and power of their physical relationship might somehow prove to her they belonged together.

Every day that passed, he saw proof of the end. The painters were gone, the roofers were finished. Books now filled the shelves in the library, utensils and pots and pans hung from the racks in the kitchen, and furniture and rugs would arrive in a few days. After that, the house would be transformed from a construction site to a home and it would all be over.

It was a day that Jordan was anxiously awaiting and one he could only dread. Why was he so afraid to broach the subject with her? Danny suspected that he wasn't ready to hear her answer.

If she was planning to walk away without a second thought, then he didn't want to know until the very last moment of their time together. She had bewitched him, and like the other victims of the *leanan sidhe,* he would pay for his desire when she let him go. Though it wouldn't be death, he might feel like it for a time.

"Why don't we just take a little break?" he suggested, nuzzling her neck. "We could go down and take a swim. Or we could go out and get an early supper."

"We're always taking little breaks from work," Jordan said.

"I don't mean that kind of break," he said, referring to their sexual trysts. "Let's just get out of the house and do something. Take a drive, take a walk. It's a beautiful autumn day and you've been cooped up inside for too long. And I want to spend some time with you. Nothing more."

"I can't leave," she said. "I have all this work to do and I—"

"I'm not asking you to take an ocean voyage for feck's sake," Danny teased.

She shrugged. "I know. But I sort of have something important to do this afternoon and I really wouldn't be very good company. And I need some time to work up my courage."

"Are you planning to go cliff diving? Or will you be jumping out of a plane?"

Jordan giggled. "No, nothing so simple. I'm going to call my father and give him an ultimatum. Either he gives me the hotel job or I'm going to quit."

A gasp slipped from Danny's throat, her statement taking him by surprise. If she wasn't working for her family then she wouldn't be tied to New York anymore. "Are you sure you want to do that?"

"Yes," Jordan said, nodding. "Absolutely. And I have you to thank for that."

"Me?"

"I've always been so careful about everything I've done in my life. Until I met you. Then I just threw caution to wind. I had sex in the middle of a fairy circle yesterday. I was naked, running around in the rain. If I can do that, I can certainly be honest with my father. It's time I stood up to him."

"And what will you do if he gives you the job?" Danny asked.

Jordan opened her mouth to reply, then paused, frowning. "I'll do the job," she murmured. "I'll do a really good job and prove that I'm just as good as any of my brothers."

"And if he refuses?"

She thought about the question for a long moment. "I don't know. I suppose I should figure that out, too." Jordan drew a ragged breath. "I guess I'll…quit."

Danny grabbed her hand and laced his fingers through hers. "Are you really ready to do that?"

"It's always been an option," she said. "I've almost done it a few times in the past, but then talked myself out of it. I can't continue like this, Danny. I should be worth something to him, as a daughter *and* an employee. Maybe it's time to find out where I stand."

"Why do you care what your father thinks? You're an adult. You don't need his approval."

Jordan laughed. "Yeah, right. Don't even try to ana-
lyze me. I've spent a lifetime trying to figure out why I
seek my father's approval. It's just something I do. My
brothers do it also. But I'm just willing to suffer more
to get what I want."

"You're suffering?" Danny asked.

"Well, not at the moment."

"I bet your brothers never had sex with one of their
employees," he said. "That's wicked suffering there."

"You're not my employee and I'm not your boss, remember?"

He grabbed her waist and set her on her feet, then
stood beside her. "Give me a half hour."

"For what?"

"A swim. We could get naked, play in the water, have
a little fun and have you back at work before anyone
knows you're missing."

"You just want to get my clothes off," she said.

"Yes, I do. That is pretty much my goal from the
time we get up in the morning until the time we crawl
into bed at night."

"Oh, so now I get the real story. You're not interested
in making gates and medallions and hinges anymore.
This is all about me and you."

"Now you're starting to understand. Finally. It's
about bloody time." He reached for the hem of her shirt.
"I'll race you. First one naked and in the water wins."

Jordan slowly shook her head. "No, no, no."

"Yes, yes, yes," he said, tugging his T-shirt over his
head. He watched as her gaze drifted over his chest,
then reached for the button of his jeans. He unzipped

them and skimmed them down his hips, kicking off his shoes before casting the jeans aside.

He was left in only his boxers and when he hooked his fingers in the waistband, Jordan sucked in a sharp breath. With deliberate ease, he slowly slid them down until he was standing in front of her, completely naked.

"All right," she finally said. "It would probably be better to call my father tomorrow. He's always in a bad mood on Tuesdays."

"That's my girl," Danny said. "Since I've had a head start, I'll let you catch up before we race to the pool."

"Here?"

Danny nodded. "Yes."

Jordan took the opportunity to perform a very sexy striptease for him and when she had him completely distracted with her naked body, took off for the door. Danny headed to the kitchen and the stairs that led down from there, but Jordan took the opposite path, taking the stairs near the front door. By the time he reached the pool, she was already treading water in the deep end.

"You have a half hour," she called, her voice echoing against the tiles. "You'd better make it worth my time."

IT WAS NEARLY 9:00 p.m. when Jordan pulled up in front of the manor house. The drive back and forth to Wexford was a long one, but her time had gone to a good cause. Over the past sixteen months, she'd visited hundreds of antique stores all over Ireland. To her delight, she'd found period fixtures for almost every room in the manor house. Today had brought a small chandelier for the upper hallway.

The only problem with a day away was that she hadn't had her regular dose of Danny Quinn. She'd grown used to seeing him whenever the impulse stuck.

But the ride to Wexford had given her time to think about all that had happened since his arrival at Castle Cnoc. Though she'd vowed to keep their relationship simple, the deeper her affections grew, the more difficult it became. She found herself fantasizing about a real future with the sexy Irishman.

She imagined them strolling the streets of Manhattan together, buying a weekend house in Connecticut, keeping an apartment in the city, enjoying everything that New York had to offer. Other times, she imagined herself living here in Ireland, raising a family and making a home with him. But always, she came to the realization that if they were to have a future, one of them would have to sacrifice.

Though she'd been determined to call her father and give him her ultimatum, Jordan had been putting it off for the past few days. Tomorrow was Friday and after that, the weekend. She'd call him at home on Sunday morning, knowing that without the pressures of the office, he might be more amenable. Plus, her mother would be there to run interference.

In truth, she was afraid of his answer. If he did allow her to quit, then she had to decide what to do with the rest of her life. At least now, everything was still in limbo. She still had choices.

As she stepped out of the car, she saw Danny standing at the front door. The scaffolding was gone and the original door was hung with brand-new hinges and hardware. Progress, she mused. That always brought a smile to her face.

"Hey, baby," he said with a devilish smile. "Welcome home."

"You've been busy," she said. "It looks incredible." He swung the door back and forth on its hinges, demonstrating how smoothly it worked. "Very nice job. Have you been waiting here long?"

"All afternoon. But I have a good reason," he said.

"You always have a good reason," she teased.

He strode up to her and picked her up off her feet, wrapping her legs around his waist. "I'm not always thinking about sex," he said. "I have other things going on in my life."

"Like what?"

Danny carried her into the house. But instead of heading back to the office, he carried her up the stairs, his mouth warm on her throat. They walked to her bedroom and then into the bathroom.

"What are we doing?"

"I'm going to draw a bath for you and then you're going to relax and tell me about your day. And then I'm going to ask you something and you're going to say yes."

"Don't I always say yes?"

"That's true. And after you say yes, we're going to have some dinner and spend the rest of the night in bed."

She slipped out of her jacket and tossed it aside, then rubbed her stiff neck. Hours in the car had exhausted her and she couldn't think of anything she wanted more than a hot bath. But her curiosity was piqued. What was he going to ask? she wondered. What was so important to him that he'd bribe her with a bath to get a positive response?

"Ask me now," Jordan demanded.

"It can wait," he said.

As the water ran into the huge clawfoot tub, Danny slowly undressed her. When she was naked, he stood back and stared at her. It felt odd for him to be fully clothed while she was naked. Not odd, she thought. Erotic. "No, I want to know now. Did you go over budget? Did you mess something up?"

"It's not about the house." He helped her into the tub, then handed her a glass of wine that he'd set on the floor.

"What is it?" she asked, sinking down into the hot water. "I want to know."

He cursed softly. "This is supposed to be relaxing and now you're all tense," he said. "It's really nothing."

"If it's nothing, than you can ask me now. Do you need a day off? Is that it?"

He reached into the back pocket of his jeans and handed her an envelope. "It's an invitation to my gallery opening on Saturday night. I'm showing a couple of pieces and I thought you might like to come with me. As my date."

Jordan stared at the invitation, warmed by his offer. "Yes," she murmured. "Yes, I'd love to go as your date."

He seemed pleased with her answer, dropping a quick kiss on her shoulder. "It's in Dublin. I thought we could go and spend the night. Maybe see a bit of the city on Sunday. Make a weekend out of it."

Though Jordan had never spent more than a day away from Castle Cnoc, she realized that time with Danny was running out. There were so many things she wanted to experience with him, but every day that passed was one less she'd have with him. By her estimate, they had less than a month left. And yet, any time spent in Danny's company was better than her solitary life in New York.

Was he really what she'd been waiting for? This wasn't supposed to be how it happened. She wasn't supposed to fall in love with an Irish blacksmith with thick, dark hair and bottomless blue eyes.

She opened her eyes and glanced at him. Danny wasn't pretty, he was sheer masculine perfection. He wore his looks the way he wore his clothes, casually, as if he weren't aware of the effect they had on her. She was so accustomed to neatly tailored men that he seemed exotic and forbidden.

"In Manhattan, gallery openings are pretty fancy affairs. Are they that way in Dublin?"

He chuckled. "You're going to see me in a proper jacket," he said. "No tie, but I'm going to look very sexy. The women will be all over me."

"I didn't ask so you could tell me about your wardrobe choice. I'll need to decide on a dress."

"I could take you shopping," he said.

"I have the perfect dress at home. I'll have it sent from New York this afternoon."

"Then it's all settled. On Saturday, we're going to Dublin." He was watching her through hooded eyes. "Now, tell me about your day."

"Chandelier for the upper hallway, monogrammed towels for the bathrooms, still looking for decent sheets. May have to do mail order from Frette. Unless I take a weekend and go to Italy for linens. Or Paris."

"Is that even a possibility?"

"Yes," Jordan said. "If that's what's needed, that's what I'll do. I'd prefer to stick with Irish linens though. Maybe if we left tonight, I could shop tomorrow in Dublin." She groaned softly and leaned back in the bath. "God, I'm so sick of shopping." She glanced over at him. "Enough about me. What did you do all day long?"

"Thought about you in the bed," he said. "Made some hinges. Thought about you in the bathtub. Worked on the garden gate. Thought about you in the swimming pool, designed a front gate for the drive."

"Really?" She laughed. "So, you had a productive day."

"Yes," he said. "So, boss, give me a job to do. I could rub your feet. Or wash your back. Or massage your shoulders."

"All of those would be nice," she murmured.

"I'll start with the shoulders." He sat down behind her and began to knead the knotted muscles. She tipped her head to the side and he pressed his lips to a spot at the base of her neck. "Do you ever wonder what you'd be doing if you hadn't come here to Castle Cnoc?" she asked.

"What do you mean?"

"Our lives seem so intertwined here. What if you were alone? What would you be doing right now?"

"I'd probably be sitting at the pub, having a beer with my brothers. Maybe tending the bar, drawing Guinness. Then a game of darts or billiards." He chuckled. "Jaysus, I had a boring life before I met you."

"Me, too," she said. "I spent my free time searching the internet for fabric and furniture and fixtures. The highlight of my evening would be my decision whether to have a ham sandwich or a grilled cheese. Dinner would be followed by whatever bestseller I was reading."

"I'd say we were damn lucky to meet each other."

"You've ruined me for other men, you know."

"How is that?"

"The sex. It's too good."

He rested his chin on her shoulder. "How can the sex be too good?"

"I never really thought sex was important," Jordan admitted. "My parents aren't very loving with each other. Our family shows affection by insulting each other. We just weren't…physical. But with you, we always seem to be touching."

"I like that," Danny said.

"Me, too. And I never thought I would. I'd sit in the subway or at the park and watch couples hanging all over each other and wonder why they couldn't contain themselves. Now I understand." She turned and kissed his cheek. "Just the tiniest thing can bring the biggest thrill."

He smoothed his palms over her shoulders and chest, then cupped her breasts. "You do have a very touchable body, boss."

Jordan moaned softly as his thumbs rubbed across her nipples. She'd grown accustomed to this power that she held over him. When he touched her, she didn't feel like a boss or Andrew Kennally's daughter or the Kennally brothers' younger sister or Kencor's "decorator." She was just a woman.

Her heart slammed in her chest and she arched to

meet his caress. Danny circled the tub and pulled her to her feet, wrapping his arms around her naked body as his lips captured hers.

Jordan was always amazed at how powerful his kiss was. He was able to take her breath away, to make her body ache, to send her heart racing, by simply covering her mouth with his. He had a way of possessing her that made her feel weak and powerful all at once.

The kiss spun out in one long, delicious encounter, growing deeper and more passionate with every breath they shared. Danny's hands smoothed over her damp skin but Jordan's touch was hampered by his clothes.

A frustrated moan slipped from her throat as she fumbled with the buttons of his shirt. She needed him naked, needed his skin touching hers. "Stop." Pressing her hands to his chest she pushed him back. "Take off your clothes."

"No," he said.

Jordan frowned, shaking her head. "No?"

"No," Danny said. "If I take off my clothes, then I'm not going to be able to stop myself. I think we should just take our time. We have the whole evening."

"Am I the boss or are you?"

"You're the boss," he said.

"Then you're supposed to follow my orders?"

"Yes, ma'am."

"Take off your clothes, Danny Quinn. And make it snappy."

With a reluctant smile, he slowly stripped. When his boxers were around his feet, he braced his hands on his hips. "Now what? Would you like me to fix that squeaky hinge or change the oil in your car?"

"Get in the tub," Jordan ordered.

He did as he was told, sliding down into the warm water. Then Jordan climbed in and straddled his waist, his hard shaft pressing against the crease between her legs. She grabbed a sponge and lathered it up then ran it over his chest.

"Isn't this considered sexual harassment?"

"Yes," she said. "And I could get fired for this."

"Really?"

Jordan nodded. "Really. But you're not going to say anything, are you?"

"Never," he said. "As long as you promise to keep harassing me, I'll keep quiet."

She leaned over and kissed him and when she moved back, Jordan shifted on top of him, slowly taking him inside her. A gasp slipped from her lips and she smiled. "I think we're going to be getting into a little overtime tonight."

"I'm ready to do whatever it takes to get the job done."

6

DANNY AND JORDAN ARRIVED in Dublin by mid-afternoon on Saturday. Danny insisted on driving Jordan's Volvo, making it from County Cork to Dublin in record time. As they raced over the curving highways, he felt as if they were setting off on a grand adventure, even though it was only a night in the city.

They weren't boss and employee now. They were a couple having a little holiday together. She was his lover, his girlfriend, his date. And it felt good to be like everyone else in the world. Just two people falling in love.

They did some shopping for linens, then checked into a room at a nice hotel. Though Jordan tried to insist on paying for it, expensing it along with the sheets, Danny refused. He wanted the weekend to be his treat and Jordan reluctantly accepted. In truth, he had all sorts of things he wanted to show her.

They got dressed for the opening, then went out for a stroll before dinner. O'Connell Street was famous for its shops, but Danny had decided to take Jordan on a sculpture tour. They began with the statue of James

Joyce and then moved on to Daniel O'Connell. James Larkin was next. The last sculpture was inside an imposing building.

"I used to come here all the time when I was at university," Danny said, holding the door open for her. "It's a pretty special place in my family history."

"What is this, a museum?"

"No," Danny said. "It's the post office."

"You spent time at the post office?"

Danny nodded. "I know. It's a bit strange, but I'll explain." They stood in the center of the lobby, Danny holding tight to her hand. "This is where the rebellion began. This is where my great-great-grandfather on my mother's side made his stand against the British soldiers. The Easter Uprising was kind of like your revolution." He pointed to the statue. "That's Cuchulainn."

"Did he fight in the rebellion?" Jordan asked.

Danny shook his head. "No, he's one of our mythological heroes. His big victory was the cattle raid of Cooley."

"He stole cows?"

"No, he protected the bull of Ulster from Queen Maeve's soldiers."

"He protected a cow—"

"A bull. *The* bull."

"And he gets a statue."

"I guess he's a martyr to cattle protection. Queen Maeve set her sorcerers on him and killed him after he saved the bull. The statue is in memory of the fourteen rebels that were executed after the Easter Uprising."

"That makes much more sense," Jordan said.

They stared up at the statue for a long time before

Jordan slipped her arms around Danny's waist and gave him a hug. "I like it. I think it's the nicest one we've seen tonight. Except for yours, of course."

"You are not required to like my work," Danny said. "The sculptures you're going to see tonight are pretty abstract."

"I'm going to love your work," she said. "I know I will."

They strolled out onto the street. There was a chill in the air and Danny slipped out of his jacket and draped it around Jordan's shoulders. "Have I told you how beautiful you look in that dress?" he asked.

"Yes. Lots of times. At least twenty since I put it on at the hotel."

"Well, then this is twenty-one. You do look incredible. You're going to be the most beautiful woman in the room tonight."

"And you're required to say that," she teased.

"No," Danny replied, shaking his head. "That's the thing about you. You don't have any idea how pretty you are. I think you've spent so much time trying to be one of the guys that you don't have any sense of who you are as a woman."

"I did feel that way," Jordan said, stunned that he'd sensed it. "You make me feel…feminine." She held up the sleeve of his jacket. "Like this. My brothers would never think to offer me a jacket if I was cold. They'd just yell at me for forgetting to bring my own along. And they'd never tell me I was pretty. They'd just make some stupid comment about my pigeon-toes or my knobby knees. Or they'd start in on my chest."

"They make fun of your chest?"

"It's often the topic around the Thanksgiving table. They think that teasing me is great family fun. I take a lot of abuse for being the only girl. Especially when my father encourages it."

Danny frowned. "Next time you have a family dinner, you call me. I'll come and stand up for you. I'm pretty good with my fists and I'm the master of the verbal put-down. Your brothers wouldn't pick on you again. Truth told, my two brothers and I could best your four brothers in a good scrap."

"That's not the worst of it. My mother tells me if I'd just get married and bring a husband home, my brothers would show me more respect." Jordan paused. "Not that I'd expect you to marry me. It—it's just what my mother said."

"Do you ever think about getting married?"

"Sure. I think every woman does. But it's not something that I'm focused on. What about you?" It was the truth. Since meeting Danny she had thought about it more than she had before; but it still didn't mean that she wanted to marry him. That would require a complete shift in her priorities.

"I don't really think about it either," Danny said. "But it's a possibility. My brother Riley met Nan and now they're going to get married and that was just this last summer." He shook his head. "It's a strange thing. A wee bit frightening. That things can change so quickly and there's nothing to be done about it."

"Marriage just hasn't fit into my plans."

"Mine neither," Danny said. *Not that it couldn't,* he thought. But he wasn't ready to say that out loud.

A long silence grew between them as they walked

down the sidewalk to the restaurant. He hadn't felt so uncomfortable around Jordan since the day they'd met. Everything had come so easily these past weeks. But maybe this was a conversation that was unavoidable. How much longer could they go on ignoring the future? Sooner or later, they'd have to talk about it.

"You should come to New York sometime," Jordan said. "We have a lot of statues and sculptures there."

"You've got the big one," he said.

"The big one?"

"The Statue of Liberty. That's one thing I'd really like to see."

"Then you'll have to come," she said. It was the closest they'd come to talking about a future together. And Danny was pleased. At least there was a possibility they'd see each other again after she left Ireland.

"What else would we see, besides the inside of your flat?" he asked.

"Depends on when you come. If you come in the fall, we'd go to Central Park. At Christmas, we'd look at the windows at Bloomie's. In the winter, there's skating at Rockefeller Center. In the spring there's baseball at Yankee Stadium. And summer is weekends in the Hamptons. And then we'd eat hot dogs and visit museums and go to Chinatown for Szechuan. We'd take a carriage ride at midnight and go to the top of the Empire State Building and have corned beef sandwiches at the Stage Door Deli and see a Broadway show."

"Jaysus, I can see why you'd want to go home. Ireland must seem like such a bore to you."

"No," she said. "I love Ireland. I didn't at first, but I

think I'm going to miss it after I leave. Who knows, I may come back for visit or two."

Danny chuckled. "I'd like that. Maybe you could find another house to fix up. Kellan's always doing that. You could do another project with him."

"Actually, Kellan talked to me about that. He offered me a job."

Gobsmacked, Danny wasn't sure what to say. Why hadn't she told him this? Why hadn't Kellan mentioned it? Was there a reason they'd keep it a secret from him? "Yeah," he murmured, maintaining an even tone. "That would be really nice."

"But, I think if I come back, I'd want to spend my time seeing Ireland first," she said. "Take some time off. Do a little trip around the country. Like your parents do. What is that called?"

"Caravanning," Danny replied. "So it's good we talked about this. I certainly feel better."

"I do too," Jordan said.

It wasn't much, but Danny did feel relieved. They'd defined their relationship a bit. They'd become so close it had been hard to believe that they'd go their separate ways and never see each other again. Now, they wouldn't.

"And we can always Skype," Jordan said.

"I don't know what that is, but it sounds like fun. Can we do it tonight? And does it involve taking off your clothes?"

"Sometimes it does involve the removal of clothing," Jordan said. "We'll talk about that later."

"Are you hungry? We can eat or we can stop by the

gallery." He pointed across the street. "It's just there. It won't be busy and they always serve finger food."

"Let's go now," Jordan said. "We can always eat later."

He took her hand and they crossed the street, then stopped short before opening the door for her. "What's wrong?" Jordan asked.

"I'm a bit nervous," he said.

"People will love your work," Jordan said.

"I'm not worried about people," Danny said, "I'm worried about you. You're the only one who matters."

He pulled her close and kissed the top of her head. And there it was. No truer words had ever been spoken. If he'd thought he could keep himself from loving Jordan, then he was sadly mistaken. It had already happened. And there was no going back.

BY THE TIME the show officially began, the gallery was packed with guests and press. Jordan had been to a number of openings in Manhattan and this was no different. There was excitement in the air and everyone milled around the pieces, wineglasses dangling from their hands.

Danny stood between his two sculptures, talking to interested guests while Jordan stood nearby, sipping her wine. He seemed like a different person in this environment, so composed and serious, not at all like the funny, teasing man she'd come to know. The suit made him look older, more respectable, and, even though he hadn't combed his hair, he was still dangerously attractive.

As expected, Jordan fell in love with the sculptures

the moment she saw them. He'd told her they were abstract, but there was something about them that brought to mind birds soaring on the air currents over the cliffs near the manor.

The sculptures had been made of copper, the thin sheets bent and crumpled and assembled to create a sense of motion. She could imagine the pieces in a museum or a private home or even the lobby of a public building. Considering the number of people gathered around Danny, Jordan felt confident that the sculptures would be sold before the night was through.

"What do you think?"

Jordan turned to find a woman standing next to her. She was about the same age as Jordan, and dressed entirely in black, her hair cropped short and trendy glasses perched on her nose.

"Sally McClary. I'm the art critic for the *Evening Post*. You seem to be captivated by his work."

"Oh, I am," Jordan said. "I think it's extraordinary."

Sally nodded. "Yes, he is, isn't he."

"Oh, I thought we were talking about his work."

"I am," Sally said. "Not his art work, although that's quite extraordinary, too."

Jordan frowned. What was this woman getting at? What other work did— "Oh, you've seen his commercial work? He's an excellent blacksmith."

"Oh, goodness, no. I'm talking about the man. The gorgeous man beneath those clothes." She took a slow sip of her wine. "He's like a fine work of art himself. Strip the clothes off of him and you could stare at him all day long, couldn't you?" She smiled slyly. "A pity he doesn't spend more time in Dublin. He has quite a group of fans here."

Jordan wasn't sure how to respond. She pasted a smile on her face. "So what do you think of the art?"

"Oh, it's fabulous, of course. But then, I've always been a patron. He needs to work more. There's not enough of his work out there to make an impact on the market. And he needs to show outside Ireland. London. New York. Even Los Angeles. Oh, they'd love him there, don't you think?"

Jordan nodded. "Yes, I suppose they would."

"Well, enjoy the rest of the evening," Sally said. "And take a look at the Deirdan etchings. He's the next big thing. Mark my words."

Jordan watched the woman weave her way through the crowds. She stopped and spoke with Danny, resting her hand on his chest as she leaned in close. He smiled and nodded and Jordan wondered at the easy familiarity. Had they been lovers?

She'd never really considered Danny's past. For all she knew, his sex life had begun the moment they met. But that was silly. He'd been seducing girls since high school and even at two or three females a year, that was still a considerable number.

As Sally walked away, he glanced over and caught Jordan's eye. Was that a trace of worry she saw in his face? Jordan watched him over the rim of her wineglass, trying to read his expression. When he excused himself, she gulped down most of her wine, and crossed the room to meet him.

"Are you all right?" he said.

"Sure. Fine," she said. "I was just talking to an art critic. Sally something."

"Right," he said. "Sally McClary. She works for the *Evening Post*. She's a fan."

"I know," Jordan said. "She told me. She seems to be a very devoted fan."

Danny tipped his head as he studied her. "What's that supposed to mean?"

"I don't know. She's the one who started the conversation with me. I got the impression that you two might have been…"

"Did she say that?"

"Not in so many words. Were you?"

He shifted nervously. "Would you be angry if I told you the truth? Because I'll lie if it makes you feel better."

Jordan set her wineglass on the tray of a passing waiter and grabbed another one. "I'm not naive enough to believe you've never been with a woman before me. What you do to me in bed I'm sure comes from lots of experience."

"Not lots," he said. "Well, maybe lots, but that depends upon what you mean by lots."

"You don't need to tell me," Jordan said.

"They don't make any difference," he said. "You're the only woman I want."

"Now," Jordan said.

"Now. Always. Any time." He gave her a seductive smile. "And that sounded really trite, didn't it?" He grabbed her arm and pulled her along to a quiet corner in the gallery.

"This really isn't necessary." Jordan put down her

glass and covered her ears. "I don't need to know. I don't want to know."

"You need to know this," he said. Danny slipped his hands around her waist and pulled her closer. "I'm glad you're here with me tonight. There isn't anyone else I'd rather have here. And I like introducing you as my girl-friend, because that's what you are. And that's impor-tant."

"Have you had a lot of girlfriends?" Jordan asked.

"No," he said. "I can count them on one hand. Ac-tually, on three fingers, counting you. And that says something about my feelings for you, Jordan. I think I'm falling for you."

Jordan slowly lowered her hands and took a quick sip of her wine. This was not what she expected. His revelation changed everything. She felt the undeniable urge to run away and glanced around, looking for an escape route.

"No," he said. "You don't have to run. It's all right. I'm just being honest. No harm in that."

"But I—"

He pressed a finger to her lips. "I know. And that's all right." He looked at his watch. "Why don't we get out of here? I've been the accommodating artist for three hours. I think I'm all right to leave."

"I could use some air," she admitted.

Danny said his goodbyes and a few minutes later, they were back on the street, strolling among the crowds of locals and tourists on O'Connell Street. Danny slipped his arm around her shoulders and they walked to the end of the street, to the river. They found a spot near the bridge and Jordan leaned against the railing and stared into the water.

"I shouldn't have said that," Danny murmured.

"No, I'm glad you did," she said. "It's how I feel, too."

"You do?"

"I do. But I don't know what it means. I guess it's not unexpected. We've been spending every minute together for over a month. It would be difficult not to develop feelings for each other."

"Exactly," he said.

"I just don't think we should have too many expectations," she said.

"Expectations." Danny chuckled softly. "That's funny. Maybe it's about time someone expected something from me when it came to romance."

"Can we just enjoy our weekend here and not worry so much about the future?" Jordan asked.

Danny nodded. "Yeah, we can do that. Come on, let's go find a pub, have a pint and enjoy ourselves."

He pulled her into his arms and kissed her, standing beneath a street lamp while the river flowed quietly nearby. For Jordan, it was the most perfect kiss they'd ever shared because it confirmed the words he'd spoken earlier.

He was falling for her. She should have been jumping for joy, shouting to the rooftops that the man she wanted felt the same way about her. But the revelation was bittersweet. It didn't make things simpler. It only made them more difficult.

DANNY GLANCED AT THE CLOCK on the bedside table. It was nearly eleven and he'd made no attempt to crawl out of bed and get the day started. After the show last night, he and Jordan had hit the town, finding a pub near the hotel and spending the night dancing and laughing and having more fun than he'd ever had with a woman.

He loved introducing her to the wonders of Ireland. Last night it was Irish art and Guinness. Today it would be a decent Irish breakfast and a stroll along the Liffey.

He drew a deep breath and closed his eyes, snuggling into her warm, naked body. From the moment he'd met Jordan, there'd been an undeniable attraction between them, a connection that seemed to be strengthened with each moment they spent in bed. They'd been so wrapped up in each other, he'd forgotten that she wasn't completely his.

Was this what Riley had gone through with Nan? His brother had fallen in love with an American tourist with a life and a career in the States. But he'd made it work, he'd convinced her to stay. How had he made that happen?

When they'd begun, Danny was happy just being with Jordan. He'd never thought about anything beyond the next time they found themselves in bed. But somewhere along the line, he'd forgotten about immediate gratification and begun thinking about the future.

She was an incredibly seductive woman. And though she claimed that he was the only one who thought so, Danny suspected the American men she'd known had seen the beauty beneath the businesslike facade. She was his inspiration, his muse, his temptress. Danny couldn't think of anything more he wanted from a woman than what he had with Jordan.

Rolling to his side, Danny wrapped his arm around

her waist and gently brushed a strand of hair from her temple. She sighed softly as he pressed his lips to her forehead. And when his mouth found hers, Jordan stirred and opened her eyes.

"What time is it?" she murmured.

"Almost eleven," he whispered.

Jordan groaned. "Why did you let me sleep so late?"

"It's Sunday. Unless you want to go to church, there isn't much else to do in Dublin. Besides, I kept you up too late last night."

"I'm going to need a vacation from my vacation," she said. "I think I've had more sex in the past month than I've had in my whole entire life. In fact, I'm quite certain of that."

"Well, now there's an accomplishment I can boast about."

"Don't you dare. Your brothers don't need to know about our sex life."

"I'm sure they've already speculated. You don't know what it's like when they get bored at the Hound." He yawned, stretching his arms over his head. "Speaking of the Hound, Riley and Nan's engagement party is coming up. Would you like to go?"

"Wow. Two dates. I don't know," she teased. "Don't you think we're moving a bit fast?"

"Yes," he said, his voice serious. "But I don't have a problem with that. Do you?"

She frowned, staring into his eyes. "No," she said softly. "Are you angry with me?"

"No," Danny said. "I'm just trying to be honest. I don't want to think about you leaving, Jordan. I'm not going to think about it. I'm just going to go on as if we're going to be together as long as we want to be together. Just like any other couple."

"But we aren't any other couple," she said. "I live across the ocean."

"Not now, you don't. Right now, you live in Ireland."

She snuggled closer to his naked body. "Yes, I suppose I do."

"We have the whole day ahead of us. What would you like to do?"

"I'll let you be the tour guide," she said, sliding her hand down his belly. She wrapped her fingers around his shaft, now hard and ready. It always amazed him how quickly that happened with Jordan. All he had to do was think about her and the blood rushed to his crotch.

Danny groaned softly as she began to stroke him, aroused by the prospect of another lazy morning in bed. "I swear to God, you do have fairy blood running through your veins," he murmured. "There's pure magic in the way you touch me."

"Maybe I do," Jordan replied, her touch now playfully teasing. "Since the fairy circle I have been feeling a bit different."

"You're not human," he said, groaning as his pleasure grew. "I'm beginning to believe that I can't live without this." Danny's breath caught in his throat. "I've never been with a woman who makes me feel the way you do."

"I can make you feel even better," she said.

"I'm not sure that's possible," Danny replied.

Jordan slid down along his body, drawing the sheet back, inch by inch. When she reached his waist, she traced a line of kisses across his belly, then moved lower still.

Danny knew what was coming and he wasn't about to stop her. Instead, he stretched his arms over his head and arched his back, waiting for the warmth of her mouth to surround him. When she finally took him between her lips, he was forced to look away. Watching her made it almost impossible to control his release.

There were many things that Jordan was good at, but she excelled at this particular activity. In fact, there were times when he wondered if it could get any better.

But it wasn't just about him. It was about the two of them sharing something so intimate that a touch replaced a word, a sigh replaced a glance. When real life was pushed aside, they had this pleasure between them and it was a powerful drug that he found himself craving constantly.

"Do you know what this does to me?" he whispered.

"Yes," she said. "But isn't that the intended result?"

"No. I'm not talking about an orgasm," he said.

She looked up at him, her hair tumbled around her face, her lips damp. "What?"

"I can't resist you," he murmured. "I don't want to anymore. You've stolen my ability to think for myself."

"That's not true."

He ran his fingers through her hair. "Ask me anything. I'll be your knight in shining armor. I'll slay dragons for you and rescue you from the tower. I'll lay down my life for you. That's what I feel when you touch me."

"Well, the next time I run into a dragon, I'll give you a call," she said, smiling. She moved back to her task, her tongue soft and warm against his shaft.

She thought he was joking. And for a moment, Danny almost let it slide. But he wanted her to understand what she meant to him, how deeply he cared about her. "It's not funny," he said. "I'm tired of dancing around it, playing like it doesn't really matter. You do matter to me, Jordan."

She stared at him. "Don't do this," she murmured. "Don't make it more difficult than it already is."

"I don't give a feck if it is difficult. It should be. It should feel like a knife to the heart, like falling off a cliff onto sharp rocks. It should make your soul bleed. I want it to be hard."

She sat up, pulling the sheet up around her body. "Why? It doesn't have to be."

"It's the only way we're going to know it was real," Danny said.

He reached out and grabbed her waist, then pulled her on top of him. She watched him, warily, all of her insecurities reflected in her expression. He shifted and then he was inside her, in the sweet warmth that had become home to him.

As he moved, Danny felt his need rise, a knot tightening deep inside of him until the ache was too much to bear. He reached between them and touched her, so that he could make her come right along with him.

Danny waited until her face grew flushed with desire, until her breath came in quick, desperate gasps. And then, when he felt her swell around him, he came. The intensity of his release was enough to make his body jerk and his muscles tense. He opened his eyes and watched her dissolve into her own orgasm, her fingers digging into his chest as she rocked above him.

And when she grew still, he pulled her down on top of him, holding her close. "Don't you dare tell me it's going to be easy," he whispered. Danny drew a ragged breath. "I'm going to do everything I can to convince you to stay."

"Please don't do that," Jordan said.

"I don't have any choice."

She fell back asleep stretched out on top of him, her thighs straddling his hips, her head resting on his shoulder. But Danny couldn't sleep. His mind was filled with desperate thoughts.

It was clear she didn't feel the same way about him as he did about her. Every time he brought up the future, she deflected the conversation. He only had two choices—convince her of his point of view or prepare to let her go. But he wasn't going to give up without a fight. He had a chance to change the course of his life, to make Jordan a part of it. And he'd do anything to make that happen.

7

Jordan carefully laid the tape measure down on the floor, measuring the width of the library. She scribbled the number on a pad of paper, then slowly measured in the opposite direction. Kellan had said that if there was a secret entrance into the house, they'd find it this way.

Drawing a ragged breath, she walked out into the foyer. What difference did it make? In a few weeks, the new owners could worry about it. They could afford to hire someone to come in and draw a new floorplan. She glanced down at her watch.

She was already an hour late for Nan and Riley's engagement party and though she was dressed and ready to go, she couldn't bring herself to walk out the front door. Everything was such a mess. The closer she got to finishing, the more confused she became. She'd put off talking to her father for fear that it might force her into a decision she wasn't ready to make. Whenever Danny spoke of the future, she deftly changed the subject. And now, she was quickly losing interest in finally finishing the house.

She pushed the button on the tape measure and it

snapped back into the plastic case. All this indecision was beginning to wear on her. She wanted to know if she had a future at Kencor. She needed to know if she had a future with Danny. It was time to ask the hard questions and get on with the rest of her life.

Jordan grabbed her pad and pencil and strode back to the library. She'd do it now. She'd call her father and if it all went bad, she'd have the party to distract her mind for the rest of the night.

Grabbing her cell phone from the desk, she quickly punched in her father's number and waited as it rang. It was Saturday afternoon in New York. He'd probably be finishing up his regular round of golf at his country club and having a few drinks with his buddies. Now would be a good time. Two martinis always made him more amenable.

The phone rang and then went to voice mail. Drawing a shaky breath, she decided to forgo a message. Maybe it wasn't the right time. But then, a few seconds later, the phone buzzed and she saw an incoming text from her father. "Busy. What do you want?" she read aloud.

"All right. Do it now," Jordan murmured to herself. Ireland job done in two weeks. I want hotel project.

"Matt already started. Maybe next time," she read.

No next time! Hotel project, now, or… Jordan bit her bottom lip, closed her eyes and said a silent prayer. This was the right thing to do. She didn't want to go on working for someone who didn't appreciate her talents.

"Or what?" she murmured.

Was she ready to do this? She was playing a giant game of poker and she was ready to go all in. …I quit. She stared at the words for a long moment, drew another breath and then hit Send. "Oh, God," Jordan groaned. "Please, please, please, let this work. This has to work."

"Hey, what's going on? Why are you still here?"

Jordan jumped at the sound of Danny's voice. She spun around in her chair. "I'm sorry. I just—I had to do this. It couldn't wait."

"What couldn't wait?" Danny asked. "I've been trying to ring you and you haven't answered. I was getting worried."

"I was trying to find the passageway," Jordan lied, grabbing the paper. "I didn't want to leave the house without—"

"The house will be fine. And I promise, we'll look for the passageway tomorrow. I'll help you. It's Sunday, it will be a good way to pass our only day off for the week."

Jordan's phone buzzed and a sick feeling came over her.

"Are you going to answer that?" Danny asked.

She shook her head. "No, not right now." She quickly stood. "I'm ready. Let's go."

Jordan smoothed her hands over the front of her dress, slipping her phone into her skirt pocket, then pasted a smile on her face. Though she'd been looking forward to the party in Ballykirk, right now she felt like crawling into bed and pulling the covers over her head. She'd never held another job. From the moment she was old enough to draw a paycheck from Kencor, she'd worked there.

When they reached the front door, Danny pulled it open, then paused. "Are you all right?"

"Sure. I'm fine." Jordan stopped short. "Wait. I forgot

the gifts. They're on my desk." She turned around and ran back through the foyer and into the library. The two presents had been neatly wrapped earlier that afternoon. But before she picked them up, Jordan pulled her phone from her pocket.

Her throat filled with emotion as she looked at the text. Don't like ultimatums. Finish Cnoc project. Send resignation letter.

That was it, Jordan thought to herself. Just a few sentences and it was over. She waited for the tears, for any reaction. But the only thing she felt was relief. She made her stand, asked for what she wanted and she'd been refused.

"Jordan! What's the holdup?"

She numbly tossed the cell phone on the desk and turned for the door. She'd figure this all out later. Tonight she'd have fun with Danny and his family, drink a bit too much and let him make love to her until nothing mattered but the feel of his body moving inside hers.

When she reached the entryway, she handed him the gifts. "Did you get these?" he asked.

She nodded. "I know it said no gifts on the invitation, but I'm not going to be here for the—" She sighed. "I wasn't going to be here for the wedding, so I wanted to get them something."

"You got them two things?" he asked.

"The smaller is a first-edition Yeats. A collection of his poems. And the other is silver. Hotel silver. It's kind of a trendy thing. You use it for everyday silverware. They're engraved with Qs and Ns and Rs."

"You got them a book and silverware?"

"Yes. I wasn't quite sure which was appropriate so I just bought them both."

"A toaster would have been appropriate."

"But that's so unimaginative," she said. "Everyone buys toasters. I bought something romantic and something useful."

"Should I have gotten a gift?"

"No. The gifts are from the two of us."

As they walked out to the car, Danny gave her hand a squeeze. "I like that," he murmured. "I like that we're a couple."

The pub was packed with barely enough room to move when Danny and Jordan arrived. She stood at his side, clutching his arm and shifting from foot to foot, trying to appear cheerful. A band played on a stage at one end of the pub and a crowd was already on the dance floor, shouting and stomping and clapping. Jordan had been to engagement parties before, but they'd always been very sedate affairs.

The song came to an end and Riley stepped up to the microphone, then pointed directly at them. "It seems my little brother has come back and with a very lovely lass on his arm."

The crowd shouted Danny's name and he chuckled beside her.

"Now, those of you who know Danny know that this is an unusual thing. But I want all of you to give our boyo a good word when you chat with Jordan. She's American and she's beautiful and I don't know what the hell she's doing hanging around my brother, but let's all pretend that he's worth it."

"Hello, Jordan!" the crowd cried out.

Jordan forced a smile and gave them all a weak wave. "Hello," she called. "Nice to be here."

"Kellan, get these two a drink. I'm going to be takin' a break for a few songs so I can go kiss my fiancée," Riley said. "And after that, I've got a special song I want to sing for her."

Kellan had saved seats for them both at the bar and Danny pulled her along through the crowd. She held tight to Danny's hand and was grateful to see a familiar face in Kellan.

"Hello," she said.

"Hi, Joe," Kellen replied with a grin. "What can I get you to drink?"

Jordan glanced around. "A large glass of whatever will get me drunk very quickly. How about one of Nan's margaritas?"

"Forget the fruity drinks," Kellan advised. "Whiskey. A double?"

"Make it a triple."

Kellan poured her a glass, then turned to Danny. "How about you, brother?"

"Nothing for now. I'm driving."

"No, you're not. You're joining in the celebration. And if you have too much, you two can stay up at your place."

"All right, then, give me a pint," Danny said.

Over the next half hour, Jordan was introduced to an endless line of people. She met Danny's parents, Eamon and Maggie Quinn, and his two older sisters and their families. And first cousins and second cousins and third cousins.

Jordan had to wonder where the crowd had come

from. Ballykirk was such a small village. But everyone in attendance seemed to know the couple quite well, considering that Nan had only lived in Ireland for a few months.

This was what family was like, she mused. One big, happy crowd of people who cared. She'd never really experienced that before, never even imagined what it would feel like to be completely comfortable with the people she was related to.

As the evening went on, the crowd became more and more boisterous and the music more raucous. This was the perfect way to distract herself. How could she feel depressed when faced with Irish pub music? It was all so cheerful and lively. Danny joined his two brothers on stage for a set and Jordan found a spot in the shadows to watch them.

"They're a wild bunch."

Jordan glanced to her left to find Nan standing next to her. "I've never seen him like this," she said. "He hums while he works, but this is a surprise. I didn't realize he could sing."

Nan gave her a long look. "Are you all right?"

"Yes," Jordan replied. "I'm…I'm fine."

The brothers finally left the stage after a rousing rendition of an Irish reel that left the audience exhausted. But Riley came back, sitting down on a stool with an acoustic guitar.

"This is a song for my lovely Nan. It's a song I wrote especially for her and I've only sung it to her once before and she promptly fell in love with me. I reckon if I sing it now, she might just marry me."

Nan leaned closer. "He's going to sing the selkie

song." Her eyes fixed on Riley as he spun the tale of a man in love with a beautiful selkie. The way he sang the ballad, it was as if the two of them were the mortal man and the beautiful creature from the sea.

Jordan watched him, amazed at the depth of emotion he conveyed to the audience...to Nan, tears swimming in her eyes. This was love, she thought to herself. Jordan could see it in Riley's eyes, in the way he smiled at his fiancée.

Riley sang two more songs, both of them sweet love songs, before he nodded to the crowd and stepped off stage, a bottle of beer dangling from his fingers. He was headed directly to Nan, but his trip was interrupted again and again by enthusiastic fans—mostly female.

When he finally reached Nan, he gave her a kiss. "Was it good?"

Her eyes shone. "It was beautiful," she said.

Jordan stood up. "Here, take my seat."

"No, that's all right," Riley said. "How are you, Jordan?"

"I'm great," she said.

Danny came up behind Riley and clapped his brother on the shoulder. "Congratulations, Riley. You got yourself a good one. Now don't do anything to feck it up."

"And you'd do well to take your own advice," Riley teased.

"I could really use some air," Jordan said.

Danny led her to the front door and then out into the cool October night. Jordan wrapped her arm around his as they strolled aimlessly toward the waterfront. The sounds from the pub faded and when they were finally alone, she spoke. "They make a cute couple. It makes me believe that love might be possible."

"You don't believe in love?"

Jordan shook her head. "I think people fall in love, like us. But I'm not sure it can last forever. Sometimes life just gets in the way."

"But then you have someone to help you with life," Danny said. "Two people against the world are a lot better odds than just one."

There were a few people wandering along the quay and they all recognized Danny and said hello. He found a spot for them to sit. Jordan felt a nervous twist in her stomach. She shouldn't have said that to him. It wasn't that she didn't believe in love. She was just used to looking at life in more realistic terms.

"I'm sorry," she said. "Don't listen to me. I don't know what I'm talking about. I never really took the time to think about romance when I was younger. I was too busy trying to keep up. I never dressed up as a bride or secretly planned my wedding or fantasized about what it would be like to find my Prince Charming."

"Love isn't a fairy tale, Jordan. It's life, as real as it gets."

"I know. But I'm supposed to be thrilled by it and it just scares me. It would change everything."

"Yes, it will. It's supposed to."

A moment later, a soft, slow ballad drifted into the cool night air from inside the pub. "There wasn't much room to dance inside. Maybe you'd dance with me here?" Danny asked.

He slipped his arm around her waist then took her

hand in his. His body was strong and hard against hers, their movement generating its own warmth. Jordan tipped her head back and drew a deep breath, then slowly let it go. This was her life, this moment in time, with this man in her arms. Nothing else mattered.

She let her hands trail over his body as she danced, creating a soothing counterpoint to the music. But this wasn't about desire. It was about comfort and protection. Even though the world she'd always known was falling apart, all her dreams disappearing before her eyes, it wasn't completely tragic.

"Maybe we should go back to the party," she said.

"We've made our appearance," Danny said. "I don't think we'll be missed. And I know you'd rather be alone."

"There's plenty of time for that later," she said. "I think maybe I want to learn another one of those Irish dances."

"Yeah?" Danny asked.

Jordan nodded. "Will you teach me?"

"I can do that." He slipped his arms around her waist, then bent closer to kiss her.

When they got back to the pub, Nan rushed up to them both. "We thought you'd left," she said. She held out the presents Danny had set on the end of the bar. "You didn't need to bring us a gift. Didn't you see the invitation?"

"Yes," Jordan said. "But I wanted to. I won't be here for the wedding, so that's what they're for. And you've given me something in return."

"Can I borrow Jordan for a moment?" Nan asked.

"Sure," Danny said. "As long as you give her back. I've grown rather fond of her."

She and Nan walked through the pub and into the kitchen. "This is the only quiet spot in the pub," Nan said. "So tell me, why are you thinking about leaving?"

"Actually, I'm not. I'm thinking of staying. But in case I don't, I wanted to give you the gifts."

"So, are you in love with him? It's all right, you can admit it to me. Believe me, I spent a long time denying it myself. But there's just something about a handsome Irishman that I find completely irresistible."

Jordan sat down on a stool next to the work table, exhaustion overwhelming her. "I've tried to keep everything in perspective," she said. "But I can't seem to help myself. I get lost in the fantasy of living here with him. It's like someone or something has put a spell on me and I'm seeing everything through magic glasses."

"I know exactly how you feel," Nan said. "But don't be so quick to write it off as a fantasy. Maybe you were meant to be here all along."

"Danny told me about your search for your father. You have a place here. I have an Irish last name, that's all."

"You could make a place for yourself," Nan replied. "It's not that hard. And with the Quinns, it seems, the more the merrier."

It wasn't difficult to like Nan. She seemed so sweet and friendly. Jordan had never had many girlfriends. She'd always been so obsessed with her career, she hadn't made time for friendships. And she'd never been interested in hanging out and talking about manicures and boyfriends and designer shoes.

Jordan was amazed at how easy it was to confide in the other woman. Though they came from completely different places, they seemed to have so much in common. She almost felt as if she would have a family here in Ireland if she stayed. "We should probably rejoin the party," Jordan said. "You *are* the guest of honor."

"We should," Nan said. "But promise that we'll see you again, soon. And if you leave, you must say goodbye."

"You should come and see the house. It's almost done. The furniture arrives this next week. Bring Danny's mother and we'll have lunch."

"Then it's decided," Nan said. "Just call when you'd like us to come and we'll be there."

Jordan picked up the presents. "Do you want to open these now or later?"

"Oh, now," Nan said. "I can't stand to wait for a surprise. And I love presents." She paused. "You said before that I'd given you something. What did you mean by that?"

Jordan hesitated, but found no reason to hide her feelings. She could trust Nan. "When I saw you and Riley together, saw how you were that first time we met, how he looked at you and how you looked at him…well, it made me think that I might find that for myself someday. And I don't think I've ever felt that way before."

"Maybe it wasn't just me and Riley," Nan pushed. "Maybe it's Danny?"

"Open it," Jordan said. "I hope you like it."

Nan tore at the paper and pulled open the box then gasped. She reached into the box and withdrew the old silver. "Oh, this is lovely. Look at the monograms. It's hotel silver, isn't it? My favorite restaurant back home uses it. I love it. It's so heavy, so much nicer than what you can buy new."

"Danny didn't understand why I was giving you old silverware." Jordan pointed to the smaller package. "Open that one."

Nan withdrew the book from the paper and smoothed her hand over the cover. Then she opened to the flyleaf. "It's a first printing?"

Jordan nodded. "I know how much you like books. And Yeats is Irish. It seemed like a good gift."

"I—I don't know what to say. It's beautiful." Nan smiled, then reached out and gave Jordan a fierce hug. "Thank you."

Jordan drew a deep breath, satisfied that she'd done well. Someday maybe she'd be planning for her own wedding and her own home. She hoped that she'd have a friend like Nan to talk to when that did happen.

"WHERE ARE WE GOING?" Jordan asked, the bedclothes rumpled around her naked body. "It's Sunday. We're not supposed to get up so early."

"Dress warm," Danny said, tugging on his jeans. "And put on a jacket and some sturdy shoes." He picked up her favorite sweater and laid it on the bed.

"Are we going on a hike?"

Danny bent over and gave her a quick kiss. "A short one."

"Shouldn't we have some breakfast first?"

He sat down next to her and brushed the hair out of her eyes. "After you fell asleep last night, I was just lying here, thinking. I have a theory and I want to check it out."

"A theory about what?"

"Our brownie problem," he said. "I think I might have figured out how they got in."

"No more brownies? I'm all for that." A smile broke across her face as she scrambled out of bed and Danny felt a small measure of relief. Since yesterday evening, Jordan had seemed so melancholy, as if the weight of the world were bearing down on her. He'd tried to coax her worries out of her, and she'd put on a smile and insisted that nothing was wrong. But Danny knew her too well.

He didn't want to think that their time together was coming to an end, or that she'd walk away without a second thought. Hell, how could he compete with a job that she loved and a family who lived on the other side of the Atlantic?

They walked out into the crisp morning air, past the walled garden and the forge and toward the rocky cliffs that separated the green from the ocean. They headed north for a few hundred yards before Danny began to look for the familiar landmark that signaled the entrance to Smuggler's Cove.

"Here," he said, pointing to the narrow pathway between the jagged rocks. "Follow me."

"Where?" Jordan asked.

"Don't worry. I've been down here before. Not for a very long time, but I know the way. Just be careful."

He carefully picked his way along the path, stepping over rocks that had fallen and tossing aside driftwood blocking the way. When he finally reached the end of the path, he jumped down the last three feet, then turned and reached for Jordan.

She stood on the sand and slowly took in her surroundings. "I never knew this was here. It's a little beach. How did you find it?"

"We used to come here when we were kids. We called it Smuggler's Cove. I discovered it. Or at least I thought I had. But if the castle was used for smuggling, then this is where the boats would have come to shore." He turned and scanned the cliff. "If there's a tunnel, it starts right there." He pointed to the cave.

"Can you swim here?" she asked, completely distracted by the prospect of her beachfront castle.

"We used to. The current is pretty strong, but if you stay close to shore, it's fine. Are you ready?"

"For what?"

"We're going to see where the other end of that cave lies. We never had the courage to explore it when we were kids, but if I'm right, it may be the entrance to a tunnel that leads to the house." He pulled a flashlight out of his pocket. "Let's give it a try."

"I'm not going in there," she said. "There might be bats. Or spiders. Or snakes."

"There are no snakes in Ireland."

"Right," Jordan said. "St. Patrick took care of that years ago."

"Maybe this is where the brownies and fairies live." Danny scrambled up the cliff to the entrance of the cave. "If I'm not back in ten minutes, call for help," he said.

Jordan frowned. "Danny, I don't think you should go in there. It could be dangerous. It could collapse and you'd be trapped."

Undeterred, Danny entered the cave. He and his brothers had explored about fifteen feet beyond the entrance before being scared away by strange noises and invisible animals. But as an adult, Danny found nothing in here that was frightening. He knew high tide was hours away and now was the time to see if he was right.

The crates that they'd brought down to sit on years ago were still against the cave wall. And a pile of driftwood that Danny had dragged inside was still where he'd left it so long ago. "Hello!" he shouted.

"Who are you talking to?"

He spun around to find Jordan standing behind him, a worried expression on her face. She squinted against the glare from the flashlight and he motioned her over. "Watch out. This first part is slippery until you get to the sand. The water comes up in here at high tide."

They slowly walked deeper into the cave, the light from the opening fading the further they went. Fifteen feet, twenty, then thirty. And then, to Danny's surprise, the cave suddenly ended. "No," he said.

"This is it?"

He examined the back wall carefully, looking for another way. But there wasn't any. "I guess I was wrong," he said.

They walked back to the entrance and he helped Jordan climb back down to the beach. Danny raked his hands through his hair. So much for his brilliant theories. He plopped down on the beach and stared out at the water. Jordan sat down beside him, smoothing her hand along his shoulders.

"It was a good theory," she said. "And I'm really glad

you showed me the beach. I'm going to see if we can build a stairway down the cliff. It's a perfect spot."

Danny leaned against her and brushed a kiss across her lips. "Stairs are going to take a lot longer than a week to build. Does this mean you're going to stay a few weeks longer?"

"I might be here longer than that," she said. Jordan folded her arms over her knees and fixed her gaze on the horizon. "I think I quit my job."

Danny's breath caught in his throat and he stared at her in disbelief. "You think?"

"Well, I'm not really sure if it's official yet. Of course, I have to finish this project. And my father wants a letter of resignation, which I haven't written. And he could always change his mind, although I don't think he—"

"This is brilliant," Danny said, drawing her into his arms and kissing her. "You won't have to leave."

"Well, I will at some point. I still have an apartment back in New York. Everything I own is there."

"Is this why you were so distant last night? Why you were late for the party?"

Jordan nodded. "I gave him my ultimatum. I told him if he didn't give me the hotel project I'd quit."

"What did he say?" Danny asked.

"He didn't say anything," Jordan replied. "I texted him. I was too nervous to talk to him. It was so much easier. He couldn't bully me and I had control of the conversation. There was no shouting, just little letters on the screen."

Danny took her face in his hands. He couldn't believe it. Everything that he'd been wishing for had suddenly come true. They had time, which meant that he had a chance. "And how do you feel now?"

Jordan frowned. "I'm not sure. There is some relief that I actually managed to express my feelings to my father. There's humiliation that it meant nothing to him. And I guess there's a lot of fear, because I'm not quite sure what I'm going to do to make a living."

"What about Kellan? You said he offered you work."

"It would probably be easier to find a job there. I don't even know if I could legally work here. There are probably all sorts of laws."

He bent closer and gave her another kiss. "But I want you to stay here," he said. "With me. What do you say?"

"I say, I'll think about it."

Danny pulled her down on top of him and settled her hips against his. In a single moment, his life had changed. They had a chance, a way to make this all work out. After Jordan was finished at the castle, she could move in with him. They'd figure out what to do about work and then they'd start a life together.

And somewhere along the way, he'd tell her exactly how he felt. Danny Quinn was in love.

JORDAN STARED AT Danny's profile, outlined by the daylight streaming through the tall windows of the bedroom. She smiled to herself then turned her face into the pillow. A giggle bubbled up and she groaned softly.

This was what it felt like to be in love. It was the most frightening, exhilarating, confusing feeling she'd ever had in her life. All the silly stereotypes were true. She felt as if her head was in the clouds, as if she was walking on air, as if nothing would ever be the same again.

Why hadn't it snuck up slowly? Why had it hit her now, while he was asleep beside her and she wasn't expecting it? Jordan's impulse was to question her own feelings, but even that didn't work. She was in love with Danny Quinn, no doubts, no hesitation.

She pushed up from the pillow and took another look. That face, those dark lashes and those beautiful lips. She'd grown so familiar with his features that she almost took them for granted.

She'd decided to stay in Ireland for a little while. Her savings could stand a year or two without work, if she was frugal. But, in truth, she wanted to see where all of this was leading.

Jordan leaned over and dropped a soft kiss on his mouth, then waited to see if he was ready to wake up. When he didn't, she kissed him again, this time running her tongue over the part in his lips.

Danny moaned softly, then opened his eyes. "What are you doing?"

"Kissing you," she whispered.

"While I'm sleeping? Don't we do enough of that while we're awake?" He rolled over on his stomach and stared at her, his cheek pressed into the pillow. "If you expect sex while I'm sleeping, then we're going to have a serious problem. I need to have some time for rest."

"That's not what I want," she said. "I need to talk to you."

"About what?"

"About the subject we've been so cautiously avoiding."

"The crazy way your hair looks in the morning?" he asked.

Jordan grabbed her pillow and hit him squarely in the face. "No." She paused. "Is it really that bad?" She crawled off the bed and ran to the bathroom. "You could have told me this sooner," she shouted, grabbing a brush.

"I'm just taking a piss," Danny replied.

"In the bed?"

"No. I'm teasing you. Making a joke. Your hair looks grand."

Jordan quickly brushed through the tangled strands, then ran back into the bedroom and hopped beneath the covers. "There. That's better."

"I love the way you look in the morning," Danny growled. He grabbed her and pulled her on top of him. He was hard and ready, his erection pressed against her belly. "So what can I do for you this morning, my fairy queen?"

Jordan stared down into his handsome face, then smoothed her fingers over his brow. She'd grown so used to this, their time together in the early morning, the quiet conversations and the lazy seductions. How would she ever live without him? "I thought we ought to talk about what's going to happen once the house is finished. We've only got a few days left. They're going to bring the furniture day after tomorrow and you'll be finished the day after that."

"Actually, I'm already finished," Danny said. "I've just been making work the past few days. I made some tools for the fireplaces. And I was thinking about doing andirons for the fireplace in the breakfast room. Even though that room had just a grate."

"No, if you're finished, then that's it."

"I don't want to be finished. I like it here. I like this bed. And I like waking up with you in the morning."

"I don't have a job after this project is done."

"You need to talk to Kellan and tell him that you're interested in his offer."

"I will," Jordan said. "I just have a lot of things to think about right now. And I've decided that I'm going to take some time before I make any big decisions. I'm going to look for a place to stay here and—"

"You'll stay with me," Danny said.

"But I should—"

"You'll stay with me," he insisted, his tone firm.

Jordan smiled and gave him a hug. "I was hoping you'd say that. I'm going to have to go back to New York at some point to sublet my apartment and move some stuff out, but that can probably wait."

"I think we should do some traveling. We could go to Paris or London or Rome. Some lady paid me a boat-load of money for my last job and I think we should spend it."

Jordan ran her hand over the rough stubble of his beard. "Paris would be fun," she said. "But we'd go Dutch. I'd have to pay my own way or I refuse to travel with you."

Danny's hands spanned her waist and he pulled her beneath him. "Do you think they have soft beds like this in Paris?"

"I'm sure they do."

Jordan closed her eyes as he kissed her, enjoying the flood of desire that snaked through her body. His palm skimmed over her naked breast and his mouth teased at the places that only he knew.

"We won't have many days left in this bed," she murmured, furrowing her fingers through his hair. "I suppose we ought to make the best of it."

"You remember, I do have a bed at my cottage. We won't be sleeping on the floor."

"I know," Jordan said. "But this was our first bed. It's special."

"We could always take it with us," Danny suggested.

"If you have an extra ten thousand pounds, I'll sell it to you," she said.

"Bloody hell. You paid that much for this bed?"

"It's a very special bed. And it's going into the master suite when the movers come."

"When are they coming?"

"Day after tomorrow. We stage the whole house that day. Top to bottom. I've hired some women from the village to help and I have seven movers coming. They're bringing everything from the warehouse. And at the end of the day, the house will be done. We'll have to be out the next morning."

"I'm going to start moving my tools back tomorrow," he said. "I should be cleared out of the laundry in a few days."

Jordan nodded. "I wish my father could see this place," she said. "I've sent him photos, but it's not the same. It's so much more impressive when you see it in person."

"Feck him," Danny said. "He doesn't appreciate you the way I do. He doesn't deserve you."

"Yes," Jordan said. "Feck him. I don't need him anymore."

"No, you don't. You're clever and talented and you can do this for yourself."

Jordan slipped her arms around his neck. "I'm glad you believe in me."

"It's not a difficult thing to do, Jordan."

They made love quietly and slowly, enjoying a long lazy morning in bed. And, through it all, there was no more fear or hesitation. She didn't have to think about leaving him. They had many more mornings ahead of them.

And on one of those mornings, she might tell him what was in her heart, how she'd fallen in love even though she'd tried so hard not to. How he'd captured her heart the very first time she'd set eyes on him.

But that could wait. She had all the time in the world.

8

THE MANOR HOUSE was dark and silent. Danny lay in bed, Jordan asleep beside him. He turned to look at her and smiled to himself. They'd come home from a leisurely dinner in the village and immediately crawled into bed. But this time, they hadn't made love. Instead, they'd spoken softly about their plans for the future.

He drew a deep breath. For now, she was going to stay. She'd furnish the house, then pack her things and move in with him. It wasn't meant to be permanent, but it was a step in the right direction.

Danny closed his eyes, unable to relax. He couldn't sleep. His mind was filled with possibilities now that Jordan was going to be a part of his life for a bit longer. It was all he'd really wanted, just a little more time.

He swung his legs off the bed, dressed only in his boxers. The air was chilly and he rubbed his arms as he walked out of the bedroom. Finny and Mogue looked up at him as he passed, but he held out his hand to stop them from rising.

He knew the house well enough that he needed no more light that the moonlight that poured through the mullioned windows. His feet were quiet against the stone stairs and he ducked into the library, heading for the small table that held a whiskey decanter.

He crossed the room and poured himself a whiskey then headed for the kitchen. Since the Shakespeare had gone missing, they hadn't found any other trace of intruders.

Danny suspected one of the workmen had come inside looking for help and left the footprint. As for the book, perhaps it had fallen out of the crate on the way to the house. Still, there were moments when he felt as if he were being watched. Ghosts. The house was probably filled with all sorts of spirits, both good and evil.

As he stepped inside the door to the kitchen, Danny froze. A figure stood at the refrigerator, the light from the interior creating an eerie silhouette. He knew immediately that it wasn't Jordan. She was sound asleep upstairs. "What the hell—"

The man spun around, a half-eaten sandwich in his hand. Danny recognized the face immediately. "Bartie?" The elderly man made a break for the butler's pantry door, but Danny was quicker. He caught him by the arm and dragged him to a stop. To his surprise, Bartie didn't offer any resistance. "What the hell are you doing in here?"

"Having myself a sandwich. I was doing a—a spot of night work in the garden and felt a twinge in my stomach."

"How did you get in?"

"The door. It was—unlocked."

"No, it wasn't. I checked all the doors and the windows. Everything is locked up tight."

"I have a right to be here," Bartie said.

"You have a right to trespass?"

"This is *my* house. *Mine*. You're the ones who are trespassing."

Either Bartie was delusional or drunk. Danny was determined to find out which it was and then find out exactly how he got inside. "Come on," he muttered. He dragged him along with him to the library. When they got inside, Danny flipped on a lamp, then pointed to a chair next to the fireplace. "Sit."

"I'm the host here. You're the guest. Don't tell me what to do."

The sandwich still clutched in his hand, Bartie watched Danny with suspicious eyes. "I could stand a whiskey," he said.

Danny strolled over to the small bar table and poured a measure into a tumbler. Perhaps it would loosen Bartie's tongue.

"Don't be stingy there, boy. A little more would be appreciated."

Stubborn old sot, Danny thought as he handed him the whiskey. "How many times have you been in the house, Bartie? I mean, before I caught you."

"I come and go as I please," he said. "It's my house."

"How is that possible?"

"I'm the heir to Castle Cnoc."

"You?"

The old man took a sip of the whiskey then returned to eating his sandwich. "My grandfather owned the place. He inherited it from his father."

"You're a Carrick?"

Bartie nodded, then wiped his hand on his pants and held it out to Danny. "Bartholomew G. Carrick the third. Pleasure to meet you."

Danny took Bartie's hand and shook it. This was growing more bizarre with every moment that passed. The man who'd been digging holes for months in the garden was the former heir to Castle Cnoc. "You've been sneaking into the house?"

He nodded.

"How? I've made sure the place has been locked up tighter than a drum. And there are the dogs."

"I have my ways," Bartie said. "Secret ways. I'm not about to tell you." He paused. "And your dogs don't bark at someone who's been feeding them bits of beef every day."

"You will tell me how you got in or I'll call the gardai. And they'll haul you off to jail. If you're honest about all this, I may let you go without reporting you to either the authorities or Jordan."

"She doesn't belong here. I do."

"Bartie, I'm not sure how it happened, but I know that this house doesn't belong to you. Not anymore."

The older man blinked at him, as if he didn't fully comprehend the complexities of property ownership. "It's been in my family for generations."

"And now it isn't. Besides, why would you want this great hulk of a place? It's impossible to keep up. It would take thousands, hell, millions, to keep it looking like this. Myself, I've always preferred a tidy little cottage."

"I have a cottage," Bartie said. "In the village. It's lovely."

"I have a place of my own in Ballykirk. Men like us don't need all these trappings. This place is like a museum. We're just regular blokes."

Bartie nodded, then drained the rest of his whiskey. He held out the glass. "Another," he ordered.

Danny decided to keep him drinking and talking. "So, you've been coming in and wandering around at night because you can't bear to part with the family estate? But what's with the holes in the garden?"

Bartie leaned forward. "I'm trying to find the treasure."

"What treasure?"

"The gold and silver my grandfather buried in the garden. Before he lost his fortune, he hid a chest somewhere on the estate, to save it from his creditors. He planned to come back for it, but he died suddenly and the family fell into financial ruin. That's when they had to sell Castle Cnoc."

Danny wasn't sure of the legalities of the situation. Would buried money belong to the current landowner or the heir of the person that buried it? Either way, Bartie would probably have some legal claim. "And have you found anything?"

He shook his head. "Not yet. But I will. I've been looking now for seventeen years. It's got to be here somewhere."

"And you've looked in the house?"

"Oh, yes, I know every inch of this house and it's not here. Once she leaves I'll have much more freedom to look. The new owners won't be around much, I reckon."

He gave Danny a shrewd look. "If you help me and we find it, I'll give you twenty percent."

"If you show me how you got in," Danny murmured, "I might consider it."

"It's a secret," Bartie said, grinning. He tapped his nose. "Only I know. A family secret passed down to the heir to Castle Cnoc."

"Of course if you're talking about the smuggler's tunnel, we already know about that."

Danny's question had the desired effect. Though there had always been talk of a tunnel out to the coast, Bartie would be the one to know. The old man's face flushed red and he seemed to grow more agitated. "Perhaps it's time to call the authorities?"

"I haven't done anything wrong. This house belongs to me."

"Bartie, you know that's not true. And besides trespassing, they might want to add some other charges as well. Stalking, harassment, theft. You could be facing ten, maybe twenty years. And what about Daisy? She could be charged as your accomplice."

"I—I—but—Daisy was only helping me search the grounds. She knew nothing about me coming into the house. And *theft*—I only took a copy of *A Midsummer Night's Dream* so Miss Kennally would think maybe there were fairies."

Danny scowled. "What about the vase? And the ring?"

"I broke the vase accidentally. And I thought the ring might be a clue. I put it back." Bartie looked offended.

"Show me the tunnel right now and I'll make sure none of this ever gets back to the authorities."

"Yes." Bartie paused. "Maybe that would be best."

"Danny?"

They both turned to find Jordan standing in the doorway, dressed in only a faded T-shirt. Her eyes went wide when she caught sight of Bartie and she pulled the bottom of the shirt down to cover her backside.

"What are you doing here, Bartie? It's late."

"Bartie is our resident brownie," Danny said. "He's been in and out of this house—what?—a hundred times since he started working for you."

"More before that," Bartie said. "It's not hard." He walked over to the center bookshelf on the far wall. "It's this center shelf. You just give it a quick shove, like this and—" He pushed and the bookcase suddenly became a door. "Simple, really. The stairway leads to a tunnel and the tunnel comes out on the cliffs."

"Why did you come in?"

"Bartie's been looking for treasure."

"First, I thought it was in the house, but I've been over this place with a magnifying glass before you showed up. Swimming pool too. Thought it might be there, but it wasn't. The garden was the next logical spot." He frowned. "It's here somewhere. I know it."

"What were you doing in my room that night?"

"Hoping to steal a key," he said. "Crawling through that tunnel's been hard on the back," he complained. "Would rather come through the front door, I would."

The three of them stood silently for a long time. "What do you want to do with him?" Danny asked.

Jordan sighed. "Just finish the garden, Bartie. I want to see roses in there before the end of the week. Stop digging holes, stop sneaking into the house. If there was

hidden treasure here, you would have found it already."
She looked over at Danny. "I'm going to bed. Are you
coming?"

"You don't want to see where this passageway goes?"
he asked, surprised.

"No! It's the middle of the night. We'll look at it tomorrow." She stumbled out of the room, grumbling, "I
can't believe Bartie was the brownie. All of that worry
for nothing."

THE NEXT FEW DAYS at Castle Cnoc were a flurry of activity. The moment Jordan got a look at the smuggler's
tunnel, she insisted that it had to be renovated before
the owner arrived: electric lighting installed, the walls
freshly painted and the tile floor restored. She would
even have the blueprints for the house redrawn to show
the new discovery.

Danny had been left to find work for himself, staying
out from underfoot as much as he could. The furniture
was being delivered that morning and though he'd offered to help, Jordan had suggested that he help Bartie
finish up the plantings in the garden.

In truth, Danny was glad to be banished from the
house. Since the movers had arrived at eight that morning, Jordan had been edgy and curt, overwhelmed with
the details of examining each piece before it was placed
in the proper room. Jordan had also hired five women
from the village to give the manor house a final polish.
They were to wash the new linens, make the beds,
unpack china and silver in the butler's pantry and carefully arrange all the bits and pieces of decor that she
had chosen over the past seventeen months. When she

wasn't dragging furniture from one spot to the other, Jordan was directing traffic and barking out orders.

Danny wandered back outside and headed to the walled garden. After the confrontation with Bartie two nights before, the old man had focused all his energy on finishing the planting. Danny felt a bit sorry for him. After years of searching for his treasure, he'd finally decided to give up looking.

Bartie had brought a crew from the village to help yesterday and they'd worked all day to get nearly a hundred rose bushes planted. Now he was spreading mulch between the plants and the crushed-stone paths.

Danny grabbed a shovel that was leaning against the wall and stepped inside the garden, ready to give the old man a hand. But as he shoved the spade into the mulch, an image flashed in his mind. There was one place that Bartie might not have searched.

"Bartie," he called, motioning the man over. "Grab your shovel and come with me."

"I have to finish. Miss Jordan wants this done by the end of the day."

"We can take a break. I'll cover for you with Jordan."

Bartie joined him and Danny headed toward the cliff. "Have you ever been down to the cove?"

"When I was a kid. Gettin' down the cliff is tricky at my age."

"And you know about the cave?" Danny asked.

Bartie shook his head. "I don't know of any cave."

"Well, I'm sure your great-grandfather knew about it. I suspect they used it to store smuggled goods until they could move them through the tunnel. I'm thinking that maybe your great-grandfather buried his treasure in that cave."

"It makes sense," Bartie said. "What if we find it?"

"We'll cross that bridge when we come to it," Danny said.

He helped Bartie navigate the narrow path down the cliffs, then showed him how to get inside the cave. The flashlight he'd used for the last trip to the cave was still in his pocket and he turned it on. "He'd have to bury anything past the reach of the water," Danny said. "You can see on the wall how far up it comes."

They started at the back wall of the cave, working in the wavering light. Almost immediately, they struck something metallic buried in the sand. Bartie looked up at him, wide-eyed, then bent down and began to brush the sand away with his hands.

Slowly, he uncovered a small metal box, the kind that usually held ammunition. Danny held his breath, hoping that Bartie wasn't about to be disappointed. "Can you get it open?" he asked.

"You do it," Bartie said. "I'm not sure I care to look."

"Let's get it into the light," Danny said.

They hurried back to the cave entrance and set the box down on the ground. It was barely rusted, the dark-green paint still visible. The box wasn't locked. Danny grabbed the top and pulled it back.

"Jaysus, Mary and Joseph," Bartie whispered. "It's the treasure. It's gold."

The old man was right. The box was filled with gold coins, hundreds of them. Danny picked one up and examined it. "It's a British sovereign," he said. "Looks like a coin from the Victorian age."

"But my great-grandfather buried the treasure in the 1920s," Bartie said.

"This might not be his treasure. This might be gold from the smugglers."

"How much do you reckon it's worth?" Bartie asked.

"I don't know," Danny said. "A lot. It's gold." He took a deep breath. "We're going to have to show this to Jordan. It was found on private property. I don't know what the law says."

They made their way back up the cliff and Danny ordered Bartie to take the box of gold to the garden and wait there. With every step he took toward the house, he thought about keeping the gold a secret from Jordan, of letting Bartie walk away with his treasure—even though it wasn't the treasure he was looking for.

Though he knew Jordan well, Danny had no idea how she'd react to this interesting development. Would she insist that her clients get the gold? Or would she find a way to compromise? The new owner was certainly rich enough. A movie star like Maggie Whitney made millions for each picture.

He found Jordan standing in the foyer, a clipboard clutched in her arms. He strode up to her and gently grabbed her elbow. "Jordan," he murmured. "I need to see you out in the garden."

"Not now," she said. "They're just bringing in the dining room table and I need to make sure they put it together properly."

"This is an emergency," Danny said.

She looked up from her clipboard. "Can't it wait?"

"No, it can't." He took her hand and pulled her out the terrace door and down the path to the walled garden.

"What is it? Is Bartie all right?"

"Bartie is fine," Danny said. "We found the treasure."

Jordan stopped short. "*What?* Where?"

"In the cave," he said. "A big box of gold coins." He squeezed her hand. "What are you going to do?"

She drew a deep breath. "What do you think I should do?"

"I think you should let Bartie keep his treasure," Danny replied. "But I'm not the boss, you are."

He watched as she thought through her options. Then she glanced up at him. "Why am I out here? There can't be anything more important than moving the furniture into the house. You and Bartie get back to work on the rose garden."

With that, Jordan turned on her heel and strode back inside, leaving Danny to wonder at what had just happened. She'd completely ignored everything he'd just told her—

He grinned, then walked back to the garden. There was a reason he loved Jordan and he had no doubt that his feelings weren't going to change.

Odd how the prospect of falling in love had once scared the hell out of him. Now, it made him feel as though he was sitting on top of the world. Danny didn't care that it had happened so fast, or that they hadn't completely decided on a future together. Jordan wasn't going home tomorrow, she was coming to live with him. Tomorrow, they'd start their life together.

Bartie was waiting for him, the box at his feet. "I guess you can just take that old metal box and everything inside it home, Bartie, and I'll finish up in the garden. Jordan isn't interested in anything you've found." Danny pressed his finger to his lips. "But I wouldn't go passing this story around the village or she might change her mind. Keep your good fortune to yourself."

"I'll do that," Bartie said, reaching down and picking up the box. "Yes, I will. I'll do that." He pulled a coin out of the box and handed it to Danny. "Here. It will bring you luck."

Danny watched as Bartie hurried off, the box tucked under his arm. He chuckled softly. Things had a way of working out just grand.

JORDAN STOOD IN THE DOORWAY. Her hair, twisted into a tidy knot earlier, now tumbled around her flushed face. Her clothes were dirty and wrinkled and she felt exhaustion overwhelming her.

"Almost done?"

She turned to look at Danny and smiled. "Almost. We're just missing a sofa. Either it never got delivered to the warehouse or they misplaced it there. But that's it. Everything else arrived in one piece, no scratches, no breakage."

Danny reached out and gathered her in his arms. "Congratulations. You did it."

"I did. Almost. I have to finish my paperwork tonight and email that to the office and then make a quick double check of my list and I'll be done."

"We should celebrate," he said. "I'll take you out tonight and we'll have some fun." He pulled the gold coin out of his pocket. "I've come into a little bit of money."

She laughed. "Don't show me that. I might ask where it came from."

"You did a good thing," he whispered, his breath warm on her hair.

"Right now, all I really need is a nice long foot massage, a hot bath and a warm bed."

Danny grinned. "I can do that," he said. "In fact, I'm good at all those things."

Jordan kissed his cheek. "We're back to the caretaker's cottage for now. I'll be out in a minute. I want to call your mom and Nan and see if they'd like to come tomorrow morning for a tour. And I have to track down that—" Her cell rang and she pulled it out of her pocket. "This might be my missing sofa."

"I'll see you in a few minutes," Danny said. He wandered through the doors to the terrace and Jordan smiled as she watched him move. She'd worried for so long over the day they'd have to part, but now, all those worries had disappeared.

Her phone rang again and Jordan looked at the caller I.D. then winced. It was her father. She hadn't spoken to him since their exchange of text messages earlier that week. She was in no mood to talk to him now. She groaned, still staring at the phone. "I don't have time for this right now."

She walked over to an upholstered bench and sat down, then answered the call. "Hello, Daddy. How are you?"

"It's not your father, Jordan, it's your mother. I want you to talk to your father and give him a chance to apologize to you. Don't argue with him, just listen."

"I don't want to talk to him, Mom," she said. "He made his decision and now I've made mine. And I'm all right with that. It's for the best. It's time for me to move on with my life."

"It certainly is not!" her mother declared. "Here he is."

"No, I don't want to— Hi, Daddy." Her heart began to pound in her chest and she took in a deep breath.

"Your mother wanted me to call. I'm sorry I was so unreasonable with you. And I've taken Matt off the hotel project and assigned it to you. You need to finish up this week and get back to New York."

"Daddy, I'm not sure I—"

"I'm not going to beg you, Jordan. Just get back here and we'll smooth things out. You'll have your project and now you're going to have to prove my trust in you is worth it."

Jordan slowly shook her head. "I'll be back in New York in a few days. I'll talk to you then."

Jordan turned off the phone and slowly walked outside. She found Danny in the cottage, sitting on the edge of the bed. His smile faded as his gaze met hers. "What's wrong? Is your sofa lost, then?"

"My father just called," Jordan said.

"Did he apologize?" Danny asked.

She shook her head. "He just offered me the hotel job. I guess after my mother heard that I quit, she was very upset. She was afraid I wasn't going to come home so she told my father he had to give me the project."

"Do you still want the project?" Danny asked.

"I—I don't know."

The expression on his face told her the whole story. This was what she'd wanted all along and now that it had been offered, Danny wasn't at all confident that she would turn it down.

"Hey, this is good, right?" Danny said, forcing a smile. "This is what you've been working for."

"I really wanted to earn it," she said. "I didn't want it handed to me like some bribe."

"You did earn it."

"No. I'm sure my mother threatened to divorce my father and take half his money. She does that when she doesn't get her own way. Only this time she probably meant it."

Danny grabbed her hand and pulled her down next to him. "You don't have to make a decision right now. Think about it. You can take some time."

"We're going to be done here in a few days. The new owners will be here for Christmas. I've hired a housekeeper and a caretaker. After tomorrow, I'm finished. He wants me to start the new project next week."

"Next week?"

She nodded.

"How long? To finish the project?"

"A year at least," Jordan said. "It wouldn't be like this project. I'd have a huge crew, lots of resources. It would be my first really major project for Kencor."

"This wasn't a major project?"

Jordan shook her head. "This is a private home. He called it my little decorating job. I could have done this in my sleep. Since I met you, I have kind of been doing it in my sleep."

"This is bollocks," Danny muttered. "How the hell am I supposed to compete with a feckin' hotel in Manhattan?"

"I don't want to go," Jordan said. "You're right. It is my choice. And if I choose to stay with you, my father will have to live with that."

Danny pulled her into a hug, raining kisses over her face. "Tell me you really mean that," he murmured. "Just tell me so I can put aside this sick feeling in my gut. I don't want to lose you, Jordan. I'm not ready to let you go."

Jordan didn't speak, but stood up beside the bed and began to take her clothes off. When she was completely undressed, she helped Danny out of his clothes then pulled him down on the bed. She didn't want to think about all of her choices right now. She wanted to lose herself in the feel of his body against hers, in the taste of his mouth.

Making love to him was the only thing that made sense right now. He made her happy, happier than she'd ever been in her life. Home was no longer in New York. Home was wrapped in Danny's arms.

9

DANNY WOKE UP LONG BEFORE DAWN, listening to the sounds of Ballykirk as the village slowly came to life. At first, it was just the fishing boats heading out of the harbor and then a lorry or two passing by.

Tossing the covers aside and swinging his feet off the bed, he stood and stretched. As soon as the dogs heard him, they scampered into the bedroom, anxious for their breakfast. "Hi, boys," he whispered, giving them each a pet.

Jordan's plane was due to leave at ten. Danny had insisted on taking her to the airport, but she'd decided to drive herself and leave her car in the car park. She'd promised she'd be back in a few days, after she'd settled everything with her parents.

In truth, Danny still wasn't sure he wanted her to leave. Even though he believed she was going to settle her affairs and come right back to him, there was a niggling doubt that her father might talk her into staying.

He couldn't imagine a future with Jordan in New York and him in Ireland. Though the two places were only a six-hour plane ride apart, there was still an ocean between them. They'd be living completely different lives. But it wasn't just their lives, it was their ideas of what constituted happiness. For Jordan, it was professional success and for him, it had become all about love in the past month.

Here in Ireland, she could be in control of her own destiny. With Kellan's help, she could build a business to be proud of. There were possibilities in the U.K., in Europe. So many interesting things to do.

But Jordan had spent her life trying to please her father and to prove her worth in her family. It was a strangely dysfunctional relationship, but one that she couldn't seem to resist.

Danny wandered out to the fireplace and threw some peat on the fire, anxious to take the chill out of the air. Her bag was open on the sofa near the fireplace, packed with a change of clothes. He sat down and picked through it, pulling out a T-shirt and inhaling the scent.

Was this all he'd be left with, Danny wondered. Just faint memories of a woman he'd once loved and then lost. He tucked the T-shirt under his arm. She wasn't going to stay long, he told himself. There was nothing to worry over.

Danny walked back to the bedroom and sat on the edge of the bed. He pressed a gentle kiss to Jordan's forehead, then drew a deep breath, committing the scent of her hair to memory. They'd spent nearly every minute together since his first day at Castle Cnoc and now, they'd be apart.

His time with Jordan had brought him a love deeper than anything he'd ever expected. Danny felt as if they had already spent a lifetime together. He'd never known a woman so intimately nor had he allowed any woman to know him in that way. Jordan had become a part of him, the part that made him feel alive and aware.

He pulled back the covers and crawled back into bed, snuggling up to her naked body. She stirred then opened her eyes. "It can't be morning already," she murmured.

"It is," Danny replied. "Although it's only been about four hours since you fell asleep."

Jordan groaned, then stretched her arms above her head. "How am I going to do without you in my bed? I'll have to just get reacquainted with my vibrator."

"You have one of those?" Danny chuckled. "Make sure you bring that back with you."

He kissed the curve of her neck. Her skin was so soft and he could feel her pulse beating beneath his lips. God, it was strange something as insignificant as a kiss would seem so important to him. Everything was important—the sound of her voice, the feel of her hand in his, the way she said his name...

The first light of dawn illuminated the room and Jordan glanced again at the clock. "I have to get up." She raked her hands through her tousled hair as she sat up beside him.

Danny watched as she silently got dressed. When she was finished, she sat on the edge of the bed and smoothed her fingers over his temple, brushing aside a strand of hair. Danny looked up at her. "You could still change your mind," he murmured. "You could take off all your clothes and crawl into bed with me and go to New York some other day."

"I don't want to leave," Jordan said. "But I have to.

I won't be gone long, I promise. I'll be back before you know it."

"What if you decide to stay?" He raised up, bracing his arm beside him and leaning closer to her. This was no time to keep his feelings to himself. He was going to say it all right now, just so she knew exactly how much he needed her. "You have everything waiting for you back there. All you have here is me."

"And that's everything," she said. "To me."

"Me, too," he said softly.

Her eyes flooded with tears and Danny groaned, pulling her into a hug. He wanted to say the words. They'd been on his lips for days now, yet he was scared that Jordan wasn't ready to return the sentiment. He loved her, but did she love him?

Danny reached out and cupped her cheek in his palm. "Promise that you'll come back to me," he whispered. "Promise you won't let your family talk you into staying."

She drew a ragged breath. "I promise."

"I'll miss you, Jordan. I don't think you realize how much."

Jordan smiled, then bent close and dropped a kiss on his lips. "I'll miss you, too, Danny."

He fell back onto the pillow and laughed, throwing his arm over his head. "I sure hope to hell you aren't *leanan sidhe* or I'm going to drop dead the moment you walk out the door."

She grabbed his face and kissed him again, a kiss filled with longing and sorrow and silent promises. "I'm not a fairy. And you're not going to die when I leave you. I—I have to go."

"Let me get dressed and I'll—"

"No, I want to leave you right here, in this cottage, all curled up in bed with Finny and Mogue asleep in front of the door. This is how I want to remember you, all rumpled from sleep and naked beneath the sheets. And when I come back, I want you to be here just like this."

"I'm actually contemplating staying in bed until you come back. I'm not sure I'll be able to do anything else, I'll be so consumed with loneliness and despair." He tried for a lighthearted tone.

"Get up and get some work done." She gave him another quick kiss and then walked to the door. Jordan picked up her bag and gave him one last look. "I'll talk to you soon," she murmured.

"Call me when you get in?"

She nodded. "I'll do that." She crossed the room and kissed him again. "Let's just say goodbye like it's any other day," she murmured. "I'll be back soon. I promise."

As she walked out of the bedroom, Danny wondered what it would be like the next time they saw each other. Would the attraction still be so intense or would it have cooled? Would they pick up where they'd left off or would they need to get to know each other again? These were all questions that worried him. Danny knew they'd have to figure out a way to get through the confusion and back to where they belonged.

He jumped out of bed and hurried to the front door, standing naked in the damp morning air. She saw him and waved from inside the car, then turned on the ignition. "Come back," he murmured to himself.

If she came back, this would become home. His family would become her family. They said absence made the heart grow fonder. Danny was counting on that to get him through the next few days.

He drew a deep breath of the morning air and then cursed loudly.

"Oh, to hell with this."

JORDAN STOOD AT the elevator and watched as the lighted numbers above the door moved downward. She'd been back in Manhattan for exactly one day, just enough time to sleep, sort through her mail and do laundry before grabbing a cab to the office.

The flight back had been uneventful, except for one thing. Whether it was the regret at leaving Ireland or the doubts she had about leaving Danny, she'd decided that it was time for her to have a serious talk with her father.

The elevator opened in front of her and she stepped inside, smoothing her hands over the designer suit she wore. She'd assumed that once she was back in her own bed, wearing her regular wardrobe she'd start to feel more like herself. But New York seemed like a foreign country now and she felt oddly out of place in the midst of all the noise and chaos.

When she stepped out of the elevator on the seventeenth floor, a familiar face greeted her. "Miss Kennally! Welcome back. You look…fabulous."

Jordan frowned at Isabelle, their receptionist. "Fabulous?"

"There's something different about you. You look… sunny."

"Well, I feel sunny," Jordan said with a smile. "Is my father in? I need to talk to him right away."

"He's in. You'll have to check with Anne Marie to see if he's available."

"Great," Jordan said. "Well, wish me luck."

"Luck," Isabelle replied. "Miss Kennally?"

Jordan turned back to her. "Yes?"

"I do hope you plan to stay. Rumor around the office was that you quit. That's not true, is it?"

Jordan smiled. "I think it is."

When she reached her office, just three doors down from her father's, Jordan dropped off her coat and brief-case. The sooner she got this over with the better. It wouldn't do to delay and lose her nerve.

Jordan glanced down at her hands, her fingers twisted together so tightly that they were losing circulation. Conversations with her father had always been very cold and businesslike. But today, she hoped to appeal to his emotions. She wanted, no, she needed his blessing.

In truth, she expected it would be much worse. He'd throw her out on her ear, maybe even refuse to pay her for the Castle Cnoc project. He'd disown her, forbid her to come to family functions. Andrew Kennally hadn't gotten to where he was today by being a nice guy.

Drawing a deep breath, she headed toward his office. His assistant was sitting at her desk and Jordan pointed at the door. "He's in?"

"Yes. But I think he's on the phone. Can I make an appointment for you?"

"No," Jordan said. "I need to talk to him right now."

"But, Miss Kennally, I don't think he wants to be disturbed."

"I'm his daughter. I'm allowed to disturb him." Before the assistant could stop her, Jordan opened the door and stepped inside. Her father was sitting at his desk, his back to her, his feet kicked up on the credenza. She listened to his conversation and it was obvious he was discussing the closing on the hotel project.

Jordan sat and waited patiently, silently going over all she planned to say. She was putting her future on the line, but it had to be done.

The entire way home, she'd thought about what she was giving up by moving to Ireland. She loved her family, but she loved Danny more. He was the one who believed in her, who supported all her dreams. Her future was with him.

Her father hung up the phone, then slowly turned around to face her. Andrew Kennally was a handsome man of nearly sixty. His graying hair was set off by a deeply tanned face. He wore custom-made suits and hand-stitched shirts and Italian shoes that cost more than the rent on a one-bedroom apartment on the Upper East Side. And all of that made him very intimidating.

"Hello, Daddy."

"You're back," he said, nodding at her. "It seems like you just left."

"I've been gone for almost eighteen months," Jordan reminded him.

"Right," he said. "Well, welcome back. I'm sure you want to jump right back into work so...run along."

"That's what I want to talk to you about," Jordan

said. "If you'll remember, we had a discussion on the phone not too long ago about the hotel project."

"Yes. I remember. It's still yours, if you want it."

"Why?" she asked. "I know you didn't want to give it to me. Why did you change your mind?"

"Your mother can be very persuasive."

"So, it's not because you trust my work. In fact, you don't think I deserve it, do you?"

"That's neither here nor there," he said. "You have the damn project. We close day after tomorrow so I'd suggest you sit down with your brother, Matt, and get up to speed. He's been doing all the preliminary work."

"I don't think that's going to be necessary," Jordan said.

"What? You think you're just going to hit the ground running?"

"No. I'm not going to hit the ground at all. I don't want the job, Daddy. I'm going to go back to Ireland. I'm quitting Kencor."

"Quit? Don't be ridiculous. You'll never find another job like this."

"I hope not. This hasn't been all that great. And you've been a horrible boss. You've always favored my brothers more than me and I'm tired of that. I proved myself capable of handling larger projects, but that didn't make a difference to you."

He shook his head. "Your mother isn't going to stand for this," he warned.

"I don't care. It's time for me to make my own way in the world. I've met a man. I'm in love and I'm happy."

"This is about a man? You're quitting your job for a man?"

"No," Jordan said. "I'm quitting my job because I need to find a place where my talents are appreciated."

"Oh, we're not going to get into all that warm fuzzy stuff. We don't do that here. I don't run around telling my employees how wonderful they are. That's not the way I run things."

"Maybe you should. People might not think you're such a jerk."

"You don't have any loyalty to me?"

"You're my father and I will always love you. But as a boss, you kind of suck. I've worked my ass off here and I deserved more than you gave me. But that's all water under the bridge. I just want you to give me your blessing and then I'll get out of your hair."

"What is this really about?" he asked. "What happened to you in Ireland?"

"Perspective," she said. "I got some perspective. I realized that there's a lot more to life than work. And I don't want to miss out on the good stuff."

"I don't like ultimatums," her father muttered, wagging his finger at her.

"I'm not giving you an ultimatum. I've made my decision, Daddy." She stood up. "I'm going back to Ireland in a few days. I'd like to come out and see you and Mom this weekend. I expect I'm going to have to explain everything to her."

"She's going to kill me, you know. She'll blame me for letting you go."

"I'll tell her that it wasn't you." She walked around his desk and threw her arms around his neck, kissing him on the cheek. "Thanks for everything. For the job.

For the opportunity. I really am grateful." She slowly straightened to find him smiling at her. "What?"

"You used to hug me like that when you were little. I liked it. I still do."

Jordan smiled, then walked to the door. She gave her father a wave, then strode down the hall toward her office. Right now, she wanted to find a quiet place to call Danny. And after she was done talking to him, she'd clean out her office, pack up her apartment and figure out how to get her things to Ireland.

She found Marcy, her assistant, flipping through a sheaf of papers on her desk. "You're back," Marcy said. She stared at her for a long moment. "You look different. Have you lost weight?"

"Actually, I've gained ten pounds," Jordan said. "I think it looks good on me, what do you think?"

"I think you look…happy."

"I am," she said. "I just quit my job. Don't worry, I'll make sure you get reassigned and get a really big raise. But I need you to do one last thing for me. Book a flight to Ireland. Make it for Sunday, if you can. I have to go out and visit my parents tomorrow."

"You're going back to Ireland so soon? Is everything all right? Did something happen with the job over there?"

"Something did happen." Jordan smiled. "I met this incredible Irishman named Danny Quinn. And I'm madly in love with him."

JORDAN GROANED SOFTLY, then sat up and turned on the bedside lamp. She picked up her pillow and punched it, then finally tossed it on the floor. She'd been trying to go to sleep for the past hour, desperate to at least get some rest before she had to face her mother in the morning.

She wanted to look fresh and beautiful and unimaginably happy when she saw her parents. Not tired and haggard and grumpy. Quitting her job had really been the easy part. Explaining to her mother why she couldn't marry one of the suitable bachelors available on the east coast would be the difficult part.

She'd tried calling Danny three times, but his voice mail had picked up each time. She'd started to worry that he'd changed his mind about her, that leaving had been a critical mistake. Jordan had even thought about calling the pub, for they'd know where he was. But in the end, she'd decided to give it another day and try him in the morning.

She imagined her homecoming in Ballykirk. She'd surprise him at the smithy. He'd be all hot and dirty and she'd throw herself into his arms and admit that she'd fallen in love with him and would never leave him again. And then they'd kiss and their life together would begin.

Occasionally, she'd think about a more gloomy scenario, still nagged by tiny slivers of doubt. She'd return, knock on his cottage door and find some gorgeous, half-naked woman in his bed.

Saying "I love you" was going to be a risk, but Jordan had decided that it was well worth it. After all, she'd taken the biggest risk of all—quitting her job and uprooting her entire life. How much scarier could things get?

She reached over and turned off the lamp and closed

her eyes. But the buzzer at her door brought her upright. She scrambled out of bed and hurried to the front door of her apartment to answer the doorman's summons.

"Yes?"

"Miss Kennally, it's Arnie. I have a man down here who insists on seeing you. I told him that you were probably sleeping, but he wouldn't take no for an answer."

Her father. He'd obviously broken the news to her mother and now had come to try to convince her to stay. She'd half expected her mother to call her by now. Jordan considered refusing him entrance, but maybe it was better to talk to him. In truth, she was starting to feel a bit guilty. "I'll be right down," Jordan said.

She hurried back to the bedroom and grabbed her robe, then walked to the elevator. As she descended, she smiled to herself. For the first time in her life, she felt like a grown-up. She'd made a decision for herself and she was happy about it. Sure, she'd miss her work, but she was setting out on a whole new chapter in life.

The elevator doors opened in front of her and her breath caught in her throat. A disheveled Danny Quinn waited for her. A gasp slipped from her lips and she rubbed her eyes. This couldn't be right. What was he doing here?

"Hi," he said, shifting back and forth on his feet.

Jordan stepped out and looked around the empty lobby. Arnie sat at his desk, watching her surreptitiously. "What are you doing here?"

"I just have to say something and then I'll go if you want. I'm not sure that I really made things clear before you left."

"You flew all the way here to say something to me?"

"Yes. I didn't really get a chance to say it the right way. And then when I realized that, I followed you to the airport, but you had already boarded your plane and they wouldn't let me get on and talk to you. So I bought a ticket, but then our plane had to stop in Iceland because of mechanical problems. And when I got here, I realized that I didn't have your address, so it took me a while to track that down, but—"

"You're here," Jordan murmured, with a smile.

"When you left, everything was happening so fast and I know we didn't get the chance to really say all the things we wanted to. I was trying to act like it was no big deal. And then, after you left, I thought, what if she doesn't come back."

"I have a ticket for Sunday, Danny. I tried to call you and let you know. I'm all packed."

"Really?" he asked, a smile breaking across his face.

"Really," she said.

He reached out and smoothed his hand along her arm. "Does this mean I get to touch you anytime I want, and I can kiss you and lie next to you and wake up with you in my arms every day?"

"Definitely," Jordan said. "I've been trying to sleep and I can't because you're not there." She paused. "I've missed you so much."

"And what about your job and your family? Won't you miss all that?"

"Of course I will. But it won't matter. I think I was throwing myself into work because I didn't have anything better to do with my time. But now, all I want to do is spend my days and nights loving you."

"You want to live in Ireland?"

She nodded.

He yanked her into his arms and kissed her deeply, his hands furrowing through her hair as he molded her mouth to his. And as Jordan lost herself in the wave of sensation that washed over her body, she realized that she couldn't live without him. His strength…his affection…his smile…

When Danny drew back, he glanced over her shoulder. "Can we maybe find someplace more private to talk? This really isn't the kind of thing that should happen in the lobby."

Jordan grabbed his hand and pulled him to the elevator. They stepped inside and she pushed the button for her floor. As soon as the door closed, Danny turned around and faced her, his gaze searching her face.

"I have something for you. But maybe I shouldn't do it here."

"What? You brought me a present?"

"I don't know if you'll want it. You might not even like it." He reached into his pocket and pulled out a ring, a beautiful antique ring with a small ruby set in a Victorian filigree.

"It was my great-grandmother's," he said. "My mum gave it to me when I told her that I was coming to see you." He drew a deep breath. "I promise that I will do everything in my power to make our lives together perfect."

The elevator door opened and Danny winced. "I should have waited. This isn't romantic."

Jordan laughed. "Oh, yes, it is." She took his hand and drew him out of the elevator. "Keep going. I'm listening."

"In the hallway?"

"All right." She ran ahead to her apartment door and by the time she got it unlocked he was behind her, his hands wrapped around her waist.

"Here?" she asked.

"No," he said, glancing around her apartment. He pointed to the sofa in the living room. "There."

When she was finally seated, Danny knelt in front of her. "All right. Here it is. Jordan, I love you. I think I fell in love with you the moment I first saw you. I know I fell in love with you the moment I kissed you."

She stared at him, wide-eyed, her hands clutched in her lap. Jordan tried to maintain a calm facade, but her heart was beating so hard it felt as though it might burst out of her chest.

"I'm willing to work hard. I'll do whatever it takes. I'm not sure I can give you what you have here, but I will make you happy. I can move to New York if that's what you want. You'll never have a day of regret, I promise."

"I know," she said. "And what about the ring?"

"Shite, the ring," he muttered, patting his pockets. "The ring. It's not something fancy, but it's a promise."

"A promise is good. And I don't need anything fancy."

He pulled the ring out of his pocket and slipped it on her finger, then pressed his lips to the back of her hand. "I want you in my life, Jordan. Forever."

"You have me," she murmured, running her fingers through his hair. "For as long as you want me." Jordan stood up in front of him and untied the belt of her robe. She shrugged out of it, letting it drop to the floor at her feet. Then she reached for the bottom of her nightgown. Grabbing the hem, she pulled it over her head and tossed it aside.

Danny reached out and splayed his hand across her stomach. "Are you trying to seduce me?" he asked.

Jordan smoothed her hand over his cheek. "Yes, I am."

"Don't you think we should talk about this a little more?"

She slowly shook her head. "We can talk later. I want to make love to the man I love."

He pulled her close and pressed his face into her stomach. "Promise me something, Jordan."

Furrowing her fingers through his hair, she tipped his gaze up to meet hers. "Anything."

"Promise we'll be together forever."

"I promise," she said, pulling him to his feet.

Danny stood to remove his clothes. When he was naked, he grabbed her waist and they tumbled onto the sofa in a tangle of limbs. When his mouth found hers, Jordan knew this was the only thing she needed in life. Danny Quinn—his heart, his soul, his body, his love.

Maybe there *had* been fairies at work in Ireland, she mused. After all, they'd found her the man of her dreams.

* * * * *

ALASKA—THE LAST FRONTIER

The nights are long. The days are cold.
And the men are really, really HOT!

Can you think of a better excuse for a trip up north?

Come on back to the unorthodox
and unforgettable town of Good Riddance and
experience some

Alaskan Heat!

Dear Reader,

Here we are, back in Good Riddance, Alaska, where folks get to leave behind what ails them.

And former marine sniper Liam Reinhardt really needs to move on. Behind him, he's left a career, a wife and a sense of purpose. And he's mad as hell.

Tansy Wellington needs a new start too. She's leaving behind a cheating fiancé and a job she's not sure she can do anymore. Needless to say, she's none too happy either.

For both Liam and Tansy, Good Riddance starts off as a sanctuary…and then turns into much, much more.

What they both quickly learn is that sometimes people have to discover their own path in life before thinking about moving forward with a partner. Sometimes even the best-laid plans get derailed. When one door closes, another one opens—all we have to do is notice it. Lucky for us, Tansy and Liam soon notice that other door…and delight in the fact that it leads to the bedroom!

I hope you enjoy the sparks that fly between this hotheaded (and hot-blooded) couple. And remember, always keep an eye out for that open door. You never know what you might find…

I'd love to hear from you. Please drop me a note at Jennifer@jenniferlabrecque.com. And, as always, happy reading!

Jennifer LaBrecque

NORTHERN
RENEGADE

BY
JENNIFER LABRECQUE

MILLS & BOON

First published in Great Britain 2012
by Mills & Boon, an imprint of Harlequin (UK) Limited,
Eton House, 18-24 Paradise Road, Richmond, Surrey TW9 1SR

© Jennifer LaBrecque 2012

ISBN: 978 0 263 89392 2
ebook ISBN: 978 1 408 96945 8

14-1112

Harlequin (UK) policy is to use papers that are natural, renewable and recyclable products and made from wood grown in sustainable forests. The logging and manufacturing processes conform to the legal environmental regulations of the country of origin.

Printed and bound in Spain
by Blackprint CPI, Barcelona

After a varied career path that included barbecue-joint waitress, corporate number-cruncher and bug-business maven, **Jennifer LaBrecque** has found her true calling writing contemporary romance. Named 2001 Notable New Author of the Year and 2002 winner of a prestigious Maggie Award for Excellence, she is also a two-time RITA® Award finalist. Jennifer lives in suburban Atlanta with a Chihuahua who runs the whole show.

ACKNOWLEDGEMENT

Many thanks to Gervais Cranston for sharing his
expertise, passion and respect for weapons…
and the time and instruction at the firing range.

1

GUNNERY SERGEANT LIAM Reinhardt, former United States Marines sharpshooter, veered his motorcycle to the left, avoiding another pothole in the pockmarked gravel road. It wasn't much better than the goat trails leading from one remote Afghani village to the next. Except, this wasn't Afghanistan and he wasn't tracking some insurgent leader through dusty mountains.

Nope, he was back in the U.S. of A. Afghanistan, Iraq and some places he couldn't divulge were his past. As was his ex-wife and an honorable discharge based on some faulty heart valve that had shown up when he was being patched up from that last mission. That assignment had been the pinnacle of his career. It was right up there with the SEALs taking out bin Laden back in 2011, only Liam's mission had had a lower profile.

Growing up, hunting in the woods of Minnesota and Wisconsin, he'd known early on he wanted to be a sharpshooter. The irony wasn't lost on him that while he'd been fully prepared that enemy fire might take him out at any time, he'd never expected to lose his life, as he knew it, due to a personal plumbing defect.

Neither had he planned on Natalie bailing on their marriage two years ago because she couldn't handle his deployments. What the hell? She'd known his career path when she married him. Now it was time to regroup because all of that was history. At thirty-one, he was starting all over. Starting what? Doing what? He'd be damned if he knew.

Rolling to a stop, he pushed up his helmet's bug-spattered visor and surveyed his immediate future. Good Riddance, Alaska, spread before him. A single road cut through the collection of buildings flanked at the rear by evergreens.

Over the throb of his bike, he heard the drone of a plane. Bush plane. It was a far cry from the sound of F-15s and recon drones or the fractured *chop-chop-chop* of a Chinook. Sure enough, a bush plane, coming in low, touched down on the landing strip to the right of the town.

A breeze carried the scent of spruce and the odor of bear. While the trees were everywhere, bears would remain scarce. For the most part, they avoided people. He knew the feeling. He wanted to be left the hell alone.

Back home in Minnesota, that had been damn near impossible with his mom hovering over him. He and she operated on different planes, and after his dad died, their differences had seemed more marked than ever.

Liam craved the solitude he remembered from when he'd visited Good Riddance as a teenager. And his uncle, Bull Swenson, a tough-as-nails vet who'd spent some time in a Vietcong hellhole back in 'Nam, had found a new start and a new life here. Liam had followed in Bull's footsteps joining the military. He figured he might as well follow Bull's lead afterward, as well. Good Riddance seemed like an all-around good decision—or at least a decent enough option to make it worth checking out.

Flipping his visor back into place, Liam rolled out once again. Within minutes and a mile or so, the piece of crap road had widened. It was certainly no mystery as to why the bush pilots had plenty of business.

On the outskirts of town, a group of kids played baseball in a clearing. Not the Little League stuff his ex-wife's nephews had played with tricked-out uniforms, brow-knitted coaches and overbearing, yelling parents. There hadn't been a thing fun about it for the kids as far as he could tell the couple of times Natalie had dragged him along to watch. Nah. He grinned. This was good old "sandlot" ball.

He caught a couple of curious glances as he parked his bike in front of the long log building on the edge of town that was both the air center, bed-and-breakfast and the only joint that sold a hot meal and a cold drink. Chances were Bull was in either the restaurant or the airstrip office instead of his hardware company.

Liam stood, feeling the stretch in his legs and back, although maintaining one position for hours was old hat to him. It was what he'd trained for and had done for a long time.

He pulled off his helmet and hung it on the handlebars, the breeze feeling good against his head. Two kids, a boy and a girl, both blond and freckled, with a sled dog at their side, sans sled, stopped on the sidewalk and eyed Liam's motorcycle with a mix of admiration and envy.

"That's a sweet ride," the boy said. Liam figured they were about seven or eight.

Liam smiled at the kid's terminology. That was one thing he'd learned—boys were boys and they liked boy toys whether it was the Middle East or suburban Minnesota or the Alaskan bush. Boss Black, as he called his Benelli, *was* damn sweet with an 1131 cc engine, matte black paint and plenty of chrome. "Thanks. I like it."

The girl piped up. "I like your helmet."

The boy rolled his eyes. "Girls."

"Shut up." She landed an elbow to his side.

Liam smiled. "Let me guess—brother and sister?"

The girl spoke up. "Twins." She shot her brother a triumphant smirk. "I'm the oldest."

That pulled a laugh out of Liam. "Me, too. I beat my brother out by five minutes." And much like this kid, he never let Lars forget it.

She looked slightly crestfallen. "Oh, I was only four minutes," she perked up, "but I was still first."

"That's because they were saving the best for last," the boy said. Obviously they'd run through this spiel a number of times before.

"Humph."

"Our grandparents run the dry goods store," the boy said, ignoring his sister's disdainful snort. "We're spending the summer with them. They can hook you up if you need stuff. The beef jerky's really good. Mr. Curl makes it himself."

"Thanks, I'll keep that in mind."

A whoop came from the baseball game down the way. "I'm playing first base."

"Uh-uh. Me."

They exchanged a look Liam recognized from swapping the same look with his twin brother, Lars, innumerable times—*not if I get there first.*

"See ya," they yelled in unison as they took off running, the dog loping down the sidewalk behind them.

The town had definitely grown since the last time he was here, which would've been sixteen or so years ago when he was sixteen and still wet behind the ears. But it still had a good feel to it. He opened the door and walked into the bed-and-breakfast/airfield office.

It was pretty much the way he remembered it. Lace-trimmed flannel curtains still hung at the windows. A couple of tables were in "the front room." The far side wall definitely held more framed photographs but the potbellied stove was still flanked by a couple of rocking chairs with a chess and checkers table between two of them.

In the far corner, a flat-screened television had replaced the older boxy model that had been there. The armchair and love seat also had a newer look than he remembered. But it still felt and smelled the same—welcoming.

Merilee Danville Weatherspoon turned from her desk to the right of the back door leading to the airstrip.

"Hi there, Merilee."

Within seconds recognition dawned in her blue eyes and a broad welcoming smile lit her face. "Liam!"

She pushed up from her desk and crossed the room, her arms already extended to embrace him. She enfolded him in a welcoming hug, giving him a squeeze. "It's so good to see you! We knew you were coming, but we didn't know when."

"That makes two of us. I took my time getting here."

"Does Bull know you're here?"

He shook his head. "I figured he was either here or next door and I knew for sure coffee was here so…"

Merilee smiled as she turned and headed for the coffee stand. Within seconds she'd poured him a cup. She was damn near as fast with that coffeepot as he was with his Glock. "Straight up?"

"Always." He grinned as he took the cup from her. That's how he preferred any situation—straight up.

"Muffin?"

"No, thanks."

"That's right. I remember you don't have a sweet tooth at all. You're looking good."

He laughed. "I need a shave and a haircut, but thanks." She was a classy lady and it was a nice thing to say. "You're looking good yourself."

"Well, thank you. That's because I'm happy. Bull and I got married."

"Congratulations! That's cool."

"It has been very cool," she said. She practically glowed.

The cynical side of him was impressed. Merilee and Bull had been an item for a damn long time. It was pretty mind-blowing she could still look like that, all soft and sweet, when she talked about his uncle. He wouldn't rain on her happy parade but her talk of marriage inevitably led him to think of his own marriage… and subsequent divorce.

Liam supposed, in retrospect, he'd never felt that way about Natalie and obviously she sure as hell hadn't felt that way about him. He'd liked being married but the truth was he hadn't missed Natalie as much per se as he'd missed having someone to come home to. And it had been a long time since he'd had a woman. Since his divorce, a few had come on to him and he'd even briefly considered an uncomplicated exchange of sex for money when a hooker had propositioned him, but he'd passed on all of it. He'd been beyond that mindless physical engagement back in his early twenties.

"How long have you guys been married?" he said.

"It'll be two years in December. We tied the knot on Christmas Day. I'll let Bull tell you the story." She grinned. "I just wanted to tell you the news."

He liked Merilee even more now than he had when he was a teenager. Although, he'd thought she was pretty damn cool then, too. She'd left her old man, driven an RV out to nowhere and founded a damn town. Now that was a woman with a pioneer spirit. Back in the day, she'd been the town mayor. He'd bet a buck she still was.

"You still the mayor?"

She nodded. "I can't find anyone to run against me. At this point it feels more like dictator-for-life." She rolled her eyes. "I've thought about stepping down so I could just relax and Bull and I could travel, but it hasn't worked out that way."

"Not your style. You're a born leader."

She grinned. "Bull says I like to have my own way. He just stepped next door to Gus's if you want to drop in over there. I imagine you're ready for a hot meal."

"I could eat a bite or two." He could get by on field rations but he enjoyed a home-cooked meal as much as the next man. Well, maybe a little more. His last real meal had been when he pulled out of Anchorage a couple of days ago. "Whatever's cooking next door smells good."

"Caribou potpie. Lucky, the guy who owns it now, does a good job."

It smelled damn good, that was for sure. "I'll go check it out and catch up with Bull." He smiled and turned to head for the restaurant that adjoined the airstrip center.

Merilee spoke, halting him. "Liam…" He turned. Smiling, she said, "Welcome to Good Riddance, where you get to leave behind what ails you."

"Thanks." Unfortunately, it wasn't that simple and he wasn't sure that was why he was here.

BASTARD. BASTARD. BASTARD.

The words had danced around in her brain all morning like some liturgical chant…which made it altogether fairly difficult to make progress on her book, which was due at the publisher's at the end of the month. And actually fairly difficult to concentrate on what her stepsister, Jenna, was saying now.

Jenna waved a hand in front of Tansy's face. "Woohoo! Hello there. Anyone home? Earth to Tansy."

Tansy shook her head to clear it and laughed, focusing on Jenna's teasing countenance across the booth of Gus's, the only restaurant in Good Riddance. It was a fun mix of a saloon from an old Western and a downhome diner. She and Jenna were sitting in a booth near the bar and front door. A mounted moose head overlooked the bar, which boasted a brass foot rail. The other side of the room held more booths and tables, a jukebox, a dartboard and a couple of pool tables. Regardless of the time of day, in the week that Tansy had been here, the local gathering spot was never without customers. "Sorry. I was wool-gathering."

"BB?"

It was simply embarrassing to admit she was allowing him to eat up her brain space. Nonetheless, Tansy nodded her head. They had dubbed Bradley, Tansy's former fiancé, Bradley the Butthead or Bradley the Bastard, which she had subsequently shortened to BB.

"Yes. Stupid, huh? He's just been on my brain this morning."

Jenna's blue eyes reflected sympathetic understanding. "I wouldn't call it stupid. I'd call it human. You guys have been an item since junior high school. He's the only guy you ever dated, the only guy you ever… well, you know. He inspired your column, your book. He's been your past, your present and, you thought, your future. I think I'd be more worried about you if he wasn't invading your thoughts."

As usual, Jenna made her own kind of sense.

"Well, technically, you know he's not the only guy I ever dated. Remember? We broke up for a while our freshman year in college?"

"You went out for pizza with one guy and the movies with another one. Once. That really doesn't count as dating."

Tansy stirred her spoon in her coffee cup idly.

"I guess."

Tansy had met Bradley in seventh grade. He had been her one and only. Those couple of dates with other guys had been enough for Tansy. She and Bradley had gotten back together from then on. Last Christmas he'd asked her to marry him. They'd done everything right. They'd moved forward cautiously, taken their time, made plans…and look where they'd wound up— Splitsville.

Heck, their history had sort of spawned her career as a love advice blogger and columnist. And then she'd started a book, *Finding Your Own Fairy-tale Ending,* that had been bought by a publisher. The book was slated for a February release, just in time for Valentine's Day, and now she was floundering because everything she'd thought she'd known about love and relationships had been turned on its ear with Bradley's infidelity. Coming to Good Riddance had been a good move on her part as she tried to find her footing with both the book and her life.

"Coming here has helped," she said.

Jenna had been totally enthusiastic when Tansy had proposed coming to Alaska for a change of venue. Plus, she'd been dying to meet her new niece, Emma. And there was the little matter of having to get this book finished.

Jenna offered a sage nod. "Yep. Good Riddance… where you get to leave behind what ails you. It's all going to be okay, Tansy."

Tansy and Jenna had been thirteen when their parents had married. The girls had formed a quick bond. Not only were they the same age but they both had parents who were addicts. However, rather than drugs or alcohol, their parents had been marriage addicts. Divorce always seemed to lead to finding the next "fix." If there was such a thing as serial spouses, Jenna's mom and Tansy's dad, to a much lesser extent, were casebook studies.

Tansy and Jenna had shared a bedroom when Tansy spent time at her dad's. Tansy had long ago come to regard Jenna as her true sister and her friend. Most of the time she didn't bother with the "step" designation and simply referred to Jenna as her sister. Not surprisingly, their parents' marriage hadn't lasted more than two years—just long enough for the new to wear off—and then Jenna's mom and Tansy's dad were off to greener grasses. Jenna and Tansy had stayed in touch, and although there were inevitable ebbs and flows in their relationship, they remained close.

"I feel like an idiot," Tansy said, impatient with herself, "wallowing in man-woes." She had never been one to wallow.

"You're not an idiot and you're not wallowing." Jenna's eyes flashed. "You found a pair of panties—not yours—in your fiancé's jacket pocket. And then there were the emails and the hotel receipt." God, she'd been painfully stupid and trusting. "There'd be something wrong with you if you weren't having days like this."

Tansy supposed. Sometimes she did okay and then sometimes it was like this. It wasn't even as if she was totally brokenhearted. She was just…pissed. Why tell her he loved her? Why ask her to marry him if he was going to be fooling around with someone else? Not only was the bastard wrecking her concentration, worse, he'd made her feel like a fraud. How could she offer up advice on love and relationships when hers had hit the skids and she was still a mess? She wrote a syndicated column, had a wildly successful webpage and her own love life was in the toilet? Small wonder she'd stalled on the book she'd been working on. She hadn't lost just her fiancé, it had been a whole damn belief in something bigger.

Admittedly, she liked it here—actually she loved it here—and it was wonderful to be with Jenna and Emma, who was cute as a bug. But Tansy had made precious little progress on her book and felt bogus every time she wrote her column. "I'll figure it out."

"You will." Jenna shook her blond head while she waved at someone across the room. "Coming here was a good thing. It would've been a million times worse if you were still in Chattanooga. We're glad you're here, even if you are in solitary confinement most of the time."

Jenna's husband, Logan, had offered Tansy the use of his new FJ Cruiser. Jenna had reassured her that Logan would never have offered it if he didn't want Tansy to drive it. So, she was staying out at a little recently renovated cabin at a place called Shadow Lake. Outside of visits to her grandfather's farm halfway between Chattanooga and Marietta, Tansy had never done remote. She'd always lived in the city. She found she rather liked it, especially as she drove in at least once a day for a meal at Gus's or Jenna's.

And while it was nice and tranquil, Bradley remained a thorn in her side…or brain, rather. And the clock kept ticking. She had two weeks to push through to the end and then it was time to head back home and deliver her book to her publisher. She was nearing meltdown mode. She put down her fork. The food was delicious but she'd lost her appetite. Tansy wasn't one to stay down for long, which made this all so confounding and annoying. "The book has to be written."

"I know. And it's pretty hard to write relationship advice when your heart is breaking…or you're still going through whatever." Jenna patted her hand across the table. "It'll all work out. Really it will. And I hate to run but I've got to get back. Nancy's got an appointment and she only wants me, plus I need to check on Emma and her daddy."

Jenna was one of those people who had been consistently underestimated. Even though she came across as slightly spacey—Tansy had even heard her referred to as a dumb blonde when they were in high school, which she had always quickly corrected—Jenna had a terrific head for business. In the year and a half she'd been in Good Riddance she'd started a small nail business, which had grown into a day spa, with her living quarters above it. Jenna was very much a hands-on owner and a seize-the-moment personality whereas Tansy was a planner and strategizer. Consequently, having things fall through with Bradley had totally thrown her for a loop. Maybe she should borrow a page from Jenna and be a little more open to spontaneity. Hey, she was here, wasn't she and that had been a fairly spontaneous decision.

"I'm glad I'm here," Tansy said. "It's wonderful to meet you for lunch and be a part of your life…and spoil my niece."

Although, three-month-old Emma Evangeline Jeffries rather scared Tansy. Emma was so little and perfect, it was almost frightening. And Tansy thought it was charming that Jenna's husband, Logan, wasn't just besotted with both his wife and daughter, but actively participated in Emma's care. The CFO of his family's mining firm, he made time to watch Emma while Jenna ran the day spa.

Sometimes seeing Jenna and Logan and their little family together made Tansy realize just how off the mark her and Bradley's relationship had been, even without the panties in his pocket and the incriminating emails.

"Come over for dinner and a movie tonight. I'm not cooking." Jenna laughed reassuringly. "Logan's got the Crock-Pot fired up." Jenna's lack of cooking skills were legendary, both back in Georgia and now throughout

Alaska. While Tansy simply didn't like to cook, Jenna couldn't seem to master it. Tansy smiled. "And we're watching *Tangled* on DVD. You know you like that movie." Tansy was a sucker for romantic fairy tales, as was evidenced by the title of her book. Now she didn't know what fairy tale, if any, was in her future. "Maybe that's what you need to lift you out of your writer's-block funk. It's a cute romance."

It was sweet of Jenna to include Tansy but sometimes seeing Jenna's little family just made the whole thing with Bradley that much more painful. That's what she had wanted. That's what she had thought she was getting. "Let me see where I am."

"What you need is a good healthy dose of a real man."

In a moment of spectacular timing, Rooster McFie practically crowed from his spot across the restaurant/bar/pool hall. The shock of red hair and beard weren't the only aspects that had earned him the Rooster moniker. He had the most disconcerting habit of almost crowing when he was excited. Dear God, she couldn't imagine what he must be like when he was in the throes of sexual fulfillment. Ugh. It was one of those things she really didn't want to imagine but crowded into her brain regardless.   ·

Truthfully, she was all kinds of open to a sweet, gentle knight showing up on a figurative white steed—yes, she was a hopeless romantic—but she simply wasn't seeing that happening in a small town in the middle of Alaska.

"I'm not holding my breath."

Jenna looked past Tansy, and a slow smile bloomed

on her face. "Don't look now, but I believe that man is just what the doctor ordered."

Don't look now had to be one of the worst phrases because it fairly begged you to do just that.

She looked…and couldn't seem to look away as something hot and real and slightly dangerous seemed to slam into her and through her, leaving her breathless and shaken.

Tansy didn't know *who* he was, but she definitely knew, at first glance, precisely *what* he was—tall, lean, dark, wounded, inaccessible and somewhere the other side of sexy.

She finally looked away, feeling flushed and disheveled, as if he'd touched her, run his fingers through her hair, brushed against her skin, marked her in some way.

She also knew exactly what he wasn't. This stranger was definitely no gentle knight on a white steed.

2

LIAM SCANNED THE ROOM for Bull. Sixteen years wouldn't
render his uncle unrecognizable. Even though he wasn't
a tall or loud man, Bull Swenson was a man of presence. Gus's was nearly full, though, so Liam continued
to search the crowded room.

And then, suddenly he saw her midscan, across the
room. The hair on the back of his neck stood at attention. Short dark hair. Glasses. Slightly round face. Aver-
age height. Lavender T-shirt. Her eyes locked with his.

It was as if everything slowed down inside him, the
same way it did when he was about to take a shot. His
heart rate slowed. His breath stilled for several counts.

And then she turned around and the rest of the room
came back into focus. He wasn't sure what the hell had
just happened, but something had. He felt shaken and
there was very little that shook his composure. It was
as if she'd sighted him in her crosshairs.

He mentally shook his head, dismissing the feeling,
and continued his scan. Bull. Four o'clock. At the bar.

Bull looked Liam's way and without a word to the
guy sitting next to him, stood. Liam met his uncle half-

way. Bull's handshake turned into a one-armed hug. "You made it."

There was a whole hell of a lot that went unsaid in those three words. Bull wasn't just talking about Liam arriving in Good Riddance. It was an acknowledgment from one soldier who'd survived combat to another.

"I did."

"I'm glad you're here. It's a good place to be."

For the first time in a long time Liam felt as if he could exhale, at least a little. He still didn't know what the hell he was going to do with his life but for now, being here felt right.

"Yeah, it seems to have treated you well."

Liam had seen some things—terrible things, but it was nothing compared to Bull's experience. As a POW in Vietnam, Bull had been to hell and back.

Bull grinned. "Can't complain, can't complain. Nice job on that mission. How's the leg?"

Liam shrugged it off. "Not a problem." The only problem had been when they'd been patching up what was little more than a flesh wound they'd found his faulty heart valve. That was the damned problem, not his leg.

Bull simply nodded and moved on to ask, "You hungry?"

Liam grinned. "Damn near starving."

"Then belly up to the bar and we'll feed you while you meet everyone."

Throughout the entire exchange with Bull, Liam had had an undercurrent of awareness, always sensing the presence of the woman sitting in the booth to his left. He would find out who she was, but he'd wait until Bull had made introductions and see if one was forthcom-

ing. Two characteristics had been honed by his training, his instinct and patience. He could wait, but in the
meantime he was cognizant of her.

Several minutes later he felt as if he'd met damn
near everyone in the joint…except *her*. However, the
blonde at the booth with her, a woman named Jenna,
had stopped by on her way out. Liam now knew the
other woman's name. Tansy. Tansy Wellington. She was
Jenna's sister and was here visiting from Chattanooga.

He'd never met anyone named Tansy. But he'd also
never reacted that way to a woman, either. In an instant
she'd slid beneath his skin. It wasn't as if his guard was
down because his guard was a permanent fixture. Nope,
she'd just slipped in, marched straight through and set
up camp. He didn't like it a damn bit.

A tall, raw-boned woman plunked a plate heaped
with a healthy portion of potpie on the counter before him. "Thanks," he said with a nod, picking up his
spoon. He turned to Bull. "So, congratulations. Merilee
says the two of you tied the knot."

He took a bite. The potpie was damn good.

"Yep. When you find a good woman you've got
to hold on to her, even if you have to spend twenty-
something years to pin her down."

Liam spoke frankly to Bull. They'd always had that
kind of relationship, even though they didn't see each
other often. Both of them were straight shooters. "I'm
surprised you and Merilee married after all this time."

"Yeah? Well, that's because the crazy woman was
still married, but just hadn't mentioned that minor de-
tail. Hell, I've been trying to marry her since I met her.
When you find a good one you have to keep her."

"No kidding? She was still married?"

"Yep. Her old man wouldn't give her a divorce. Picture an asshole with control issues. She kept thinking she'd get a divorce at any time and then it just became a thing. He showed up a couple of years ago engaged to Jenna, the woman who just left."

Jenna had mentioned her husband and a baby. "Merilee's ex lives here and they just had a kid?"

"Hell, no. Merilee ran his ass out on the rails once she got her paperwork signed." He grinned and nodded his satisfaction with his woman's actions. "Jenna decided to stay. She married a guy she knew from high school last year. Nice fellow. Speaking of marriage and divorce, sorry to hear about Natalie."

"How'd you know about Natalie?"

"Dirk. He rolled in last September, stayed a couple of months and then rolled back out."

Liam's cousin Dirk did that. He'd show up for a while and then vamoose. Dirk was something of a rolling stone. And they'd had some damn good times together as kids and teenagers. Dirk was a year younger than Liam and Lars and a year older than Liam's baby brother, Jack. The four of them had spent many a summer vacation and holidays fishing, hunting, making slingshots, four-wheeling, skinny-dipping, generally doing a bunch of fun stuff at their grandparents' spread in upper Michigan.

And that Dirk would know about his and Natalie's divorce made sense. Liam's mom didn't get along with her two brothers, Bull and Dirk's dad. However, Natalie and Dirk had grown up next door to each other and their moms were good friends. Hell, that's how he'd met Natalie in the first place.

In fact, Natalie had been a sore spot between Liam

and his cousin. Liam hadn't known he was encroaching at the time, and the truth was, it probably wouldn't have made any difference. Dirk thought Liam had stolen Natalie from him, and it had definitely driven a wedge between the two of them.

Liam felt sure that Natalie's mom had been the one to tell of his and Natalie's breakup. You knew you were in a crazy family when your former mother-in-law was the one telling your kin about your divorce.

"How long was Dirk here?" Liam asked. He was sorry he'd missed his cousin. He hadn't seen him in probably six years or more.

"For a couple of months."

Behind him, Tansy stood. He sensed her movement. The mirror beneath the stuffed moose head mounted on the back wall over the bar merely confirmed it.

Unlike nearly every other person in the room, she didn't approach them for an introduction. He looked over his shoulder at her retreating backside as she headed for the door. Bull followed Liam's gaze.

"So, what's her story?" Liam said.

There was no point in anything other than cutting to the chase. Bull would see straight through it.

"She's working on a book. She caught her fiancé fooling around on her and came here to get away for a while and finish up her work. She got here last week and she'll be heading out at the end of the month."

"Ah. One of those scorned women hating on men."

"I wouldn't say that. She strikes me as a nice gal. Now when she asks if you're one of those scorned divorced men hating on women, what should I say?"

"What makes you think she'll ask?"

"Oh, she'll ask. What should I tell her?"

She'd sighted him in her crosshairs. She'd peered down her scope at him. He didn't like it one damn bit. "Tell her it's none of her business."

TANSY STEPPED OUT INTO the September sun and hesitated as the door to Gus's Restaurant and Bar swung shut behind her. Indecision washed through her. She really should just head back to the cabin and get to work. However, focus didn't seem to be her strong suit these days. If she went back out there now without knowing who the stranger with the magnetic gray eyes was, well, she'd simply sit around and wonder.

Jenna was going to be tied up with a client so asking her was out, and the need to know burned inside her.

"What's up, Tansy?"

Lost in her own indecision, she'd missed Alberta's approach. Which merely proved how distracted Tansy had been by the nonverbal encounter with the stranger because Alberta was one hard lady to overlook.

Alberta was, in a word, "colorful." A flowered kerchief covered some of her bright red hair. A brocade vest topped a mutton-sleeved cream blouse. Full, multicolored panels comprised her handkerchief-hemmed skirt, which ended right above her lace-up ankle boots. Turquoise eye shadow, Popsicle-orange lipstick and purple nail polish rounded out her full presentation of the color spectrum. There wasn't a color known to God or man that Alberta wasn't wearing today.

"Not a lot on going on," Tansy said. "I just grabbed a bite to eat with Jenna. How about you?"

"Can't complain." Alberta issued a gap-toothed grin. "Me and Dwight still in that honeymoon stage."

The thought that she, Tansy, wouldn't have a honeymoon because Bradley was a liar and a cheater, crossed her mind. She brushed it aside, focusing on Alberta and the conversation.

That was the remarkable thing about Good Riddance. Tansy had only been here a week, but between Jenna's weekly emails and being here, she felt fully tuned-in to the town and its people.

Alberta, a traveling Gypsy matchmaker, had shown up in Good Riddance back in May. She'd wound up marrying the man who'd commissioned her to find him a wife.

Dwight Simmons had spent most of his life prospecting and his latter years playing chess and checkers with his prospecting partner, Jeb Taylor. When Jeb died, Dwight decided he was ready for a wife and sought Alberta's expertise. She'd found him one all right—her.

At eighty-one, it was his first marriage. Dwight was Alberta's sixth husband. It was all rather mind-boggling in a charming way.

Actually, Alberta had proven comforting. Within two days of Tansy's arrival, Alberta had corralled her and told Tansy not to worry about Bradley. According to the psychic/matchmaker, Bradley wasn't the one for Tansy and his infidelity was a reflection of him, not her. It was all standard comfort-your-dumped-friend verbiage. Tansy had found some solace in being told she hadn't fallen short as a woman because it was all too easy to feel inadequate when you'd expected to spend your life with a man while he was busy seeking the next best thing.

It was sweet to hear Alberta talk about her new marriage. "A honeymoon stage is good."

"You'd better believe it." A sly wink and an elbow

nudge accompanied her words. "I'm on my way to check in on my stud muffins. Why don't you walk over and say hi with me?"

Dwight and Lord Byron, Alberta's three-legged tom-cat, both hung out at the airstrip center office. Tansy couldn't exactly see either Dwight or Lord Byron as stud-muffin material, but, as with beauty, reality was in the eye of the beholder.

It sounded good to Tansy. She wasn't ready to get back to work and perhaps if she knew who the stranger was, she could shake off the impact of those few seconds when his eyes had pierced hers. And the surest source of information was Merilee.

Tansy trailed along with Alberta to the door halfway down the front of the building.

They stepped into the airstrip office, the scent of cookies and coffee in the air. Merilee and one of the bush pilots, a pretty, newly married brunette named Juliette, had their heads together over paperwork at Merilee's desk. Juliette and her husband, Sven, were her neighbors out at Shadow Lake. Juliette's husky puppy, Baby, sat waiting patiently between the two women. Baby actually flew in the plane with Juliette on trips. It was cute.

The object of Alberta's affections sat across the room, staring at the chess table before him. Dwight not only had a new wife, but a new chess partner had materialized in Jefferson Walker Monroe.

According to Jenna, Jefferson had simply walked into town one day and sat down in the rocking chair on the other side of the chess set and that had been that. It turned out that the only relative Jefferson had left was Curl, the town's taxidermist, mortician and barber.

Curl hadn't actually known he had a long-lost relative, particularly a man of color who recounted stories of playing the saxophone with greats such as Count Basie and Louis Armstrong and playing studio sessions with Billie Holiday and Ella Fitzgerald. However, Curl had embraced Jefferson, as had the rest of the town's people.

Tansy had looked him up on Google. Jefferson Walker Monroe was the real deal.

In so many ways, Good Riddance was like the collection of Santa's misfit toys from the Rudolph the Red-nosed Reindeer TV classic. Maybe that's why Tansy felt right at home.

Dwight and Jefferson sat on opposite sides of the chessboard. They were a study in juxtaposition, their only commonalities white hair and lined faces. Both men had witnessed the change of seasons for more than eight decades.

Dwight's long white beard and fringe of white hair rested against the collar of his checked flannel shirt. Long summer days and harsh winters had weathered his skin to a permanent ruddiness. Tall and thin, his carriage bore a permanent stoop. His overalls, while clean, were as worn and weathered as his face.

Across the table, Jefferson bespoke a sophistication of a bygone era of well-dressed couples, two-olive martinis and a husky-voiced chanteuse in evening wear. With his close-cropped white hair, wire-rimmed spectacles and well-pressed suit he should've appeared ridiculous in a town ruled by work boots and flannel. However, he simply looked like a man comfortable in his own skin, waiting to be called onstage to play the next set.

Lord Byron, who was possibly the ugliest cat Tansy had ever seen, but had survivor written all over him, lay curled on top of the empty potbellied stove.

"Hey, sweet thing," Alberta said loudly to Dwight, whose hearing wasn't so good these days.

The cat's ears pricked but he didn't open his eyes.

Before Dwight could respond, Jefferson smiled, mischief glinting in his eyes. "I've told you not to talk to me that way in front of your old man."

"Hey, beautiful," Dwight said to his wife. Most assuredly a case of beauty in the eye of the beholder. He turned back to his chess partner. "Don't make me call you out, talking to my wife that way."

"Won't make any difference if you're not any better at fighting than you are at chess. And if you don't have better moves behind closed doors than you do on the chessboard...."

Dwight grumbled beneath his breath and moved a chess piece.

Tansy laughed at the byplay as Merilee looked over her shoulder. "Afternoon, ladies."

Tansy waved. Alberta spoke up. "What's shaking, Merilee? Juliette?"

Juliette opened the back door. "I'm off to Wolf Pass for a pickup. See you guys later." Baby trotted out behind her.

Merilee stood, stretching. "Bull's nephew Liam just got into town. We haven't seen him in years. We knew he was coming but we just didn't know when." Merilee looked at Tansy, a question in her eyes. "He was just over at Gus's."

Liam. Tansy turned the name over in her head. It fit. It was unusual, and the man himself, in that brief moment of eye contact, had struck her as just that—unusual.

"I saw someone with Bull, but there are still people in town that I don't know. Or rather who live out of town." There were a number of people, men mostly, who lived out in the wilderness surrounding Good Riddance.

"Liam's a nice name," Alberta said.

Merilee nodded. "He's a nice guy. We don't know the whole story but he just got out of the Marines. He was a sharpshooter. I'm surprised he's out—don't know why—but I'm glad he's here."

Something slid over Tansy. A sharpshooter. The man's sole purpose had been to kill people. Hard. Dangerous.

"When did he get out of the military?" Alberta said.

Merilee shrugged. "All we know is Bull got an email from his sister saying he left in May setting out for here. His sister's not the most reliable source. We thought for years Liam and Lars had joined the Army. Where he's been in between or what happened, I have no idea."

"So, I guess he's not married or he wouldn't have left his wife behind?" Alberta pursed her lips in consideration.

"He's divorced. His cousin Dirk told us when he was here. Liam's got a twin, Lars, who's also a Marine and a younger brother, Jack, who's a Navy SEAL, but beyond that—" another shrug from Merilee "—is a mystery. Bull and his sister have been estranged for several years now. She's an odd bird and doesn't seem to play well with others."

None of it should matter to Tansy any more than any of the other people she'd encountered here, but strangely it did. There was something about the man that attracted her, drew her, from the moment she exchanged that glance. She felt unsettled inside…well, even more so than before. And it wasn't just a curiosity. It was a sexual attraction, a wanting that had been instant, and it was a feeling that she simply wasn't accustomed to. She'd felt desire with Bradley, but that had been a culmination of getting to know him, of wooing and bonding that grew as she got to know who Bradley was inside. Although she'd obviously been way off the mark with what was inside Bradley. How could she have been so wrong about him? She wanted to just wake up and have things the way they used to be. However, she kept those thoughts to herself, not even sharing them with Jenna.

But how could she be attracted to a stranger when she still felt that way about Bradley?

"Interesting," Alberta said, and for one disconcerting moment Tansy thought the other woman was commenting on what had been rolling through Tansy's head. But then she realized Alberta was merely commenting on Merilee's rundown on Liam. "Where's he gonna stay?" Alberta said.

"Bull and I have talked about it and discussed it with Skye and Dalton. We knew he was coming, just not when. He's going to stay in the other cabin out at Shadow Lake." Merilee smiled at Tansy. "Liam's your new neighbor."

MALLORY KINCAID GNAWED on the end of her pen—a bad habit, that—as she stared at the blinking cursor on her computer screen. The air conditioner hummed in the background, working overtime in the humid heat of Louisiana's Indian summer. She could close the blind on the hot sun slanting through the window but she liked the feel of it against her skin.

Good Riddance, Alaska. The satellite image showed a small town, with one main street running through its center and surrounded by trees. Lots and lots of trees.

That's where Liam Reinhardt was now. She quit gnawing on the pen and placed it on top of one of the piles on her desk. He obviously wasn't trying to hide. It'd been easy to follow him via his credit card usage.

He'd left Minnesota and headed southwest, rolling through South Dakota, Wyoming, Idaho, back north into Montana, west again to Washington and finally Alaska via Canada. He hadn't been in any hurry. He'd spent four months traveling, alternating between motels and campgrounds.

He might pick up and move on tomorrow, but Mallory had a feeling he'd finally arrived at his destination. His uncle lived in Good Riddance. Bull Swenson owned a hardware store/sawmill and the deed to several parcels of land in addition to an interest in the airstrip and the local eatery—public records were a beautiful thing.

The remoteness of the Alaskan wilderness seemed to fit Liam Reinhardt perfectly. She just couldn't imagine a man like him settling down in the suburbs.

It'd been a crapshoot when he was discharged. She figured he'd either land at Quantico as a civilian adviser or he'd go to ground. Apparently he was going to ground.

She opened another tab and typed in flight information. She winced at the results. She hadn't thought it would be cheap, but it was going to be damn expensive to get herself there. However, she had to do what she had to do. A couple of keystrokes later and she was printing her boarding pass for a flight tomorrow.

And that was the easy part. Adrenaline surged through her. The challenge lay in getting Liam Reinhardt to actually talk to her. And part of that adrenaline surge was due to the fact that she was admittedly infatuated with and fascinated by the man.

She came from a military family and had pursued a career as a military historian. She'd grown up surrounded by men in uniform and had always considered them a cut above the rest, but there were always a handful of men who stood out even above them. Liam Reinhardt was one of those men.

He'd performed brilliantly in what was his final mission. It hadn't gotten a lot of coverage in the media, which was the way the corps had wanted it, but those with military knowledge knew the importance of what had gone down, and that Reinhardt had been the one to deliver the goods. She had seen him a year ago in a video conference when she'd been in a Marine general's office on a documenting assignment and had been smitten from the moment she'd seen him and heard his voice—online, that is. Since then she'd followed his career, researched him and come to realize he was the man meant for her.

She glanced at his framed picture sitting on her desk. Those eyes, the hard glint of his stare, the line of his jaw. She smiled and reached over and traced her finger against the glass that separated her from his image. She'd found it of him in military files and had the photo printed. There was also one sitting on her nightstand.

He was only one of the best sharpshooters in military history, right up there with legendary sharpshooter

Carlos Hathcock of Vietnam-era fame. He was precisely what she'd always dreamed of in a man. Handsome yet rugged, highly accomplished and self-contained—how could a woman not be in love with a man like that?

While getting him to share the story of his last mission with her might be a challenge, she knew that once they met he'd recognize her as his fate, as surely as she knew he was hers.

As mere mortals neither of them could deny a force stronger than them—destiny.

They were meant to be together.

3

"GOT ANY PLANS?" Bull asked as they stepped outside. A truck with more rust than actual body parts passed and Bull automatically waved. It was that kind of town.

"Thought I'd just chill for a while." The words almost stuck in his throat. He had no purpose. He was rudderless. He was well acquainted with stillness and quietness of being—it had been vital to his job. This was different. He'd be damned if he knew what to do with himself.

Bull nodded. "Think you might be interested in some seasonal construction work? Sven Sorenson can always use an extra set of hands, and he's up to his eyeballs in work these days."

"Is it hard labor?"

"It can be."

"Then count me in." He needed to work himself into exhaustion. Maybe then he could actually sleep at night.

The airstrip/bed-and-breakfast door opened and the woman from the booth, the woman who'd seemed to sink into him—Tansy—stepped out onto the sidewalk.

"See you later," she called over her shoulder, closing the door behind her.

Both Bull and Liam stopped, but the sun must have been in her eyes, because she walked right into Liam. Instinctively he grabbed her to deflect the impact.

Every sense inside him went on high alert, which translated to everything slowing down to utter awareness. The wind from the northeast carried her scent of woman—vanilla and a hint of spice. Her skin was soft and warm beneath his hands, her flesh firm to his touch. Her eyes, somewhere between blue and almost purple, widened behind her glasses in surprise and a flash of recognition.

Something wild and hot sprang between them. Liam wasn't used to wild and hot. It wasn't his modus operandi. He did only a controlled heat. Her eyes widened even more and he felt a tremor chase through her. She recognized it as well, and he fully suspected it was outside her normal range, too.

He released her.

She dropped her gaze.

"Thank you."

Her voice, low, husky and damned sexy resonated through him. What the hell was wrong with him? What was it with this woman?

"Steady there," Bull said from his side, ending his loss of composure. He'd totally forgotten Bull was even there. Crap. "Tansy, meet Liam Reinhardt, my nephew. Liam, this is Tansy Wellington."

"Nice to meet you," he said automatically. He didn't offer his hand and neither did she. It seemed unnecessary, considering they'd already touched. And because he wanted so badly to touch her again, he wouldn't.

"It's nice to meet you, too." There was a softness to her that made him want to taste her. The thought crossed his mind that her honeyed sweetness might mitigate some of the bitterness and anger inside him. He pushed aside the notion. "I hear you just got into town," he said.

She smiled and it knocked him for yet another loop, lighting her face and transforming her from ordinary to extraordinary in the blink of an eye. "I just arrived last week. I'm not one of the regulars."

"So I hear."

"You'll both find," Bull said, "that news travels faster than the speed of light here."

Her laugh held the same husky sexiness that made him think of lying in bed with her, both of them naked. That and the way her T-shirt clung to the roundness of her breasts and followed the curve of her waist to her full hips.

"I understand we're going to be neighbors," she said.

What the hell? "We are?" Liam looked to Bull.

"Janie—" God, his mother hated that name, preferring the more formal Jane "—gave us the heads-up you were heading this way. Me and Merilee figured you'd want a little privacy, so we made arrangements for you to stay in one of the cabins at Shadow Lake, outside of town. Tansy's staying in the other cabin." Bull looked at Tansy. "Nice place, isn't it?"

She nodded. "It's beautiful. The cabins overlook a lake surrounded by mountains."

He could almost feel her encroaching on him. She painted a scene of tranquillity at odds with the seething inside him. He wanted solitude to embrace his anger, not dispel it. He didn't want to be seduced by her dulcet tones, her ripeness, her sweetness. He wanted dis-

tance from her. "How many cabins are there?" he said
to Bull, knowing damn well he was bordering on rude.

"Only the two. They belonged to two old maids who
built them next to one another. They're within spitting
distance. There's even a crude intercom system that
was left in place. Sven just overhauled them a couple
of months ago. They're nice enough, but not fussy. It
should suit your needs."

How the hell would Bull know what his needs were
when he wasn't even sure of them? All he knew was
that he needed to be alone and he needed time. But how
could he be alone, with this woman right next door?

As if he'd gained some inside track on what was
going through Liam's head, Bull added, "Trust me on
this."

If there was anyone in this world, other than his twin,
whom he trusted, it was Bull Swenson. He looked at
Tansy Wellington standing there in the sunshine.

He was in trouble....

TANSY SETTLED IN on the couch with her laptop. A small
desk sat against one wall, but she preferred propping
her feet on the coffee table and working from there. It
wasn't exactly balmy outside. She'd thrown on a car-
digan over her T-shirt and would start up the potbellied stove in a bit. She loved the smell of wood smoke
against the crispness of the autumn evenings here. For
now, the front door stood open, with the screen door
guarding against bugs and anything that might wan-
der up.

She would get to work. She would power through
this. Five minutes later she'd gotten a big fat nowhere.
And now instead of Bradley burning into her brain, she

had both Bradley and Liam occupying that space. Actually, Liam was pushing Bradley to the background.

She sighed, frustrated with herself, and set aside her laptop. Wrapping her sweater around her, she walked out to the front porch and sat on the bottom step, soaking up the sun. It glinted off the lake's surface. Snow capped the mountains that stood as a backdrop. They appeared close enough to touch, but were actually quite a distance away. It was tranquillity incarnate. She sighed again and leaned her head against the porch post.

She didn't want this man in the cabin next door. And it *was* right next door. He was hard and wounded…and she was attracted to him. The feel of his hard palms against her had set off an unwelcome need to have more. She'd been relieved, yet disappointed, when he'd dropped his hands from her arms.

The roar of a motorcycle approaching disturbed the quiet. It was him. She didn't know that he drove a motorcycle, but it fit. She heard the downshift as he turned onto the driveway from the main road. She forced herself not to get up and go inside. She would not run, scurrying inside like some frightened little mouse, despite the temptation to do just that.

He emerged from the stand of trees on a black beast of a motorcycle. She openly watched his approach. It would be silly to pretend she didn't see or hear him.

He, however, ignored her as he drove past to park in front of the cabin next to hers. He killed the engine and climbed off. He was tall and lean, yet broad shouldered, and she'd have to be dead not to notice that he had a nice derriere in those jeans. She most assuredly wasn't dead.

He pulled off his helmet and without hesitation

crossed the expanse separating them. She thought about remaining seated, but that would put his crotch directly at eye level, which didn't seem the best idea.

She rose and tamped down the urge to wrap her arms around her middle. He was intimidating in his black leather jacket. Actually, it wasn't even the jacket. It was the attitude. She, however, refused to be intimidated.

He cut to the chase. "I came here for privacy."

What the heck? "So did I."

"I don't want a neighbor."

For a moment his sheer nerve and arrogance rendered her speechless. And then that moment passed. "News flash, Captain Sharpshooter—"

"That's Sergeant Sharpshooter."

Whatever. "You didn't corner that market. I came here for privacy and I don't want a neighbor, either. And if I did, it sure as heck wouldn't be you. However, churlishness isn't in my nature, so I will make the best of what has become a bad situation."

"Really?" He crossed his arms over his chest, and she had the distinct impression, despite his dour expression, that she was amusing him. "So how do you plan to make the best of what you term a bad situation? Are you going to move in with your sister?"

"Hardly. If anyone were to seek alternative arrangements, that would be you. I was here first. So are you going to move in with your aunt and uncle?"

"Nope. I told you I want privacy."

"Have I invaded your privacy? I was sitting here minding my own business and you walked over to my cabin."

"I wanted to make my position clear."

"It's crystal clear. And I hope you're not suffering any confusion as to where I stand, either."

"I don't want any company or milk and cookies or any of that neighborly crap."

"I don't bake, so no worries. And if I was seeking out company, it certainly wouldn't be yours."

"Same here, sister."

She wasn't sure whether she wanted to cry or throw something at him. Both were atypical behavior and neither was a viable option.

"Good," she said.

"Great."

"Better than great." By God, she'd have the last word with this moron.

"By the way, I don't plan to alter the way I do things on your behalf."

Merilee was seriously confused if she thought Liam was a nice guy. He was a jerk. "I don't recall asking you to." And then curiosity got the best of her. "Like what exactly? Should I expect you to howl at the moon?"

"I only howl occasionally, but I do swim in the nude."

He swam in the nude? She didn't know whether he was just trying to shock her or if he was serious. Either way, she felt her face heating with a blush. Nonetheless, she called his bluff. "Yet another news flash, Sergeant." She looked around as if checking that no one else was nearby and lowered her voice to a conspiratorial whisper. "I've seen nude men before. I think I'll manage to contain myself."

"I just don't need a jilted man-hating woman taking out her frustrations on me."

Really? Seriously? That had just come out of his mouth? *Jerk* didn't begin to describe him. She gathered every ounce of self-control and smiled sweetly at him. "I am shocked, simply shocked, that you're not married. Such gallantry and charm—you're such a catch it's unfathomable you arrived alone. It will require great willpower on my part, but I think I can manage to not show up on your doorstep, craving your fun-loving, witty company, or throw myself at your nakedness when you go for your swim."

His expression remained implacable. "I think we've come to an understanding." He turned to go.

Almost. "One more thing, Sergeant…"

He gave a quarter turn to face her again. "Yes?"

"I don't know, and quite frankly I don't care, what your problem is, but you need to find another whipping post. Stay the hell away from me."

SON OF A BITCH. That tactic had failed miserably. Well, it hadn't been a total wash from the standpoint that she'd certainly give him a wide berth now, but it hadn't sent her packing, which had been the overall plan. She was still within spitting distance.

He'd underestimated her.

There was a tactic that when a soldier found himself outmanned and alone, he pulled out all his weapons and went on the offensive, guns blazing. He might get gunned down, regardless, but odds were the enemy would turn and flee, sure that anyone on such a certain attack had reinforcements behind him. Liam had dubbed it "playing crazy." He supposed he'd dub what he'd just done "playing super-bastard." He'd gone on the offensive and been incredibly abrasive and rude.

He'd fully expected her to turn tail and run. He'd counted on her to quail and take cover by moving into town, away from him. Instead, she'd not only stood her ground, but returned fire, volley for volley.

She was a worthy adversary.

He found himself whistling as he emptied his backpack and stored his meager provisions.

The cabin was comfortable, just the other side of utilitarian. He preferred no frills, and this place provided just that. He immediately noted the entrances and exits—one door in the front, one in the back on the other side of the kitchen.

A single room accommodated a kitchen and sofa with a small desk. A television sat against the opposite wall. The two other rooms were a bathroom and a bedroom. The bathroom held a double bed, small dresser, nightstand and standing wardrobe for clothes. A large braided rug covered a good portion of the wood floor in the main room, with a smaller version of the same color and design in the bedroom.

Framed nature prints hung on the walls. An eagle at roost. A pair of loons on the water. The unblinking stare of a bull moose. Some purple flowers. Spruce hanging heavy with snow.

Nice.

Bull had contacted Sven Sorenson, who had stopped by to meet Liam. Liam would start working with Sven's crew tomorrow. He'd asked for the most physically demanding job Sven could throw his way.

Liam craved a workout. He ran every morning, but it wasn't enough—he needed to push himself to the point of physical exhaustion. The sun seemed to wink off the water in invitation. Liam had met the other two couples who lived here—Skye and Dalton Saunders and Sven and Juliette Sorenson. They were all at work.

Liam was going for a swim. It was brisk, but he'd swam in much colder water. As boys in Wisconsin, he and his brother had always swam in the altogether when they could get away with it. Maybe this would send her packing.

He tugged off his boots and socks and stepped outside, clad only in his T-shirt, jeans and underwear. The grass was soft beneath his feet. It had been a long time since he'd walked barefoot on a carpet of green like this.

The water would be cold. That was fine. He'd embrace the cold, adapt to it, push through it.

The hair on the back of his neck prickled to attention. She was there. He felt her watching him. Dammit—he wanted to her *gone.* Methodically, without fanfare, he stripped.

He waded in, the bracingly cold water lapping around him, and he kept going. Once he hit waist-deep, he began to swim. He focused on the strokes, the rhythm, mentally calculating his distance until the physicality of it freed his mind.

TANSY STOOD ROOTED to her spot behind the screen door, mesmerized by the sheer beauty of the man moving through the water.

The water rippled about him as his powerful strokes cut through the surface. Muscles rippled along his arms, shoulders and back. The effect rippled through her.

He'd disturbed her surface. He'd broken her calm… well, what little calm she'd had. He'd shattered it in spades.

Watching him strip on the shoreline—and yeah, she'd watched—had been something else. Yes, she'd seen a naked man before…and Bradley hadn't looked like that. Hard and muscled, Liam's body bespoke discipline and rigor. She had no doubt that whatever physical demands he encountered, he was up to the task. He didn't have the bulk and bulge of a weight lifter, but sleek, honed definition. The man didn't carry an ounce of fat and if she'd thought his derriere was impressive in jeans, it had been beyond compare in the altogether.

She'd called his bluff and he'd delivered.

He'd told her he would do what he would do and wouldn't change anything up for her. And he had.

She opened the screen door and stepped out onto the porch, into the waning sunlight. Leaning against the post, she openly watched him. If an unattractive, albeit boorish, man chose to strip naked and swim in the lake in front of her temporary home, then she chose to watch. Plus, she was curious as to just how far and long he'd swim.

Another plus in the equation was it really was rather akin to poetry in motion to watch his movements in the water. Fluid and powerful, he seemed at one with the lake. And last but not least, given how impressive the rear view had been, she readily admitted she wanted to see how the front view stacked up.

There was something about that argument and then subsequently watching him disrobe that had only heightened the sexual attraction she'd felt from the instant she'd seen him. And in a way, she had enjoyed that blowup. She'd welcomed the anger and outrage. He'd been a distraction and an outlet. For the entire time she'd been arguing with him, she hadn't thought of Bradley, not in any portion of her brain, except when the butt-head had mentioned her being jilted or whatever nonsense he'd said. But then she really still hadn't thought of Bradley—it had been more about her.

And it had been good to feel something more—even if it was anger and outrage…and this sexual tingling—than the numbness that had permeated her since she'd walked away from Bradley and his infidelity.

Lost in her own musings, she realized his pace had slowed. A few yards from the shore, he stopped swimming and stood. Her breath caught in her throat and her heart rate accelerated as he began to walk to the water's edge. Wet, dark hair was scattered over his chest, a taut belly and then—oh…my…goodness. She swallowed hard, a white-hot heat arcing from her brain straight to her sex. Sweet mercy. It was chilly, the water was cold… and he was still impressive. Certainly more impressive than what she'd seen in her other views of male nudity. What he hadn't been gifted with in the way of manners he'd been given in physical endowments because…well, wow. He was a jerk, but a well-hung jerk.

Maybe that was part of his problem—too much testosterone. She'd always favored gentle, academic men who tended to be a little on the soft side. There was nothing gentle, academic or soft about the naked man retrieving his clothes from the ground.

He straightened and she wasn't surprised at all that he made absolutely no attempt to cover his nakedness. She made absolutely no attempt to avert her eyes.

He strode audaciously, surely, toward his cabin. She watched boldly, the play of muscles in his thighs, the weight of his penis between his legs, the slide of water over his golden skin.

Neither of them spoke a word. He stared straight ahead. She stared straight at him, silently challenging him to say something to acknowledge her presence when he'd vowed to ignore her.

Actually, he didn't have to speak to acknowledge her. Awareness arced between them; sexual tension fairly sizzled in the air.

Insanely, if he detoured and his path led him naked to her, despite his earlier behavior she wouldn't turn away. She fairly hummed with a newfound sexual energy…that suddenly needed an outlet.

But he didn't detour and come to stand before her. He went inside his cabin and closed the door behind him.

She sank to the top step, feeling both weak-kneed and energized at the same time. She felt alive and turned on.

He wanted a war? She'd give him a war.

Tansy smiled to herself and reached into her pocket for her cell phone.

She knew just the next move.

4

LIAM TURNED OUT THE LIGHT and stretched out on the bed, his hands folded beneath his head. Why the hell did everything have to be so damn complicated?

All he'd wanted was a military career, and that was gone. It'd been easy not to think about Natalie and her leaving him when he'd had his job to fill his mind. His job had always come first. Now his failed marriage was horning into his thoughts.

There was the woman next door. And he'd gotten an email from Lars. His twin had leave coming up and was heading to Good Riddance.

He pushed up off of the bed and crossed to the window. It wasn't exactly hot but he'd spent so much time bunking down in tents and out in the field that he slept better with a little fresh air circulating around him. He raised the blind and opened the window a couple of inches. Cool night air seeped into the room and a slice of star-scattered sky was visible with the blinds raised.

He settled back on the bed, his hands once again folded beneath his head. Peripheral movement caught his eye. Next door, the lights had gone out in the main part of the cabin. Seconds later the lamp switched on in the bedroom. With the light on and the blinds down, she was like a shadow puppet as she moved about the room.

And then she really caught and held his attention when she, in outline, tugged the T-shirt over her head. The woman had a classic hourglass figure. She was built the way women were supposed to be built, with curves and a little extra padding here and there.

He rolled to his side and watched while she slid her jeans over her hips. Turning one-hundred eighty degrees, she reached behind her and unhooked her bra. She stood there for a moment, outlined in cock-hardening relief, the fullness of her breast, the slight sag that said they were real and the thrusts of her nipples all clearly detailed in the play of shadow.

She slipped her panties off and there was the curve of her belly and ass, the faint unevenness of pubic hair. He lay transfixed, his breathing growing as heavy as his cock, when she lightly ran her hands over her breasts, palming the points. Then she slid one hand down her belly and dipped her fingers between her thighs and he could almost feel the moisture gathered there, smell the scent of her arousal in the air.

She sank to the bed and extinguished the light but he knew what she was doing and as surely as he knew triangulation, he knew that she'd been turned on by him. She wasn't thinking about whatever Joe Blow she'd been engaged to. When she'd touched herself, Liam had been the man in mind.

And it was hot to know she was next door thinking of him while she fingered herself. She was hot. It had been a while since he'd been with a woman and he wanted her. He closed his eyes as he wrapped his hand around

his cock. He didn't think he'd ever been this horny. He
let his mind drift....

*Her eyes glittering the way they had earlier in the
day, she lowered her head to his waiting penis. She
dragged her wet tongue up one side and down the other,
then she took him into the wet warmth of her mouth and
sucked on him. Her mouth felt so good wrapped around
him. He was damn near at the point of exploding. He
dragged her off of his cock and flipped her to her back,
lapping at her tight, taut nipples, suckling her while he
filled his hands with her soft, full breasts. He couldn't
wait...couldn't hold back... He nudged the head of his
dick against her, coating himself with her slick juices
and then buried himself deep inside her tight channel...
again...and again...and again until he unloaded deep
inside her while she spasmed around him, milking him
with her orgasm.*

Spent, he lay there, his breathing heavy and ragged.

And in his fevered brain, in the quiet of the night,
he could've sworn he heard the faint echoes of her own
cries as she found her release.

THE NEXT MORNING TANSY stood in her T-shirt and panties, scrambling eggs at the stove. She'd had the best
night's rest since she'd been here. Masturbation didn't
even come close to a man's touch, the slide of skin
against skin, the fullness of a man's penis inside her, but
her orgasm as she'd imagined hard, rough sex—which
was unlike any sex she'd had before—with Sergeant
Alpha-Male Sharpshooter next door had been great.
She'd slept like a baby and woken up ravenous.

The screen door slammed and she glanced out the
window. Liam wore running shoes, shorts and a sweat-

shirt. The man boasted some nice legs, that was for sure. She'd sort of missed that yesterday, she'd been so busy checking out other parts of his anatomy. Nicely muscled. He was just altogether a fine specimen of a man.

He took off at a jog on the trail to the left of the cabins that skirted the lake. Swimming. Running. It all explained that nice hard body. With a start she realized she was scorching her eggs. She yanked the pan off the burner. His arrogant self would probably love the fact that she'd nearly burned her breakfast because of him.

Regardless, she ate the eggs, at least the ones that hadn't stuck to the bottom of the pan, and headed into the bedroom to get dressed. She eyed her meager wardrobe, hesitating in a way she never did over what to wear. Defiantly, she pulled on her least favorite shirt she'd packed and a pair of jeans. She might be in some crazy heightened sexual state over the man next door but she'd be damned if she'd alter her routine because of him.

Ten minutes later, face washed, teeth and hair brushed, minimal makeup on, she settled on the sofa with her laptop. She opened her document and got herself oriented in the work.

Engrossed, she heard the motorcycle roar to life. She glanced at her clock. She'd been at it for an hour and a half. And she'd accomplished more today than she had since her arrival last week. She supposed she should've tried a head-to-head argument and masturbation earlier. Infuriating man.

With a grin, she got back to work, the sound of the motorcycle fading in the distance.

Midmorning, she'd just stood to stretch when the truck rumbled down the driveway. She went out onto the front porch. The driver, an older man with salt-and-pepper hair and beard, rolled down the window. "Name's Clyde. Bull sent me."

"Hi, I'm Tansy. If you could just put it right there." She pointed to the area separating the two cabins.

Clyde climbed out of the cab. He picked up the first bag of sand out of the cargo bed. "You want me to spread it around or something?"

"No. You can just put them there."

She'd called Bull yesterday to see if he stocked sand and some rope. She was in luck on both counts. She'd planned to drive in but he'd offered to have Clyde stop by with it on his way to deliver supplies to Sven's crew. It worked for her.

"Whatever you say." He stacked the bags where she'd indicated and added the length of rope she'd also ordered. "So, you making some kind of beach or something here?"

His look clearly said he thought she'd lost her mind. She wasn't too sure that she hadn't. Her plan was a little out there. It might have to do with being in Alaska, or at this cabin, or maybe it was her experience with Bradley, or even something to do with Liam that had sparked something in her. On the other hand, like the last box on a multiple choice test, it might be all of the above. Whatever the reason, the idea had just popped into her head, and although she normally would've dismissed it, she was going with it.

"Not a beach. Just something."

"Alrighty then. Bull said to leave the shovel, as well, so here ya go."

"Thanks so much." Tansy tried to press a five-dollar tip into Clyde's hand.

"Sorry, can't take that. Bull wouldn't like it."

"Tell him I said thank you so much and I really appreciate it." Clyde was heading out to the construction site where Liam was working. "Oh, yeah, and remember not to say anything because this is a surprise for Sergeant Reinhardt."

Clyde grinned, obviously delighted to be part of a surprise, even if he did think she was nuts. "My lips are sealed."

An hour later, Tansy's shoulders ached and she'd worked up a sweat. Stepping back, she eyed her handiwork.

Perfect. Absolutely perfect.

"You do good work," Sven Sorenson said.

Liam had spent the day carrying and hanging Sheetrock. They were building a bed-and-breakfast on the outskirts of town. They'd all headed over to Gus's for some lunch and while the place had been crowded and he'd seen Jenna, Tansy hadn't been there. Sven's crew, however, was a good group of guys.

"Thanks." Liam liked the big blond guy who could've doubled as a Viking stand-in in an action flick. "So do you." Sven had remodeled/updated the cabins out at Shadow Lake.

The other man smiled. "I try. So, same time tomorrow? I can use you if you're up for it."

"I'll be here." Liam nodded and walked over to his motorcycle. A few minutes later he was opening the throttle on his bike, relaxing into the ride. It had been hard work, but it hadn't pushed him to his limit, not even with the run he'd gotten in ahead of time.

He drove along the road that had been cut through

the towering evergreens. Clouds dotted the expanse of blue sky. The wind felt good against his skin. It was one of the best days he'd had since he'd been told about his discharge. It was good to be in the company of men all working toward a common purpose, even if it wasn't defeating the enemy.

Tansy had drifted through his thoughts throughout the day. Her front door had been closed when he went out for his run this morning and it had still been shut when he'd headed out to work. But she'd been there and she'd been up. He'd sensed her, felt her looking at him when he'd set out on his morning run, the way he'd always felt a countersniper sighting him.

He turned onto the road leading to the cabins and there she was, sitting on the front step, the same as she'd been yesterday when he'd arrived. A part of him had wondered if she might have left, but the greater part of him had known she'd still be around.

The late-afternoon sun glinted in her hair, picking up threads of red. She wore jeans and a striped T-shirt, but the clothes really didn't matter because now he knew exactly what curves lay beneath her attire. All that was left was to fill in the details…and he'd more than like to fill in those blanks in his mind. The desire he'd felt yesterday and last night had been simmering beneath his surface all day and now seeing her was like throwing gasoline on an ember—it exploded inside him.

Caught up in her, he didn't notice it until he was almost upon it. What the…? He wanted to throw his head back and laugh. The woman was crazy, mad as a hatter. It was the same kind of crazy tactic he'd employed last night.

He pulled up in front of his cabin, killed the engine

and climbed off. Pulling off his helmet, he walked over to the strip of sand that ran the length of the cabins with a length of rope down the center of the sand. General Wellington, he quickly designated her, had literally drawn a line in the sand.

"And what's this supposed to be?" he said, walking forward until the toe of his boot rested against the rope.

She approached on her side until mere inches, and the line, separated them. She brimmed with smug self-satisfaction…and sexuality. "You're a smart man. I'm sure you know exactly what it is."

God, she smelled good, like sunshine, woman and some bath stuff. Her lips were as full and ripe as the rest of her. He ached to kiss that smirk right off of her face, but that didn't seem to be the best tactical move right now. "So what happens if one of us crosses the line?" he asked in a low tone.

A slight breeze ruffled her hair. The exchange took on a whole new meaning. The shift wasn't lost on her, either. Her eyes widened behind her glasses and the air between them sizzled.

She rimmed her lower lip with the tip of her tongue, a nervous gesture, but it immediately brought to mind his fantasy last night of her mouth on his cock. Her proximity and that memory had an instant hardening effect on him.

"Crossing the line is a very bad idea. Just know there will be dire consequences."

He smiled. Smiling in the face of an enemy messed with its mind. "Is that a fact? I've faced dire consequences before and lived to tell it."

"Clearly," she countered. "Do you always state the obvious?"

"Only to reinforce a point." He inched his boot forward until it rested on the line, nearly over. "What are you going to do about it, Wellington? Or should I call you General Wellington?"

She arched one eyebrow? "Really? You consider this your Waterloo? And if I'm General Wellington, that puts you on the losing side, doesn't it?"

Ha. So, she'd paid attention during world history classes. "What are you prepared to do if I invade your territory?"

"You're the one who made such an issue of your privacy. So, why are you standing here now when we agreed to stay out of each other's business? To ignore each other?"

Jesus, he wanted to touch her, taste her, bury himself in her.

"You're avoiding the question. You drew the line. You never draw the line if you're not willing to back it up with action."

"Don't try me, Reinhardt." He'd never wanted to try a woman more, try her on for size, texture, fit. "It's not a dare. It's just the boundaries you made such a big deal about."

"What are you afraid of?"

"I'm not afraid."

"I call bullshit on that because you can't handle me."

"Maybe I can and maybe I can't, but I can promise you I'll go down trying." I'll go down…her warm wet mouth encompassing him… Dammit, he was throbbing for her. "Just watch me if you—"

"Watching you was a pleasure."

For a second she froze. "You…when…"

He leaned down until her hair brushed against his

face, his lips nearly touching the shell of her ear. "Last night. You were outlined against the blinds. How was it?"

"Oh, God."

"Did you think about me?" He paused and while it might seem for effect, he had to struggle to collect himself. He was far from immune to her nearness. She tested his mettle, his self-control. "I thought about you."

"You…you're reprehensible." But there was no venom behind it, merely a breathless desperation.

"And it doesn't matter, does it, Tansy, because I turn you on, just like you turn me on."

"You don't…" She petered out. "I don't like you."

He respected the fact she didn't deny he turned her on. That took some guts. Wellington was no wimp beneath her soft facade.

"I know. I don't want you to like me."

"Why not? What are you afraid of? What are you so angry about?"

"My business is none of your business."

She stood her ground. "Then don't make it my business." She looked down at where his boot rested on the orange mark. "I'd suggest you continue to toe the line and leave it at that."

Smart-ass. And then he did laugh. "I'll outmaneuver you every time, Wellington."

"It doesn't matter—" she paused deliberately "—Reinhardt. I outrank you. You're just a sergeant—" her grin socked him in the gut "—I'm a general. You're out of your league."

She turned on her heel and walked back to her cabin. He let her go. It wasn't a retreat, but rather a triumphant march. He stood there until the door closed behind her.

Outranked? Perhaps. Out of his league? Never. He'd felled an opposing general with a single shot from a mile away.

General Wellington should be quaking in her proverbial boots.

MALLORY SET HER TRAVEL case at the foot of the quilt-covered double bed in the Good Riddance Bed & Breakfast, which was located on the second floor of the airstrip office.

"Come on down when you get settled and let me know if there's anything you need," Merilee Swenson said.

"Will do. I'm just going to freshen up a bit. It's been a long day."

"Traveling all the way from Louisiana will do that." She shook her head, smiling. "That was some timing that you called just after we got that cancellation. We're at full capacity." She laughed. "All four rooms." She crossed the threshold. "See you in a bit and holler if you need anything." She closed the door behind her.

Mallory sat on the bed's edge and reoriented herself. It had been an exhausting, yet invigorating, day— airports and connections and then the bush plane flight out to here. She'd never been to Alaska before and all the Google images and pictures couldn't begin to do justice to the breathtaking splendor of the Alaskan wilderness.

And she was one step closer to initiating contact with Liam Reinhardt. He hadn't moved on, but then again she'd been sure he wouldn't. He was still here. And in a town this size and given they were both newcomers, an introduction was inevitable. For all she knew, he could be staying in the room next door. And she took it as a providential sign that a room had opened up just before she called.

There had been so many signs that had made the rightness of her and Liam impossible to ignore. She'd taken it as a sign that she'd been able to...well, *hack* was sort of an ugly word, she preferred *access*...access his personnel files so easily. She knew he was divorced, she knew how much money he'd made, and once she had his Social Security number, with a little computer ingenuity, she even knew his net worth. But those weren't the really important things she'd discovered. Knowing both his zodiac sign and his year of birth, she'd run compatibility reports on her and Liam as a couple, both astrological and Chinese horoscope. It had been another green light when the reports said she and Liam were a well-matched pair. If that wasn't an important sign, she didn't know what was. She might be a military historian and know her way around a weapon or two and combat tactics, but she was a woman and a romantic at heart. The stars had ordained them as a couple.

She glanced around the room, which imparted a peacefulness. She ran her hand over the cotton squares, her fingers encountering the tiny ridges formed by rows of small, straight stitches connecting them. The squares were a soothing mix of florals and stripes in faded shades of lavender, yellow and rose. Ecru lace curtains hung at the window. A small yellow-and-rose braided rug was on the wood floor next to the bed. A lone framed watercolor hung on the wall. Snow-laden spruce branches bowed beneath their winter weight, while chickadees perched on the branches. A snow-shoe hare sat poised on the snowy ground. Rather than icy cold, the place embodied serenity. A small bowl of fresh lemon slices and dried lavender on the bedside nightstand perfumed the air.

She crossed to the window, pushing aside the lace curtain to look down at the small town nestled against a surreal backdrop of evergreens, distant mountains and blue sky. The sounds of life drifted up—childish laughter, a barking dog, the distinct hum of a diesel-engine truck, adult voices. A bird—she didn't know if it was a hawk, vulture or eagle, as bird identification wasn't her forte—seemed to float on a wind current in the distance.

Biting back a sigh at the utter tranquility around her, she made her way down the hall to the communal bathroom Merilee had pointed out. Ten minutes later, she was back downstairs in the airstrip office and had gotten the rundown on the restaurant/bar next door and the rest of the town's accommodations and attractions.

"I think I'd like to book a massage at that day spa." She might as well make the most of her time here.

"You can either drop by or I can call for you."

Mallory hesitated. "I'll just drop by."

"Sure. It's easy to find." Merilee Swenson laughed. "Everything here is easy to find."

There was much to be said for easy to find but that didn't always get you what you wanted. Liam Reinhardt had been easy enough to find. Yet another indication they belonged together. Once they met, she was sure he'd know it, too.

5

TANSY BRUSHED ON another coat of mascara and checked herself in the mirror, leaning in close to peer without the aid of her glasses. Good, no clumps. The screen door slammed next door.

She left the bathroom and went to the kitchen window. Liam was heading toward the lake, barefoot again. She checked her watch. Yep, same time he'd gone for a swim yesterday. Sheer cussedness kept her at the window. She'd always had a streak of cussedness but something about Alaska was really bringing it out in her. Perhaps it was because everything seemed a little more authentic, a little stripped of the veneer of polite society here.

Okay, and she had to be honest with herself. She wanted to see him naked again. Who was she kidding? She wanted to feel him naked against her, in her. And the dreadful man knew it. And she didn't know if she was appalled or gratified that he wanted her, as well.

He'd watched her last night, seen her touch herself. And the beast had known she was thinking of him, imagining his fingers plying her slick folds, wanting him on her, in her, taking her hard and fast.

The intensity, the raw sexual want she'd seen in his eyes today... Bradley had never looked at her like that. No man had ever looked at her like that. And it was heady, potent, thoroughly confusing stuff.

She watched him now, even though she should turn away and go about her business. Again, he methodically disrobed and stood tall and proud at the water's edge. Broad shoulders, trim waist, a perfect butt giving way to strong thighs and muscled calves.

Want warred with reason. Want won. Arousal, barely held at bay, gripped her. She'd been wet with desire ever since that encounter at the line today. Simply the heat of his breath against her ear, the scent of sweat and man, had nearly driven her mad as she stood toe-to-toe with him. She wanted to know the feel of his skin beneath her fingertips, against her belly and thighs. She longed for his taste, for the warmth of his breath against her skin, his mouth on her breasts, the press of him inside her.

He walked into the water and she turned away. She was losing her mind to so desperately crave the touch of a man she didn't even like. He was angry and hard and who needed that bundle of trouble? Certainly not her.

Tansy reconsidered. She wasn't losing her mind. It was simply that Bradley had screwed with her head. He'd undermined her sense of self. Her attraction to Sergeant Reinhardt was rebound, pure and simple.

Determined to get over herself...and Bradley...and the odious Liam...she marched back into her bedroom and changed into the prettiest dress she owned. She was short and needed to drop ten pounds but the flowing cut of the dress accentuated her waist and camouflaged her excess baggage below. She slipped her feet into matching flats and, deciding to go for broke, put in her contacts. She usually didn't bother, but tonight she was on a mission. Tonight, if she was in rebound mode, she'd find someone other than Liam to rebound with, on, or whatever the appropriate preposition might be.

Thursday nights were karaoke night at Gus's and she'd had a heck of a good time last week. Tonight, she, Jenna and Jenna's husband, Logan, were meeting there for an early dinner and then karaoke entertainment. Thursday night was Jenna and Logan's date night. Baby Emma had a sitter. So, she'd meet them and maybe, just maybe, she'd meet another rebound candidate that would get her off of this path of hell-bound insanity with Liam.

She brushed on a light coating of lip gloss and took stock of herself. Not bad. Good, in fact. She looked pretty. She felt pretty. She was ready to set forth and conquer. For good measure and extra fortification, she spritzed on some perfume.

She picked up her purse and walked out the door, locking it behind her. She paused as she opened the door to her borrowed vehicle.

Liam was still swimming laps, his arms slicing through the water, his shoulder and back muscles rippling like some athletic verse of poetry. Under different circumstances, she would've been neighborly and invited the idiot in the water to go with her, offered him a ride into town. But they weren't different circumstances, so she left him to his own devices in the lake and climbed into the FJ Cruiser.

She didn't glance back as she drove down the driveway.

She hoped he drowned in his own solitude. Well, metaphorically speaking, not literally.

Let the lout wonder just where she'd gone…and if she'd be back.

LIAM ENTERED GUS'S, once again in a brooding, dark state. Finally, Wellington had vacated the premises but he'd foolishly allowed Bull and Merilee to talk him into joining them for dinner tonight. He'd figured he at least owed them that much since they'd hooked him up with a place to stay and a job.

The joint was hopping. Games were going at a couple of pool tables in the back corner and a dartboard. Most of the tables and all of the booths were taken, as were most of the stools at the bar. On the jukebox, Elvis sang "Love Me Tender." He figured Gus's ranked two steps below a honky-tonk—it sure wouldn't qualify as fine dining.

The question as to where Wellington had taken her quirky, well-rounded ass was quickly answered. Despite the crowded room, he spotted her immediately across the way. The woman had a way of showing up front and center in his scope.

She sat at a table with Jenna and a dark-haired man Liam hadn't met. Maybe he was Wellington's date.

She was certainly all dolled up tonight, although Liam preferred her wearing her glasses. There was something kind of sexy about her specs—that school-teacher/library male fantasy thing. The scent of her perfume had hung in the evening air when he'd walked back to the cabin from his swim.

Maybe she'd take the man beside her back to her cabin tonight. Better yet, maybe the man would take her to his place and Liam would have the whole parcel of land to himself, just the way he wanted. Yeah, that'd be grand. Perfect.

She was laughing at something the man said when she spotted Liam. She deliberately turned back to her date, as if she hadn't seen Liam at all. Good.

Rather belatedly he noticed Merilee and Bull sitting two tables over. Merilee waved him their way. Liam made his way through the tables to them. The two empty chairs faced Wellington…and her date. No biggie. He sat down. "Evening," he said.

Merilee reached over and placed her hand on his. "I'm so glad you're joining us this evening." She squeezed. "I'm glad you're here."

"So am I. Thanks for the invite tonight." There wasn't much else he could say under the circumstances.

Merilee shook her head. "I wasn't thinking. You and Tansy could've shared a ride. I should've known she was going to meet Jenna and Logan here tonight. Have you met Logan yet?"

Logan must be the date. Wellington had certainly pulled out all the stops for him. "Not yet."

"Well, there's no time like the present," Merilee said. Merilee was really into that introduction business. Liam actually had no interest in meeting Logan. She was in the process of pushing back from the table when Bull spoke up.

"It can wait, Merilee," Bull said. He nodded at Liam across the table. "Liam's going to be here awhile. He can't meet everyone at once. Let him settle in first."

"Okay." She pushed her chair back into place and said to her husband, "You're right." She rolled her eyes across the table at Liam. "Sometimes I hate it when he's right."

Bull nodded with a grin. "I'm always right."

Liam laughed. Bull and Merilee were good together. He and Natalie had never been that, never had between them what his aunt and uncle seemed to have. Hell, they'd been together for twenty-five years. And who exactly was this Logan? "Sure. I can meet him later. Who is he?"

"He's Jenna's husband," Merilee said. Ah. "He splits his time between here and Georgia but he's mostly here since their baby arrived in June."

If Logan wasn't Wellington's date, then who the hell was she all gussied up for?

"You'll have to meet baby Emma, too," Merilee said. She caught herself. "You do like babies, don't you?"

Well, he didn't actually know. He'd never spent much time around them. He and Natalie had talked about maybe starting a family one day, but that day had never come. He figured it was just as well considering how their marriage had turned out. He sure as hell wasn't at a point in his rudderless life right now where it was even on his radar.

"Uh, I guess I like babies well enough." He grinned at Merilee. "I don't dislike them, so does that count?"

He could feel Wellington watching him. He kept his attention trained on Merilee.

Merilee chuckled. "We'll give you points for not disliking them."

The waitress, a pretty redhead appropriately named Ruby, stopped by and took their drink orders. "You ready to order dinner or do you need a minute?"

"We might want to get it in now. They're pretty slammed," Merilee said.

"We've got lasagna, caribou stew and bison burgers with fries."

"Because Thursday nights are so popular, there are only three choices," Bull explained to Liam. "The caribou and bison are local."

Liam had noticed Wellington working on a burger at her table. And the woman soaked a fry in catsup. It was almost sexual the way she ate her fries. Damn distracting was what it was.

Liam, Bull and Merilee all opted for the burgers and Ruby hurried off.

"Everything go okay with Sven today?" Bull said.

"Oh, yeah. He's a good guy. He's got a top-notch crew, too."

His uncle nodded. "I thought it'd be a good fit."

"And you're happy with the cabin at Shadow Lake?" Merilee joined in.

"Couldn't ask for anything nicer."

"Isn't Tansy just a doll?"

Liam glanced over at the doll in question and then back to Merilee. That wasn't quite how he thought of Wellington, but the easiest, least red-flagging course of action was to agree. "Absolutely."

"So, you two are getting along okay?"

He glanced her way again. A smile, directed at Logan, lit her face. Liam looked away. "Like a house afire." There was definitely heat there, white-hot heat.

Merilee smiled. "When I heard about the sand, I wasn't too sure."

How'd she know? Shadow Lake was a couple of

miles out of town and set back from the main road. It was pretty much to itself.

Bull looked at him. "Son, I told you yesterday, news travels fast here."

Damn. No kidding it spread fast. "It was a joke." He shot another look over at Wellington, who was chatting up a storm. "She's got a heck of a sense of humor." It *had* been damn funny. She did have a sense of humor.

Merilee smiled. "That's a side of her I haven't really seen, but a sense of humor goes a long way in life."

Every now and then the husky notes of Wellington's voice would drift over, not that he could actually hear what she was saying, not that he wanted to.

"I hear Lars is coming," Bull said. "You mind if he stays with you or would you rather us put him up with us?"

Crap. He'd forgotten that his twin was taking leave and coming to see him. How the hell could he have driven all the way to Alaska and still not manage to get away from life and everyone? But since Lars was coming to see Liam, the onus fell on him. "He can stay with me."

Ruby arrived with the bison burgers and they all dug in. Between carrying Sheetrock and his swim, he'd worked up an appetite. Half an hour later they'd finished dinner, the meal having been spent on conversation about the town. Merilee had recounted how she and Bull had finally gotten hitched in a Christmas Day ceremony a year and a half ago.

She knew how to spin a yarn. Liam gave her kudos for not asking him the questions about him and Natalie that were lurking in the back of her eyes. Sooner or later she would, but he was glad it was later. He didn't want to talk about the past and how he'd wound up where he was now—no career, no wife and no home.

Throughout the meal, Wellington had remained in his line of sight, in the distance, beyond the gap between Merilee and Bull. A couple of different people had stopped by their table to chat, but no one had dropped into and stayed in the seat next to her. Maybe Wellington didn't have a hot assignation after all.

While Tansy had been on his central radar, the sixth sense that had served him so well in combat had been prickling from another area of the room. He turned. A woman, tall with straight blond hair that fell just past her shoulders, sat at the bar. He'd never laid eyes on her. She shot him a smile. He smiled back and then turned around. He wasn't interested.

In the far corner, near the pool tables, a long-haired Native fellow he'd met yesterday, Nelson Sisnukett, hopped up on the small stage tucked there. He picked up a microphone. "Welcome to karaoke night at Gus's."

Hell, no. He was just about to excuse himself when Merilee beamed in his direction. "This is fun. Everyone really gets into it."

He could hardly leave on that note.

Nelson continued talking. "We're going to start out with a real treat tonight. Jefferson Walker Monroe is gonna blow his horn for us."

The well-dressed man with the white hair who'd been on the other side of the chessboard took the stage, saxophone in hand, to a rousing round of applause.

Merilee addressed someone over Liam's shoulder as the smoky notes of the saxophone carried through the room. "Hi. Are you having a good time?"

"I am." It was the blonde from the bar. "There are lots of interesting people here."

"Why don't you join us, unless you're already with some of the folks at the bar?"

"I'd love to, if I'm not intruding."

"Not at all," Merilee said. "This is my husband, Bull Swenson, and our nephew Liam Reinhardt. Liam, Bull, this is Mallory Kincaid. She just arrived from New Orleans today."

She had the classic girl-next-door look. Shoulder-length hair, slightly square jaw, nice complexion. A smattering of freckles dusted her nose. Liam would put her in her mid- to late-twenties. Damn nice figure, too. Tall, athletic build.

She was strikingly pretty. And he didn't feel even a remote interest in her. Given all his sexual energy earlier, none of it transferred to the pretty woman next to him.

She nodded a greeting as she slipped into the empty seat. "Mr. Swenson, Mr. Reinhardt, it's nice to meet you."

"Liam just got into town yesterday," Merilee said.

"Oh, really?" She turned her gaze to him. Her eyes were shamrock-green. "Is it just a visit or are you here to stay?"

"Not sure yet. How about you?"

"Oh, I'm just here for a few days to enjoy the Alaskan wilderness."

He didn't know the woman but there was something studied about her casualness. She'd approached their table deliberately. He was pretty damn sure she'd manipulated the invitation.

Even though she was a stranger, he couldn't shake the sense she had an agenda and it involved him.

"Did you get by the spa for an appointment?" Merilee asked.

"I sure did. I'm down for the works tomorrow at two."

Across the way, Wellington was checking out the blonde, surreptitiously, but checking her out nonetheless.

Jefferson finished his sax solo and the first singing act took to the stage. An older woman started her version of an old Patsy Cline tune, "Crazy." It wasn't as bad as it could have been. She actually had a decent voice.

He stayed through the song and then pushed his chair back. He'd fulfilled his social obligations and then some. Tansy was still sitting with Jenna and Logan. However, she wasn't smiling now. Her expression was definitely tight. He supposed "Crazy" was a hard song to sit through when a breakup was still fresh. Regardless, he was getting out of here before the next act started.

"I'm heading out. Early morning. I enjoyed dinner." He nodded to Mallory. "Nice to meet you."

"Nice to meet you, as well. Maybe we'll bump into each other again."

"Maybe."

He stood and made his way toward the door.

He was halfway there when the door opened and his cousin Dirk strolled in. Damn, what was this, old home week? He hadn't seen his cousin since Liam and Natalie had tied the knot. He knew Dirk had been in town, but then he'd left for parts unknown. Dirk looked rough. Liam almost didn't recognize him. His hair was down to his shoulders and an unkempt beard covered his face. But beneath all the hair, the square of his jaw and his eyes remained unmistakable.

A smile that didn't bode well curled Dirk's lips. "I heard you were here."

Jesus, he might as well have taken out a full-page ad.

"I heard you'd been here."

"Yeah? Well, I'm back. I've got something for you. This is for Natalie."

The last thing Liam knew was an exploding pain as Dirk's fist connected with Liam's face.

6

TANSY JUMPED TO HER FEET, along with pretty much everyone else in the room. The music stopped. All eyes were trained on the doorway and the drama unfolding there.

One minute Liam had been standing, the next he was laid out on the floor. The big hairy man who'd punched him simply stood there rubbing his fist with his other hand.

Bull made his way through the gawkers and walked over. "You feel better now, Dirk?" he asked. "I hope so because that's enough. You're done."

On the floor, Liam showed signs of life. He sat up, shaking his head to clear it, his hand to his jaw. Blood trickled down his face. He'd caught his cheek on a chair edge on the way down.

Dirk looked from Liam to Bull. "Yep, I'm done. I said what I needed to say."

Merilee had gone to stand beside Bull. "Say?" She raised an eyebrow.

Dirk grinned unrepentantly. "You know actions speak louder than words."

"You gonna take that, Reinhardt?" a male voice from somewhere behind Tansy called out.

A chorus of male murmurs followed.

"Quit crowing, Rooster," Merilee said to the man in the back. "And the rest of you hush up, too."

Dirk stepped closer to Liam and held out his hand, offering him help up. Liam looked from Dirk's hand up to his face. "We're even."

Even though it wasn't a question, Dirk nodded his agreement. "We're even."

Liam took the proffered hand and rose to his feet. Blood running down his face, he grinned. "You just used your free pass." He rubbed his hand over his jaw. "You've obviously been working out."

"Been up on the pipeline."

"I hate to break up the family reunion here," Merilee offered drily, "but you're dripping blood on Lucky's floor and this is an eating establishment." She handed him a paper napkin to staunch the blood.

"Sorry," Liam said, holding it to the cut on his face.

Nelson approached, having turned his karaoke emceeing duties over to a short balding man. "Dr. Skye's out delivering a baby who decided to show up early but let's step next door and get you cleaned up. You might need a stitch or two."

Dirk, Bull, Merilee, Liam and Nelson all exited through the door that connected the airstrip to the restaurant/bar. And the pretty blonde woman—Merilee had said her name was Mallory Kincaid and she had just arrived in town today—after a second or two, followed them into the airstrip.

Tansy's stomach felt as if it was tied up in a knot.

She sat back down, as did everyone else, and the conversation resumed, ramped up a notch with the drama.

"That was interesting," Jenna said.

"It was definitely unexpected. Who was that? What was it about?"

"I know they're cousins, but I have no clue what that was about."

Logan laughed. "No worries, honey. You will. Before midday tomorrow," he said.

Jenna flashed him an impish grin. "I know." She looked at Tansy. "I saw that look on your face. Mallory's staying at the bed-and-breakfast. That's why she went in behind them."

Right. Tansy said, "Did you see the way she was looking at Liam?"

"I sure did. She was watching him from the bar like a hungry cat eyeing a canary."

Logan looked from Jenna to Tansy and back to Jenna. "I think I missed something."

Jenna rubbed his shoulders. "Of course you did, sweetie. You're a man. But if there's one thing women don't miss, it's when another woman is interested in a man. And Mallory Kincaid is interested in Liam."

He shook his head. "If you say so."

Jenna laughed. "I know so."

Tansy felt kind of queasy inside. She must've eaten too much of Lucky's delicious bison burger and fries. Mallory Kincaid was everything Tansy wasn't—tall, thin, blonde—and Liam hadn't pulled his hostile act with her. "Yeah, she was definitely putting out signals."

"It won't do her any good."

"Why?" Obviously Jenna knew something Tansy didn't.

"Because he's not interested in her."

"He didn't seem not interested in her," Tansy said.

Jenna cocked her head to one side and looked at Tansy as if she'd just climbed off of a spaceship. "How could he be interested in her when he was busy watching you all night?"

"No, he wasn't." He'd looked at her when he'd walked in and then ignored her all night.

"Tansy Patrice Wellington, the man couldn't stop looking at you all evening. Of course, you didn't see because you were so busy trying to ignore him." Jenna looked at Logan. "Am I right?"

Logan held up his hands in mock surrender. "I have no clue. You know I'm not good at that stuff. In fact, I'm going to go over and check with Leo on a new stock offering."

"You do that, honey, but don't talk business too long. We'll wrap up our girl business soon."

Jenna's husband was all about finance and had found a kindred spirit in retired insurance salesman turned general store owner Leo Perkins. Logan simply shook his head as if he didn't quite know what to make of his wife and headed to the other table. Jenna scootched her chair closer to Tansy's.

"Now, while Logan's gone, tell me what's going on with Liam."

"I told you last night when I called about the sand, he's got some issue with me being out at Shadow Lake. He thinks I'm going to compromise his privacy. He's a jerk."

"Really? I think he's the best thing that could've possibly happened."

Jenna was a smart lady, but she seemed off the mark

this time. "I'm obviously missing a piece of some puzzle here. How's that?"

"You got a lot of work done today, even with the sand being delivered, didn't you? You haven't been thinking about Bradley nearly as much, have you?"

That was all true. "How'd you know?"

"You haven't mentioned either work or Bradley tonight. If you're not mentioning work, it means it's good. If you haven't mentioned Bradley, it means you're not thinking about him. And I think you're not thinking about him because you're distracted by Liam." Jenna beamed. "I think he's just what you need to get you over Bradley and finish your book."

A delicious shiver ran through her at the remembered heat in Liam's eyes and the fire he stoked in her. Trepidation followed fast on the heels of anticipation. "You mean, like a rebound?"

"Sure. It's the way things work. You throw a basketball against something and what happens? It bounces back. It rebounds. Sooner or later you've got to rebound. Liam could fit that bill."

"I don't know if I want to rebound yet or if I'm ready."

"Don't sweat it. You'll know when the time is right." Jenna smiled and waggled her eyebrows à la Groucho Marx. "But there is that saying that there's no time like the present."

Before Tansy could comment, and quite frankly she didn't know what to say to that, Merilee slipped into the chair next to Tansy. "Nelson says Liam doesn't need stitches, just a butterfly bandage, but he really whacked the back of his head. He doesn't think Liam should drive. That, of course, has made Liam act like a bear with a sore paw. Can you haul him home since he's right next door?"

Oh, joy. He'd definitely be difficult now, but she could hardly say no. "Sure. No problem."

"Well, not to cut your evening short, but Nelson's almost done with him. I think if he's left to cool his jets too long, he'll just get on his motorcycle and go."

Tansy gathered her purse. "I was just about to leave anyway. I need to let Jenna and Logan get on with their date night."

Jenna laughed, looking around the crowded room. "Oh, yeah, 'cause you were keeping us from being alone. Go take the wounded soldier home. Why put off to tomorrow what you can do today?"

Merilee looked a little confused but pretty much everyone was used to not fully following Jenna conversationally at some point or another.

Tansy, however, knew exactly what her stepsister meant.

THE LIGHTS OF GOOD Riddance faded in the side view mirror as Wellington headed out to Shadow Lake. Neither of them had said a word since she'd met him at the door outside of the airstrip/bed-and-breakfast.

Her perfume, her very presence, seemed to wrap around him in the confines of the SUV and the night.

"Go ahead and say it, Wellington," Liam said, his injured cheek throbbing.

Her profile was etched darker than the dark of the night. "What is it I'm supposed to say, Reinhardt?"

"Don't you want to know why he hit me? Don't you want to crow that I've dogged you about you being next door and now you're taking me home?"

"I don't do smug." Her voice sounded huskier than usual in the dark.

"Right." She'd been so smug about her line in the sand she could hardly stand herself.

"As to why your cousin knocked you out—" she *would* have to phrase it that way "—that's between you and him. I don't want to interject myself in your business. I know how you feel about your privacy."

"I'm beginning to think there's no such thing here." The gossip would be all over Good Riddance before sunrise.

"It didn't help that he did it in front of everyone in Gus's on a crowded night. Since there'll be all kinds of speculation and your privacy's already shot to heck, I'll bite. Why'd he hit you?"

"He thinks I stole his girl."

"Did you?"

"Not knowingly. I didn't know at the time he was interested in Natalie. Dirk's not the best communicator."

"It must run in the family," she said with a note of teasing. Touché. She followed it with a laugh. "He expressed himself pretty clearly tonight." She glanced at him and then looked back to the road. "What happened to Natalie?"

"We got a divorce."

"Oh, wow. You didn't just steal his girl for a date, you *married* her and then it still didn't work out."

Wellington didn't sugarcoat it, but that was fine, he didn't need sugarcoating. But he would set the record straight on one point. "I didn't steal her. I don't poach on other men's territory."

"No, you don't seem like the type of man who would," she said quietly. Her hands were small and dainty against the steering wheel. Her bare arms were graceful.

"By the way, you look nice tonight."

Was that faint sound an indrawn breath?

"Thank you. He must've hit you harder than I thought. You actually said something nice to me."

"But I like you better with your glasses on."

"That's more like it, Reinhardt."

It was the truth so why'd she sound as if her nose was suddenly out of joint? "So, did you have a date tonight who didn't show?"

"No. I did not get stood up, thank you very much. I did not have a date."

"Why else would you get all dolled up?"

"Maybe because I wanted to and I can. I don't have to 'doll up,' as you call it, for anyone but me."

Natalie had had some book about men being from one planet and women from another. He'd thought it was a bunch of crap at the time she'd run around quoting from it, but honestly women just didn't make sense sometimes. "So, you didn't have a date tonight?"

She turned onto the private road leading to the cabins.

"I'm going to cut you some slack because you suffered a concussion." Actually, Wellington was proving to be good entertainment. "No, I did not have a date tonight. And what business is it of yours?"

She threw the vehicle in Park and killed the engine.

"None. Just passing time." He opened the door and got out while she did the same. She rounded the back end of the SUV and he headed to his cabin as she mounted the stairs. He paused to make sure she got in without mishap. She opened the door.

"Thanks for the ride," he said, his foot on the bottom stair of his cabin. "Oh, and feel free to undress in front of the window again tonight. I enjoy the view."

"Wait up for it," she responded with a sweetness he didn't trust. The door closed behind her.

Half an hour later he lay in bed, in the dark, his blind up and window cracked, doing just that. He waited to see what Wellington would do, because she would do something.

Five minutes later she snapped on the bedside lamp, her blinds drawn, throwing her into relief the same as last night. However, unlike last night, this time she climbed on the bed on her knees. He swallowed hard. Damn.

The intercom next to his bed rang, the one that looked like an old-fashioned phone and ran between the two cabins, and he picked it up. "Yes?"

"Are you watching? Are you up?"

He was both. "Yes."

"I just wanted to make sure." The intercom clicked in his ear. She'd hung up.

He watched, waiting, unblinking.

Slowly, languidly, her movements heavy with deliberateness, she raised her right arm and his breath stuck in his chest.

Her movements still seductive, she presented her hand…and then her middle finger.

He blinked and burst out laughing as she extinguished her light. Damn. Laughing hurt his head.

Wellington had flipped him off.

It had been better than another striptease.

He settled against his pillow. Well, *almost* better than a striptease.

THE FOLLOWING AFTERNOON Tansy dropped by the airstrip office to say hello to Merilee after her lunch at Gus's. Alberta was parked in the chair next to Merilee's desk, while Dwight and Jefferson, Lord Byron on the floor between them, contemplated life and the chessboard.

"How's it shaking, sugar?" Alberta quipped as Tansy crossed the room.

Tansy laughed, feeling more carefree than she had in some time. "It's shaking just fine. And you?"

"The sun rose this morning and me and Dwight lived to see it. Can't ask for much more than that at our age, except for a good roll in the sack now and then." She winked. "How's that man of yours after his beat down last night?"

Tansy felt the heat of a blush creeping up her face. "He's not my man," she said, "but he was fine on the way back last night. I heard Sven stop by this morning and pick him up for work."

He'd been out for his run before that. Apparently a knockout didn't stop Liam Reinhardt, even if it had kept him from driving the previous evening.

Merilee shook her head. "Men. Liam and Dirk were just fine afterwards."

Tansy laughed. "It gave the town something to talk about. Gus's was buzzing just now." Jenna hadn't been available for lunch but Tansy had just listened to all the chatter around her. No one was malicious, but the place had been rife with speculation. Tansy had simply kept her mouth shut. Reinhardt's news wasn't hers to tell.

Her days were beginning to take on a nice rhythm. This morning she'd actually made more headway rather than floundering on her work. Coming in for lunch at Gus's had been a nice break rather than the escape from writer's block that it had previously been. She'd found some measure of hope that she might actually make her deadline with some decent material to boot. And on a larger level, she had the sense that she was reorienting herself in her life.

Alberta was about to say something when Mallory Kincaid came down the stairs from the bed-and-breakfast upstairs. Merilee introduced them.

Tansy shook the other woman's hand, her stomach knotting. That little measure of Zen she'd come in with dissipated in the other woman's presence.

"It's nice to meet you," the blonde said.

"Nice to meet you, as well." Tansy did not find it nice to meet the other woman, but she'd been reared too well not to be polite. Something about Mallory bugged her. There was just something that didn't quite sit right with her.

Mallory was even worse in person. She possessed a lilting musical voice, arresting green eyes and at least five inches, maybe six, on Tansy's meager five-foot-four stature.

"So, are you off to Jenna's for your spa date?" Merilee said.

"I am." Mallory smoothed her hand over the edge of her shirt. She looked casual but put-together. "I'm really looking forward to it."

"I'm sure you'll love it," Merilee said. She added, "Tansy and Jenna are sisters."

"Oh." Mallory's green eyes widened in surprise. "I would've never guessed."

The other woman wasn't being bitchy, but somehow her genuine surprise stung more than if it had contained an element of cattiness. "We're technically stepsisters, which is why there's no resemblance."

"Ah." Mallory nodded. "I have a stepsister, as well, and her mom is Asian so Dina and I seriously don't resemble each other. Do you live here?"

"Just visiting for a bit."

"She's staying in one of the cabins out at Shadow Lake along with Liam," Alberta said with a mischievous gleam in her eye.

"Oh. I didn't realize…"

That caught Mallory even more off guard than the Jenna situation. Tansy cleared up the misunderstanding. "She means he's in the cabin next to mine."

"Oh, I see." Tansy so did not imagine the flicker of relief in Mallory's eyes and the faint shadow of hostility. "Shadow Lake sounds interesting. Perhaps I could stop by one afternoon to check it out."

Ha. More like check Liam out…and Tansy considered it pretty darn pushy. Not that Liam was any of Tansy's business, but she wasn't about to have her work interrupted, especially when she was finally cranking on it again, just so some strange woman could put herself in the man's path. No, thanks. "Sorry, I work long hours. If I'm not here in town, then I'm working."

"Well, perhaps we can work something out on a day you won't be too busy. Maybe tomorrow."

Good grief. Was she going to have to tattoo *no* on her forehead? The woman was relentless. "Sorry, but I really need to stick with it. I'm avoiding distractions." And pushy strangers she didn't care for. Settled. Done. She didn't like this woman.

"Well, better run. I don't want to be late for my pampering."

"Enjoy," Merilee said as Mallory was walking out.

Juliette came through the door, her pup, Baby, by her side, passing Mallory on her way out.

"She's definitely not shy," Alberta said with a snort as the door closed behind Mallory.

Juliette looked bewildered. "Did I miss something?"

"Just a little woman-to-woman standoff," Alberta said with a smirk.

"It was nothing," Tansy said. She had yet to see Juliette without the pup. She and Sven were funny. Baby was with her today and Sven's dog, Bruiser, went to work with him every day. Tansy had run into the couple and their canines twice last week when she'd gone for a late evening hike along the lake. Juliette and Tansy had sort of clicked and Tansy enjoyed chatting with the couple while the dogs cavorted. It was cute, but then again, Sven and Juliette made a cute couple. They obviously adored each other. Come to think of it, there was a lot of that going around in Good Riddance.

She bit back a sigh. It had been rather painful a week ago but now it was just nice. She supposed she was getting used to being split with Bradley and rethinking her life without him.

"Oh, okay," Juliette said, her gaze encompassing the room. She looked at Tansy with a quiet smile. "I just popped by Gus's looking for you, since I missed you at the cabin. I know it's last minute but Sven and I decided to cook out tonight and we thought you might want to come over for dinner." The last time she'd ran into them Sven had mentioned she ought to come over for a cookout before she left. "Would you care to join us?"

She'd be more than happy to get to know them better. "That sounds nice. What can I bring?"

Juliette shook her head. "Don't worry about bringing anything. I know you're not particularly in cook mode while you're here. And we're just doing simple."

"I can make brownies. I picked up a mix at the dry goods store when I first got here just in case a chocolate craving struck in the middle of the night." Or she needed to drown her sorrows in chocolate. However, Jenna had kept her stocked in cookies thus far.

Juliette laughed. "Okay. Sure. Bring brownies. Around seven? That gives Sven time to clean up after work."

Tansy was dying to know if they'd also invited her next-door neighbor but she could hardly ask. Part of her hoped he was there, part of her hoped he wasn't. And what she hoped didn't matter—if he was, he was. If he wasn't, well, then, he wasn't. Either way, she was going.

"Seven sounds perfect. I'll be there."

7

LIAM WALKED OUT his front door, a bottle of sparkling water that the dry goods store stocked specifically for Juliette tucked beneath his arm. Merilee had given him the heads-up on that one.

Wellington was just walking down her front steps, looking as pretty as she had the previous evening. She had on a purple dress that hit her right above her knees—Wellington had some nice, shapely legs. The dress flared out from the waist and sort of flowed over her hips. The color looked nice with her dark hair and olive-tinted skin.

Sven had said she was coming when he extended Liam's invite. Although socializing had been the last thing on Liam's want-to-do list, he felt somewhat obligated as Sven had given him a job. He'd show up tonight, as he'd shown up last night for dinner with Merilee and Bull, and then his obligations should all be satisfied and he could retreat back into solitude. Plus, he'd be damned if he'd have Wellington think his not showing up was retreat or defeat on his part. He was almost looking forward to the evening.

"I think you're going my way," he said. "Want a lift?"

She cut her eyes from him to the motorcycle and back to him. "On your motorcycle?"

"No, on my back. Of course on my motorcycle. It's how I get from point A to point B."

"You're so gracious, Reinhardt. Really. But I suppose it's asinine to take two vehicles."

"Hey, it's a nice evening. Just think of mine as a convertible without all the sides."

She laughed and the sound flowed over him, through him. "That's a different take, but okay. You certainly have a unique perspective on things."

"You might want to grab a jacket for the ride back."

"Okay. Hold the brownies. Wait. I can't hold on to the brownies and you at the same time."

"Got you covered. Go get your jacket." She looked ready to balk and he added, "Please. I'm starving, Wellington. I'm not nearly as fun-loving and carefree when I'm hungry."

"Well, we definitely want you at your best" was her smart-ass response as she handed off the brownies and turned to go back inside.

He put the brownies, along with the bottle of seltzer, in a backpack and strapped it to the bike.

Tansy returned within two minutes. The woman was efficient, he'd give her that.

She eyed his bike and then him. "So what do I do?"

"You've never been on a bike before?"

"Not a motorcycle."

"You'll like it."

"How would you know?"

"You will." He climbed on and looked over his shoulder. "Now you climb on the back and just hold on."

"I'm wearing a dress."

"Wellington, just shut up and climb on. Mind the pipes. They get hot fast."

She climbed on and cautiously settled her hands at his waist. However, there was very little room on the seat and he felt the press of her thighs against his hips and her breasts against his back.

"Don't we need helmets?"

"We're going about a mile and a half. It's fine. Just relax. Tuck the hem of your dress down or it's going to be up around your waist. Of course, with your exhibitionist tendencies, you might like that."

"Poor you. Considering how you like to watch, you'd miss the show. Speaking of, how'd you enjoy last night?" She dropped her voice to a lower seductive pitch on the last part. Pipes weren't the only thing on the bike getting hot fast.

"It was almost as good as the night before. I can't wait for tonight."

"Last night was the final curtain call."

"But your audience demands an encore. And you should always play to your audience and make sure they're satisfied."

"My audience is on their own."

"I never pegged you for a quitter."

"Funny. I never pegged you as a watcher. I'd have thought you were more a man of action."

"The key, Wellington, is in waiting until the right time to take action."

And that just about summed up life.

TANSY SIPPED THE lime-flavored seltzer and sank back into the Adirondack chair overlooking the lake. Sven and Liam were over tossing horseshoes in the horse-shoe pit. An array of wind chimes in assorted sizes, made of various materials, played in the breeze drifting off of the lake. The puppies, Bruiser and Baby, had exhausted themselves and were piled in a heap next to Juliette's chair.

"Dinner was delicious and this is just wonderful—very relaxing, very tranquil. I love your wind chime collection."

Juliette looked pleased. "Thanks. I make them."

"Seriously? They're lovely."

"It's just a hobby."

"Wow. Would you ever consider making them for other people? If I paid you, would you make one for me? My mom would love something like these."

"I never thought about making them for anyone else, except I did make one for Sven as a wedding gift."

"Nice. It's okay if it's not something you're comfortable with. I just think yours are really nice."

"Thanks. I'm glad you came for dinner. Sven and I are pretty quiet and sort of keep to ourselves but the weather's been so nice and he got a new grill so he's just been chomping at the bit."

Tansy laughed. "He was really into grilling." Sven and Liam had approached grilling as if it were some delicate maneuver to be executed under stringent conditions.

Juliette smiled, her feelings for her husband all over her face. "They're just such men, aren't they?"

"You got that right. There's lots of testosterone floating around over there."

Juliette sighed. "It's great, isn't it?"

"Uh, yeah, I guess."

"Once you get used to all that testosterone, you'll never go back to the metrosexual side."

Tansy paused for a moment and then she just burst out laughing. Juliette simply smiled. "I...that was just..." Tansy said once her laughter died. "I so didn't expect you to say that."

Bradley was so very metrosexual, which had been one of the things she'd loved about him—his quiet, gentle spirit, the fact that she could use his hair gel and didn't have to bring over her own. And there was a part of her that felt a bit of a panic that he was slipping away from her. She really hadn't thought about him all evening. She'd been totally tuned in to the here and now. She'd found that Liam actually did have a charming side. She'd nearly fallen over when he'd pulled out and held her chair at dinner, when he'd paused and allowed her to precede him through a door. He had charm and he had manners, when he cared to pull them out and dust them off. His leg had brushed against hers beneath the table at dinner. Now and again his arm had glanced against hers, or he'd leaned in at the same time she had and his breath had been warm against her skin. And always there was the memory of his hips against her thighs, the expanse of his back against her breasts, his scent in her nose, the press of his shoulder against her face, blocking too much wind from her. There was the memory of the ride over...and the promise of the return trip to the cabins.

And much as she didn't want to admit it, there had been a "couple" feel to the evening. It had been like some aberration of a blind date, except they did sort of know each other.

The evening drew to a close. Juliette had the weekend flight schedule, so Tansy and Liam made their way back to his motorcycle.

"We'll have to do it again sometime soon."

"That would be fun. I really had a good time."

Liam climbed on the bike and she climbed on behind him. She liked the wind in her hair, the throb of the motor, and heaven help her but she also liked the press of him against her.

They pulled into the yard, the headlight picking out the bright eyes and rounded shape of a porcupine. The animal took off in the other direction. Liam killed the engine.

They both climbed off of the bike. Tansy thought she should just say thanks and walk away. What was she, a glutton for punishment, that she didn't just walk over to her own cabin, where the light on the porch spilled over the edge of the rail? Instead, she was reluctant for the night to end. There was something almost anticlimatic about quietly retreating to her cabin at the end of the evening.

"Thanks for the ride."

"You liked it?"

"I did."

"I knew you would. Maybe one afternoon we could go for a long ride."

Why was he asking her? "I think I would like that."

"Wellington…"

"Reinhardt…"

"I think we called a cease-fire this evening."

"I never declared war in the first place."

"But you drew the line in the sand. And look, now you've crossed the line, Wellington, which leaves me only one thing to do."

Her heart pounded in her chest. "What's that?"

"This…" Liam threaded his fingers through her hair, fitting his palm to the contours of her scalp. She tingled all over with anticipation—oh, yes, she knew what was coming, what she'd wanted for what felt like an eternity but in actuality had only been a couple of days.

His touch was surprisingly gentle. Tansy placed her palm against his chest and slid it up to his shoulder. She would not retreat. She wanted this thing too badly. However, she would not simply submit. She would meet him, participate.

His lips settled against hers, firm, warm. She sighed into the kiss and returned it, her lips seeking, exploring.

And then the kiss detonated. Like some time-released action, it exploded into heat and passion and fire, which raced through her, threatening to consume her. He pulled her hard against him and she pressed closer still.

Liam pulled away, his breathing ragged. "Good night, Wellington."

And then as quickly as it had started, it was over and she was still standing rooted to the spot when he quietly closed his cabin door behind him.

LIAM PACED ACROSS THE floor of the cabin, his boots resounding on the wood in the night's quiet. He was tight and hard and wanted Tansy Wellington. And the fervor with which she had returned his kiss made it fairly apparent that she wanted him, as well. And for this point in time, wanting her outweighed his need for privacy. She was leaving in a couple of weeks, so why not just go for it? It would be an uncomplicated win-win scenario.

He made up his mind and crossed to the door. Yanking it open, he found her standing on the other side, her hand raised to knock. Without a word, he pulled her inside and closed the door.

She leaned back against the door. "I want more," she said.

"How much more?"

"Just what you're willing to give for now." She drew a deep breath. "I need a distraction. You make me forget…other things."

Her former fiancé? He could live with that. Being a distraction was perfect. She wasn't asking for something he couldn't deliver.

He nodded, bracing one hand against the wood behind her, and plied his thumb against the soft round of her cheek. "I understand wanting a distraction. I could use the same thing."

He leaned in, summoned by her scent and the woman herself. Liam nuzzled the soft skin below her ear, enjoying the play of her hair against his face. He felt her tremble. He wasn't sure if it was excitement or fear, or perhaps a bit of both. It didn't matter. He wouldn't hurt her and inherently she knew that or she wouldn't have come seeking him, the same as he had been on his way to find her.

He kissed her. Her lips welcomed him, greeted him, opened to him. She wound her arms around his neck, finding the edge of his hair with her fingertips. She tasted like brownies and sweet, sweet woman.

Liam deepened the kiss and she opened her mouth to him, her tongue meeting his. He pressed against her, wanting to lose himself in her softness, the fullness of her breasts, the curves of her hips, the plumpness of her thighs.

She murmured indistinctly into his mouth and leaned into him fully.

Liam wrapped his arms around her and, mouths still fused, worked their way to the sofa. She touched him as if she couldn't get enough of him. She ran her hands beneath his shirt, her fingers as eager and seeking as her tongue in his mouth.

He explored the curves of her hips with his hands. He dragged his mouth down the column of her throat to the ridge of her collarbone. She felt, tasted, smelled so good. It had been so long. And she was as frantic as he was. He wasn't going to last long at this pace... but he wasn't sure he could slow down. But he'd damn well try. He pulled away from her, panting, as if he'd just run a half marathon in full battle gear.

"Tansy...I... Give me a second.... It's been a while...."

"Same here. I'm ready. Bring out the big gun, Reinhardt."

"What I'm trying to tell you is it's locked and loaded."

"Good. That's what I want. Now."

"Bedroom?"

"Too far."

He didn't need a second invitation. He freed himself from his jeans and underwear while she pulled down her panties. Her eyes glittered with heat and arousal.

"Oh, my. It *is* a big gun."

He leaned back and looked at her, the same as she was looking at him. She had a full bush and her pink sex glistened.

He'd always taken his time. He'd never simply had a woman after just a kiss or two—but then again, he didn't think he'd ever wanted a woman quite the way he wanted Tansy Wellington.

He positioned himself between her legs…and froze.

"Liam? What?"

"Condom. I don't have one."

"My purse. On the floor."

She reached down beside the couch and in less than a minute presented him with the cellophane-wrapped prophylactic. "You were saying…."

"Are you still—"

"Ready? Yes."

She looked wanton with her prim glasses and her legs splayed, her dress up around her thighs, eager for him. Damn this woman turned him on.

"You are one sexy woman."

She simply smiled and pulled him into position between her thighs. And then he was inside her. She was wet and tight and it was as if all the good things in life were right there between her thighs, wrapping around him, encompassing him.

"You feel good," he said.

"So do you. So. Do. You."

Liam stroked in and out. Hard and fast, which seemed to be what she wanted. She rose up to meet each of his thrusts with her own.

He gritted his teeth. He tried to hold out but it was futile. She felt too damn good.

He did something he'd never ever done before. He came too fast.

8

Tansy lay beneath Liam, on the brink, but not there yet when he obviously had found his release. He had warned her ahead of time that he was in full firing position. It was, nonetheless, disappointing. Well, *frustrating* was a more apt word.

He rolled off her. "Hold that thought. I'll be right back."

He disappeared into the bathroom. She suddenly felt cold and exposed, the tweed fabric of the sofa rough beneath her bare skin. Disgruntled, she'd pulled her panties on, tugged her dress down over her thighs and sat back down on the couch. She'd wait until Liam returned before she left. That had been the most disappointing end to a most promising beginning. Forget sitting on the couch. She slipped her purse strap over her shoulder and stood, her legs not quite as steady as she would've liked.

He emerged from the bathroom, paused and then crossed the room to her.

"You don't follow orders very well," he said, but there was no sting in his comment. He reached out, slid her purse strap off of her shoulder and tossed it to the floor. "That is definitely not holding the thought."

He reached for her and she sidestepped him. "You're not obligated."

"No, I'm not *obligated*. I *want* to satisfy you, the way you satisfied me. I just got my round off too fast and needed to clean up." He took her by the hand and tried to lead her but she held her ground.

"I'll just head home."

"Tansy, we can do this my way or we can do this my way, but you are not walking out that door yet. Now, quit sulking and come here."

"I'm not sulking."

"Yes, you are. Damn, woman, it was embarrassing enough that I didn't have more willpower not to come so soon." She hadn't thought about it being embarrassing for him. And she hated that. It was one thing to both be in the throes of passion together, but now that he wasn't so hot and bothered, it just felt awkward. "But I'm not through with you yet."

It was possibly the least romantic, most straightforward verbal exchange she'd ever had regarding sex. Bradley had always been all about flowery phrases and candlelight. Oddly enough, Liam's *I'm not through with you yet* kind of turned her on.

"You're not through with me yet?"

"That's right. Actually, we're just getting started. Let's go to the bedroom."

Just getting started sounded promising, while walking out the door seemed a whole lot like cutting off her nose to spite her face. Tansy stepped forward and said, "Okay."

Liam's cabin was a mirror image of her own. Her

heart thumping against her chest, she followed him into the bedroom. The room furnishings were very similar to those next door. A double-bed was covered in a hand-made quilt, the headboard obviously hand-carved. A matching wardrobe was positioned against one wall in lieu of a closet. A single nightstand and a braided rug completed the furnishings. Unlike her bedroom next door, however, he didn't have any personal items scattered around. It was neat as a pin. The waning light filtered through lace curtains at the window, bathing the room in a mix of shadows and soft light.

He stopped by the bed. "Now, you were holding a thought," he said as he bent his head and kissed her neck. His mouth was warm, his lips firm against her sensitive skin. His whiskers rasped deliciously against her. The same sense of urgency, of want, she'd had before swept through her once again. She thrilled to the smell of him, the taste of him, the feel of him and the sound of his voice.

He pulled back the covers and they sank to the mattress's edge. He gentled her back onto the bed. While he kissed her, he ran his hand over her hip and beneath the hem of her dress. His touch, although sure and firm, wasn't in the least rough. Tansy sighed, relishing the stroke of his fingers against her flesh.

She arched up against his hands. Liam caught the edge of her panties with his finger and pulled them down her hips and the length of her legs. The air rushed cool against the heated flesh between her thighs.

He kissed the edge of her neck, the scrape of his whiskers sending shivers through her. He brushed his hand over her thigh as his mouth found her lips. Tansy wrapped her hand around his neck and pulled him closer, wielding her tongue against his. The intensity with which she wanted him increased, which she really hadn't thought was possible.

Liam stroked and touched her thighs, her lower belly, her hips. With one finger, he traced along the edge of her pubic mound. The maddening man touched everywhere but the one place she wanted him to touch the most. She pulled away from his mouth, panting. "Liam, you've got to—"

He shook his head and continued to circle her with his finger. "Patience."

Pouting, she fired back, "We've seen how much patience you had."

The infuriating man laughed at her. "Extenuating circumstances. Now, close your eyes."

"Maybe I don't want to."

"Just do it. For once, can you just do as instructed and not argue the point?"

Fine. If that's what it took for him to give her what she wanted.… She closed her eyes. He teased his tongue against the ridge of her collarbone, and the sensation arced through her, heaping fuel on the flame that was already burning inside her. Her eyes fluttered.

"Keep them closed," he said.

It really was more intense that way.

He captured her nipple in his mouth, clothes and all, and she sucked in her breath as the sensation shot straight through her to the aching need between her thighs. She dug her fingers in the muscles of his shoulders and moaned. He teased at her nipple with his teeth and she gasped. Tansy was nearly writhing with want when he finally touched his fingertip to her slick folds.

"Yes."

"Hmm." His sound of satisfaction reverberated through his mouth as he suckled her. He plucked and stroked at her flesh and she spread her legs farther apart, opening herself to his ministrations, her orgasm building. He slid a finger inside her and then another while he found her clitoris with his thumb.

She bit her lip when he curved his fingers inside her and rubbed a sensitive spot she hadn't even known existed. At the same time, he worked his thumb against her clitoris.

"I…oh…yes…please." Her cry of satisfaction reverberated around the room as waves of pleasure echoed through her body.

THE FOLLOWING DAY, MALLORY sighed in frustration as she rolled to her back and settled under the sheet, naked. Soothing flute music drifted on the air and candles lit the room. Jenna's spa was on par with any facility she'd find in the big city and certainly not what you'd anticipate in some backwoods town that didn't even have a traffic light. And she'd been comped her massage when she'd been bumped to today due to an overbooking. It was fine by her.

Ellie Sisnukett, newlywed and talented massage therapist, poured more warm oil into her hands. Ellie had a gifted touch. She'd told Mallory that she used to be a schoolteacher before she began working massage in Jenna's spa. If Ellie was half as good at teaching school as she was at massage, the little kiddies were missing out.

"You are so tense. Do you want to talk about it? Is it a man?"

"Isn't it always about a man?" She was getting a big

fat nowhere with initiating contact with Liam Reinhardt. Well, she'd met him but he was clearly not interested in small talk or chatting. It had been terribly disappointing that he hadn't immediately picked up on the rightness of her and him. Mallory, however, was convinced enough for both of them. So, it was simply time for her to lay her cards on the table. She'd tried subtle but subtle wasn't getting her anywhere. Liam was both personal and professional for her. "How did you meet your husband?"

"Nelson likes to say it was when he found me naked in Mirror Lake." Ellie laughed. "It's a thermal lake and I was there one night in the water naked when he showed up, but we'd known each other long before that. I actually dated his cousin Clint for a while. I'd always had a crush on Nelson but he'd never seemed to really notice me. But he noticed me then. We talked and really got to know each other and it just went from there."

"But what if a man is interested in someone else?"

Mallory had banked on Liam feeling the attraction for her that she'd experienced when she'd seen him. But he seemed distracted by Jenna's stepsister, Tansy, the short brunette who was staying out at Shadow Lake. Mallory knew Tansy didn't like her. She found her pushy and abrasive. Mallory was well aware of the other woman's reaction—it was her business to read people. And Mallory *had* been pushy. And then there was the little matter of Tansy not liking her because Tansy knew Mallory was interested in Liam. But that was too damn bad and not Mallory's problem because the stars had fated her and Liam. Liam was meant to be hers.

Her problem, professionally speaking, was in getting Liam Reinhardt to grant her an interview, to talk about his military career and experience. The man had summarily turned down a couple of interview requests—not from Mallory, but from other sources. As a military historian, she desperately wanted this interview with a man who arguably deserved to go down in history as one of the greats of his era in military sharpshooting. It was a shame that he had been discharged, but his experiences needed to be recorded for posterity and she wanted to be the one to do so. And yes, she could've called but she wanted to bask in his presence, to see the look in his eyes when he recognized what they could be to and for each other.

"Well, sometimes what we think we want isn't meant to be. You just have to let it play out."

Perhaps in some circumstances but not with them. Mallory *knew* she and Liam were meant to be.

She finally relaxed and let Ellie work her magic.

Mallory would simply show up on his doorstep. He couldn't ignore her—or their intertwined destinies—then.

LIAM WASN'T SURPRISED when Dirk slid into the seat opposite him at Gus's the following day. He'd known his and Dirk's business wasn't done, although there shouldn't be any more exchanges of blows. At least he hoped not. If there was a next time, Liam would hit back.

"How's your face?" Dirk said.

"Your face looks a whole helluva lot better." He'd lost the wild mountain-man face with a shave and a haircut.

Dirk laughed, looking more like the guy Liam knew. "Yeah. I didn't want to scare any of the little kids in town so I dropped by Curl's and he hooked me up. Your face okay?"

Liam ran his hand over his own chin. "Still intact."

Ruby, the pretty redhead, dropped by for their orders. She was attractive but she wasn't Wellington. They ordered and she left to get their drinks.

Dirk tilted his head to one side in inquiry. "So, what are you doing here?"

"I guess the same as you. Rolling." If anyone would understand aimless wandering, it was Dirk.

He nodded with acknowledgment. "How long you going to stay?"

"Hell if I know. I've got no plan, except to get out of bed every morning and who knows, I may decide to change that up." Liam wasn't into gambling, strip clubs or booze—three money drains for some guys—so he'd just socked away his cash each month. Financially, lying around in bed for a while was an option if that's what he wanted.

"Damn, skippy. That's a different song and dance for you."

"Life changes." And Liam didn't want to talk about his defunct career and lost sense of purpose. He was more than happy to talk about Dirk for a while. "How long are *you* staying?"

Ruby showed up with Liam's water and Dirk's beer. "The food'll be out in a minute."

Both men nodded and she left.

"I'm thinking I'll hang here for a while," Dirk said, picking up the conversational thread of how long he was hanging out in Good Riddance. "I've got some time off up on the pipeline and some dough tucked away.

If you're interested, I could probably get you on. The money's pretty good."

"I'll think about it." But it really held no interest for him. He figured when something struck him as right, he'd know it. "I'm good working construction with Sven for now. Look, since you slugged me over it, let's clear the air about Natalie. I didn't know I was poaching or I'd have never gone there. That's not my style."

Ruby placed a burger platter in front of each of them. "Anything else?"

Both Liam and Dirk shook their heads no. Liam continued. "If you still feel something for her, and you obviously do, you should look her up."

Dirk was suddenly fascinated with adding a small lake of catsup to his plate. Liam wasn't sure whether he planned to drown his fries or eat them. "She made her choice."

"Yeah, well, I obviously was the wrong choice."

Dirk glared at him across the table, as if he might take another swing. "Did you do right by her?"

Damn, but his cousin was hung up on Liam's ex-wife. That much was obvious. "If you were anyone else," Liam said, "I'd tell you it wasn't any of your damn business, but you seem to care about her so, yeah, I did as right by her as I knew how to do. I didn't screw around on her if that's what you mean. As far as I know, she didn't screw around on me."

"Natalie wouldn't," Dirk jumped in.

Damn. Dirk was definitely a head case over her. "No. She's not that kind of woman. She said she couldn't take me being gone all the time. It takes a different kind of woman to live those long stretches with her man gone. It just got to her, to us. She said I was married to the military first and her second." Liam shrugged. "She was right. She said she wanted to come first with her man. You should give her a call."

Dirk dredged a fry in catsup. "Did you ever think that you should give her a call now that you're out?"

"Nah, that ship has sailed for both of us," Liam said. "Damn, man, you care enough to knock me out in a room full of people and now you want to push me back into her life?" He shook his head. "That's some screwed up thinking."

The big man across the table scowled. "I just want her to be happy."

"Then give it a shot yourself, idiot."

Dirk turned a dull red. "I might look her up. We'll see. So, what happened that you're out?"

"I'm out of the military. It's the past so it just doesn't matter."

"I call bullshit on that. If it didn't matter then you'd talk about it. But, it's cool."

There wasn't much to say to that because Dirk was correct—it did matter, but he damn sure didn't plan to discuss it.

THE SOOTHING SOUND OF the waterfall in the reception area and flute music greeted Tansy as she walked into Jenna's spa late in the afternoon. The small reception desk in front of the waterfall was empty.

Ellie, her glossy black hair in its signature single braid, came down the hall. "Hi, Tansy. Are you looking for Jenna?"

"If she's not busy."

"She popped upstairs to check on Logan and Emma."

"Thanks." Tansy headed for the door marked Private. Jenna wouldn't care if Tansy dropped in for a few minutes.

She walked up and knocked on the door at the top of the stairs. "Come on in," Jenna sang out.

Tansy walked in. Jenna's home was beautiful. Huge windows let in light and offered awe-inspiring views of towering evergreens against a backdrop of distant snow-capped mountains and blue sky. Inside it was cozy and homey with a pink-and-yellow chintz sofa and love seat. A leather recliner added a masculine touch. A breakfast bar separated the den from the sunny kitchen.

Jenna sat curled up on the couch, Logan next to her. Jenna's blouse was unbuttoned and Emma nursed nois-ily, her dark head in contrast to her mother's pale breast. It was a sweet moment and a longing inside Tansy un-furled.

"Have a seat," Jenna said.

"I'm just on my way out," Logan said, rising.

"I don't want to interrupt."

"Seriously, you're not interrupting anything. Emma's still chowing down and Logan's on his way out."

"Bye, punkin. Keep your mama straight until Daddy can get back."

He dropped a kiss on Emma's head and then Jenna's forehead. As he headed out, he called, "See ya, Tansy."

"Bye, Logan."

The door had barely closed behind him when Jenna nodded, a big smile on her face. "You slept with him, didn't you?"

"Oh, God, don't tell me it's all over Good Riddance already."

"No. But it's just a matter of time. You've got that look about you…relaxed, kind of a glow…."

"Oh, please."

"What? Am I wrong?"

"Well, no...." Tansy laughed. "You're right. I don't know about glowing, but I do feel relaxed."

"I work with skin. Trust me, you're glowing."

"Well, I've got a bit of a dilemma."

"You need condoms."

"How did you know?"

"You came here brokenhearted. He came here pissed off. Neither one of you was likely to have been anticipating sex, so it stands to reason you need condoms and you don't want to go shopping over at the dry goods store for something like that." Jenna laughed. "Your mouth is hanging open."

"That's just plain scary."

"No. Just logical. I keep a big supply in the closet downstairs. So does Merilee. We like to keep the women in Good Riddance happy...and safe. However, we all know that condoms aren't one-hundred percent fail-safe, as little Ms. Emma is here." She giggled, much like she used to when she and Tansy were tweens and breaking in training bras and braces. "Thank goodness."

She transferred Emma to her shoulder and started patting the baby's back. "She is a cutie," Tansy said.

Emma issued a resounding burp. "And a delicate little thing, too," Jenna said with a proud-mama grin.

"Let me put her down for her nap and then we'll hook you up so you aren't having your own bundle of joy nine months from now."

Tansy laughed but it stirred all kinds of emotions inside her, not the least of which was a longing for what

Jenna, Logan and Emma had…and the realization that life was altogether too complicated.

But in the meantime, she and Liam would have a very good time.

LIAM SPOTTED HER THE MOMENT he rolled down the road. She was sitting on his porch step, obviously waiting. She'd parked a pickup—wonder who she'd borrowed that from—to the right of his cabin.

Mallory Kincaid, the sun glinting off of her blond hair, issued a small wave of greeting. He didn't wave back.

His first thought was they were about to get to the bottom of something. Obviously his instinct hadn't been off when he'd sensed her interest was beyond casual. His second thought was she was bold as he had neither encouraged her nor invited her. Close on the heels of all of that was the thought that he couldn't seem to get people to leave him the hell alone.

He parked his bike and walked toward her. He stopped short of the porch.

She stood, smiling. "Good afternoon."

"What do you want?" he said.

She looked slightly taken aback, but not intimidated. If anything, she appeared faintly amused. "That's blunt."

"I don't see the point in being otherwise." He wanted his swim, Tansy and dinner…and in that order. He didn't want an uninvited, unwelcome visitor. "What do you want, Ms. Kincaid?"

"Mallory. Please call me Mallory."

He ignored that. "I didn't invite you here. You've got

two minutes to tell me why you're here and then I'm going in that door. You can waste your two minutes on bullshit or you can state your case." He glanced at his watch. "Your two minutes start now."

She shrugged and nodded, as if accepting his terms. "I'm a military historian. My family has a long history of service that dates back to the Revolutionary War. My uncle served in Vietnam with Carlos Hathcock. My oldest brother was in Kosovo and Afghanistan. I want to document your contribution—"

"No."

"But—"

"No."

"It's important. And you're one of the greats."

He was not going to feed her curiosity and the curiosity of others as a "has-been." Four months ago, he would have talked. Now, she could get the hell out of his face.

"Your time is up." He walked past her and she turned, watching him. He paused at his door. Her two minutes were spent, but he had some questions of his own. "How did you know where I was?"

She shrugged. "It's not hard to find people."

"I don't like being stalked."

She shifted, leaning casually against the porch rail and post. "I don't consider it stalking. I consider it doing my job."

"Well, hopefully you can get a nice little vacation out of your time here. Otherwise you've wasted your time and your money tailing me."

She didn't bat an eye. "I don't give up easily."

"You're spinning your wheels and, as I said, I don't like being stalked."

"At least look at my work," she countered. "I'll do a great job of portraying your contribution without hyperbole or conjecture."

"Leave me alone." He enunciated clearly.

"An hour. I'm only asking for an hour." She raised her chin. "I'm going to write about you regardless because you're too important not to. You can either give me insight and the straight scoop or I'll do the best I can on my own."

That gave him pause. He didn't like being strongarmed but there was something to be said for making sure facts were presented correctly. And dammit, he could see it in her eyes. She fully intended to write about him. If she got it wrong, he could sue but that wasn't really his modus operandi and retractions didn't mean shit. What initially was in print was what people remembered. While he didn't particularly give a rat's ass what people thought, at least the record would be straight.

"I'll think about it."

"I leave in three days."

"I said I'd think about it."

She reached into her pocket and pulled out a business card. "My cell number is on there. You can search me on Google. I'm legit."

He took her card but didn't look at it. "I get final editing say-so."

"No." She shook her head as she delivered her immediate, firm denial. "That's censorship and I won't be censored. I suggest you check out my work online."

He felt a grudging admiration. She was ballsy and she wasn't backing down on her brave front.

He would think about it. He held her card up between two fingers. "I've got your number." He opened the door and stepped inside. "I expect you to be gone when I come back out."

She smiled. "I'm already on my way." She walked down the two steps. "I look forward to hearing from you."

Liam closed the door on her without replying. He had a lot to think about.

9

TANSY TURNED ONTO THE ROAD leading to Shadow Lake
and was taken aback when she met another vehicle.
Secluded and off-the-beaten-path in an area that was
already remote, Shadow Lake got virtually no traffic.
Mallory Kincaid waved from behind the wheel of a
pickup truck.

Tansy returned the wave even though her gut somersaulted, a sense of betrayal washing over her. And
then she realized it was a response that came from her
experience with Bradley and this wasn't Bradley. This
was Liam and she knew in her gut, deep inside her, that
whatever business Mallory Kincaid had had with Liam
it hadn't been monkey business. Liam had been in bed
with Tansy last night and now Mallory had been out
here, but she knew as surely as she knew her name he
wouldn't have gone there. Some men just enjoyed the
chase and once the hunt was over, it was on to other
prey. She didn't have that sense with Liam. He might
be abrupt and abrasive at times but he was a man who
reeked of integrity.

And even though they were two ships passing in

the night, Tansy expected to be the only ship sharing docking space with him, even though they were short-term. The fact that she was so sure she was the only one docking with him was either a testimony to Liam or an indication that she was in fact recovering from Bradley's betrayal.

She'd seen Liam as a rebound, as a recovery from Bradley, but her feelings about Bradley were still all tangled up. She still hadn't really let go of the notion of them as a couple. She still had this little fantasy going in the back of her mind where Bradley showed up, full of contrition, vowing undying love and begging her to come back home to live happily ever after.

She parked and was walking toward her stairs when Liam stepped out onto the porch next door. "Did you see the Kincaid woman?"

Tansy hoped she managed to keep her expression neutral as she nodded. "I did."

He crossed the small yard to where she stood and rubbed his hand over his face. "She was waiting on my doorstep when I got home."

Well, hell. Tansy wasn't quite sure what to say to that. "Oh. Uh…that's different." She had struck Tansy as bold and well, that was bold. And she'd been right—Mallory was interested in him. Showing up on his doorstep was definitely interested. And all of that aside, there was something about the other woman that just raised the hair on the back of Tansy's neck. Tansy just got a weird vibe from Mallory.

"She wants an interview," Liam said.

That was so not what she'd expected. It took her a hot second to assimilate what he'd said. "An *interview?*"

"Yeah. She's a military historian and she wants to interview me about my time in the service."

Tansy's level of relief verged on the ridiculous. She couldn't stop the smile that bloomed on her face. "That's cool." Although why she'd had to fly all the way to Alaska and then into the backwoods for an interview was a question that begged asking. But hey...

Liam's scowl, however, clearly said he didn't find it cool. "I told her I'd think about it."

"Why not just say yes?"

He crossed his arms over his chest, his expression set. "Because it's done."

Together, they wandered up to her porch.

"Well, that's why it's history," she said. "I'm not sure I get your point."

"No, you wouldn't, would you?" He was as controlled as ever but the air practically vibrated with his frustration. "I'm a has-been. I didn't retire. I was medically discharged because of a faulty heart valve."

"Hold on a second. You run every morning and swim like that every evening and you've got a faulty heart valve?"

"I'm fine. It's fine. The doc said it wouldn't keep me from doing my job but since it's on record, it does technically keep me from doing my job, hence my discharge. Is that some bullshit or what?"

"Wow." She didn't even know what else to say.

"All I ever wanted to do was be in the military and now I don't have a damned thing to do." He squared his shoulders. "The only reason I'm thinking about letting her interview me is she said she would write about me one way or another."

"I don't see that you're a has-been. That implies that

you're all washed up." Tansy was just sort of thinking aloud.

"Do you see me in active service? Do you see me doing my thing? No. I'm carrying Sheetrock instead of a rifle. Do you have any idea how that feels?"

He wasn't the only one who found himself floundering professionally. "I hate to rain on your pity party but yeah, I kind of do have an idea of how that feels. I write a column that is carried all over the world, giving advice on love and relationships, and I'm working on my first book on finding your fairy-tale ending. Then I find out my fiancé was cheating on me. Do you have any idea how bogus that makes me feel? You haven't exactly cornered the market on professional and personal disappointment."

"It's not the same. No one took your column away from you."

"True, but then again, no one took your skills away from you. Just because you aren't in the service anymore doesn't mean you don't know your way around a rifle. Put it to use otherwise. There have to be other outlets."

"I'm not going to be a gun for hire."

"Who says you have to?" An idea popped into her head. "You're up here in Alaska. Why don't you do some wilderness training thing? You know, one of those survival camp deals? That would appeal to the kind of people who make Alaska their holiday destination."

Liam all but sneered at her idea. "Those that can, do. Those that can't, teach."

His outlook exasperated her. "Oh, really? Then it's a good thing that there are plenty that can't and teach what they can't do. That's some jackass thinking there, Reinhardt."

"What, Wellington? Are you thinking you'll change to career counseling since you're not doing so hot these days in the love department?"

She flinched inside, but remained outwardly poised. She knew enough about people to know he was striking out because he was so frustrated with his situation. It did not, however, mean she had to be his whipping boy. "That was uncalled for, Liam."

She used his first name deliberately, bringing the interaction back to a more personal level.

He looked somewhat contrite. "Yeah, I guess it was. Sorry."

It wasn't much in the way of an apology, but it was actually more than she'd expected from him. He obviously wasn't in a good place, which she fully recognized as she was sharing that same not-in-a-good-place designation. "No worries. But for the record, I think you should talk to Mallory—" even though Tansy still didn't much care for the woman "—and think about a survivalist skills camp."

"I'll think about it." And she had the impression that he would. "You keep writing your column and your book."

It felt like a peace offering for his earlier churlishness. She took it. "I will." She grinned. "It's how I pay my bills."

"Do you have any dinner plans?"

"No…" Was he actually asking her out?

"Want to make some dinner while I get my swim in?"

Really? He was serious. No teasing glimmer shone in his eyes. Yeah, she could make some dinner all right.

"I can make dinner *plans*—as in I can change clothes so you can take me to dinner at Gus's when you finish your swim."

He considered it for a couple of moments and then laughed. "Okay. You want to drive or you want to go on my bike?"

"I like your bike, but maybe I should drive."

He grinned. "Then I'll stop by in about an hour and a half. Does that work for you?"

"I'll be ready."

She had a date. It was a nice change.

Bradley who?

DAMN. NONE OF THIS WAS going according to plan. First, the Kincaid woman had been parked on his doorstep and then Tansy threw out the career idea and now they were going out to dinner. What had happened to his quiet home-cooked meal and hot sex afterward? Hell, he'd even sought out Bull after lunch to track down condoms. Thus was life in a town the size of a gnat on a map.

He supposed it was all good, except the Kincaid woman. Didn't anyone understand he didn't want his life delved into, that he simply wanted some privacy to lick his wounds? Apparently not. Although, it had been kind of nice to talk to Tansy about his situation. While she hadn't been particularly sympathetic, she had given him a different perspective. And, while they weren't in exactly the same situation, she did seem to understand.

The thought came out of left field that she at least got it in a way that Natalie wouldn't have. He and Natalie got along well and he'd loved and respected her and she'd seemed to feel the same about him, but he didn't think they'd ever really understood each other. Hindsight was twenty-twenty, but they would've been far better off just remaining friends than trying the husband-wife thing.

He knocked on Tansy's door. "Be there in a minute," she called out.

He waited, hearing her moving around inside. Finally she opened the door, looking fresh. A slight flush colored her face. She wore the same dress she'd had on at Gus's on Thursday evening. It looked as good on her now as it did then. "You look nice." He leaned in and kissed her cheek. Her skin was soft beneath his lips.

"Thanks. So do you."

He laughed at her handing it back to him. "Thanks."

She tilted her head to one side, perplexed. "What's so funny?"

"That you think I look nice. I trimmed my hair but my clothes choices were limited to my least worn jeans and T-shirt." He looked down at his jeans and boots. "I only brought what I could carry on the back of my bike. That's one thing you learn in the military—just take what you can't live without and pack light."

Her chin took on a stubborn tilt. "Well, I still maintain you look nice."

He grinned. "If you say so." He caught her hand in his. "Ready to head out? I'm starving."

Fifteen minutes later they walked into Gus's, Liam opening the door for Tansy and then ushering her to a booth with his hand resting slightly in the small of her back. More than a few looks came their way, some speculating, some smug. Merilee and Bull waved from across the room, where they sat at a full table.

He and Tansy had just placed their drink orders when

Mallory Kincaid approached their booth, speculation and perhaps a bit of consternation in her eyes. "Evening. Mind if I join you?"

Liam spoke up before Tansy could. In fact, he didn't even glance at Tansy. "Yes, we do mind."

Even the fairly unflappable Mallory Kincaid appeared somewhat taken aback. Her smile faltered and then she firmly pasted it back in place. "Uh, okay. See you later. Enjoy your dinner."

Tansy eyed him across the table as Mallory retreated. "That was blunt."

And her point was? "I am blunt. What? Did you want to have dinner with her?"

"Well, no."

"Okay. Neither did I. What's the problem?"

"You didn't even bother to ask me. Would it have mattered if I did?"

"Let me lay this out for you, Wellington. All day I've wanted to have dinner with you and then move beyond where we left off last night. Now, if I'd looked over to you for approval on her joining us for dinner, your sense of common courtesy would've kept you from saying you didn't want her to eat with us. So, then my and your private dinner would've been ruined. The only one at the table who would be happy with the situation would be her and I'm much more concerned with you getting what you want and me getting what I want. Dinner would've been spoiled and there was just no point in spoiling dinner for the sake of being polite. Somebody had to be in charge and I decided it was me. If you did want to eat with her, then you could always make arrangements to share a meal with her some other time, couldn't you?"

"That's true. However, next time I get to be in charge."

Liam laughed. "Fair enough." From the bar area, Dirk caught Liam's eye and pushed away, heading toward them. "Have at it. You're in charge."

It was a repeat of the Kincaid woman scenario. "Hey, slide over and I'll eat with you," Dirk said.

Liam kept his mouth shut and looked at Tansy.

She flashed Dirk such a warm, sunny smile that a twinge of jealousy bit Liam in the ass. "Maybe some other time. I want him all to myself tonight."

"Well, damn." Dirk looked at Liam. "You need to give me lessons, tiger."

Tansy laughed. She was damn sexy when she laughed. Actually, she was just flat-out sexy. "I think Ms. Kincaid was looking for a dinner companion."

"I'll see you later, then." Dirk headed toward the blonde.

"See?" She was cute even when she was smug. And he was suddenly extremely glad that she was being smug with him and not some other man. "There's blunt and then there's finesse."

Liam laughed. "That was well executed, but this was why I suggested you cook…unless you particularly want to have dinner with someone else. This place is like Grand Central."

Tansy shook her head, her dark hair swinging against her cheek. "It is Grand Central for Good Riddance. Why don't we have an appetizer here and get dinner to go?"

He trusted she'd meant it when she'd told Dirk she wanted him all to herself for the evening because he was damn sure finding himself unwilling to share her with anyone else. A bite or two would tide him over.

The woman across from him had main course…and dessert…written all over her. "That sounds like a plan."

"COME HERE," LIAM SAID, as she locked the front door and he placed the take-out containers on her kitchen counter.

A shiver ran through her. The glimmer in his eyes echoed how she felt.

"Are you in charge again?" she said. She actually found it pretty darn sexy.

"What do you think?" He leaned against the counter, looking hard, sexy, commanding.

"I think I might let you *think* you're in charge," she said as she slowly approached him.

"Are you trying to outmaneuver me with mind games?"

"Perish the thought." She stopped a foot away from him.

"Come here, woman." He pulled her to him.

"Hmm. I think I like it when you're in charge." She nuzzled against his neck. "It turns me on."

And it did.

"Keep your dress on. I wanted you the first time I saw you in it. Does that offend you?"

"No. It turns me on."

She felt as if she was on fire for him. It was as if all the other times, with Bradley, they'd had to build up to it. But with Liam, there was just this chemistry, as if when she was around him something crazy but real happened inside her. Him simply being him turned her on.

She ran her hand down the front of his pants and cupped the ridge of his erection. She rubbed her palm against the prize. "Unzip your pants. Does that offend you?"

"Not in the least." He unzipped.

She knelt in front of him and he groaned aloud. "It turns me on to have you on your knees in front of me."

Tansy licked the length of him from base to top and then took him in her mouth. She swirled her tongue around his shaft. The taste of him, the fullness of him in her mouth, excited her. Liam tangled his hands in her hair. She was so wet, so hot for him.

He gasped. "Enough."

He didn't have to say any more. She knew he was reaching his limit and he wanted the same thing she wanted. She wanted to feel his lovely cock inside her.

She rose and took his hand. "Bedroom." She'd left the bedside lamp on.

Liam quickly stripped out of his clothes, pushed her onto the bed, pulled her panties down and off and leaned back. "You're beautiful," he said as he rolled on a condom he took from his pocket. "Open yourself for me."

She touched herself and he shuddered. She spread herself for him and he entered her slowly. She savored the feel of him, inch by delicious inch. He was seated deep inside her and she tightened around him.

"Oh…" he gasped.

She wrapped her legs around him, pulling him deeper, harder into her. "Yes," she said.

He set up a slow rhythm of out and in and out and in. Tansy closed her eyes, letting herself go into the motion, the sensation. Liam pulled out of her and rolled to his back. "Your turn."

Tansy smiled and climbed on top. She settled onto his erection and sighed in pure pleasure, grinding down and around on him. She rode him facing him for a few minutes and then she turned her back to him and set up a thrust-and-retreat rhythm. Something in that hit just the right spot and she began to gasp as the beginning wave of an orgasm rolled through her. It seemed to resonate from somewhere deep inside her, with an intensity that left her spent and light-headed.

LIAM LAY ON HIS BACK and let the aftershocks quiver through him. Last night had been a relief and a release after a long period of celibacy, but tonight, this, her... She was incredible, felt incredible. He'd always enjoyed sex, but he'd never known it could be this good.

He drew her down to his chest to lie on top of him and pulled the cover over both of them. "Hmm." She snuggled in contentment against him, her head tucked in his shoulder, beneath his chin.

"When I can muster the strength to move, I'm going to take that dress off of you."

Tansy laughed softly against him. "Unless you just have some particular attachment to undressing me, I can take the dress off now."

"Hmm. Now would be good."

She shifted and wiggled and pulled the dress up and over her head.

"I can handle the rest."

She laughed. "The only thing left is my bra."

"Exactly. I can handle that."

Wrapping his arms around her, he unhooked her in the back. He slid the straps down her arms and took it off her. He realized it was the first time he'd seen her totally naked. Her skin was soft and smooth. Her breasts were full yet her nipples were a little on the small side, soft-pink eraser points atop her creamy mounds.

Liam teased one fingertip around the flat areola and felt her quiver. "Tired?" he asked.

"Content. You?"

"Satiated…but a little hungry."

"I'm glad to hear you say that, because I'm a lot hungry. I'm starving."

Liam chuckled. Most women wouldn't admit to having an appetite, especially a naked woman. It was refreshing. "How does dinner in bed sound to you?"

"Decadent. Fun. Satisfying."

"Wait…I think you've already skipped ahead to dessert."

"Shut up and get our food. And can you give me a T-shirt, second drawer on the right side?"

He levered out of bed, pulled out a T-shirt from the wardrobe and tossed it to her. "Thanks."

When Liam returned with the take-out boxes from Gus's, Tansy was sitting cross-legged against the pillows and headboard. He rather liked that she'd opted for that instead of putting her dress back on.

He passed Tansy a box and settled into the spot next to her.

"I think this is where we're supposed to exchange personal information," he said.

"You really don't ascribe to a whole lot of social skills, do you?" She opened the lid to reveal bison pot roast with mashed potatoes and green beans.

"Not particularly." He opened his container, as well.

"Well, for goodness' sake, I won't burden you with a lot of useless information about myself. God forbid that you might want to know something about me as a person and not just a convenient warm and willing female form who happens to be next door. There's nothing quite as gratifying for a woman as knowing she's merely a handy vagina." She took a bite of mashed potatoes.

"Why do I get the feeling I just said the wrong thing?"

"Ya think?"

"Let's try this again. Why don't you tell me about yourself?" The pot roast was delicious.

"Maybe it'll work better if you pretend it's a military interrogation and you ask what you want to know. I, however, reserve the right to not answer every question. I think we've already covered name, rank and serial number."

Liam laughed. "You and Jenna are stepsisters?"

"Yeah. Her mom and my dad got married when I was thirteen. My folks had been divorced for two years and I lived with my mom, but Jenna was there on my weekends and holidays when I was there to see my dad. We just sort of clicked. I had an older brother but I'd always wanted a sister, so it worked out even though things didn't work out between my dad and her mom."

"That's good that you and she stayed close even if things didn't work out with your folks."

"Jenna's mom is nice and she was always good to me, but she's either on her fifth or sixth husband. I can't keep up. It's like she's searching for something in someone else that she just can't find in herself."

"What about your mom? She remarry?"

"She's been in a long-term relationship. Mom left my dad because she finally came out of the closet. She's a lesbian. She and Dorothea have been together now for eighteen years."

He wasn't quite sure how he was supposed to respond to that. "Oh."

"It's all good. It was a bit of an adjustment at thirteen and kids at school can be really ignorant. Actually, people can be really ignorant in general, but you've just got to find the good things in life and let go of the rest."

Spoken like a true optimist. He wasn't sure anymore if he was capable of finding the good when the bad was so damn prevalent. "There's a whole lot of bad out there. Really, really bad. Sometimes finding the good is like looking for a needle in a haystack."

"I know you've seen a lot of bad."

"I've seen enough bad to last me a lifetime." And dammit, he'd been instrumental in stemming the bad, that had been part of his job and he'd be damned if he could find the good in the way that worked, in no longer being a part of the checks and balances out there.

"Then maybe that's why you're here now." Her comment tapped right into his head. "There are just some things that are outside of our control. What about your folks?"

"My dad died when we were kids. My mom never remarried. She's okay but she's difficult. She wants to manage everyone's life. I stay out of her business so she'll stay out of mine. I've got two brothers, a twin and a younger brother. And no, we're not identical. We all went into the military."

"And now you're starting a new phase of your life."

"It looks that way, doesn't it? What about your life? You came here for a bit, what happens next?"

"I came here to get some clarity and I guess accept that things didn't turn out the way I had thought they would. I thought Bradley and I were something we obviously weren't. I thought we had something we obviously didn't. So, I've regrouped. I know a lot of it is me, but in some ways, being here has made a huge difference. The town motto is something about leaving behind what ails you and it's true. There's something very healing about this place. I guess it sort of bears out the finding the good and letting the rest go."

"If you say so."

She laughed. "I just did."

10

TANSY FINISHED UP HER column and saved the file. She'd let it sit for a while and reread it before she submitted it via cyberspace. She'd never suffered these doubts as to the advice she doled out to others. But now she felt like a poser, a fraud, because, dammit, she was still so unsettled about Bradley and now Liam was on the scene. It had taken her all day to work through that column.

And she may not have her personal business in order, but she could at least maintain some semblance of order in her home away from home. She went into the kitchen and had just run hot water into the sink when her phone rang. It was Jenna's ring tone.

"Hey, you. How's it going?"

"Are you sitting down?" Jenna said.

Jenna didn't sound upset but Tansy's heart leaped into her throat. "Is something wrong?"

"No, no. Everyone's okay, but you might want to find a seat."

"Okay." Tansy crossed the room and sank onto the couch. It seemed the easiest thing to do. Her heart was thumping like mad in her chest. "I am now. What is it?"

"Bradley is here."

Tansy felt light-headed. She curled her fingers into the cushion, needing to grasp something, hold on to something. "Bradley? Here? In Good Riddance?"

"Yeah. Merilee just called me so I could give you the heads-up." Oh. Dear. God. "He's at the airstrip center and Petey's on his way to pick him up and take him out to you."

Petey, a part-time prospector and part-time mechanic, ran the "taxi service" in Good Riddance, which mostly meant he ferried people about in his Suburban for a token fee when needed.

Tansy sat, thankful for the sofa beneath her, stunned. Bradley was here. He had made the trip cross-country to see her. It wasn't as if he was just in the neighborhood and dropped by. He was here.

"Tansy?" Jenna cut into her reverie. "Are you there?"

"Yeah. I'm here."

"Are you okay?"

Oh, yeah, that was the question. She wasn't sure. "I think so. I don't know."

"Do you want me to come out? I can be there in a few minutes."

Jenna was a sweetheart but this was between Tansy and Bradley. Whatever was going to happen, whatever needed to be said, needed to happen with just the two of them. "No. No, I appreciate it, but I don't think so."

"Do you need to talk?"

"Not right now." She needed to pull herself together. "I need to organize my thoughts before he shows up, but I really, really appreciate the heads-up."

"Anytime. Call me if you need me. I'll keep my cell with me."

"I appreciate it."

"You'll call me after he leaves?"

Tansy laughed, as much from nervousness as amusement. "I'm sure you'll be hearing from me—probably before the taillights have faded. I'm going to run now."

She hung up and drew a deep breath. Forget about the dishes in the sink. Leaving the phone on the sofa, she hurried into the bathroom. While she rushed through brushing her teeth and hair and slapping on some makeup, her brain was running a thousand miles a minute.

She didn't know how she felt. Part of her wanted to see Bradley. Another part of her was dismayed. And what about Liam? Would he care? Would it make a difference?

She pulled on the much-worn dress, the one in shades of lavender, that she knew looked good on her, that played up her eyes. She had enough feminine pride that she wanted to "present" well. She hesitated and then defiantly pushed her glasses more firmly onto the bridge of her nose. Bradley had always preferred her wearing her contact lenses. She might put on the makeup and dress, but she was keeping the specs. Liam thought they were sexy.

She had just closed the door on her bedroom when she heard the sound of a vehicle coming down the drive. For all of her frantic thoughts and activity, a calmness descended over her. She sank onto the couch and waited. She wouldn't anticipate him at the door. He could knock...and wait.

The idea finally popped into her brain that she could actually refuse to see him. However, she didn't want him to think that she was afraid to see him or too vulnerable or still licking her wounds. No. She'd see him.

She heard his footfalls on the steps and then his knock on the door. Recognition rippled through her. The familiarity of his knock threw her for a loop, took her back to when they were an item. A sense of nostalgia and longing ripped through her. All the times she'd heard that knock before, all the good times that had followed. She shook her head, dispelling the memories. It was the past, water under the bridge. This was the here and now.

He knocked again, this time calling out, "Tansy?"

She didn't call out to him in return. Instead, she rose to her feet and crossed the room. Drawing a deep breath, she opened the door.

Bradley stood there...and she felt nothing. No anger. No wave of nostalgia. Just numb.

He motioned Petey to leave. Tansy motioned Petey to stay. He stayed, his motor running in the driveway.

"Hi, Tansy."

"Hello, Bradley." His sandy hair was short and well-groomed, as always. Uncertainty and contrition shadowed his blue eyes. There was a small spot on his cleft chin—she'd always found it rather endearing that he couldn't seem to shave without nicking himself there. Now, it was simply a thing—not endearing or otherwise. He wore a pair of pressed khakis and a collared light blue shirt—a combination she'd always found classy and sexy. He smelled like the Paco Rabanne he'd always favored and which she'd always found such an olfactory turn-on.

Now, it just was. He simply was.

Bradley shifted and she noted the Dockers on his

feet. He looked well put-together, albeit a little haggard around the eyes. He'd obviously taken the time to change before catching a ride out with Petey, considering he would've been traveling for a minimum of half a day, probably more.

"You look good. Alaska agrees with you."

"Thanks."

He shifted from one foot to another, as if unsure how to proceed. He looked beyond her, to the cabin's interior. "Aren't you going to invite me in?"

She hesitated and then made up her mind. She didn't want him in her cabin. She'd traveled more than a thousand miles to put herself in a place that didn't hold memories of him, of them. And she and Liam had been together here. "No. I'm not."

She reached behind her, stepped outside and closed the door.

"Ah. I see. You're not going to make this easy for me, are you?"

"It's not about making it easy or difficult for you. I simply don't want to invite you in." And that much was true. She didn't want him in her cabin.

He nodded, reaching out as if to touch her and then dropping his hand to his side. "You're still mad and I don't blame you."

It had been, still was, so much more than simply being mad. Try searing, soul-deep hurt, betrayal. And she didn't owe him any explanation and she certainly didn't care as to whether he faulted her for it. Tansy shrugged. "I don't care whether you do or don't."

A group of chickadees dive-bombed a feeder to the right of the porch and an eagle circled in the distance. A slight breeze teased her hair against her cheek. She stopped herself from wrapping her arms about her waist and instead kept her hands by her sides.

Bradley ran his hand over his head, his shoulders slumping forward. "Tansy, I know I hurt you. It was the most stupid thing I've ever done in my life." He looked deep into her eyes, as if he wanted to peer into her heart. She kept that door closed. "I've lived with regret and missed you like hell since you left."

She simply looked at him, a detached part of her noting that his eyes were nearly the same hue as the sky behind him.

He reached between them and took her hands in his, his fingers curling about hers. His touch, his skin, bore the familiarity of the hundreds of touches between them in their past. It shook her to her core. "I want you to come back with me. I want to fix things. I want us to get back to where we were."

She shook her head and disentangled her hands. She didn't care how it looked, she wrapped her arms about her middle. "There's no going back." It was a declaration as much for her as for him. "There's only moving forward."

He nodded eagerly, hope glimmering in his eyes. "Then let's move forward together. We'll see a couple's therapist. We'll work on it. You're the best thing that ever happened to me and I screwed up big-time."

She bit the edge of her tongue, just to make sure she was fully awake. It was nearly verbatim every grovel-and-beg-for-her-back fantasy she'd indulged in when they'd first split.

But this was no fantasy. This was real. Bradley was flesh-and-blood standing before her. Where was the sense of vindication she'd anticipated? Where was any sense of elation?

Despite her off-putting body language, Bradley wrapped his arms around her, pulling her to his chest. He pressed his cheek to the top of her head. It was hauntingly familiar...and disconcerting rather than comforting. "God, Tansy, I've missed you." He pulled back enough to stroke her jaw tenderly with his hand, his eyes drinking her in. "At least say you'll think about it. Will you at least give me that?"

She felt awkward and uncertain and a little trapped. And she heard the thrum of Liam's motorcycle at about the same time it appeared.

"I'll think about it," she said, trying to extricate herself from his embrace.

He, however, wasn't letting her go that easily—she supposed either figuratively or literally.

Liam killed his engine and climbed off of his bike. He walked toward the porch, a marked contrast to Bradley. Liam, in jeans, T-shirt and work boots, was dark and hard.

He looked Bradley over in cool appraisal and then looked away, clearly dismissing him. His eyes tangled with Tansy's. "I could use a back rub after my swim. I'll make dinner tonight."

Liam was definitely marking territory and drawing his own line in the sand. And she had no intention of changing her current plans, which had been to spend the evening with Liam, just because Bradley had shown up. And there was a big portion of her that was delighted that Bradley knew he wasn't the only game in town. "Okay."

Bradley's eyebrows drew into a straight line as he

frowned, looking between Tansy and Liam and then training his gaze on Liam.

"Who are you?" Bradley asked with more than a hint of belligerence.

Liam ignored Bradley. "Call me if you need me," he said as he turned on his heel and walked away.

Bradley looked back to Tansy. "Who is that guy? Obviously you haven't wasted any time." He had the nerve to look wounded.

Things should have been crystal clear, but Tansy had never felt quite as conflicted as she did at that moment.

When it was clear she had no intention of explaining Liam, Bradley continued. "I thought we'd have dinner together."

"I obviously have plans."

"What do you mean you have plans?"

"Just that. I have plans."

"Tansy, I flew across the country to see you."

"Bradley, I didn't ask you to come."

"Fair enough. I know I hurt you."

She nodded. He had hurt her.

He rubbed his hand over his brow. "Okay, I'll head back to the bed-and-breakfast and leave you to whoever he is, but will you at least sit down and talk to me while I'm here? I think we both owe it to ourselves and what we had to at least talk about it and try to work things out."

She hesitated, taking a minute to think. She didn't want to just send him away. She *couldn't* just send him away. She looked at his feet. "Did you bring some other shoes?"

He looked at her as if she'd lost her mind. "Yeah."

"Come back tomorrow at eleven. We can go for a hike and talk then."

For a second he looked as if he was going to argue with her. She didn't know whether it was the waiting until eleven or the hiking that he had issue with. She didn't care. He could come back at eleven and they could hike and talk or he could sit around and then go home. He wisely decided to roll with her plans—she saw it in his eyes. He nodded. "Okay. I'll be back at eleven." He glanced at the cabin next door. "Who is he? What is he to you?"

There were two issues here. One, she wasn't exactly sure what Liam Reinhardt was to her. Second, she didn't owe Bradley an explanation as to what Liam was to her—Bradley had forfeited the right to know when he'd cheated on her. The first question, however, was easy enough. "He's a former Marine sharpshooter, a sniper who is living next door."

"Oh. What is he to you?"

"That's private."

Bradley narrowed his eyes but nodded nonetheless. "We'll talk tomorrow."

LIAM ADDED A CAN OF TUNA to the pasta noodles and stirred it all together. It wasn't gourmet by a long shot, but it was dinner, after a fashion.

The Suburban had been gone by the time he'd gone out for his swim. Something had crawled over him, gone through him, when he'd driven up and seen—what was his name?—Bradley, with his arms around Tansy. He'd been a little disturbed and curious. It was like finding out the enemy had broached your perimeter. Although Bradley wasn't exactly the enemy. Tansy was simply a short-term thing, nothing more and nothing less which suited him just fine considering where his life was at this juncture. He was too unsettled and at a loss for her to be any more or any less.

He heard her door close and shortly thereafter her footfalls as she mounted his steps, then her knock. The first thing he noticed when he opened the door was that she'd changed into a pair of jeans and a T-shirt.

"Hey," she said.

"Hey, yourself," he said with a smile. He stood aside to let her in. Desire, hot and swift, flared inside him at the cling of her jeans to her hips and the way her T-shirt hugged her breasts. "You okay?"

She didn't pretend to misunderstand him. "Yeah. Still a little surprised, but I'm fine."

"You didn't know he was coming?"

Tansy's laughter held a note of incredulity. "Uh, no. We haven't kept in touch. I haven't heard from or seen Bradley in over a month."

"You still up for dinner?"

"A girl's got to eat." She smiled. "But maybe you could take a rain check on the back rub. And I'm not sure I'll be the best company."

"I can live without a back rub. And don't worry about whether you're good company or not. We'll just eat, okay?"

"It's a deal. Thanks."

"Have a seat and I'll dish it up. You may want to hold the thanks, though, because it's just stove-top tuna. It's one of only a couple of things I cook. My big criteria in the kitchen is quick, easy and some semblance of nutrition."

She sat down at the small kitchen table while he spooned up the food. "Water or milk?"

"Water, please."

Liam brought the food and drinks to the table and then settled in the chair across from her.

"Dig in."

"It's good. Kind of like comfort food. My mom used to make something similar when we were kids and she got in late from work."

"Glad you like it. So, was it a nice visit?"

"I can't say that it was nice. It just was. Is."

"I see. Is he sticking around for a while?"

"Jenna says he's here for two days. We're going for a hike tomorrow."

Liam nodded. "I'm guessing if he came all this way he wants you to go back with him."

"That's what he says."

"I see. I guess you've got some decisions to make."

She shrugged. "I guess I do."

"Just so you know, Wellington, I don't share."

"I didn't think you did. You don't strike me as that type. Neither do I, Reinhardt. I'll let you know if things change."

"Fair enough." He didn't want things to change. He wanted them to roll along the way they were until she left. He enjoyed her company and the sex was good, too…make that better than good. And there wasn't a whole helluva lot more to be said on that topic. "So, you never did say how you got started writing a column for the lovelorn."

"You never did ask."

"I'm asking now."

"It's really kind of crazy the way it all happened.

My degree is in art history with a minor in psychology. I know, they're not even remotely related. I always seemed to be the go-to girl when my girlfriends needed relationship advice and it always seemed to work out pretty good for them when they listened to me. It almost became something of a joke. As a lark, one of my friends set up a webpage and before I knew it, I went viral. Agnes, my friend who'd set up the page, suggested selling ads. Well, at that point we didn't have to sell anything because we were being approached by advertisers. I loved doing that a whole lot more than the job I had and I was being stretched pretty thin, keeping up with the website and my day job so I dumped the day job and started working the website full-time."

"You ever hear from people who say your advice sucked?"

"Occasionally. But it's mostly a case of people sometimes not wanting to hear what you have to say. The thing I love about it is I feel as if I make a positive difference in people's lives. Even if I tell them what they don't want to hear, it's really to get them to a healthier place."

"So you can really live anywhere. Work anywhere."

"As long as I've got an internet connection, I'm in business."

"That's a nice freedom."

"Yeah. I guess it is. I hadn't really thought about it. I always liked where I lived. But when my relationship with Bradley went down I came out here to get away for a while. Plus, I hadn't seen Emma yet."

"Do you miss…where is it…Chattanooga?"

"Not as much as I had thought I would. But it's one

thing to go away for a visit and a whole different ball game to think about moving for good."

"Yeah. I understand."

He got up and moved behind her. He put his hands on her shoulders and rubbed. "You're tense. Relax. I'll give you the back rub and you can catch me up another time. Deal?"

"That's a nice offer, but you know what I'd find much more relaxing?"

She caught his hand in hers and brought it to her mouth, pressing a kiss to his knuckles. Half an hour ago, he'd have turned her down, but then half an hour ago she wouldn't have made the offer because mentally she had been somewhere else, her mind wrapped up in her ex. Now, he didn't need to be asked twice.

"That works for me." He helped her to her feet and wrapped his arms around her, pulling her close, simply holding her for a moment. He kissed her, slow, deep, thoroughly, testing the weight of his lips against hers, discovering the recesses of her mouth, the texture of her tongue. He pulled away from her.

"Let's go to the bedroom." He didn't feel the franticness he'd felt before, last night and the night before. He wanted slow time with her.

"Okay."

They went into the bedroom and silently, of one accord, undressed. Unhurried. He pulled back the covers and they climbed into bed together. He touched her cheek, her neck, feeling the beat of her heart, the rush of her blood, beneath his fingertips. Still silent, she smoothed her hand over his jaw, palmed his chest.

He kissed the ridge of her collarbone, weighed the fullness of her breasts. He traced the darker circle of her areola and then teased his tongue against her ripe nipple. He lapped at her and then took the turgid point in his mouth and suckled as she plied her fingers through his hair and moaned in the back of her throat.

He kissed his way down her torso to the softness of her belly. He nuzzled at the curves of her hips.

"Liam." She spoke his name softly, almost a sigh.

He felt the fullness of her thighs, the firmness of her calves, and tested the delicate arches of her feet with his hands. Then he made his way back up to the soft, wet folds beneath the fullness of her bush.

He pulled on a condom and eased into her. She was beautiful, her dark head against his pillow, the softness overlying the steel that was her, welcoming him inside her. She draped her legs over his shoulders and he wrapped his hands around her thighs, going deeper, harder, as if he could get to the core of her, meld with her.

He felt her tense, felt the tightening of her around him. She fisted her hands in the sheets. He came with her, riding the orgasm that seemed to come from some place inside her, inside him.

11

THE NEXT DAY, TANSY GLANCED at the clock on her computer—almost eleven.

Despite dinner and the incredible time with Liam, which had rendered her beyond relaxed at the time, she hadn't slept worth a damn last night. If anything, the great sex with him had further complicated everything. She'd lain awake for what felt like all night, thoughts whirling through her head like a dervish.

She needed, wanted, some clarity but she was just as unsettled and confused as she had been. Actually, more so. Her plan, at this point after turning over both Liam and Bradley in her head all night, was just to hear Bradley out. She'd let him have his say and then figure it out from there.

It didn't mean he was in charge, but she was curious as to what was going on in his mind, his heart. She'd like to say she didn't care, but now that the shock and numbness had worn off, she did.

The sound of an engine coming closer heralded his arrival. The door slammed and the vehicle retreated as Bradley's footsteps reverberated on the porch steps.

Her heart tattooing against her ribs, she opened the door and stepped out onto the porch. "Morning," she said.

"Good morning." Even though his jeans and T-shirt were neat and pressed, he looked as if he hadn't slept any better than she had.

She found his haggardness gratifying. She had cried a veritable river over him, especially early on, so it was somewhat mollifying to see that he'd lost at least one night's sleep over her. She also found it slightly endearing.

"You ready?" she said.

"I don't even get invited in?"

No. She still wasn't ready for Bradley's energy in her space, even if it was a temporary space. That had been one of the reasons she'd come here in the first place. She'd move forward very cautiously. "I asked you to go for a hike, not sit in my den."

He wasn't particularly happy with her answer but he didn't have much recourse. He nodded. "Okay."

She walked down the porch steps and out into the bright day. Bradley followed her. The sun was warm against her skin. The light sparkled on the lake like diamonds scattered across its surface. The air, crisp and clean, sifted through the trees. Birds called to one another as if celebrating the day. At the end of the dirt path that led to Liam's cabin, Tansy hesitated.

Several trails ran through the property. The best-marked trail was the one she and Liam had taken the evening they'd spent at Juliette and Sven's place. It skirted the lake and offered stunning views of both the water and the mountains. However, she chose a more rugged path that ran perpendicular to that trail and led through the spruces to a clearing.

"This way," she said.

"You've become a regular nature girl, huh?" His laugh held a forced note.

Tansy didn't answer, letting the silence stretch between them as the towering evergreens filtered the sun to an arboreal twilight. She was giving him an audience, but it didn't mean she was going to make it easy for him. He didn't deserve an easy path, either figuratively or literally.

He stumbled over a root. "You're not going to make this easy, are you?"

The man did know her fairly well. "Life isn't fair or easy a lot of times, is it? I guess you make the most of whatever opportunity you find yourself given."

"I don't really know where to start."

She said nothing, continuing to put one foot in front of another. That had been all she'd been capable of when she'd first arrived here, simply putting one foot in front of another. Bradley would either find the words he wanted or he wouldn't.

The tall evergreens blocked the sun, save for the occasional shards of light that pierced the green canopy. The smell of his cologne struck a discordant note with the scent of fresh loamy earth and the trees. Ahead of them, the path and twilight gave way to a small opening of meadow. Tansy had often wondered what had occurred that nothing but grasses grew in the small space. She walked to the center and sank to the ground, wrapping her arms about her knees, the sun warm against her shoulders and back. Bradley lowered himself to sit beside her.

"This is beautiful. Remote but beautiful."

"I know."

He drew an audibly deep breath. "Okay, I screwed up. Actually, that's an understatement." *No kidding.* He paused and plunged on. "It was a couple of drinks and temporary insanity. That's no excuse, just what happened." He looked at her. "God, if I could go back and take it back I would but I can't. I've missed you like crazy." Real pain thickened his voice. "I've missed the sound of your voice—" he paused as if at a loss "—your head on the pillow next to mine in the morning, talking to you…just being with you."

His words resonated with her. She'd felt all of that herself. Some men weren't great communicators, but that had never been Bradley's problem. Words came easily to him. The fact that he was struggling now spoke volumes in and of itself. She didn't doubt his sincerity at all.

"Would you please, please say something?" he said, desperation echoing in his words.

She responded honestly. "I've missed you." And she had, dreadfully. He had haunted her days and nights… until she'd met Liam.

"God, that's a relief. I've missed you…been so lost without you. I was so scared…and then when I saw that guy yesterday. Damn, lambchop, I didn't sleep at all last night."

Guilt assaulted her. He *really* wouldn't have slept if he'd been a fly on the bedroom wall. She pushed aside the guilt. She and Bradley weren't an item anymore. He had torn that apart when he'd climbed into bed with that other woman. And he'd said it was a case of a few drinks and bad judgment.

"Are you saying it was just that one time?" she said.

"Does it matter?"

Did it matter? She wasn't sure. Either way it couldn't be undone. "I don't know."

"It was twice. I swear it was only twice."

It felt like a knife going through her. Twice with the same woman or twice under those circumstances? "The same woman?"

"God, yes."

She felt sick inside. So, it wasn't as if one night and one mistake had been their undoing. He'd seen her again, another time. "Okay."

"What does okay mean?"

It was funny how a sense of betrayal could uncoil inside you all over again. "Just that. Okay."

"So, this guy next door to you…you've slept with him?" There was no missing the edge to his voice. Good. Let him feel a little of what she was feeling, not that it was the same or even close to the same. She'd betrayed nothing when she'd slept with Liam because there'd been nothing to betray.

"Yes."

"More than once?"

She gave him back his earlier words. "Does it make a difference?"

"Then we're even," he said.

Tell her that hadn't just come out of his stupid mouth. "Really?" Outrage escalated her voice an octave. She swallowed hard and strove for her normal tone. "There's no 'even' to it. We're not engaged anymore." She held up her hand. "Do you see a ring on this finger?"

"That's why I'm here." He shifted, digging in his jeans pocket, and pulled out a small velvet-covered box.

He opened the top and the ring, her ring, sparkled in the sun. The night he'd proposed, the night he'd first shown her the ring, a symbol of promise, a declaration of love and fidelity and a lifetime of ever-after, the joy—it all rushed back at her and it all seemed little more than a mockery now. "Because this ring isn't on your finger and that's wrong." She determinedly looked away from the ring. It was just a thing. "I want to make things right. I want this ring back on that finger. I love you. I want us to fix things. I want us back together."

She stood, unable to sit any longer, a restlessness gripping her. She hadn't expected the ring. She looked down at him and absently noticed his bald spot on the top of his head had grown. She'd known it was there and it hadn't mattered. Ring still in hand, he rose to his feet.

"Put the ring away before you lose it," she said.

"If I put it on your finger then we'll both know where it is."

She shook her head. "Put it back in your pocket. I'm not sure that's what I want anymore."

"Shh. Don't say anything else right now." He did, however, close the box and return it to his pocket. "Tansy, will you at least think about it? I'm begging you to give me another chance."

She wavered. She didn't know if she had it in her to give him a second chance. However, she found that she just couldn't walk away from him. She didn't know what she wanted.

She spoke slowly, weighing her words. "I'll think about it. You've got to give me some time."

"Thank you." He pulled her close and inhaled. "I've missed the way you smell." He nuzzled down her face and murmured, "The way you taste." For the first time in what felt like a lifetime his mouth was on hers. He smoothed his hand over her hip and pulled her closer to him. There was no missing his erection against her.

She pushed away. "Bradley..."

He tried to pull her close again. "I want you, lambchop. In every way."

She stepped back, out of his reach. "I said I'd think about us, but we're not just picking back up where we left off."

"I know. It's just hard, lambie." She could attest to that firsthand. And she'd always loved it when he called her that pet name, but it was sort of working her nerves right now. "I've missed you." He stepped behind her and wrapped his arms around her, pulling her back hard against him. His breath brushed against her neck as he murmured in her ear. She had always loved it when he did that. "I could make you feel so good." He cupped her breasts in his hands. "Let me kiss your vajayjay. You know I know just the way you like it."

She grabbed his wrist and forcibly moved his hands, stepping away from him. "Whoa, whoa and whoa." She turned to face him, taking another step back for good measure, putting physical distance between them. "I don't know if I even want to kiss you again. The vajayjay isn't a remote possibility." Good grief, give the man an inch and he would take a mile. How he went from her thinking about forgiving him to cunnilingus was mind-boggling. And insulting.

"Ever?" He gave her his puppy-dog look. She used to find it endearing. Now it was just sort of annoying.

"Drop it, Bradley."

He threw up both hands in mock surrender. "Okay, okay. What about dinner tonight?"

She spoke without hesitation. "No."

"It's that Marine, isn't it?"

"Bradley, I answered all the questions about Liam that I plan to answer. And I was generous when I did that. You don't have any right to quiz me about anything."

"You're right. I just—" he ran his hand through his hair "—I can't stand to think… It makes me crazy."

She knew exactly how he felt as she'd lain awake her fair share of nights thinking of him in bed with someone else. He'd live. "You'll just have to deal with it."

"You've changed."

"I have, haven't I?" She was stronger, more sure of who she was. She and Bradley had been an item for so long, she'd been so young when they'd become a couple. Who she was had always been tied up in "them." She'd had to find who she was without him. "You say that like it's not a good thing."

"I don't know."

She realized with a start that it really didn't matter whether Bradley liked the new her or not. She liked her.

LIAM WALKED INTO Gus's and it seemed as if the conversations died at once, everyone turning to look at him. He looked back. It was just a few seconds and conversations resumed but it was a weird feeling.

Obviously everyone was busy speculating on what was happening between him and Tansy now that her fiancé had turned up.

Bull motioned Liam over to a corner booth. "You sitting down or is it a grab and go?"

"Grab and go. Sven's pushing to get this phase done so he sent me over to pick up lunch." Being the least seasoned on the crew when it came to construction meant Liam was essentially the gofer.

Over Bull's shoulder, Mallory Kincaid smiled a greeting that held an invitation. Liam acknowledged her with a slight nod and then turned his attention back to Bull. "That woman's a pain."

"She seems nice enough."

"She's pushy as hell."

"She's got a job to do and she wants to do it well." Liam shrugged at Bull's assessment. He had more immediate things on his mind. "You met Bradley?" Bull said.

"After a fashion. I saw him. I wasn't impressed. Tansy said he was coming back out today."

"He went. He's back in town now. Petey picked him up about fifteen minutes ago." Bull looked over Liam's shoulder. The hair on the back of Liam's neck stood at attention. "Speak of the devil... He just walked in from the B and B."

The room didn't come to a standstill, but a hush settled, voices lowering to a murmur. Liam didn't turn around. He knew all he needed to know about Bradley—he hadn't treated Tansy right. He'd hurt her. The guy was an asshole and Liam would be just as happy to smash his face as look at him, but this was Tansy's call.

"Approaching," Bull said, spotting for him.

"I know." Liam felt Bradley closing in on him. He kept his back to him. Around them, the room quieted once again. The only sound was a soap opera running on the wall-mounted television. And then someone muted that and the only sound was something frying in the open kitchen.

Bradley stopped and called him out. "Reinhardt."

Liam turned, looked the other man square in the eye and stared him down. "Yes?"

"I'm Tansy's fiancé." In one of those moments where life was stranger than fiction, Tansy walked through the door, stopping dead in her tracks at the sight of him and Bradley facing off. "Stay away from her," Bradley said.

"The way I understand it, you *used* to be her fiancé. And it's Tansy's call whether or not I stay away from here."

"I plan to marry her."

Liam smiled without humor. "Is that a fact? Once again, I think that's up to her."

Tansy stepped forward and spoke up. "First, don't talk about me as if I'm not even here. Second, have you both lost your minds?"

"Bradley started it. Liam was minding his own business," someone piped up from the back of the room.

Tansy glared at her ex. "Okay, so Bradley, you've clearly lost your mind."

He shook his head. "I'm lost without you."

Damn. This guy was a pathetic excuse of a man. What the hell had Tansy ever seen in him? Liam wasn't much when it came to love and romance, but even he could see this guy wasn't right for the General.

"Oh, brother," someone else said from another corner of the room.

Tansy covered her face with her hands and shook her head. She dropped her hands to her sides. "Oh, my God, this is like some bad soap opera or reality TV show."

"This is way better than a soap," said a tall man with red hair and a shock of red beard.

"Shut up, Rooster," someone called out.

"Which one do you want, Tansy?" Rooster asked. "We've got some bets going."

Bradley spoke, holding out his hand. "Tansy—"

She cut him off. "Do not say another word." He opened his mouth and she glared at him. "Nothing. Nada."

What the hell? He hadn't done anything but respond to the guy, but she seemed thoroughly put out with both of them, which he put down to general embarrassment that she was being publicly discussed. Oh, well.

And Bradley, spineless wonder that he was, turned tail and headed back over to the bed-and-breakfast. Meanwhile, Tansy marched across the room, head held high, back ramrod straight, to the counter. "I'd like whatever today's special is. To go."

The waitress nodded. "Sure thing." She looked over at Liam and called out, "Your order is ready."

Liam crossed the room, heedless of the looks being thrown his way. Behind him, Bull called out, "Turn the TV back on."

At the pick-up counter Tansy ignored him. Giving her space seemed a wise tactic. Liam picked up the cardboard box containing the crew's lunch and silently left.

Sometimes the wisest course of action was retreat. It did not escape his attention, however, that Tansy had left the question of who she wanted unanswered.

"HOLY MOLY," JENNA SAID, shaking her head from behind the reception desk in the spa lobby as Tansy closed the door behind her.

Jenna had obviously already heard about the spectacle that had just played out. "Okay, that was fast, even for Good Riddance. I came straight here from Gus's."

She'd covered the distance from Gus's to Jenna's spa in about five minutes, seriously needing to talk to her sister.

"Alberta was texting me from the restaurant," Jenna said, stepping from behind the desk and hugging her.

Tansy hugged back and then shook her head, still feeling as if she'd just had some out-of-body experience. "Jenna, it was surreal."

Jenna nodded. "Kind of bizarre, too."

Uh, well, that's what surreal was but Tansy just kept it to herself. Jenna was a genius at business but sometimes in other areas...

Jenna slid her arm around Tansy's waist, as if sensing her sister was still in some kind of oh-hell-did-that-really-just-happen shock. "I've got ten minutes before Rachelle Richardson comes in for a set of nails. Ellie's in the massage room and they can't hear." She led her to the nail area. "We can talk over here."

Tansy sat in the seat across from Jenna, the small nail table between them. She recounted the walk in the woods with Bradley...down to the nitty-gritty details.

Jenna's mouth dropped open and she leaned across the table, lowering her voice even though she'd reassured Tansy there was no one around to overhear them. "You mean he offered to go down on you in the woods?" Jenna's blue eyes were as big as saucers. "Like he just rolled into town and said—"

"Uh-huh. Unbelievable." It was funny how a little distance and a different man had given her a whole new perspective. She'd been so wrapped up in Bradley as an ideal that she hadn't seen him clearly before. Her Prince Charming wasn't so charming after all.

"Seriously?"

"Yep."

"And you said no?"

Tansy laughed and shook her head at Jenna. "Jenna…"

"Well, I'm just saying you could have…"

Tansy grabbed her head with both hands. "I feel like flushing my head down a toilet. I don't know what I want anymore. Maybe somewhere inside, all this time I've been hating on him, I've wanted him to do exactly what he's doing now—well, show up that is, not make a scene in Gus's. I don't know. In a way, I moved on, but I think some part of me was waiting for him. I wanted him to come for me the way Logan came after you. I thought that's what I wanted. But somewhere along the way, without realizing it, I did move on."

"Liam?"

"He was definitely part of it. But it's me. Bradley said today that I've changed and I have."

Jenna pursed her lips. "So, what are you going to do?" She leaned in, her eyes sparkling with excitement as if she'd just had a great idea. "Are you going to sleep with both of them? Sort of a test run at the same time?"

Both exasperated and amused, Tansy laughed. "Jenna, I swear. You won an award for probably the oldest virgin in the state of Alaska when you finally slept with Logan, but now, girl, you are sex-crazy."

Her sister's grin was infectious. "It's fun. It feels good. At least it does with Logan. I wouldn't know about anyone else but that's okay because if it was any better than it is with us, I think I'd probably just expire from satisfaction and Emma needs her mommy." Jenna rubbed her hands together. "So, are you? Boy Toy One and Boy Toy Two test-drives?"

"As much as I hate to disappoint your lascivious little soul, no I'm not going to test-drive them. And they're both too old or I'm too young, but whichever way you look at it they're not boy toys."

"All right, already. So, what's the plan? Because failing to plan is planning to fail."

"My plan is to take a break from them so I can think."

"Exactly what do you mean take a break? Not have any contact with them?"

"Well, I'm definitely not going to sleep with either one of them right now. Sex won't do a thing but muddy the waters for me and I'm not sure if I even want to sit down and have dinner with either one of them. When I'm with one, the other is just going to be hovering in the background—I mean that figuratively, but Good Riddance is so small, it'd be literally, as well."

"What has Liam said about Bradley being here?"

"He really only had one thing to say last night."

"Which was?"

"He doesn't share. And I know what he means because he and I are casual, but I don't share, either."

"Are the two of you casual?"

"Of course. We haven't known each other very long. We just fell into a thing. I think we were both convenient for each other at the time."

"Maybe or maybe not. Maybe it's always been more than just that or maybe it started out as just that but has changed."

"I don't know. I can't even think about it right now."

Jenna laughed. "I beg to differ. I think it's exactly part of everything you have to think about right now."

"This is all so complicated. How is it that you think

you know what you want, and then when it happens, you're just not sure if it's really what you want? I know Bradley and I can never go back to what we had and that's a good thing because there were holes in our relationship that I didn't see before. But now I don't know if I want to move forward with him, either. And it's really not an either-or situation with Liam or Bradley. Just because I do or don't want Bradley doesn't mean I do or don't want Liam. That sounds so convoluted. Do you know what I mean?"

"Hey, those are the conversations I'm best at following. I know just what you mean. Maybe you don't want either one of them eating crackers in your bed."

Jenna had a unique way of putting things. "Exactly."

"So, maybe just because you don't want Liam, it doesn't mean that you do want Bradley, or vice versa. Do you still love Bradley?"

Did she love him? He'd been a part of her life for so long that while she'd hated him at first, she'd found some healing in time and this place. "I don't hate him. I don't still wish terrible things on him like I did at first. But I'm not sure if I'm still in love with him."

"How do you think he really feels? Could you ever trust him again? If you can't trust someone, you don't really have anything."

"I do think he loves me and that's not just wishful thinking on my part. But one thing I've figured out is that the other woman…that was about him, not me. I know it took a lot for him to come here and I do think he's desperate to have me back, otherwise he wouldn't have made that scene today with Liam in Gus's. And Liam… I just don't know. I don't know about any of it."

"Well, the good thing is, you don't have to make a

decision now or even today. You don't have to make a decision until you're ready."

"That's true enough. It's up to me to decide, but I do know I don't want to drag this out. For me, not knowing is always worse than making a decision or finding out one way or another and then dealing with those consequences. Plus, Bradley is going to be pinging around like a loose cannon until I give him something, one way or the other. It was mortifying to have him and Liam discussing me in public today." She wrapped her hands around one knee and rocked back and forth. "What was it like when Logan showed up here, after all that time?"

"I knew inside the moment I saw him even though I tried to deny it. It's funny. I still feel that rush when he walks into the room. It's not as intense as it used to be, but it's real and it's there. I think the rush will always be a part of me, of us."

Tansy nodded, intuitively knowing exactly what Jenna was talking about. She'd felt the same thing... the first time she'd seen Liam Reinhardt.

12

THE FOLLOWING AFTERNOON, Liam decided to forgo his ritual after-work swim in lieu of a visit with Bull. He hadn't seen hide nor hair of Tansy since she'd ignored him in Gus's yesterday, which wasn't surprising. The woman had a lot on her mind. So did he. The crazy, disturbing thing was he'd actually missed Wellington last night. What the hell was up with that?

He parked his bike in front of Bull's hardware store and went in. The metallic smell of tools and the sweet scent of sawdust greeted him. Bull sat on the other side of the counter whittling.

"Got a minute?" Liam said.

"Got lots of them," Bull said, working the wood chunk, which had yet to take on any particular shape. It sort of seemed symbolic of Liam's future, which was why he was here now. "What's on your mind?"

Liam leaned against the counter. "I wanted to run an idea by you."

"Sure thing." Seemingly focused on the wood and knife in his hands, his uncle waited.

"I've been thinking about something Tansy mentioned the other day. She suggested a survivalist training camp since I have a special ops background. She said this area invited that kind of person in the first place. The more I think about it, the more I think it might work." Bull nodded and Liam continued. "I appreciate Sven hiring me on but I can't see me doing that for more than a season. And dammit, I've got to do something." He pushed away from the counter and gave voice to the frustration that ate at him, that had been eating at him since he'd been handed his discharge papers. "I'm thirty-one years old and wondering what to do with my life now that I don't belong in the military anymore."

Bull whittled on.

Liam continued, "I had it all planned, but with that discharge… What the hell. I don't know what to do with myself."

"Life has a way of doing that." He stilled his knife and looked at Liam. "I was eighteen and had all kinds of plans…then I was drafted to go to Vietnam. That didn't quite go according to plan, either. I just wanted to do my rotation and get back home." He pointed to the scar on his neck with the knife's point. "It didn't quite work out that way and when I finally got back, all those plans I'd had before just didn't fit. So, yeah, sometimes you've got to punt on the goal line. I know your frustration."

"I've just been pissed…so pissed I don't know what to do with myself…and I didn't have the experience you did. How'd you handle it?"

Bull folded the knife and crossed his hands on his still-flat belly. "I went around angry for a long, long time until I finally figured out that wasn't getting me anywhere. Plus, I met Merilee and knew she was the damn best thing I'd ever come across. Finally figured out if all that other shit hadn't happened, I wouldn't have wound up meeting her, so maybe I should be glad for all the crap that came before because I sure as hell am glad for her. She's the best thing to ever happen to my life, bar none. Once I started looking at it that way, I could let the other stuff go."

He had a whole lot of respect for Bull but that struck Liam as some faulty logic. "But maybe you'd have met her if all the other stuff hadn't happened."

"Maybe. Maybe not. I'll never know because it did happen and it was the reason I wound up here and I met her here so, there you have it. Sometimes it's damn hard to see a door opening in your life because you're so pissed over the one that just slammed shut on you and caught you in the ass and hurt like hell while it was closing."

Liam wasn't convinced. "I suppose."

"You've got to open your mind to possibilities."

"I guess I'm getting there since I'm having this conversation with you. I've been so angry, all I could think about was how angry I was."

Bull grinned. "Tell me something I didn't know. Your mom thought you were coming here to heal. I called bullshit on that the second I saw your face. You just came here to wallow in the shit you found yourself in."

Liam winced. "Guilty as charged."

"Nothing to feel guilty about. But I'm glad to see you're ready to quit wallowing and get on with life. The survivalist camp is a good idea. With your reputation,

I think you could be booking out a training camp and having people on a waiting list."

Excitement stirred in Liam in response to Bull's enthusiasm. Bull wasn't a man given to hyperbole.

Liam had been turning the logistics over in his head. "I'd need a big tract of land that would still be close enough to transport participants and supplies."

"If there's one thing we've got up here, it's land," Bull said with a grin. "You might find yourself with fairly primitive conditions, but land isn't a problem."

He'd done primitive. Hell, he'd sat out the enemy for days at a time without any provisions. "If it's survivalist training, no one should expect the Hilton."

Bull grinned. "Have you given any thought to bringing someone in with you on the operation? You're going to need a second-in-command."

"I'd need some help, but I haven't gotten that far. I just wanted to toss it around with you first."

"Can I make a suggestion?"

"That's why I'm here."

"Dirk."

Instinctively Liam rubbed his hand over his jaw. "What about him?" Surely, Bull wasn't thinking...

"You should bring him in with you on this."

"Dirk's a loose cannon. He knocked the hell out of me."

"Yeah and then he helped you up and you guys were okay. I know Dirk's always been a rolling stone but that's because he's got all the qualities of a second-in-command. He's just been looking for a commander and a spot he fits in."

Right off the top of his head, he wasn't seeing it,

nonetheless he respected Bull and his opinions. "I'll think about it."

"Just turn it over in your head a bit. Now, what about Tansy?"

"Wellington as part of my crew?" Damn, if Bull wasn't stretching the bounds of rationality there.

Bull chuckled. "No, Tansy just as Tansy."

"She's an interesting woman."

Bull stood and clapped him on the back. "You may be surprised at all the doors you find opening."

TANSY LEVERED HERSELF up off the couch. She was tired of her own head and her own company. She'd done nothing but think, think and think some more. Jenna had kept her updated on what Bradley had spent his day doing—warming a seat at Gus's, shooting a few games of pool and nursing beers. He'd called and texted. She wasn't being a bitch, but she needed some time away from him to think, which was ironic considering she'd had a couple of months away from him. But this was different thinking. He was just a few minutes away. And he wanted her to go back with him. And she wanted to think about something else. She wanted a distraction.

Night had settled around the cabin and over the lake. An owl hooted in the distance. Farther away still, a wolf howled. Within a few minutes another wolf answered. The scent of woodsmoke drifted in on the night air. She wandered outside and around the back of the cabin.

Liam sat near a fire pit where wood snapped and popped, casting an orange glow. A mat on the ground held various pieces of what looked like a rifle. He glanced over as she approached.

"Hi," she said. "Are you up for some company or are you enjoying your solitude?"

"Company is fine. Have a seat."

Tansy settled on a log to his right. It wasn't exactly cold, but the autumn nights had grown chilly and Tansy welcomed the fire's warmth. She hugged her arms to her knees and watched as he deftly cleaned the part in his hand. He had nice hands. Strong, capable. Sexy. Her body hummed, remembering the feel of them against her, gripping her thighs, testing the weight of her breasts.

"You have enough light to do that?" she said.

"I could do this in the dark blindfolded."

"Ah." She shifted. "I'm sorry about…well, yesterday at Gus's."

"You don't owe me an apology because you didn't do anything."

She had been angry at finding them discussing her but in retrospect, she realized Liam had simply been in the wrong place at the wrong time. Bradley had been the one who made her business public. Given his privacy issues, Liam had probably found it as embarrassing as she had, perhaps more so. "Bradley was—"

"You're not responsible for him. You didn't do anything so you don't owe me an apology."

"Okay. Nice fire. Reminds me of when I was a Girl Scout. You don't have any s'mores fixings, do you?"

His teeth flashed in the firelight. "Fresh out. So, you were a Girl Scout?"

"Of course."

"I bet you sold a lot of cookies."

"My fair share. Were you a Boy Scout?" She wasn't seeing it.

"Nope. That just wasn't my thing."

"I didn't think so, but I thought I'd ask anyway."

"We were too busy playing in the woods, hunting and fishing."

They exchanged tales of childhood misdemeanors, silly stories that made each other laugh. It was quiet and relaxed. There was something comfortable about his voice, the warmth of the fire and the night's darkness. They talked about a little bit of everything and a lot of nothing but it was nice.

"Do you want to go inside?" he said.

"No. I just wanted to share the campfire and some conversation."

"I understand." He hesitated. "I don't want to be presumptuous, but don't make any decisions based on me, Tansy. I'm trying to figure out my life. I don't have anything for anyone right now."

"I'm not." And she wasn't. "This is between me and Bradley, which is why I don't want to cloud the water with anything else." For all of his gruffness, abruptness and lack of adherence to social dictates, he really was a very nice man. "Can I ask you a very personal question, and it's really none of my business, so feel free to tell me to mind my own business."

"Ask and I reserve the right to not answer."

"Were you faithful to your wife?" The question hung in the night air and she found herself holding her breath as to whether he'd answer.

He did. "Yes. There was never another woman. There was my career and long separations, but there was no one else. I'm a man of my word."

She was somewhat surprised he'd answered. However, his answer itself didn't surprise her. It simply confirmed what she'd thought of him and his character. "That's what I thought. Thanks for answering."

"You'll figure it out, Wellington. I have great faith in you."

There was nothing left to figure out. She had all the answers she needed.

MALLORY CLICKED HER TAPE recorder to the Off position on the kitchen table. "Thank you."

Liam had left it down to the wire but he'd finally contacted her and granted an interview. She'd extended her stay. She'd known that day that she'd left his cabin that he'd come around, if for no other reason than to make sure she got her facts straight. But there was so much more to it than that. He had to have finally tuned in to this cosmic connection between the two of them. Her inner self was so tuned in to him, he *had to be* equally tuned in to her.

They'd arranged for her to come out to his cabin. He'd said it was simply for the sake of the interview not being interrupted. The only other real choice had been her room at the bed-and-breakfast and that didn't really work. There were a few tables that overlooked the main street in the front of the airstrip office, but that place had a steady flow of people coming and going so that had been out. Mallory, however, was certain he'd simply wanted the time alone with her, to get to know her better.

And now the business portion was finished—he was the kind of man who'd always take care of business before pleasure. They'd spent a couple of hours on the interview.

She'd dressed carefully, wanting to look professional

but also wanting to strike a feminine, alluring note. She packed away her notes and the recorder. She'd been in love with him from before she ever met him face-to-face here. Her friend Yvonne had dared to tell Mallory she was obsessed. Mallory, however, had known she'd found her soul mate. She and Yvonne were no longer friends. Just as she'd known he'd be, Liam, in person, was even more potent than on the video she'd seen, and the dry facts in his personnel file and other records hadn't done him justice, either.

"Can I buy you dinner?" she said as she stood to leave.

A perplexed frown furrowed his brow. "I thought you got all the information you needed."

Ah, he wanted to play a game with her, because him not being attracted to her simply wasn't an option. One of her girlfriends had told her once that she was pretty without being so gorgeous that she scared men off. It seemed to be true enough because sitting at home on a weekend night wasn't an issue. However, most men bored her. As a military historian, she dealt with men who were larger than life. Heroes. Most ordinary men simply couldn't measure up. Her last love interest had been a retired lieutenant colonel in his fifties. There was something about that combination of authority and power that did it for her. Liam Reinhardt was a man of incredible skill, valor, and he was damn hot to boot. Her man.

She was used to going for what she wanted. If you didn't ask, if you didn't throw the line out there, you didn't get. She cast her line. And this wasn't simply want—this was destiny. "This isn't business. You're very attractive, and one of the most fascinating men I've ever met."

He paused and she found herself holding her breath. "I'm flattered—" that foreshadowed a big old *but* "—and you're very pretty, but I'm going to pass. It's been a long day and I just want to kick back."

What? She couldn't just give up on them, on the future she *knew* they were meant to have together.

"I totally understand kicking back. I'd be glad to bring over takeout or I make a mean spaghetti sauce."

She saw it in his eyes before he even opened his mouth. "Thanks, but no."

No. No? It was that Wellington bitch next door. She'd clouded Liam's thinking, his perception. Mallory was for him. She recognized what a hero he was. She loved him, dammit. She was what he needed, not Tansy Wellington.

Mallory wanted to cry and kick and scream. Instead, she nodded. "I'll be in touch then if I find I missed anything."

And that was that...for now.

TANSY WALKED INTO THE airstrip office. Alberta had a tarot-card reading going over in the corner with a tourist. Dwight, Lord Byron and Jefferson were all huddled around the chessboard. Merilee and Dalton Saunders, the other bush pilot, were going over a schedule.

Merilee looked across the room to Tansy. "He's out of here in two hours."

"I know."

Merilee nodded. "Room three. All the way at the other end of the hall, next to the bathroom."

Tansy mounted the stairs. She'd slept on it, waited

until the last minute, had searched her heart one last time before she drove over here. She walked down the hall, her shoes echoing on the wood floor. She knocked. Bradley opened the door. "Come on in."

He looked terrible. There was a time, when she was so angry at his betrayal, she would've been near gleeful. Now she simply felt sad.

"Dammit, Tansy," he said, tears gathering in his eyes.

She didn't even have to say it. He saw it in her eyes, on her face. "It's just no use, Bradley. I care about you, but I just can't... It's not going to work."

"So does that mean you never loved me? Because if you loved me, you could forgive me. Is this just your way of punishing me?"

She shook her head. "This has nothing to do with punishing you. It told me something about the man you are and something about the woman I am and you're right, it did change me. I can't regret it because I grew from it. It was definitely growing pains, but growth nonetheless. So, we're not the same people we were and the people we've become don't belong together. It's time for both of us to move on."

She wrapped her arms around him and kissed him softly on the cheek. "Thank you for coming, Bradley. You set me free. I was stuck and you've unstuck me."

Tansy could see it in his eyes. He didn't get it, not even a little bit, which was even further proof that the two of them didn't belong together, not that she doubted it.

He grabbed her wrist, but not too tightly. "It's that Marine, isn't it?"

"No. How I feel about you has nothing to do with Liam."

"If I had gotten here a week before him——"

"It wouldn't have made any difference. This is about you and me, not me and him. It wasn't an either-or situation. And you and me aren't going to work."

That particular lightbulb still wasn't going off for him, but it really didn't matter. She'd said what she had to say and it was time for them to permanently part ways.

"Travel safe, Bradley. I wish you well."

"Yeah, right."

She simply shook her head as she closed the door behind her. Now she had one more piece of business to set in order.

She went downstairs and cut through the connecting door to Gus's. She really, really wasn't into making her life a public spectacle but within no time everyone would know Bradley had left without her and she wanted to make one point clear.

She made her way to where Rooster was sitting. As far as she could tell, Rooster's main income stream was operating as the local bookie. Rooster took bets on anything and everything and people placed bets on anything and everything. Some places had dog-track racing, some places had horse racing, Good Riddance just had the ins and outs of life that they bet on.

Norris, a retired newspaper reporter, and her boyfriend, a short man whose name Tansy never could remember, were sitting at the table with Rooster. Good, they could vouch for the information. "Hello——" she didn't see any point in beating around the bush "——I know there are bets placed and soon enough it'll go around that Bradley is leaving alone. I need to clarify that just because I didn't choose Bradley, I haven't chosen Liam, either."

"Let me get this straight 'cause it makes a difference in how the bets are paid out. You didn't choose Bradley and you didn't choose Liam. You didn't choose either one of them. Got it." He looked beyond Tansy's shoulder. "You got it?"

Tansy knew before she turned, before she heard the voice.

"Got it," Liam said.

Well, that was one way for him to find out.

13

LIAM FINISHED UP HIS NOTES and supply list with a renewed sense of purpose. He didn't still feel so angry that he couldn't think anymore. Talking to Mallory Kincaid had ultimately been a good thing, even though he'd been getting a kind of weird vibe from her, especially after the interview. The interview, however, had been a good thing.

He'd gained a perspective on his time in the military. It was the past, just like his marriage was the past. He'd always been so sure that a career in the military was his destiny, was where he belonged. And if he went with Bull's philosophy, that clearly was the case. So, he could go around being angry at the world and the unfairness of life or he could regroup. Nope. Life wasn't particularly fair. There wasn't a damned thing fair about life as far as he could tell. He'd seen too much of it to be that naive—there was no equity in the way some of the villagers lived in Iraq and Afghanistan. There was no equity in the way some Americans lived. What had been fair about Bull being a POW for two years? What had been fair in guys losing body parts to roadside bombs and living as half men? Nope. He could safely say fair wasn't part of life.

He could also safely say that he didn't have any control over having been kicked out—okay, discharged on a medical—but the thing he could control was what he did from this point out. He could sit around in his own crap, stinking up himself and the world, or he could get up, clean up and move forward.

That interview with Kincaid felt like moving forward. Making plans for his future, finding a purpose, felt like moving forward. He'd talked to Bull and was moving forward on exploring setting up a camp. He'd spent some time looking over topographical maps and he'd scheduled a reconnaissance flyover for tomorrow.

He picked up the two-way handset and "rang" Tansy next door.

"Wellington, how's your schedule looking day after tomorrow? Want to take a trip?"

"What kind of trip and for how long?"

"Just a couple of days. We'd be gone two nights and it'd be camping with no facilities. Just thought I'd ask, but no problem if it's not your thing."

"Keep talking. You've got my interest."

"I'm going to go look at a piece of property for that survivalist camp you mentioned. Either Dalton or Juliette will fly me in. I'll take a couple of days to hike around and get a feel for the terrain and then they'll pick me up a couple of days later."

"I see. So, like no running water, no toilets, no beds."

"A stream runs through the property. I'll pack a latrine shovel. And there will be a tent and sleeping bags with bedrolls under them. Gourmet freeze-dried rations. Deluxe accommodations."

"What about snakes and bears and other wildlife?"

"All possible. Fairly probable, in fact."

"What if something happens or there's an emergency?"

"We radio base and they fly in and pick us up. You ever been camping before?"

"Hel-lo. Remember, I was a Girl Scout. All Girl Scouts go camping at one time or another. We stayed in these little teepee things with platforms for our sleeping bags."

"Bathroom and showers?"

"Not in the teepees. We had to walk to get there and all the showers were in a row."

"But you've never done any wilderness camping?"

"Well, not exactly."

She'd be perfect. If she could do this, then greenhorns could. She'd be a good barometer. "You need to know, though, that if you go I'm not going to babysit you. You have to carry your own gear and keep up."

"When do we go?"

"Day after tomorrow."

She swallowed. "Okay. What do I need to do to get ready?"

"I'll pull together your gear. You put together some clothes and I'll look them over. Remember, you've got to carry everything on your back. How about I come over tomorrow evening and sign off on your clothes."

"I'll see you then."

"Are you going to feed me or do I need to bring dinner from Gus's?"

"I'll feed you."

"One more thing, Wellington. Now that Bradley has gone, are we still on a sex moratorium?"

"That's just so…romantic…really, Reinhardt."

"Would that be a yes or no?"

"That would be an I'm-still-thinking-about-it."

THE NEXT AFTERNOON, Tansy stirred her soup with one hand and answered the phone with the other.

"Please tell me the grapevine is wrong," Jenna said without preamble.

"I was going to call you but I got on a roll with the book today and just went with it." And she'd known Jenna would flip a gasket.

"Have you lost your mind?"

There went the gasket. "It'll be an adventure. When am I going to get this opportunity again?"

"Hmm. And it doesn't have anything to do with the fact that you're going with Liam?"

"Of course it does. He knows what he's doing. In fact, he and Bull went out or up or whatever you call it with Dalton, looking at it from the plane."

"I know that. Everyone knows everything here. I did not, however, know my sister had signed on for the trip."

"I swear I was going to call you in a bit."

"I'm not worried about that. I'm worried about you. Is it safe?"

"I'm not sure I'd feel safe going with anyone else. Like I said, when will I get this opportunity again? Plus, it was my idea he do this camp thing so it'll be pretty cool to be checking it out."

"I suppose if you're going to do something awful like that, he's the best guy to be with. But better you than me. When are you getting back?"

"Sunday afternoon."

"I'm holding a spot for you for a massage and a mani/pedi on Monday. You're going to need it."

Tansy laughed. "I'm up for all of the above even when I'm not coming in off of a wilderness experience, so thanks. I'm sure I'll be ready for it."

"No doubt. I bet you break at least one nail out there."

"Who knows? Once Liam gets this off the ground, you'll probably be signing up for one of the sessions."

"Sure. When aliens take over my body I'll be right there."

Tansy laughed and a knock sounded on her door. "Gotta run."

"Yeah, Emma's got a dirty diaper over here. Later. But you'd better stop by on your way out tomorrow."

"Will do."

Tansy opened the front door to Liam and her heart thudded against her ribs just at the sight of him.

"What was so funny?" he said.

"Jenna. She thinks I've lost my mind going on this adventure."

Liam grinned and her heart sort of somersaulted in her chest. "She would. I bet she's worried you're going to break a nail."

How'd he know that? "That was exactly what she said."

He leveled a look at her. "Your sister runs a spa and nail salon, of course that's what she'd say."

She almost blurted out that she'd missed him. She didn't realize until right now, with him next to her, just how very much she'd missed him. Her heart felt happy for the first time in a long time…. Actually, her heart had never felt happy this way ever.

Ever practical, Liam said, "Okay, let's take a look at what you've got."

Tansy led him back to where she had her clothes laid out on the end of her bed.

Within seconds he'd reduced her pile by two-thirds. "That's what you need to bring."

"But—"

"No nightgown. You need to sleep in your clothes so you can be ready to roll out at a moment's notice. You only need one extra pair of panties. No bra change. One shirt and one extra pants, three pairs of clean socks and a rain poncho. No makeup. No perfume. Leave everything but your toothbrush here."

Tansy bit back the urge to lobby for some additional items. This was his area of expertise and she'd respect that. "What about a hair brush?"

"A comb would be better. It weighs less and takes up less room."

"Okay, a comb it is."

"You nervous?"

"A little. Mostly excited."

"Want to see a topographical map?"

It was kind of sexy the way that sounded when he said it. "Sure."

Pulling out a map, Liam opened it on the bed. He showed her where they were and where they were going. "See, the great thing about this piece is that it straddles the tree line so you have some barren areas and some wooded areas, which makes for a nice mix of training opportunities."

"I see." What she saw was the way the hair covered his forearm, the way his biceps bunched when he pointed. She ran her finger down his arm. "Speaking of straddling…"

"Oh, yeah?" He grinned and tossed the map to the

top of the pile of clothes on the other side of the bed. He turned and in one swift movement, sat on the bed and pulled her on top of him, which did, in fact, leave her straddling him in intimate proximity.

She linked her arms around his neck. "Yeah." She nipped at his jaw and then his lips.

Gazing at him, realization clicked into place. She loved this man. In one short week she'd found something she'd never had with Bradley, never felt with Bradley. There was nothing conventional or convenient or even seemingly rational about the way she felt about, with or for Liam.

She wasn't ready to say the words and he definitely wasn't ready to hear them. But she could show him.

And she proceeded to do just that with her body... and her heart.

GENERAL WELLINGTON WAS a trouper, he'd hand her that.

"We'll set up camp for the night here," Liam said. It was a nice, small clearing that was relatively flat. They were a decent distance from the stream and would re-cross it in the morning to refill their water, but they were far enough away to keep some distance between themselves and the wildlife that would be drawn to the water.

"Okay." She shrugged out of the pack she'd carried all day and put it on the ground.

Actually, he'd hand her a whole hell of a lot. She hadn't whined or complained all day, even though they'd covered a good bit of ground. Liam was used to operating on his own, but it'd been nice having her along. She was a good person to bounce ideas off of.

"You gather up some firewood while I pitch the tent

and set up the rest of camp. We need small sticks for kindling and bigger pieces to keep it going."

She propped her hands on her hips. "I know that. Sheesh. I was a Girl Scout. Remember?"

Liam laughed. "Okay, Girl Scout, get to it."

"Yessir, sir." She offered a smart-ass grin and a mocking salute as she started reconnoitering the area.

An hour later, Liam passed Tansy a plate of reconstituted beef Stroganoff. "Here you go. The finest in freeze-dried meals."

She took a bite. "Oh, my God, that's good. I didn't expect it to be so tasty."

Liam laughed. "That's what hiking all day will do for you. It wouldn't taste nearly as good if you were sitting in your kitchen at home."

"So, is this what it's like when you're out in the military?"

"In some ways."

"Tell me about it." She smiled at him, her spoon poised over her plate, across the campfire. "You know that's what Girl Scouts do when they camp. They sit around the fire and tell stories."

"Yeah? That's what soldiers do, too. What kind of stories do you want?"

"Whatever you want to tell. If you don't want to talk about the nitty-gritty parts, then just tell me the other."

"The interesting part is that you have these guys who are from different places, different backgrounds, a whole range of personalities, but you're all working toward one common goal." He told her about the guys in his outfit, about Renwald, his spotter who had been his eyes out on missions. Once he started talking, he found he couldn't stop. And it was different from talking to Mallory Kincaid. With Tansy it became personal. He found himself opening up, sharing a part of himself he'd never shared before, not even with Natalie, because Tansy seemed to get him, to understand.

"I like your stories," she said.

"I'm not usually much of a talker."

"You're a good storyteller."

"You're a good listener." He pushed to his feet. "Let's get this cleaned up and the packs in the trees."

"Packs in the trees?" she said as she stood.

"Yeah. We need to clean up away from camp and then hang the packs in the trees to keep out bears and other wildlife. And no food, not even gum or mints, in the tent. Nothing with any scent." He shook his head at her expression. "Guess your troop leader didn't cover that in training, huh?"

She eyed the tree line. "If she did, I forgot. Let's get it done. I really don't want any four-legged visitors."

"Yep. Don't worry. We'll be fine."

They went to the other side of the clearing and into the woods a bit and washed up. Then they backtracked to the other side and he made quick work of rigging their packs up high enough off of the ground and far enough out on a tree. "That should be fine."

Walking back to the camp, she said, "Liam, I have a question."

"Shoot."

She grinned in the descending darkness. "Exactly. Would you teach me to shoot a gun?"

He was only a little surprised by her question. "Have you ever fired a weapon before?"

They were back by the campfire where their tent sat

a short distance from the fire. He sat back down on the log and she did, as well.

She shook her head. "No. I'd like to learn, though."

"Sure. The first thing you need to do is learn about the weapon itself before you do anything else. We could do a basic lesson if you want to."

"That would be awesome."

He unholstered the Glock and took out all the ammunition and then double-checked again that it was empty. "The first rule of thumb is you always handle a weapon as if it's loaded, even when it's not. Don't ever point it at anyone unless you're planning to use it."

He gave her a rundown of the components and basic operation. In the flickering firelight, her gaze was intent. She asked intelligent questions and most importantly, when he handed her the weapon, she wasn't tentative, but she also wasn't careless and cocky.

"You've got a natural grip and you seem pretty comfortable with it," he said.

"It is comfortable. It's not as heavy as I thought it would be."

"Be careful where you're aiming it, but go ahead and practice the grip."

"How's this?" She followed his instructions to a T.

He was impressed. "Not bad, Wellington. In fact, damn good. Is it still comfortable in your hand?"

"I like the way your gun feels in my hand."

She didn't know what she was saying, which made it all the funnier.

"What? What's so funny?"

"There's a saying—this is my weapon, this is my gun. One is for fighting, one is for fun."

A purely sensual smile lit her face and eyes. "Hmm. I

see. Well, I like the way both your weapon and your gun feel in my hand…and the gun in other places, too. In fact, maybe it's time for me to handle your gun again."

"Hand me my weapon." She did, adhering to his safety rules. He reloaded it and put it away while she waited silently. "Now, come here, woman, and handle my gun."

TANSY NURSED A CUP of hot coffee the next morning while Liam cooked breakfast. She was fairly amazed by how well she'd slept considering it was in a sleeping bag on a bedroll on the ground in a tent. She'd felt safe in a tent with Liam. She'd even been okay to get up this morning without a shower and take care of her business behind a bush. All told, she was actually having a great time roughing it.

"I'm pretty happy we made it through the night without being visited by any wild animals."

He grinned at her over the small cookstove. "I don't know. I was pretty into the wild animal in my tent last night. That was fairly spectacular."

"It was, wasn't it? Having fired your gun a couple of times, maybe you could teach me to shoot your weapon if we have some time this morning."

"We could do that. We have time. Now, keep your strength up and eat."

"How much ground do you want to cover today?" They'd hiked about five miles yesterday, which didn't sound like a lot but it had been rugged, somewhat mountainous terrain and they'd been trailblazing. It had been arduous but invigorating.

"We should cover about twelve miles today but it'll be different. We're moving north so once we get through the first three miles or so, we're going to be in much more open terrain with sparse trees. You'll need to layer on your other shirt tonight."

"I'm glad you asked me to come."

"Yeah? We'll see if you still feel that way tomorrow." There was no sting in his words and he grinned. She supposed it was early and they still had a lot of ground to cover. "Let's clean up, break camp, and then we'll get in your firing round before we start."

Half an hour later, Liam looked at her, admiration glinting in his eyes. "You're a quick study, Wellington, and a natural marksman. You sure you never did this before?"

It was ridiculous how good his praise made her feel, and it was all the more meaningful because she knew he wasn't one to hand out praise lightly or blithely. Plus, coming from a man who was one of the best at what he did… "No. Never before."

"Damn good job. Now, you reload the way I told you…that's right…barrel pointing down…yep…now, safety on. Good job. And you remember the most important thing about handling a weapon?"

"Yep. You don't have it if you aren't willing to use it."

"That's right." She passed the weapon to him and he holstered it. "Okay, sharpshooter, ready to march?"

Happiness, contentment and excitement surged through her. Good grief but she loved this man. "Lead on…as long as I don't have to sing cadence."

It was a spectacularly glorious day.

14

THE HAIR ON THE BACK of Liam's neck stood up. Something wasn't right. He couldn't shake a feeling he'd had for a while, and the deal was, when you couldn't shake a feeling, you listened to it because it meant something wasn't right. It had saved his ass more times than he could count.

He didn't want to alarm Tansy but he looked around for an area to take cover. Already the vegetation was less dense, the trees increasingly sparse. According to the topographical map, they were going to be in open terrain in about half a mile and that wasn't feeling safe at this moment.

Something, or someone, was watching them. If it was a friend, they'd have made themselves known by now, which only left him to surmise he was dealing with an unknown foe.

"Let's take a break over here," he said, eyeing a small boulder in a clump of trees. It had become increasingly rocky.

"We can keep going. I'm really not tired."

"We're breaking." He took her hand and steered her none too gently.

Tansy glanced at him. "I was just saying. Okay."

He'd hurt her feelings. It was all in her voice and all over her face. He'd slipped back into full military mode but she was still in aren't-we-having-a-good-time-in-the-woods mode. He had a bad, bad feeling that was all about to change.

His sixth sense, on red alert, led him to grab her and pull her down behind the boulder's cover.

"What are you—"

He'd heard the crack-bang. Any marksman recognized the bang of a rifle being fired and the crack as it impacted its target. The bullet lodged in the tree to their left.

Reflexively, he already had his rifle out and in his hands. "Someone's shooting at us." Actually, the shot had been aimed at Tansy. Had he been the target, the bullet would've landed to the right.

Her eyes widened and the color drained from her face. "What? Why?"

"I don't know why. Do everything I tell you, when I tell you. Got it?"

She nodded mutely. He listened. It was faint, but there. A branch cracked. Based on the shooter's probable position per the entry angle of the bullet into the tree and that crack, he was circling to their left.

Liam motioned Tansy over farther behind the boulder. He unholstered the Glock and passed it to her. She shook her head.

He nodded and pressed it into her hand. "I may need you to back me up and you may need to protect yourself," he said directly into her ear, his voice low. "Just make damn sure you don't shoot me."

A resolution joined the fear in her eyes. Her lips a straight line, she nodded. There was an off chance that the shot had been fired by a hunter who had mistaken them for game. He didn't think so, but he had to cover their bases. To call out wasn't giving away their location, because their location was already known. And whoever had fired that shot was working with a rifle and a scope, which should have given the shooter a clear view. Nonetheless, he wasn't moving them out and being mistaken by some overzealous hunter again.

"Hey," he called out. "Hold your fire. People here."

His words echoed through the woods and were met with nothing but silence. The woods were too sparse for the shooter not to have heard. To get off a shot and have it land that close, and based on the fairly straight entry line of the bullet into the tree, Liam estimated it had been fired from no more than one hundred and thirty-seven meters, definitely close enough for the person to hear him call out.

He scanned the woods through the scope. Nothing. He lowered his rifle. They were going to have to move. It would've been a whole helluva lot easier had he been by himself, or if Tansy was trained personnel. He had worn his BDUs but Tansy was in jeans and a red shirt. He pulled off his pack and yanked out his extra military-issue brown T-shirt, then took her pack off of her back. "Take off your T-shirt and put this on."

Thank God she had the sense not to question him. He reached down and grabbed a handful of dirt, smearing it on his face and arms. He motioned for her to do the same to her face, arms and neck. She did. He shrugged back into his pack.

"We're going to move out now. Leave your pack." He could handle his. Hers would slow her down. Plus, she was only carrying her clothes and sleeping bag. "Stay low. Be as quiet as possible. We're going to backtrack in a zigzag pattern, using the trees and brush as much as possible for cover. Got it?"

She nodded. "I'm scared."

"You should be." She was taking this seriously. She should. Someone was stalking them.

TANSY'S HEART WAS THUMPING so hard she could hear the blood rushing in her ears. Fear like she'd never known before coursed through her, filled her mouth with a bitter metallic taste.

She squatted behind a bush while Liam scanned the area behind them. He pointed to his left and she nodded. Another dash for cover when all she really wanted to do was sit and cower and have this all be over. They made it to their next destination and he motioned for her to drop and stay. Gladly. A bullet whizzed past her to her left. Liam was positioned to her right.

Liam eased into a prone position and pulled out his binoculars. He scanned the woods again. He'd done that each time. His hands were steady. His breathing slow. His face impassive, devoid of any emotion. She was shaking like a leaf. She felt as if she was running a marathon.

She thought about all the things she wanted to do and it wasn't die in the woods in the middle of nowhere. Anger kicked in, tamping back the fear. This was madness. She'd descended into a hell she didn't understand.

Calmly, methodically, he braced his rifle on a branch
and used his scope. He positioned himself with one leg
under him, his upper body off the ground. It was as if
he quit breathing, his body grew so still, and then he
moved his finger against the trigger. She jumped at the
shot, even though she knew it was coming.

A terrible screeching filled the air.

"Got him," Liam said. "And now I want some answers."

"How do you know it's safe? There might be more
than one."

"If there was more than one, we'd be dead. I didn't
aim to kill, just to wound. I want answers and a dead
man can't talk."

The screeching gave way to sobs and moans. "You
can stay here—"

The thought nauseated her. And she was infinitely
relieved it wasn't her or him, but was some nameless
stranger. Bile rose in her throat and she lay there and
puked. Fear, and everything else, spilling out of her as
she emptied her stomach. Liam waited, his hand on her
shoulder. When she was through he passed her a ban-
danna. She wiped her mouth.

He sat up and pulled her to him. Fear roiled through
her again. "Get back down," she said frantically, trying to get both her and him back to the ground safely.
She felt exposed sitting up.

"Do you hear that thrashing? That's someone with
a serious injury trying to get away. His trigger arm
and hand is disabled. And I want some answers before
whoever it is loses too much blood and can't give any
answers."

She pulled herself together. "Okay." She handed him back his Glock.

He holstered it. "Once again, follow my instructions. He's wounded, which will make him still dangerous."

They moved fast, Liam with his Glock drawn.

The thrashing had ceased but it wasn't difficult to follow the trail of blood. He motioned her to his left, to take cover behind a tree. The shooter lay propped against a tree, eerily outfitted in camouflage gear, face paint and a camouflage hat. The chest was still moving up and down but the right arm hung useless, blood flowing steadily from a debilitating wound. There was something vaguely, disturbingly familiar about the figure slumped against the tree. At Liam's approach, the shooter looked up.

"She needs to die so we can be together," Mallory Kincaid said, pain and madness shining in her eyes. "I love you."

LIAM WRAPPED THE LAST of Tansy's shredded T-shirt into a makeshift bandage and stood. "She's lost a fair amount of blood but she's young and strong. Her pulse and heart rate are steady, so that's a good sign."

Tansy nodded but said nothing. After her initial horrified expression when it had become clear that Mallory, mentally unstable and clearly obsessed with Liam, had set out to kill her, Tansy had pretty much shut down.

She'd dutifully helped organize the supplies and assisted him in stabilizing the other woman, but she hadn't looked at Mallory and she hadn't spoken other than monosyllabic responses. Acute stress reaction. He'd seen it time and time again.

He put his arms around her and held her close.

"Tansy, it's okay. You're fine. I'm fine. It's all going to be okay."

"What do we do now?"

"Now that she's bandaged, I'm going to secure her to the tree with our rope, just as a precaution. I needed your help stopping the bleeding, but now you can stay away from her. It would probably be best."

Tansy shivered. "The three of us are going to be out here together tonight, aren't we?"

He patiently went over it again with her. At least she hadn't descended into hysteria. "Hopefully not. She needs medical attention. Hopefully they can pick us up north of here, where it opens up."

He got on the two-way and Merilee came back to him. As briefly and concisely as possible, he outlined the situation. He waited while she arranged for an emergency medical chopper.

Tansy sat on the ground, her arms wrapped around her knees, staring in the other direction.

Within minutes Merilee came back with an evacuation ETA and pick-up coordinates. It would be four hours until the medevac helicopter would arrive…and in the meantime Liam and Tansy had to get Mallory to the designated area. It would be too late for her to be portaged out after the chopper arrived.

Liam approached Tansy and explained the situation. "I can rig together a stretcher but I'm going to need your help in transporting her. Are you up to that? If not, I'll manage but if we're working together, it'll keep her stabilized. I understand if it's something you can't do."

For a moment he wondered if she had even heard him as she stared straight ahead. Finally, she turned to look at him, squaring her shoulders as she stood. "Tell me what we need to do."

In fairly short order he and Tansy had fashioned together a stretcher of branches and sleeping bag. He used the other sleeping bag as a blanket. Although it was a warm enough day, Kincaid didn't need to go into further physical shock from her trauma. He secured her to the stretcher with the other rope.

"If you'll carry her feet, I'll take her head." The feet were much lighter and he wasn't even sure that Tansy was going to be up to that. "Use your legs to lift, not your back. Ready? On three. One. Two. Three. Lift."

It was slow going as the terrain was uneven and there was no designated path. Not once did Tansy complain or loosen her grip, although she did request a break a couple of times near the end. Her arms had to be burning with exertion. Mallory Kincaid wasn't overweight, but she was a tall woman with an athletic build—she was no lightweight.

Mallory drifted in and out of consciousness. Tansy remained quiet and Liam simply reassured her they were getting her help. She obviously needed more than medical attention but medical care was his primary objective at this point.

They had reached the clearing and rested about ten minutes when he heard the approaching *thwack-thwack-thwack* of rotors. He stood but Tansy remained seated some distance away from where they'd deposited Mallory.

The chopper touched down and an emergency team disembarked, heading toward Mallory stat. Within minutes they had her loaded onto the helicopter.

Tansy had stood and watched everything unfold from

a distance. Liam approached her now. It was time for her to go.

"Come on, let's get you loaded on the chopper."

She looked at him. "What about you?"

"There's only room for one of us, so on you go."

She shook her head. "I'm not leaving."

"Tansy, be reasonable."

"I came with you and I'm not leaving until you leave." A fierceness pierced the numbness in her eyes.

"I'm used to these kinds of conditions. I'm used to operating alone. I'm ordering you to get on that helicopter."

She crossed her arms over her chest. "And I came with you and I'll leave with you."

He shook his head at the pilot and gave them the liftoff signal.

General Wellington was a helluva woman.

TANSY FELT NUMB, DETACHED. The whole thing had been surreal. No one had ever tried to kill her before. It wasn't a good feeling. The thought was so ludicrous she had to tamp down the hysteria that wanted to surface at the mental understatement.

Liam mercifully interrupted her thoughts. "We need to set up camp, Tansy."

She wanted to do something, needed to do something. "I'll gather firewood."

"Good. I'll pitch the tent."

She walked back to the edge of the woods, suppressing a shudder at all that had unfolded in there. She was grateful—grateful to have something physical to do, grateful that things had turned out the way they had, grateful that she was alive, grateful that she'd stayed behind with Liam rather than leave him, grateful that he thought she was strong enough to move forward and contribute rather than treat her like a helpless invalid.

She picked up sticks for kindling and then rounded up some bona fide firewood. Half an hour later they had a campfire going and dinner was served up.

"What happens next?" she said. The routine and the food was restoring some sense of normal for her.

"The Alaska State Troopers will come out first thing in the morning. They'll want to inspect the scene, gather statements. At some point we'll both have to show up in court."

She nodded and he continued. "Tansy, I had no idea that was what she was thinking. She came on to me at the end of our interview. I turned her down." He shook his head and ran a hand through his hair. "I never led her on. I never touched her."

She sat for a moment, digesting his words. It seemed fairly incomprehensible that Mallory would've gone off the deep end without provocation. However, she believed him. He was a man of integrity, which was a boat Bradley had fallen short of boarding. Then there was the madness glimmering in Mallory's eyes. Shuddering, she nodded, accepting his word as the truth. "I believe you," she said.

"Thank you. You've been through a lot today. I've seen men not handle it as well as you have. You okay?"

"Yeah, I suppose I'm fine." She got up and moved to sit next to him, suddenly wanting, needing, his solid strength beside her. "I guess this...today...was what it was like for you all the time." She had a new appreciation for who he was, what he was, what his job had entailed. How did someone live with that kind of fear, facing death as a part of their job? And yet, that's what men and women in combat did every day, every hour.

"Yes and no. Today it was personal." He slid his arm around her, pulling her hard and tight to his side. She was more than happy to be there. "Especially when I realized you were the target, not me."

"How'd you know?"

"Where the shot landed. It was the tree nearest you. If I'd have been the target, it would've been the one behind me or to my right."

So, he'd known. "Did you have any idea it was Mallory?"

"No. As far as I knew, she left after Bull and I did yesterday. At that point it didn't matter who it was, the person just needed to be stopped. I knew it was someone who had a working knowledge of tactics, but not a lot of practical experience. I also knew it wasn't a professional. It was too personal, based on the number of shots fired. A professional would've sat tight and bided their time to get off a kill shot. She wasn't operating with a cool, detached head and it came through."

Tansy suddenly didn't want to talk about or think about Mallory and her madness. "Tell me about going out on missions."

He talked and she let it wash over her and through her, bringing a new sense of understanding. Of stalking the enemy, but for a cause, a greater purpose, the end result ultimately to save lives by neutralizing the enemy. She didn't ask how many men he'd killed. It didn't matter, except for the toll it might have taken on him.

They cleaned up their dishes, hung the packs and then it was simply the fire, the night sky and the two of them. Tansy came to him and wrapped her arms around his waist, holding him close, her head resting against his chest. She offered him comfort, solace, and sought the same in return.

She was suddenly infinitely grateful for the man he was. He smoothed a hand over her hair, his breath whispering wordlessly against her hair. He laughed softly against her. "This has been a hell of a day and a hell of a trip—certainly not what you'd anticipated. I bet you wish you'd stayed at Shadow Lake."

She didn't have to think about it, there in the shelter of his arms, offering support to him while she took her measure of the same. She stepped back and looked him in the eyes. "No, I don't regret being here. I could be at Shadow Lake now, if I'd wanted to."

"Why didn't you get on that helicopter and leave?"

She shook her head. "I didn't want to leave you," she said.

"I would've been fine."

"I know." He was a lone wolf. A man unto himself. Yet, she'd wanted to stay. Staying had felt right.

And it was as simple and as complicated as that. She'd been operating on adrenaline, numbness, instinct, and she hadn't wanted to leave him. Quite simply, she loved him.

He sighed, twining his fingers in her hair. "You know we don't have any sleeping bags. They went on the chopper."

There'd been no question of transferring Mallory to another stretcher. They'd simply started an IV, assessed her medical state, loaded her on board as she was and left. However, Tansy hadn't actually gotten as far as thinking they were sleeping bagless. And in the big scheme of life and death, it really didn't matter.

"We'll layer on all the clothes we have, put our bed-rolls next to each other and share body heat," Liam said. "It'll get cold tonight but we should be okay in the tent together. I would've never let you stay otherwise."

"I know that."

She realized she trusted him implicitly, with her safety, her life, but more important, with her heart. She hadn't been looking to fall in love with Liam Reinhardt. She hadn't wanted to fall in love with him. But she had.

And in her book love was meant to be shared, to be offered freely, without expecting anything in return, but her heart told her he wasn't ready. He wasn't ready to hear it, to receive it. Plus, there was the little matter that one crazy woman had already declared her love for him today. Tansy figured that was enough for any one man, even one as extraordinary as Liam, in any one given day.

Plus, she knew him well enough, the way his mind worked, that he'd write it off as gratitude or mistaken emotion based on him saving her life. Nope. She knew her own heart. She'd perhaps known it from the moment she'd first seen him but her head and her heart hadn't been ready. And he wasn't ready. For now, she'd hold her own counsel…and love him nonetheless, because her heart hadn't given her any choice in the matter.

15

LIAM WATCHED OUT THE window as the town of Good Riddance came into view. It had been a long night. He'd stayed awake all night, which had felt like being back on alert on a mission, but this time it had been different.

He'd held Tansy, kept his arms around her, keeping her warm, keeping her safe, while it danced through his head over and over just how damn close she'd come to being killed because of him.

He'd done a lot of thinking through the night. He'd never put Natalie first. She'd been right about that. What he'd finally realized last night was that he'd never wanted to put her first, never allowed himself to make that commitment, that leap.

He didn't want anyone to mean that much to him. He could face down the enemy all day, but the thought of allowing someone to mean that much, to matter that much, to be that vulnerable—no. The very idea struck a fear in him that he'd never been willing to acknowledge. He didn't want to be that vulnerable to losing someone. And fast on the heels of that thought had come the thought that what he'd felt for Natalie was a drop in the bucket to what he felt for Tansy.

Tansy *could* mean that much to him, *could* be that important to him *if* he opened himself up to it…and he wasn't going to. He couldn't. He wouldn't. So now she was back in Good Riddance and they could both get on with their lives.

He'd been damn glad when dawn had broken and they'd been busy breaking camp, packing in anticipation of the state troopers' arrival. They'd answered questions, retraced the events of the day before and then all loaded up on the chopper and were touching down now.

Chaos erupted when they cleared the rotors, damn near the whole town turning out to welcome them back. Jenna, her eyes red and swollen from crying, embraced Tansy, holding on to her as if she would never let her go, her husband and their baby right there, as well. Bull, Merilee and Dirk all surrounded Liam. Merilee's tears fell wet against his neck.

"I'm fine," Liam said. "It's over."

Merilee nodded mutely, which spoke volumes for a woman who was always composed with an inner core of steel. He realized Tansy possessed that same inner core of tempered metal.

Dirk clapped him on the back. "That was a hell of a trip, huh?"

Bull stood silently, letting Liam know he'd be there when Liam was ready to talk, when the dust had settled.

Surrounded by the jostling crowd, he felt Tansy's gaze seeking him out. He didn't acknowledge it, didn't acknowledge her. It was time for each of them to move on…in separate directions.

TANSY SETTLED BACK IN the cushioned seat while Jenna worked on her nails. "I knew you'd break a nail, but I didn't expect this. You wrecked your manicure."

"Jenna, do you know how crazy that sounds?"

Her sister grinned. "It does kind of, doesn't it?"

Last night had been a whirlwind of activity and conversation. Merilee had done a great job of keeping the media at bay. Tansy and Liam had each released a statement that essentially said they each had no comment and that had been that. She'd spent a couple of hours on the phone reassuring her mother that she was fine and that no, her mom didn't need to hop on the next plane to Alaska. Jenna had insisted Tansy have dinner with her, Emma and Logan and she'd been more than happy to bask in the safety of their family nest.

Tansy hadn't gotten back out to Shadow Lake until long past dark settling in. She'd seen the lights on next door but knew instinctively that Liam needed some time to himself. And she needed the night to herself, as well. She'd known as surely as she'd known her own name that they each needed their own space to process the past couple of days.

She'd spent the morning immersed in catching up on her work and the afternoon being pampered at Jenna's spa. Ellie had given her the best massage she'd ever had in her life and now Jenna was fussing over her nails. Admittedly, all the pampering felt good.

"I don't want to go back," she said quietly to Jenna.

"Then you can hang out upstairs with Logan and Emma-bug for a while and have dinner with us again."

"No. I mean I don't want to go back to Chattanooga."

A smile blossomed and wreathed Jenna's face. She dropped Tansy's hand and circled the table to hug her.

"You don't know how happy that makes me. I don't want you to go, either. It's been wonderful having you here. I've been hoping and hoping you'd stay. We can talk to Sven about building you a place—"

"I don't want to stay in Good Riddance, either. I will if I have to, but that's not what I want."

Comprehension dawned in Jenna's eyes as she settled back in her seat and once again picked up Tansy's hand. "Liam?"

Tansy nodded. "Yeah. Liam. Do you think I'm crazy?"

Jenna sat, gnawing at her lip, while she filed Tansy's ragged nail. Jenna spoke slowly, obviously choosing her words with care. "I don't think you're crazy, but five days ago you thought you were still in love with Bradley. You know you and Liam just shared a traumatic experience and what you're feeling could be…well, you know, kind of mixed up in your head."

"You make a lot of sense and those are valid concerns. At another point I would've agreed. But I had to work through my feelings for Bradley to see what was in front of my face. I've never been surer of anything. No doubts. Liam, and what I feel for him, feels right in a way Bradley never did. I finally figured out the difference between loving someone and being in love and when you have both…it's just…" She petered out, not even knowing how to put it in words.

She didn't have to. Jenna's smile showed she totally understood. "I get it. Trust me, I get it. And I can see it all over your face. So, how does Liam feel about you?"

"Well, that's still to be determined. He's not an easy man to read and I wanted to give him a little time."

A frown niggled at Jenna's brow. "Not to rain on your parade, Tansy, but I think you need to protect yourself."

She smiled like the fool in love that she was. "It's too late for that, Jenna. Way too late for that. There's nothing quite like being stalked in the woods to make you realize just how short and precarious life is. All I could think about was how much I didn't want to die, all the things I had left undone. And telling Liam I love him, well, I can't in good conscience leave that undone. All I know to do is offer him my heart. I hope he loves me, too. I think we can have a good future together. We work well as a team. For the short period of time we've known each other, I get him and I think he gets me. The only thing I know to do is tell him how I feel. I think he loves me. Maybe he doesn't, but it still doesn't change the way I feel about him. I damn sure hope he loves me because the other thing I know for certain is that he's ruined me for any other man. No one else can compare to him."

"I'll keep my fingers crossed for you, honey. And what's the plan if he's not buying into your plan? Will you go back to Chattanooga then?"

"Nope. No running away, getting away. I'll stay here and get on with my life. I just hope it's with him."

Liam came in from his after-work swim. Finally, things were settling back into a routine. Nothing had changed, yet everything had changed. He'd gone for his run this morning, shown up to work with Sven and moved forward to buy the property.

He went inside, showered and had just finished dressing when he heard her knock at his door. He recognized her knock. Hell, he knew her walk, the way she looked when she was sleeping.

He opened the door and she stood on the other side of the screen door, wearing that dress he liked so much.

She smiled and he steeled himself against the way his body tightened in response. "Hi. Did I catch you at a bad time?"

For a second he thought about saying yes, but instead he stood aside. "Come on in."

She smelled fresh and sweet and against his better judgment, he reached for her, pulling her into his arms, tight against his body. Damn, he'd missed her. The way she felt next to him, her smile, her scent, every damn thing about her.

Wordlessly, she took him by the hand and led him to his bedroom. She slipped her dress over her head. She was naked beneath. He took off the clothes he'd just put on.

Together, they climbed into his bed. There had been something close and intimate in the past night in the woods, when he'd held her wrapped in his arms and stood silent sentinel through the night as she'd slept. And now he told her with his body, with his touch and his kisses, how damn glad he was that she was still part of this earth. But he wouldn't allow her to know how much she meant to him.

Afterward, she propped on one elbow and traced a nothing pattern on his chest with her fingertips. He saw it in her eyes, knew it was coming but couldn't do anything to stop it.

"I love you."

Her words didn't take him by surprise. Funny, but he'd known it, felt it before she'd said it.

"What about Bradley?"

Her eyes pierced him, calling him out. "Evasive

maneuvers, Reinhardt. He went back to Chattanooga. Alone. I made that decision based on me and him. He's a nonissue at this point."

They both knew Liam was in retreat-and-regroup mode. She waited. The next move was his. He wanted to tell her, he almost said it, that they could take it one day at a time, but that wasn't fair to her. She was putting her cards on the table. He owed her the same.

"Tansy, I don't have anything to offer you. I'm just getting back on my feet, starting down a new career path."

She simply looked at him. They both knew that wasn't the issue. "Dammit, Tansy."

He pushed out of the bed and pulled on his jeans. He tossed her dress to her. Her nakedness was distracting.

She pulled on the garment and sat up against his headboard. "I've decided to stay in Good Riddance."

"I haven't asked you to stay."

"No, you haven't. You also didn't ask me to stay when that helicopter was leaving the other night. I stayed then and I'm staying now."

"What are you, some glutton for punishment, Wellington? I can't give you what you want."

"And just so we're on the same page, what is it that you think I want, Reinhardt?"

"What I'm willing to give is what we've got. It works, but that's not going to be enough for you, is it?"

"No. You're right. I'm not going to settle for half measures. I don't care that you're moody and ill-tempered and have the social skills of an armadillo." An armadillo? "I can live with all of that, but I want all of the good parts, too. I want the part that you deny and keep under lock and key. I want the whole man. It's the only way to have a healthy relationship."

"And I'm telling you I'm not a whole man. You want something I don't have to give. Ask my ex-wife."

"I don't have to ask your ex-wife. I know you. I know the heart of you. For such a man of courage, the notion of fully loving someone leaves you quaking in fear and denial. Whether you *choose* to be a whole man, well, that's a different story."

Dammit. She made it sound so easy and there was nothing easy about it. "What are you going to do, Wellington? Move out with me to that remote location? How long do you think that would last? A month? Maybe stretch it to six? I'll be gone for a week at a time. You'll be out in the middle of nowhere alone. You'll see me maybe six days out of a month. How does that fit into your plan?"

She eyed him with cool disdain. "Do you think I'm an idiot? Of course I know that. And it actually sounds great to me. I like a certain amount of alone time. I can always fly in and out with the supply plane when I want some time away. It's not like I'd be in lockdown." She assumed the same stance she had at the sand line. "I want a partner, not a shadow or a hovercraft."

"You've got an answer for everything, don't you, Wellington?"

"Pretty much, Reinhardt. Those six days out of the month that you were home would be good, damn good. And I want a dog."

Why did she have to paint a picture that made it all sound so good? Why couldn't she have just left well enough alone? "Jesus. Next you're going to be throwing in a couple of kids."

She lifted her chin, her eyes unyielding. "In due time. I happen to think you're good genetic material and would make a good dad."

A boy, a girl, one like him, one like her. And what about when the isolation and lifestyle got to be too much and he was way the hell more invested than he'd ever been with Natalie? Hell, he was already more invested than he was with Natalie. No. "So, what is this? A take-it-or-leave-it proposition?"

"On the table."

"And if I can't meet your terms, are you going to leave? Head back to Chattanooga?"

"No. I don't want to leave you, but I also like it here. I like the people. I love my sister and I can be a part of my niece growing up. I'm staying, with you or without you."

"I could come into town in between gigs. We could—"

"No."

"I'm not going to be coerced."

"I'm just leveling with you."

"So much for your profession of love. You don't get your way and suddenly you don't love me."

She laughed and he'd be damned if he saw what was so funny. "No, it'd be nice and tidy if it worked that way but it doesn't. I'm going to love you regardless. My heart didn't leave me any choice in the matter. However, I still have a choice in how I live my life and I'm not settling for half measures."

It reminded him of that damn load of sand she'd had delivered and then drawn her line. "So, I guess you've drawn your line in the sand once again."

"I guess I have."

Damn stubborn woman. She'd see it his way in due time. "Then you stay on your side and I'll stay on mine."

TANSY REMINDED HERSELF that she wouldn't actually expire from a broken heart. She'd hurt like hell but she'd survive. People did it all the time. And the damnable part was she didn't think for a minute he wasn't capable of love. Actually, she didn't think for a minute he didn't love her. And that wasn't arrogance or self-delusion. The tenderness in his touch wasn't just about sex, and it was something she didn't think intensely private men like Liam Reinhardt shared often.

But she couldn't move the man past himself. She'd put it out there and the rest was up to him. In the meantime, she'd get on with her life. She was ever so tempted to cave, to give in, to take what he was willing to give, but she stood firm. She wouldn't settle. Life was too short to settle.

She called Merilee and booked herself a flight out. She had business to attend to in Chatanooga—namely closing out her life there and clearing out her apartment so she could make the move to Alaska. Plus, she wanted to spend some time with her mom. While she wasn't as close to her dad, she wanted to at least have dinner with him. She was ready to move on with a new phase of her life.

And a woman could always hope that the man of her heart would stop being an idiot and come through.

She parked the FJ Cruiser at Jenna's and her sister met her at the door. "Emma-bug and I will see you off. You want her or you want me to carry her?"

"I'll take her."

With a smile, Jenna handed over the flannel sling

that went around Tansy's neck and then placed Emma in the pouch. The sleeping baby grunted and nestled closer in the fabric, next to Tansy's midsection, and kept sleeping. Tansy welcomed Emma's warmth and weight against her.

Together they walked down the street. Quietly, Jenna reached for and held her hand. "It'll all work out in the end, Tansy. Give him some time and you know we'll be waiting here for you."

"I know. I'll be back in a month."

They walked into the airstrip office to find the regulars there—Alberta, Lord Byron, Dwight, Jefferson, Bull and Merilee. Liam wasn't there. She hadn't expected him to be there. Nonetheless, she had hoped. He knew she was leaving and he'd steadfastly kept his distance. He hadn't answered her knock on the door last night when she'd stopped by to say goodbye. She supposed he figured they'd said everything there was to say.

Merilee smiled and took Emma. "Here's my girl." She looked at Tansy. "We'll have you all set up when you get back. Don't you worry, honey, we'll have a place for you to stay other than Shadow Lake."

Housing was an issue in the small town and while she'd enjoyed the accommodations at Shadow Lake, she couldn't continue to live next door to Liam for a number of reasons. One being, the cabins at Shadow Lake were temporary and Skye's folks were coming in for a visit in November. Plus, she wanted a fresh start and there were too many memories there. It would be too easy to fall into and settle for whatever Liam was willing to give.

There were a couple of options on the table—

sharing the apartment above Gus's with Ruby, the waitress who was staying there, staying with Jenna and her family, and there were a couple of other things Merilee and Bull were working on. Of course, she was hoping it was a matter of none of the above and Liam came to his senses.

"I know," she said to Merilee.

Alberta patted her hand. "It's all going to be fine. I knew when you sent that Bradley fellow packing, you were going to be A-OK. No hooking up with him while you're in Chattanooga." She cackled at her own joke, coaxing a smile out of Tansy.

"Not even a remote possibility."

Bull, standing quietly in the background, as was his way, caught her eye. "Time, Tansy. Give him time. It has a way of letting things unfold."

Tansy nodded, holding Bull's words close to her heart, finding comfort in them, even more than anything anyone else could say to her now. Bull knew Liam as well as anyone.

Juliette came in the back door, Baby in tow. "Okay, we're ready if you're ready. There's a storm blowing in but we should beat it out."

Tansy hugged her goodbyes and crossed the airstrip. She'd be back. She had no choice. Her heart was here.

16

"I OUGHT TO KNOCK the hell out of you again," Dirk said, without any hint of animosity as he, Liam, Sven and Bull gathered around rough drawings on Bull's counter in the hardware store. They were designing the main building for Liam's survival camp.

"Then you damn well better make it good, because I'm going to swing back this time."

Unperturbed, Dirk shrugged. "Well, hell, someone's got to knock some sense into you."

"You're trying my patience, Dirk."

The big man laughed. "You've got to be kidding. Like you haven't been trying everyone's patience for the past month. You're like a damn bear with a sore paw."

"Mind your own business."

"It is my business. I have to work with your sorry ass and you are one miserable son of a bitch, and since shit rolls downhill, I'm catching yours."

Bull spoke up. "The man has a point."

Attempting to get back to business, Sven wisely changed the subject. "We should do what we did on

Jenna's place and build up with a little more room to accommodate family quarters."

Liam considered Sven's suggestion. It'd be tight, but he should be able to swing it.

And damnation, he missed Tansy. The woman haunted him. Her smile, her voice, the sex—he even missed their quiet talks while sitting around the fire pit behind the cabin. And she was smart. More than once he'd wanted to know what she would've thought about the plans—he'd have liked her input. But there was that line in the sand and she'd laid out the terms of crossing it.

So, here he sat, one miserable son of a bitch. Dirk had called that right, being dogged out by the three of them. It'd been the longest month of his life…and now she was back. He'd caught a glimpse of her in Gus's. Then there'd been another "sighting" when he'd been on his way to Bull's for this meeting, but they'd each taken and were holding their positions. General Wellington had dug in. He'd sort of thought it'd be better once she was back, but really it was worse.

When she was gone, there was distance separating them. Now, the only thing separating them were her terms, which required unconditional surrender. She was a most unreasonable woman…and a damn fine general…considering she was outflanking him and outmaneuvering him.

He looked at Sven. "Do I want to know the odds?"

Sven was known to follow Rooster's betting and Liam had known for some time he and Tansy were the biggest bet going.

The big blond grimaced, his eyes sympathetic.

"They're weighted pretty heavily. You're a long shot at this point."

He eyed the three of them. "You all got money riding on this?"

At least they had the decency to look sheepish. Bull? Even Bull? His uncle shrugged. "Hey, I had to throw a couple of bucks at it."

"So, you've all got a vested interest."

Dirk laughed. "Hell, no. It's weighted so heavily in Tansy's favor, the most I'm going to pick up is a couple of bucks."

They all eyed him with a mixture of pity and amusement, as if they knew he was fighting a losing battle but were humoring him nonetheless. "I've lived through firefights where the odds were stacked against me."

Dirk rolled his eyes. Sven laughed. Bull clapped him on the back. "Opening doors, son, opening doors. Sometimes you've just got to lay down your weapon and surrender your gun."

The subtlety wasn't lost on him. Bull winked. "It worked out well enough for me. I set siege for twenty-five years."

"Look," Sven said, as if reasoning with a simpleton. "I thought I'd never settle down and look at me. Juliette's the best thing that ever came my way. And I damn near lost her."

Dirk wasn't about to be left out. "I had my head up my ass and let you waltz Natalie right out from under me. By the way, I talked to her last week."

He'd had enough. He pushed back from the table, standing. He reached in his pocket and pulled out a Ben Franklin and tossed it on the table in front of Dirk. "You've got five minutes to get that to Rooster."

"You can't bet on yourself," Dirk said.

"I'm not, dammit. Put the money on Wellington."

He pulled on his jacket and walked down the street to the airstrip, beelining for Merilee. "I need something white," he said, cutting straight to the chase. "Anything."

Merilee grinned and walked over to the table beside the love seat and picked up a lace doily. "That's the best I can do for you. That or underwear."

"I'll take this."

"She's at Jenna's."

He wasted no time heading back down the street.

TANSY HEARD HIS FOOTSTEPS on the stairs leading to Jenna's house. She had time to utter one word to her sister before his knock at the door. "Liam."

Jenna smiled. "I'll just step into the bedroom."

"You don't have to."

"Oh, yes, I do."

Tansy opened the door and silently stood aside for him to enter. He walked in, past her and tossed something on the table. A white lace doily?

He faced her, back straight, shoulders up. "You sighted me in your crosshairs the moment I met you. I have been outmaneuvered, outflanked and outranked. I concede the firefight, Wellington."

"You are the most unromantic man I know."

"True." He stood unyielding. He nodded toward the white lace. "I surrender."

"You know the terms."

"We need to negotiate those."

She crossed her arms over her chest, holding her line. "Let's hear them."

"Two dogs. Three kids."

She waved a dismissing hand. "That's never been the sticking point."

"I suppose you want a ring on your finger."

"It'd be nice, but I'm still waiting."

"You don't give a man any quarter, do you, Wellington?"

"There's not a lot of room for negotiation on the major term."

He stood there, tall and proud, and she waited, her heart thumping in her chest. He was a man of integrity. A man of his word. He wouldn't give it lightly, which made it all the more important.

"I love you." The words hung between them. "All of me. Heart, body, soul, I'm yours."

She wanted to ask if it'd really been that hard to say, but she didn't have to. She knew it had. "Thank you. I love you, too. I'll stand by you, with you."

She picked up the lace doily and handed it back to him. "I don't need this. The way I see it, it's not surrender at all, we're just combining forces. We've always been on the same side, Reinhardt. You just needed to figure it out."

"Come here, woman."

She willingly, eagerly, stepped into his arms, kissing him with all the passion and longing she'd kept to herself for the past month, week and two days—and yes, she'd counted. She felt the same thing in his kiss...and much more. His lips silently spoke of promise and a future and a here and now beyond compare.

He rested his forehead against hers. "It's going to take time for me to get this off the ground. I think it'll work, but it's not going to be easy. I don't have anything to offer you, honey, except for a lot of hard work."

"The things worth really having usually aren't easy.

God knows, you haven't been. But we'll travel that path together and you've offered me everything—you and a future together. How did I get so lucky?"

He shook his head. "I've been asking myself the same thing. I guess doors have opened while others have closed, while our paths have led to each other's."

"Are you getting philosophical and sentimental?" she asked.

"I have my lapses." He looked down at her, his eyes glittering with a look she had longed for on all her lonely nights since they'd been apart. "Now why don't you leave that dress on, but—"

"Liam—" She stopped his wandering hand.

"Tansy?"

"Jenna's in the other room."

"Hi, Liam," Jenna said, poking her head out the door. "Welcome to the family."

"Thanks. I'm going to take your sister now. She has building plans to look over."

Jenna laughed. "Okay. Her suitcase is here, though."

"We'll come back for her things later," he said, already ushering her toward the door. She could feel the sexual tension radiating from him. He was as ready for her as she was for him.

"He's in charge," she said to Jenna over her shoulder as they walked out the door.

She wrapped her arm around his waist, feeling the quiet strength of her strong man. At least she'd let him think he was in charge. It just worked better that way.

* * * * *

A sneaky peek at next month...

Blaze®

SCORCHING HOT, SEXY READS

My wish list for next month's titles...

In stores from 16th November 2012:

☐ Red-Hot Santa — Tori Carrington

& Lead Me Home — Vicki Lewis Thompson

☐ The Mighty Quinns: Kellan — Kate Hoffmann

& Feels So Right — Isabel Sharpe

Available at WHSmith, Tesco, Asda, Eason, Amazon and Apple

Just can't wait?

www.millsandboon.co.uk/freebookoffer

Or fill in the form below and post it back to us

THE MILLS & BOON® BOOK CLUB™—HERE'S HOW IT WORKS: Accepting your free books places you under no obligation to buy anything. You may keep the books and return the despatch note marked 'Cancel'. If we do not hear from you, about a month later we'll send you 4 brand-new stories from the Blaze® series, including a 2-in-1 book priced at £5.49 and two single books priced at £3.49* each. There is no extra charge for post and packaging. You may cancel at any time, otherwise we will send you 4 stories a month which you may purchase or return to us—the choice is yours. *Terms and prices subject to change without notice. Offer valid in UK only. Applicants must be 18 or over. Offer expires 31st January 2013. **For full terms and conditions, please go to www.millsandboon.co.uk/freebookoffer**

Mrs/Miss/Ms/Mr (please circle)

First Name

Surname

Address

Postcode

E-mail

Send this completed page to: Mills & Boon Book Club, Free Book Offer, FREEPOST NAT 10298, Richmond, Surrey, TW9 1BR

Find out more at
www.millsandboon.co.uk/freebookoffer

Visit us Online

0712/K2YEA

The World of Mills & Boon®

There's a Mills & Boon® series that's perfect for you. We publish ten series and, with new titles every month, you never have to wait long for your favourite to come along.

Blaze®

Scorching hot, sexy reads
4 new stories every month

By Request

Relive the romance with the best of the best
9 new stories every month

Cherish™

Romance to melt the heart every time
12 new stories every month

Desire™

Passionate and dramatic love stories
8 new stories every month